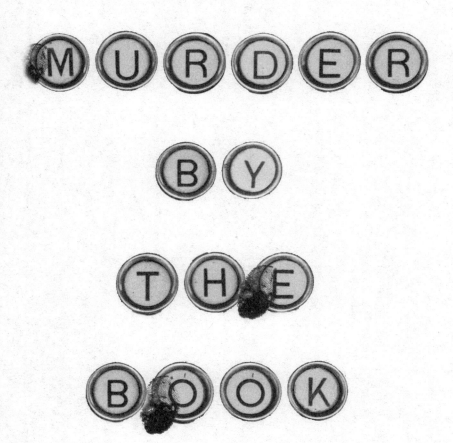

AMIE SCHAUMBERG

/II MIRA

MIRA

ISBN-13: 978-0-7783-8750-3

Murder by the Book

Copyright © 2025 by Amie Schaumberg

Recycling programs for this product may not exist in your area.

All rights reserved. No part of this book may be used or reproduced in any manner whatsoever without written permission.

Without limiting the author's and publisher's exclusive rights, any unauthorized use of this publication to train generative artificial intelligence (AI) technologies is expressly prohibited.

This is a work of fiction. Names, characters, places and incidents are either the product of the author's imagination or are used fictitiously. Any resemblance to actual persons, living or dead, businesses, companies, events or locales is entirely coincidental.

For questions and comments about the quality of this book, please contact us at CustomerService@Harlequin.com.

TM is a trademark of Harlequin Enterprises ULC.

Mira
22 Adelaide St. West, 41st Floor
Toronto, Ontario M5H 4E3, Canada
MIRABooks.com

Printed in U.S.A.

To my sister, Landy—my first reader and biggest supporter.

Chapter 1

A strand of yellow crime scene tape had broken free and struggled in the wind as Ian Carter trudged down the low hill to where an old barn waited in the long grass. The deserted farmyard was busy with law enforcement personnel weaving in and around each other like a well-rehearsed ballet corps, each one focused on their own part of the dance. The previous night's steady rain was dissipating, leaving charcoal-smeared clouds hanging low in the sky and rippling puddles reflecting a cold gray light across the landscape. The face of the barn was weather-beaten; remnants of red paint just visible on the faded boards marked the building as a relic of another time. Ian felt like an intruder as he crossed toward it.

At the center of the scene, his partner, Mike Kellogg, squinted into the hazy morning light as he watched Ian's careful progress down the hill. At forty-five, Mike was about a decade older than Ian, but his heavy body, strained by stress and hard use, made him look twice that. His flat, brown hair was thinning above a round face incongruously dusted with freckles.

"Morning, starshine." Mike's deep baritone echoed crudely above the noise of the crime scene.

"What have we got?" Ian asked.

"What, no small talk this morning, Carter?" Mike caught Ian's eye, and he sighed. "Caucasian female, early twenties. No ID. Some high school kids found the body when they came out to the boondocks to enjoy a little beer and some weed. We've got some uniforms canvassing, but it's unlikely we'll get lucky there." Mike waved his hand across the empty field surrounding them.

"Cause of death?" Ian pulled a pair of latex gloves from his coat pocket.

"Waiting on the ME, but . . ."

"But, what?"

"Better if you see it yourself," Mike replied enigmatically, striding away from Ian. "There aren't words for this one."

"That bad?" Ian asked, jogging after his partner.

"Not so much bad as, well . . ." Mike slowed to a halt as he searched for a description. "Whoever did this is a special kind of batshit." He shook his head and continued toward the inner perimeter of the crime scene, Ian following at his heels.

Ian paused at the threshold of the barn, letting his eyes adjust to the dim light within. He scanned the large structure slowly: well-worn boards pulling against rusted nails, scattered hay too old for use, a battered wooden ladder leaning against one wall, bits of twine and leather lying helter-skelter, petrified chunks of manure, and a few abandoned tools rusting from disuse. It smelled of dust, mold, and the soft, sweet scent of decay. A swarm of scene-of-crime techs clustered at the far end. A few others paced slowly in parallel lines along the length of the barn, pausing periodically to mark and record something they thought might be important. The constant activity created a humming undertone that played beneath Ian's thoughts like the drone of a bagpipe. As he approached, his steps slowed as he tried to decipher the scene before him. Mike walked a careful path to the back of the barn, leaving Ian to follow.

This part of the structure was different. The area was meticulously clean, the detritus having been swept from a large rectangular section by the rear door. The door itself had been painted with a bright mural, an idyllic scene that was jarringly at odds with the dim interior of the building. The image of a broad-leafed tree stretched from the ceiling to the floor, the board's texture giving it a discomforting realism. A frothy stream curled around the tree's roots and disappeared into the distance, its banks alive with a vibrant swath of flowers—a tangle of purple, yellow, white, and green. One of the painted tree's long limbs dipped nearly to the water, and from it hung what looked like a rope of the same flowers that colored the ground, braided and tied around the branch. It dangled partway down the trunk, coming to a severed end a foot above the water. Centered in front of the painted door sat an old metal water trough. It looked to have been scrubbed clean, with dull metal showing through where rust had eaten away at the lining. Golden hair spilled over the rim, and Ian could just see the blue-white skin of the victim's knees visible above the dented metal.

He moved closer, looking down at the immobile body of a young woman. The trough was partially filled with water, covering her stomach and shoulders. Her face rose above the surface as if she were taking a final breath. Her beauty had turned waxy and shrunken beneath the harsh lights illuminating the crime scene. Heavy-lidded eyes stared blankly from a rounded face, still almost childlike despite the full curves revealed where the water trapped her clothes against her body. Her lips were parted slightly as if she were sighing.

Ian had learned to anticipate the worst in his cases and expected—feared—that he would find the girl naked, but instead, she was dressed in a long silver gown embroidered with beads or some sort of metallic thread that glinted through the murky water. Her knees were pushed up, and the heavy material of her skirt gathered at her pelvis and coiled around her pale thighs. The slender arms were bent at the elbow so that her hands floated near her shoulders, the palms and fingers breaking the water's surface. Her hair floated in a corona around her, sliding across her collarbone and catching on her upturned fingers. A knot of plants wound around her neck. Ian leaned in to see it more closely: purple, yellow, and white flowers tangled against her skin.

Ian stared at her for a silent moment before pulling on the gloves and crouching down to examine the floor beside the trough. Several gutted candles sat at uneven intervals around the base. They had burned just long enough for slim streaks of wax to melt down the sides. The killer had not just lit them and left; he had stayed to watch them burn around his victim before snuffing them out. A paperback book lay before them, opened to reveal darkened pages, some roughly torn out. An old-fashioned inkwell lay on its side, the spilled liquid leaving a deep red stain on the grayed flooring.

Ian glanced over his shoulder. "Has this all been photographed?" he called to a nearby CSI tech.

"Yep. We've got overalls and close-ups, and everything's been documented. Have at it."

Ian squatted down, leaning close to the stain. The viscosity and color suggested that the pooled substance was blood. The pages, too, were coated in it, obscuring any identifying words. Using the end of a pen he pulled from his jacket pocket, Ian gingerly flipped the book closed so that he could see the cover, but the thick paper was saturated and unreadable. The image of what might have been a skull was the only distinguishable marking. Ian rose as he heard someone walk up behind him.

"What'd I tell ya," Mike's voice rumbled. "Special kind of batshit."

Ian glanced over his shoulder with a noncommittal shrug before staring at the victim again. He was reminded grotesquely of a passage from a Raymond Chandler novel where the narrator sees a stained glass window depicting a knight rescuing a bound woman—rather ineffectually, as the narrator points out. He wishes that he could rescue her himself, knowing that is impossible.

For a moment, in the girl's staring blankness, he saw another face. He reached down and brushed a dried strand of hair from the girl's cheek.

"See something?" asked Mike, misinterpreting the tender gesture.

"I, uh . . ." Ian leaned toward the body to disguise his sentimental lapse and studied the flowers. "The flowers look hand braided," Ian stated, narrating his thought process aloud, "not a store-bought decoration. Specific. They match the painting." He handled the woven strands gently, plucking them away from the girl's skin and revealing a purplish welt along her neck. "Ligature marks. Looks like she was strangled."

"Very good, Detective," came a throaty voice from behind him. "You gonna tell me time of death, too?"

"That's all you, Ivy," Ian responded without looking up.

A shadow darkened the girl's torso, and he turned his head to see the medical examiner standing at his shoulder. She snapped on a latex glove with more force than necessary. Ian stood and looked down at her. Dr. Ivy Wollard was in her midforties and stood at barely five feet, with close-cropped dark hair and a surprisingly lithe build. Her manner of dress and general attitude seemed to work actively against the potential beauty that lay in her face. She was blunt, short-tempered, and fiercely territorial about her job.

"Finished yet?"

"Just about." Ian knew he would have an ample supply of photos to which he could refer, but he bent down once more and thoughtfully studied the girl's face. He noticed something odd about the set of her lips.

"I think there's something in her mouth," he said, reaching forward. Ivy smacked his hand as if he were a naughty child.

"Don't," she said shortly, pushing past him to stand nearer the water trough. She accepted forceps from an assistant who had fetched them without being asked and gingerly pulled an object from beneath the girl's tongue. "Paper."

Mike gestured at one of the CSI techs. "We need an evidence bag." Turning to Ian, he asked, "What do you think?"

"There are pages missing from the book," Ian stated simply.

"Huh." Mike shook his head. "Bag and tag, guys. Then let the doctor get to work." The scene-of-crime technicians collected any evidence that might be disturbed and then moved it aside. Ivy methodically examined the body in situ before gesturing to her waiting staff. The gloved assistants lifted the body and lowered it onto a waiting gurney. The girl maintained her rigid position as she was moved.

Ian watched the puddles grow around the gurney as water streamed from the folds of the girl's dress, not looking toward Ivy's efficient movements. He was used to death and rarely upset by what he saw, but something about the scientific precision of Ivy's work always made him uneasy.

"Can you tell us anything?" Mike asked impatiently.

She stared at him for a long moment, then shrugged. "The water complicates body temperature, but I'd say she's been dead eight to ten hours, right around dinner last night. I'll check the stomach contents to see if anything is identifiable. Rigor's begun but isn't fully set. Lividity's fixed, though; discoloration on the legs suggests she was killed first, lay prone for an hour or two, and then was placed in the trough before rigor set in. Posed more accurately. Whoever did this put her in the position where she was found."

Mike nodded. "You drop a body in a trough, that's not how it lands."

Ivy cut him a sharp glance, and her mouth tightened. "No. It's not."

"Was the water an attempt to disguise time of death?" Ian asked.

"Possibly, although there are more effective methods." Ivy surveyed the scene. "My guess? Whoever this was, he wasn't interested in hiding what he did. He wanted to display it. The water means something."

"What?" Mike asked.

"That's your job, *Detective*," she responded dryly, signaling her people to pack up. She glanced at Ian. "I'll know more once I get the autopsy done. I'll keep you posted."

"Thanks." Ian watched as the body was rolled slowly out of the barn, the medical assistants maneuvering skillfully around the debris scattered on the floor. He turned his attention back to the mural and the now vacant water trough.

"She's right, you know," Mike said, approaching. "This guy's not trying to hide."

"No," Ian said, thoughtfully studying the mural. "He wants everyone to know what he's done."

Chapter 2

The reverberations of the tolling bell shimmered through the steps as Emma Reilly ran upward. Ignoring the sharp rap of her book bag against her hip, she picked up speed. She was late to class, the second time already this quarter. Emma hated how easily she fell into the absent-minded professor trope, but despite an elaborate system of calendars, sticky notes, and phone alarms, her brain had fallen into a quicksand of interesting ideas, and she hadn't pulled herself out in time.

She slammed through the door of the small attic room with a wave and a panted apology. "Sorry, sorry."

"Get lost in some Shakespeare again?" a brunette named Olivia asked kindly. She was bright and pretty, with just a touch of the ruthlessness that came with popularity. She'd impressed Emma last term with a blistering takedown of the main character in *Mill on the Floss*. Olivia had taken several classes with Emma during her two years at Carlisle College and had apparently chosen to find Emma's scattered existence endearing.

Emma smiled at her. "Poe." She pulled their textbook from her bag and waved it. "So, at least I was on topic."

Emma skirted around the rows of desks to her own place at the front of the room. She paused for just a moment to look out of a small round window that splashed light across the floor. A wide expanse of green stretched below them, a teasing glimpse of summer's end. Emma sighed and turned away. She used the excuse of unpacking her bag to hide her face from the waiting room and pulled in a slow breath. She settled a pleasantly interested expression across her face, looked up, and opened her book.

"True!" Emma exclaimed, startling a few of the students as they scrambled for their texts. Emma chuckled lightly. "Page thirty-three for those who want to play along." She lowered her voice dramatically, dropping to a hiss. "'True!—nervous—very, very dreadfully nervous I had been and am; but why will you say that I am mad?'"

Twenty-three sets of eyes dropped, tracking her words as they skittered across the page. Emma watched the students in front of her, having read this page often enough that she didn't need to look at the text. The room was, strictly speaking, not a classroom. But a boom in enrollment had caused the college to creatively reallocate its spaces, and Emma's literature class was moved from the liberal arts building to a room at the top of the main hall used mainly for storage since the sixties. She had nodded along with the other faculty when they griped about the administration remodeling the business building while Liberal Arts fought over rooms with working clocks, but Emma secretly loved it here. The old wooden floors and gabled roof made her feel like a governess in a Gothic novel rather than an English professor at a midsize college in a midsize town in rural Oregon.

She finished the passage, then waited in silence as the students processed the words that floated between them. Emma eyed a boy who was drawing what looked like the human muscular system in an open notebook. He was new this term but had shown himself to be a bold debater.

"Why do you think Poe begins with this declaration on the part of his narrator?" Emma racked her brain for his name. "Ah, Ethan?" The student's dark head jerked up, startled. Emma smiled gently and raised her eyebrows.

"Uh, because the guy's nuts?"

"He could be faking it. He doesn't seem exactly trustworthy," Olivia retorted.

"Why would he do that?" The dark-haired boy—Ethan! Emma reminded herself—scoffed.

"Because he doesn't want to say, 'Hey, I straight up killed a guy.' He wants us to think he's insane, but insisting that what you're saying is true is a dead giveaway that you're lying. 'The lady doth protest too much, methinks,'" Olivia retorted, smug as she quoted Shakespeare at him. She met Ethan's eyes with a challenge.

"He killed a guy because he thought his eye looked weird. That's crazy." Ethan's smile bordered on flirtatiousness. Olivia quirked an eyebrow.

Emma smiled. "Well, I wouldn't use the word *crazy*, but mental illness is a solid theory for the murderer, Ethan. Let's see if the text agrees with you. Remember, there are . . ."

"No right or wrong answers," a redheaded boy finished from the back of the room with a grin. He was another repeat student.

"Point to Aiden. As long as you can justify your interpretation with textual examples, then it's a good one. So, let's see what the text tells us." Emma directed them to the line that Ethan had referenced and then slowly guided them through the rest of the story. She pushed until the comments ran dry, then glanced at the clock. Fifteen minutes left.

"So, what do you think now? Can we, the readers, trust what we are being told?"

"I don't think so," a soft voice in the third row offered.

Blake, Emma thought but wasn't sure enough to say it aloud.

He rarely spoke, instead watching intensely and noting down every word. He trailed Ethan in and out of the room but always chose a seat behind rather than beside him.

"Olivia was right," he continued, his glance flicking toward Ethan. Ethan raised an eyebrow but gave a slight nod. "He's trying to convince us he has a reason for what he did so that we don't think he's just plain evil. I mean, there are a lot of killers who just . . . kill. Because they want to. Because they can."

"Right," Olivia added. "The narrator talks directly to us like we're a jury. He wants us to believe that he's craz—mentally ill because that makes him less culpable. But there is no real reason. He wanted to kill that man, so he did."

Ethan smirked, but before he could speak, another voice joined the debate.

"Or maybe the old man had it coming." All the students turned toward the door, where a lanky man with tousled sandy-blond hair lounged against the door frame.

Emma shook her head in mock disapproval but couldn't stop a reflexive smile. "Everyone—please welcome a distinguished guest, our very own Dean of Arts and Media. Provocative reading, Dr. Tamblyn. Care to explain?"

"What if everything Poe tells us is one hundred percent true?" He looked around the room, his voice tinted with just a touch of theatricality. "What if the old man was genuinely evil, and the heart really was beating beneath the floorboards? Maybe the blue curtains really are just blue."

"What curtains?" A slender girl next to Olivia whispered.

"There are no curtains, Hallie," Emma replied, trying to hide amusement. "Dr. Tamblyn is demonstrating irony by using a metaphor to argue for a literalist interpretation."

"Touché." Rory grinned unapologetically. "And the blue curtains refer to what I believe you all call a meme."

"How do you do, fellow kids?" Olivia said sotto voce, earning her a few discreet laughs.

Something uncomfortable flickered across Rory's face before he smiled again. "Well, let me make amends for commandeering your discussion by getting you out of class a few minutes early."

The students glanced at Emma, a few already reaching for their bags. "Alright, everyone, take off. We'll pick this up next time. And don't forget your first essay assignment is posted. Ask questions early and often."

The students dumped their books unceremoniously into their bags, scrambled out of the classroom and on to the next chapter of their educational experience.

"Sorry to interrupt," Rory said, strolling in.

"No, you aren't," Emma retorted, her voice warm. "You love making a scene."

"I do at that." Rory exuded a puckish quality that made him seem boyish despite his current role as head of the department. He was nearly a decade older than Emma's thirty-three, but careful sartorial choices disguised any hints of aging.

"Maybe you should have dedicated yourself to treading the boards instead of lowly academics," Emma teased.

"I still hold out hope that my art will bring me wealth and fame. Preferably while I'm still around to enjoy it and without losing an ear. Besides, you're the actress here."

"One school production of *Midsummer* does not make me an actress."

"Your daily performances outshine the grand dames of the stage. Most people just don't notice."

Emma frowned. "It's not a performance, Rory. I just . . ." She shook her head, unsure how to explain the second skin she'd learned to wear.

Rory looked immediately contrite. "Sorry, Em. I meant that as a compliment."

"It's fine. I'm fine." Emma took a deep breath, then settled a smile on her face. "Did you need me for something?" she asked, her voice all politeness.

"Always. But right now, I just wanted to see if you're free for lunch today. I'm feeling neglected." He gave her a smile that would have beguiled Da Vinci.

"Oh, I can't today. I . . ." Emma trailed off as a movement caught her eye at the back of the room. "Yes, Ethan?"

The boy was standing centered in the doorway, watching their exchange. His friend shadowed him, standing just out of the light.

"Sorry," Ethan said with a grin. "I hate to interrupt. But I think you dropped this?" His voice lilted up as he cocked his head in a question. He crossed the distance between them, holding out a folded paper to Emma. Rory stepped forward to take it from him.

"Not mine," Rory told him, thrusting it back.

Emma took it from him gently, narrowing her eyes reprovingly. The pale paper was surprisingly thick between her fingers. One side read simply: *You're Invited!* in a swirl of letters. Emma flipped it over.

Light and Darkness in the Pre-Raphaelite Brotherhood,
A Special Exhibition: Friday, August 17th, 6:00 p.m.

"I don't think it's mine either, Ethan." She had one just like it, though, on her desk—Emma replayed the frenzied dash from her office, shuffling books and papers into her bag. "Or maybe it is. Thank you for returning it."

"No problem. I've heard it's going to be really interesting."

"Oh?" Rory's dry tone was a clear challenge to the boy.

"Yeah," Ethan said, his chin lifting. "My girlfriend told me about it. She's really into art."

"Yes, I'm sure that her expertise in Victorian reform movements is considerable," Rory retorted.

"Well," Emma interjected, "the Pre-Raphaelites drew significant inspiration from the literature of the time. You might enjoy it from that perspective, Ethan. The brotherhood actually formed around the same time that Poe was beginning to publish his work. You, too, Blake," Emma called to the other boy, still in the hallway, hoping that actually was his name.

Ethan considered Emma for a moment. "So, if I go and maybe . . . write something. Could I get extra credit?"

"Just focus on your regular credit," Emma told him gently. "Thank you again, Ethan." She lifted the invitation in a clear dismissal. The boy left with a shrug, nodding at Blake to follow as he passed.

"So, does that mean that you're going to the exhibit?" Rory asked when they were alone. "I'm short a plus-one." He shrugged a little awkwardly.

Emma made an unintentional face. "Honestly, I was kind of looking forward to a quiet night at home."

"Playing Emily Dickinson again? I mean, I admire her, too, but the agoraphobia isn't what I'd emulate." Rory's voice teased, but Emma could hear worry beneath it. "You don't need to hide yourself, Em."

"I'm not . . . I just don't like crowds."

"Come on," Rory coaxed. "It's just one night. Even the most dedicated misanthrope needs some time off. Don't make me go alone."

"I just don't think I'd enjoy it, Rory."

"How is that possible? Champagne, music, masterpieces of art, beautiful people in beautiful clothes . . ."

"I spend all day around people." Emma absently massaged a muscle beneath her ear. "People exhaust me."

"You can give up one night of reading yourself to sleep to spend a little time with the Pre-Raphaelite Brotherhood. There's an original Rossetti sketch, a study for his *Marina*. *Marina*, Em. Dead painters drawing inspiration from dead playwrights—it's everything that you love."

"I'll think about it."

"Really?" He smiled hesitantly, both peace offering and supplication.

Emma returned it with a small sigh. "Really, I'll think about it."

"That's all I can ask." Rory reached out and softly squeezed her hand. "I don't need the performance, you know. Backstage Emma is pretty great." He cleared his throat and looked away. "But for now, I have to run to yet another exceptionally dull meeting in a perfectly timed escape from my own mawkishness."

Emma laughed, letting the tugging emotions dissipate. "Still enjoying your time as dean, then?"

"*Interim* dean. I am being held against my will."

"I'll notify the UN."

She let her smile fade as he dashed off. Despite Rory's frequent invitations, Emma rarely went to the gala events, preferring to view the museum's collections in the relative privacy offered during public hours. Truth be told, she rarely went to any events. She'd never been particularly social—large groups made her want to crawl beneath the floorboards—preferring the solitude of reading even as a child. She'd cultivated that love as she grew up, studying literature, earning her PhD, and eventually turning her escape into a career.

But seeing herself through Rory's eyes, she realized how small her world had become. She had moved here just a year after grad school—Carlisle College was her first full-time job—and worked hard, earned tenure, and found her place and role at the college. It was a public institution but sufficiently provincial to bill itself as *intimate* in the glossy brochures. The limited budget led to the lecture hall freshman classes taught by teaching assistants and adjunct-heavy course offerings. But the full-time faculty were fierce in dedication to their disciplines. Emma's students often followed her from semester to semester, and she loved that she got to see their knowledge and thinking grow with each new text they encountered. She felt grounded here, valued, but—Rory's voice snuck in again—she didn't stray from the bounds of campus much. Her house was mere blocks away. Her regular grocery store, coffee shop, and bookstore all sat in between.

Carlisle wasn't exactly the proverbial ivory tower, but it largely kept itself separate from the surrounding town of Colchester, which had found itself in the midst of an identity crisis over the last few decades. Its role as a logging town had faded into the past, and a larger, more diverse population replaced those historical roots as the college had grown beyond its agricultural beginnings. Hidden in a valley and bound by forests, the community—still too small to be considered a city outside of the rural west—was now largely supported by the money the student population brought in. The college had slowly become a source of controversy among the generational residents as its success brought both new economic possibilities and perspectives to the expanding populace.

Emma frowned as she left the classroom, locking the door behind her. She was a bit socially awkward, she had been told, but had never considered herself a loner. Rory clearly saw her that way, though, and the thought bothered her. They had met soon after Emma had moved to Colchester and had briefly attempted a romance during her first year, but it had ended as an easy friendship rather than a passionate affair. Rory was one of the few people that Emma could count on. One of only a handful of friendships, mostly work friends really, but she was close to her family—although they all lived back East—plus . . . her students? Maybe Rory was right.

She jogged down the stairs to the ground floor, stepping into the soft light of fading summer. Campus echoed with the usual sounds of laughter and chatter as she crossed the quad to her office. Students were scattered across the still-green grass, singly and in groups, like post-storm debris. They leaned and loafed on every surface. Those on their way to class moved in eddies around others enjoying the last of the summer weather. Hard light had scattered the morning clouds and mottled the ground with soft shadows of not-yet-fallen leaves. It was the third week of the term, and the students knew that the warmth would be short-lived; the previous night's storm had already scented the air with the sharp tang of autumn. Some were laughing, some taut with concentration, but they thrummed with life and potential. Emma felt a sudden longing for that feeling, for the warm days when everything was colored by a surety in the world's possibilities. She wanted to stand at a precipice, bracing for the next step.

The bell in the clock tower began its sonorous summons and propelled them all into action. With a sigh, Emma left the sunlight for the cool recesses of her office.

Chapter 3

Ian was itemizing evidence, noting the descriptions and statements that would begin to form their investigation. He and Mike were both running on just a few hours of sleep, having stayed at the barn until the darkness drove them home, and arrived at first light this morning, an unspoken urgency pulling them from their beds. The girl in the barn was far from their usual domestic cases, and Ian felt a slick sense of guilt at the soft excitement rising in him. If asked, he told people he was a cop because he believed everyone deserved justice. He'd joined the force to speak for those who couldn't speak for themselves. But he admitted to himself that righteous dedication had chipped and peeled beneath the perpetual tedium of small, senseless crimes and small, senseless people. Justice alone wasn't enough to motivate anyone outside of the movies. Some cops stayed on the job for the power, some for the pension, and some for lack of a better plan. Ian stayed because he wanted the win. He liked outthinking the other guy, whether a criminal, a witness, a defense attorney, or another cop. He came to this job every day, with all its darkness, grime, and banal human cruelty, because of that moment when they realized he wasn't what they thought he was. But this case felt different. This killer was playing a game, laying out the puzzle pieces and issuing his challenge. That alone was enough to keep Ian awake.

And there was the girl.

There had been no ID, no license on the body, no prints in the system. It would come down to luck—and Ian's ability—to solve the puzzle. They would need a witness to come forward, or a missing person's report, which seemed possible, as this most likely was a student. Hopefully, Ian thought, while the grieving family could still ID her too-quiet face. If not, they'd need to use dental records, a grim but too-likely prospect for the girl currently bearing a small white tag labeled Jane Doe. He looked up from the file he was creating as Mike tapped a pencil to get his attention. The second floor of the police department where they were seated was designed for function rather than aesthetics, with sturdy desks and mismatched chairs filling the space. The precinct was unusually quiet as Ian and Mike worked. Their desks, which faced each other, were covered with precisely labeled documents and files; slightly out-of-date desktop monitors created a barrier between them. Mike would have been happy relying on digital files, but Ian liked the tactile process of sorting and organizing physical files. There was satisfaction in the slow accrual.

"Initial toxicology came back," Mike said. "We'll have to wait for the full report, but it looks like our Jane Doe from the barn picked the red pill *and* the blue pill. Nothing illegal, though—assuming she had a prescription."

"Quick turnaround," Ian said. He gave his partner a disapproving look. It made him uncomfortable when Mike bent the rules and jumped the line.

Mike shrugged. "I'm persuasive."

Ian shook his head. "What'd they find?"

"Nothing recreational. A pain reliever and a sedative, enough to knock her out pretty good. The amount suggests that she was drugged for a few days prior to death."

"Traceable?"

Mike shook his head. "All of it's easy to get a hold of. I've got the same pain meds in my bathroom cabinet from when the kids convinced Brian to try snowboarding and he messed up his knee."

"I'll put you on the suspect list," Ian said dryly.

"Me and every other middle-aged guy." Mike glanced up. "Brace yourself."

Ian turned. Ivy Wollard was crossing the precinct toward them with clipped steps and definite intent. "Persuasive?"

Mike grinned unabashedly.

The diminutive woman reached Mike's desk and slapped a manila envelope down in front of him. "Autopsy report. Crime scene report. Stop harassing my people." Ivy turned on her heel and started away.

"Can you give us a rundown of the basics?" Mike asked in a lazy drawl designed to antagonize her. "We coppers aren't really up on all that . . . science."

Ivy inhaled and exhaled sharply through her nose before turning back. She stared at Mike for a long moment before turning very deliberately to Ian. Mike smirked.

"Her hyoid was broken, indicating strangulation. Ligature suggests that she was strangled with a small, thin object—baling twine, judging by the fibers collected from the wound. Probably found at the scene."

"Strangled, not hung?" Mike asked.

Ivy stiffened. "She was strangled . . . manually."

"Any defensive wounds?" Ian asked.

"No. She was likely sedated at the time of death."

"Could it have been an accidental overdose?" Ian asked.

"It's possible but unlikely." Ivy paused. "These aren't recreational drugs."

"Huh," Mike said lightly, "I said the same thing."

"Every clock, twice a day," Ivy retorted.

"What did the crime techs find?" Mike asked too casually.

"It's in the report." Ivy glanced down at him dismissively and turned back to Ian. "One point of interest: she was drugged but well cared for before she was killed. No signs of physical or sexual assault. She was well hydrated, well-groomed, and had eaten within the last day. Whatever his reasons for keeping her for that long, it wasn't torture. Or rape."

"Practically a saint then," Mike added, sotto voce.

Ivy ignored him. "If you have questions, email."

"Thanks, Ivy," Ian said, an apology in his tone. She nodded in acknowledgment, then turned and walked, straight-backed, from the room.

Mike grinned at Ian. "Always a delight."

"You know there are other detectives whose cases you disrupt when you pull that shit."

"You know that the mayor's already called the lieutenant twice to check for updates? Pretty blonde girl gets murdered and posed like a Barbie—it's going to be front-page news across the country by tomorrow, and we're going to be part of the twenty-four-hour news cycles until this is solved. Not to mention fucking social media. Crazies will be coming out of the woodwork."

"You think we should get special treatment because our vic is pretty and blonde?" Ian knew the accusation was unfair but couldn't leave it unspoken.

Mike didn't take the bait. "I'll send the other detectives a card with my deepest regrets. Okay, Boy Scout," Mike dismissed him. "Let's see what Little Mary Sunshine brought us." He flipped open the crime scene report. "Trace suggests she was killed in the barn; too much debris there to find much of use. The flowers around her neck were generic, the kind you can get at any craft store. No identifying marks on the gown." Mike glanced up. "I'll get Jones to check with local costume shops, community theaters, and the like, but five will give you twenty he got everything online."

"Hard to check that without a suspect first."

"No shit."

"Anything on the kids who found her?"

"Teenage stoners. Apparently, the barn isn't a regular spot, but some guy told them there'd be a party that night."

"Some guy? They didn't know him?"

"No. Said they'd seen him around, he'd bought from them occasionally, but they couldn't give us a name."

"Description?" Ian asked.

"Medium height, medium build, brown or blond-ish hair, white."

"So, every third guy out there. Was it a setup, do you think? They wanted the body found?"

"Seems like. He'd need to have her found reasonably soon; that scene wouldn't have lasted."

"Unlikely we'll get anything off of that description, but let's have them make a sketch to send around." Ian tapped his pen thoughtfully. "Anything on the paper under her tongue?"

"Size and paper type match the book found at the scene, but the page was folded and degraded from being in her mouth. They can't tell yet what's on it—if anything."

"Can they tell what the book is?"

"No such luck. The pages are covered in blood, congealed to the point that it's unreadable. They could scan it, might be able to see what's underneath."

"Suggest that to Ivy. I bet she'd appreciate the help."

Mike cast a mocking look at Ian and went back to the report. "Blood's animal, not human. Pig, most likely."

"Prints?" Ian prompted.

"Two partials on the rim of the trough. Ran 'em through IAFIS. Nada."

"Couldn't be that easy."

"Nope. But they match a latent collected from an assault case up in—" Mike checked his notes "—Northport. Back in June."

"I'll put a call into the precinct and see if they have anything useful. He might have started there before coming to us," Ian offered.

"Well, it was unlikely this was his first kill. No one starts out this pretty."

Ian glanced up to see if his partner was making a crude joke, but Mike's face was passive as he continued reading over the file.

"Speaking of pretty, shouldn't you be heading off to the ball, Cinderella?" Mike asked, still not looking up.

"Shit." Ian glanced at the clock. He was going to be late. He mentally calculated the time it would take to get home, change, shave, and get to the museum. He was definitely going to be late. He snatched his jacket from the back of the chair.

"Are you sure you don't need me . . . ?" Ian asked as he shrugged it on.

"Not much more we can do tonight. Enjoy your champagne, Boy Scout."

Chapter 4

Her face ducked low against the rain, Emma dashed up the stone steps leading into the museum. She bundled her skirt in one hand while the gathering puddles soaked the toes of her satin shoes. The final summer warmth had fled as another storm crept over Carlisle. Her duck-handled umbrella battered against the multicolored blockade of rain-savvy patrons, sending splinters of water lashing back at her. She stepped over the threshold of the broad, glass doors into a well-lit room, her skin pricking in the air-conditioned cool of the gallery. Shaking off as much water as she could, she stuffed her umbrella into a plastic bag provided by a clearly bored coat check attendant, and left that, along with her coat, at the counter.

"Purse," the attendant said, holding out her hand.

"No thanks, I'll keep it."

The woman shrugged, and Emma tugged the purse up on her shoulder, mentally deriding her lack of pockets and the impracticality of women's formal wear. She tried not to fidget with the narrow strap.

"Fun," she told herself on a breath. "This will be fun."

Moving with the crowd to the designated starting point, she automatically paused to take in her surroundings, centering herself as the press of people threaded a knot of discomfort in her chest. The sharp details of the brightly colored images stood in stark relief against the matte white walls. Pleasantly unobtrusive music floated through the room as expensively dressed guests moved from painting to painting, conversing in hushed tones. The faint scent of designer perfume and damp cloth surrounded Emma as she moved farther into the gallery. Each wall was decorated for both aesthetics and efficiency.

Emma hovered near the edge of the crowd, doing her best to find space in the room, and picked up a tastefully designed program announcing: "Light and Darkness: The Pre-Raphaelite Artists of Victorian England." She thumbed through it briefly, dog-earing the paintings she especially wanted to see, and accepted a glass of champagne proffered by a black-vested server who could have been no more than twenty. She mentally ran through her class rosters to see if he had been one of her students. She couldn't place him but smiled politely, just in case. Emma had always had a memory for texts, memorizing passages easily and recalling illustrations in minute detail. People, though, never seemed to stick.

The crowd shifted forward to a painting of a beautiful young woman, eyes downcast, with golden hair flowing down around a Renaissance-style dress. Emma leaned close to study the precision of the painted pearls grasped in the girl's hand. An overeager museum docent sidled toward her, and Emma wrapped the fingers of both hands around her champagne flute to show that she could be trusted not to slosh its contents onto the century-old work of art. She felt a firm pressure on her arm and arranged her face into amicable politeness in anticipation of the inevitable acquaintance wanting to exchange greetings. Rory was grinning down at her. Emma relaxed, feeling a beat of gratitude that she'd be able to postpone the ritual of small talk with a stranger for a few more minutes.

"You came," he said excitedly, his voice a touch too loud.

"I came." She looked up at him, hoping her enthusiasm was convincing. "I just . . . decided you were right. I could do with a night out."

Rory snagged a glass of champagne from the tray of a passing waiter—not his first of the night, Emma guessed. He slid his hand to the small of her back, then immediately lifted it as she tensed. She could smell a light musk of sweat, alcohol, and the dense spice of his cologne.

"I'm glad you came," Rory said. He studied her face for a moment, then stepped back. "What have you seen so far?"

"Not much. I just got here."

"Well, it's not the Tate, but I'm pleased with what we pulled together. The bigger works are all by less known artists—there's a few 'in the school of' as well—but we've got a small Burne-Jones sketch, there's a Hunt on loan from a private collector, and they did a great job with the photography exhibit—the Cameron stuff is excellent."

"It's great, Rory. Really. You and the rest of the board should be proud."

He smiled at the praise, but his attention shifted across the room before he could reply. "Damn. I was hoping to show you around, but I'm technically here in an official capacity, and it appears that a few of my underlings need attention."

Emma turned to see a group of students who looked just on the wrong side of tipsy.

"Go. I'm good at flying solo."

"No fleeing to the sculpture garden; we can't afford to lose you to the darkness."

"Don't worry. I have enough small talk saved up to survive one evening. Lunch next week?"

"I'll have Caro block off my calendar." He dropped a light

kiss on her cheek and turned into the crowd. "Skip to the third painting—it's one you'll want to spend some time with."

Emma took his advice and wove through the crowd as knots of people paused in front of the next two paintings—a rather staid portrait of a girl in white and a still life of sword hilts—glancing at them only briefly. At the third, she felt a swell of warmth in her chest. On the canvas was a beautiful honey-haired woman in a golden gown rising from her seat at a loom. Colored threads slipped from her fingers, tangling around her wrists and catching in her pooled skirt as she rose and turned from her work. A tapestry of a medieval village sat unfinished beside her. She stood in profile, gazing longingly out of a window. Her body tipped forward slightly, and one hand came upward as if she were straining toward the outside world. Through another window, just over her shoulder, a small boat was moored, waiting. A cracked and blackened mirror behind her reflected a jagged image of what had so captivated the young woman: beyond the window, an armored knight and palfrey were just discernible in the glass fragments. Emma felt oddly voyeuristic as she examined the painting.

"I feel as if I shouldn't be watching." A low voice echoed her thoughts.

Emma glanced up from her reverie, too startled to construct her expression. A tall, wiry man studied the canvas, his eyes seeming to settle on the boat in the distance.

"*The Lady of Shalott*," Emma offered. Then, after a pause to consider her companion, she added, "Do you know the story?"

The man looked at her directly, and Emma was momentarily startled. His eyes, sharp and unblinking, were the palest blue, almost frost-colored, and gave the unnerving impression that he wasn't seeing her at all.

"Tennyson, right?" he asked. "She was cursed to live in a castle tower, weaving images of the world around her, but only able to see real life through her mirror. But then, she decides that's not enough and leaves. The mirror cracks, the curse is triggered, and she dies." The man returned his gaze to the painting.

"'The curse is come upon me,'" Emma quoted with a frown. "She sees Sir Lancelot and is overcome by love. It's all-consuming. World-shattering. But it's not just him—it's what he represents. He's freedom, joy, hope, life—she can't bear to stay in her tower once she knows what the world outside can offer. She chooses knowledge over security. All she can do is write her name on the boat and hope, as it carries her body toward Camelot, that someone understands." Emma, too, turned back to the painting.

"Like Eve with the apple."

"What?"

"You said she chose knowledge over security. Like Eve."

"Very like." Emma gave him an appraising look. Something dark passed beneath the ice-blue eyes, and Emma felt a burst of nerves. "The Pre-Raphaelites were fascinated by tragic love stories like Tennyson and Shakespeare and, and . . ." Emma's mind blanked as she looked up to see those eyes on her once again. His skin was fair, with the faintest etching of stubble across a slight but firm jaw. Her breathing quickened slightly from attraction or nerves—Emma wasn't sure. She slid her fingers along her purse strap, accidentally pulling it from her shoulder.

"And?" His lips quirked as she dropped the purse and awkwardly stooped to catch it.

A blush crept across her cheeks. "Centuries of stories tell us that love will only end in heartbreak. We keep trying anyway. Maybe she thought it was worth it." Emma looked back at the doomed woman on the canvas.

"Maybe it was." His voice was soft and slightly sad as he studied the textures and color of the paint, lost in the web it created.

Emma glanced up, then away, catching her bottom lip between her teeth. She stepped quickly to the next painting, trying to elude the feeling of ineptness that was spreading over her. The man moved with her, standing close as the other patrons undulated around them. They stared together at a depiction of Shakespeare's Ophelia. Most artists captured the distraught girl sinking beneath murky waters, lost in grief. This Ophelia, though, stood at the end of the stream, flowers cradled in her skirt, as she looked directly back at those who studied her. She had wildly streaming hair and bare feet, but something in the pose suggested all was not yet lost. Emma imagined that her eyes were pleading—for help? Forgiveness? Emma leaned in to study the doomed woman's expression. The man brushed close and moved away again as he stepped past the crowd. Emma could smell the clean scent of his laundry detergent twined with something headier, warm skin and spice. Emma caught sight of a familiar flicker in his eyes as he studied the painting in silence.

"Did she die for love, too?" he finally asked.

"In a way," Emma responded, her voice soft. "She was Hamlet's beloved, but he spurned her when he chose a path of vengeance. Arguably, he did it to protect her—pushing her away to keep her safe."

"He White Fanged her?"

"Yes. But then he killed her father, so he loses a few chivalry points there."

"That would make for an awkward Christmas dinner."

Emma smiled, surprised by how much she was enjoying the banter. "Well, it was an accident, but she didn't know that." Emma reached a hand toward the painted flowers, her own fingertips hovering near the dying girl's.

"She's . . . compelling," the man said, his voice uneasy. "What happened to her?"

"She was overcome by grief. To Shakespeare's audience—and the Victorians—those flowers would have told the whole story. Crowflowers represent mourning, nettles mean pain, daisies for innocence—Ophelia's story gathered by her own hands. 'There is a willow grows aslant a brook, that shows his hoary leagues in the glassy stream: There with fantastique garlands did she come, of crowflowers, nettles, daisies, and long purples. There on the pendant boughs, her coronet weeds, clambering to hang; an envious sliver broke. Her garments, heavy with her drink, pulled the poor wretch from her melodious lay . . . to muddy death.'" Emma quoted the lines from *Hamlet* gently, lost in the words.

"You seem to know the play well," he said.

"Sorry." Emma's face flushed. "I do that. Bad habit."

"It wasn't a complaint." Silence enveloped them. Emma began to fidget with her purse again, then pulled her hand sharply down.

The man smiled as he caught the gesture and moved to the next painting, a rather flat-looking portrait of a woman clothed in reds and oranges, holding a small treasure box. Emma followed a step behind.

"That's Pandora, who released all of the evils of the world," Emma offered.

"Another woman who chose knowledge over safety."

"Hesiod interpreted the story as a warning against the evils of women."

The man shrugged. "You tell anyone not to touch something, they're going to want to touch it."

The man had spoken while looking toward the painting, but Emma felt her skin warm. With Rory's gentle worry fresh in her mind, she had taken pains with her appearance that evening. Her auburn hair was curled and brushed away from her face, held loosely in a jeweled clip. She had chosen the deep blue of her floor-length gown, with a matching stone glinting in the hollow of her throat, to complement her English coloring. He turned toward her, and the fabric suddenly felt stiff, heavy, and awkward.

"Ian Carter," the man said, leaning in so his voice wouldn't be lost in the din.

"What?" Emma spoke on a startled inhale as she felt his breath against her cheek.

He moved back slightly and raised his voice. "I'm Ian Carter."

"Emma. Emma Reilly."

"Do you teach, Emma?" At her blank expression, he added, "You seem to know a lot about all of this."

"Yes. I, um . . . literature, at the college." He looked at her, clearly expectant, but she couldn't think of anything to add. "What do you do?" she blurted finally.

"I'm a detective." He hesitated. "Homicide."

"Oh." Emma looked up at him, playing the last ten minutes back in her mind. "I'm so sorry." He flinched back a fraction. "No! Not, sorry for you. Or about you. Sorry that I kept talking about . . . dead people."

Ian's stance softened. "Don't be. This was interesting. And I got far more information than I would have just reading the placards."

"Well, I team-taught a course that included a trip to London last summer. One of our art professors discussed the, well, art, and I covered the literary aspects. It was actually a fascinating interdisciplinary approach . . ." Emma's rush of words broke off as she saw Ian's focus shift.

"I'm sure . . ." Ian's glance flicked toward her as he spoke, but she could tell she didn't really register. He was watching something, or someone, across the room.

Emma fought down a confusing sense of disappointment.

"This is going to seem extremely rude and . . ." His gaze flicked behind her again. His face had closed down into a cool, hard mask, and his body tightened as if readying for a confrontation. He jerked his chin toward the other side of the room. "Something is going on over there, a girl . . ." Emma followed his glance but didn't see whatever had compelled him. He looked over again. "I need to see if I can . . . do anything. I'll try to find you when I can."

"Okay," Emma replied feebly. "I'll see you later . . . I guess."

Ian strode quickly away, with none of the awkward ambling suggested by his long frame. Emma scanned the room but saw nothing particularly interesting—the usual throng of wealthy donors in evening wear standing separate from the less refined academics whose combined donations and passion were enough to earn them invitations. As Ian faded into the crowd, Emma's brain began to catalog all of the moments of awkwardness in their interaction—every fidget, overshare, and too-eager explanation. She quickly shut it down, suppressing the well-recognized voices of criticism, but the colors of the evening had dulled. She turned back to the paintings, telling herself each story again, unwilling to explore the shadow of regret that settled over her.

Chapter 5

Ian stepped into the maze of people, each seeming like an obstacle to overcome—silken dress hems, polished shoes, waving hands with champagne glasses eager to be spilled. He moved as quickly as possible, a familiar charge running along his skin as he pushed toward the scene that had caught his eye. It had been just a flash of a moment, a scared look across the face of a young blonde woman; she couldn't be more than twenty by Ian's calculation. A man a bit older had reached out and grasped her arm, a seemingly innocuous gesture, but the woman's reaction had been clear, even from across the room. A shifting of weight, tension in the muscles, eyebrows raised, mouth tight, arms crossed—the image of a victim facing a predator. Ian couldn't see the young man's face, but his body straightened and broadened as he moved toward her with an equally unmistakable response. He was drawn to her fear.

Then, in an instant, the postures reversed. Her face smoothed into a haughty stare, her shoulders pulled back, and her eyes ran along the man defiantly. She jerked her arm away from his touch. The man stepped back so quickly that he almost fell. Ian stopped his progress, searching for the cause of the sudden shift, when he noticed five people approaching the girl. There were three girls and two boys, all of a similar age. None had apparently seen the moment or the blonde's reaction to it, but their presence created a palpable wall of support for the girl to lean on. One of the young men, an athlete Ian judged by his build, stepped up and tucked the girl against his side. The blonde woman's face was triumphant. The athlete leaned down and said something Ian couldn't hear from where the sedately moving patrons hemmed him in.

The girl responded to her new companion, but her eyes stayed on the man who had grabbed her. He froze before them, his bravado melting until he looked almost hunched. The group rippled with laughter. The blonde tossed a comment out, and the laughter grew. Ian moved forward instinctively, but an older woman with a cane elbowed him sharply back, muttering about young people with no manners as she stepped past him. The girl turned toward the safety of her friends, and the young man disappeared into the crowd. Ian realized uneasily that he didn't have a clear image of the man. His suit had been a bit rumpled, generic and dark, his hair a bit long and blandly brown. He had a medium build and was medium height. Ian felt a sudden sympathy for all of the eyewitnesses who had described an assailant as "just ordinary."

"Shit," he said aloud, startling a silk-wrapped woman at his elbow. She glared.

He mumbled an apology and turned away. He retraced his steps, trying to shake the threads of adrenaline that still shivered along his skin. He tried to convince himself that he'd sensed something, that some instinct from his years on the force had told him that the blonde had needed help. But he was lying, and he knew it. He'd overreacted. That girl had been fine, and he'd—Ian took a breath to clear away the mingled dust of emotion and memory. That girl wasn't Zoey, he chastised himself. Playing hero now wouldn't change his choices then, the help he hadn't offered when she'd needed it.

It hadn't been his fault, a voice in his head reassured him. But it was Mike's voice, not his own, and he struggled to believe it. He glanced back over his shoulder to the space where the girl had been. She was gone.

So, he realized with a very different emotion, was Emma. He surveyed the room for a bright swirl of blue that would announce her presence but found nothing. Ian scanned the paintings systematically, trying to conjure her next to each of them. He finally spotted her near the main doors. Pleasure sparked like a static shock. She looked isolated, even as other people churned around her. Ian followed at a distance for a moment, compelled by her. She paused briefly before each painting, never looking at the descriptive placards, keeping her hands carefully close. There was something—not frightened, Ian thought—wary about her movements. She wasn't comfortable here. But Ian could see in the careful lines of her body and the mild smile that she carried at all times that she was trying to blend in. Emma turned toward the entrance, and Ian increased his pace. As he worked through the crowd, he planned his approach, his opening line, ran through possibilities for her response—then stopped short.

She'd turned with a smile, but it wasn't for him. A man approached, obviously someone Emma knew. He was catalog handsome, with sandy blond hair that curled in intentional messiness around his tanned face. He had sharp green eyes and a firm chin. She knew him and, Ian noted, clearly liked him. Her body had softened just slightly, her smile shifting from the painted mask to one of genuine pleasure. Their body language was familiar but—Ian convinced himself—not intimate. Emma dropped her head. Coquettishly? No—Ian recognized relief in the gesture.

Ian resolutely turned away, pushing down a sharp sting of disappointment. He worked through the flow of people back to the painting of Ophelia and continued his tour where he'd left off, trying not to critique the museum's program notes against Emma's much more engaging discussion. He knew the story, of course—murdered king, angsty prince, evil uncle, tragic deaths—but he'd forgotten poor Ophelia in all the bloodshed. The graveyard scene, he remembered, and Hamlet's famous conversation with the skull. But Ophelia and her flowers . . . he stepped closer. She had a softly rounded face and long auburn hair dancing around her shoulders. Her green eyes caught his, and he saw Emma reflected in those gentle features, remembered the soft touch of rose scenting her skin. He turned away, suddenly troubled that he hadn't remembered what had happened to Ophelia.

Chapter 6

Emma had continued around the exhibit after Ian disappeared into the crowd, trying to avoid small talk with other patrons until the gala began to wind down. She collected her coat and umbrella—still slightly soggy as she pulled it from its plastic cover—and joined the other attendees on the museum's portico. Tucking the now crumpled program into her purse, she scanned the crowd, half hoping to see Ian. Instead, Rory appeared beside her. She turned, smiling.

"Having fun, Em?"

"I was—am."

"It looked like it." Rory flashed a dimpled grin.

Emma felt her skin heat. "I wasn't, I mean . . ."

"No worries, love. I had my shot. It's nice to see you playing so well with others."

"I'm not a child, Rory." Emma's embarrassment made her voice harder than she had intended.

"No, you most definitely are not. I didn't mean to infantilize. You just looked like you were genuinely enjoying yourself, and since I'm the one who talked you into coming . . ." He trailed off, his expression questioning. He smiled at Emma's sheepish glance, risking a gentle quip. "Did you lecture at him?"

"Oh, god." Emma dropped her head forward. "I did. So, so much."

"Good. That's when you're at your best."

"Just because you find social awkwardness endearing doesn't mean that the rest of the world does."

Rory leaned close. "Then fuck the world. They don't deserve you." He reached for her hand and pressed it gently. "Lunch this week, don't forget." Emma watched him jog down the stairs into the dark night and felt a pull of longing. Their brief romantic relationship had fizzled quickly, and Emma wondered—not for the first time—if she'd made a mistake ending it. If it would have worked out if she'd just been able to . . . be something else. Emma sighed. A floppy-haired boy brushed by her, running as if he were trying to catch up with someone. Rory glanced over his shoulder at the boy but didn't adjust his quick pace.

Emma flipped up her coat collar, opened her umbrella against the still-falling rain, and descended to the glistening sidewalk without enthusiasm. She turned away from the crowd as the departing guests flowed toward the adjoining parking structure, heading in the opposite direction down a tree-lined sidewalk where the streetlamps struggled to break through the damp and drear. She had parked several blocks away to avoid the exorbitant fees that always cropped up on gala nights but regretted it with each step, her heeled feet already sore from the marble floors. She made it two blocks at a limping pace before she caught the heel of her shoe in a crack in the sidewalk. The shoe jammed against her foot, and she lurched sideways, her clutch and umbrella scattering as she fell. Emma caught herself against a tree trunk, feeling the skin of her palm snag as she gripped the rough bark. Hissing in pain, she tucked the sore hand against her stomach. She spotted her umbrella just to her left and the purse farther down the sidewalk, haloed in the light of a streetlamp. Abandoning her good shoe next to the broken one, she stepped gingerly away from the tree toward her belongings, trying in vain to lift her gown away from the muddy ground.

As she bent for the umbrella, a weight against her back sent her skidding forward. Her legs tangled in her heavy skirt, and she fell onto her hands, collapsing to her elbows as her muscles instinctively pulled the raw palm of her hand away from the pain of impact. Emma rolled to her side, shoving her damp hair back and bracing for further assault. She registered the brief blur of an arm grabbing her dropped purse, then the splash and clack of footsteps moving rapidly down the puddled sidewalk.

Watching as the running figure grew ever more abstract in the angling rain, Emma struggled to right herself in the soggy grass. Her breath echoed harshly in the air, and cold tremors traced her limbs. She slipped, sitting down hard, then pulled her knees to her chest. She closed her eyes, trying to shut out the world enough to calm her breathing and slow the pounding of her heart. As she felt the panic settle into a dull throb, footsteps approached quickly from behind. Fear immediately spiked again, and she scrambled backward into the darkness. A figure stepped into the uneven light of the streetlamp.

"Emma," Ian said, slightly breathless. "Are you alright? What happened?"

He shifted forward and dropped onto his heels to see her better. Moving slowly as if she were a skittish animal, he gently pushed a strand of hair back from her eyes. Goose bumps rose along her skin. "Take a deep breath. Tell me what happened."

Emma dug her fingers into the wet grass, using the coarse textures to ground herself. "Someone . . ." Emma trailed off as she shifted away and pointed up the now empty street. The dim lights illuminated the sweeping rain, turning the dark street into an impressionistic watercolor. "Someone came up behind me, pushed me down, and took my purse."

"Are you injured?"

Emma shook her head. "They didn't really hurt me, just shoved me down."

"Good. That's good." Ian reached out, gingerly taking her bloodied palms and helping her to her feet. He stood silent for a moment as he took in her dishevelment, then glanced around. Spotting the abandoned umbrella, he scooped it up, slid it open, and gently tugged Emma beneath its cover.

"You'll want to make a report."

"My phone was in the purse and—damn it!—my keys." Emma shut her eyes. "Damn it," she repeated softly.

Without responding, Ian pulled his cell phone from an inner jacket pocket. He called the police station, tersely explaining that he was on sight with a mugging victim and needed an officer to take her statement. He looked around briefly and then gave the address of an all-night diner up the street.

"Come on," he said, taking Emma by the elbow, "let's get out of the rain."

The police officers—a weather-beaten older woman and a round-faced man young enough to be at home in one of Emma's classes—arrived just as Ian set two cups of hot black coffee down on one of the diner's Formica tables. The reflected lights from the diner's neon window sign colored the porcelain mugs in muted tones that rotated as the sign blinked. Ian nodded a greeting and slid into the vinyl booth opposite Emma, gingerly lifting his cup to his lips. Emma left hers alone. She had been to the bathroom to clean up as well as possible, wiping smudged makeup from her face with coarse paper towels and tugging her fingers through her hair, but she was very aware that, under the fluorescent lights, she looked like Viola after the shipwreck in *Twelfth Night*.

"So, ma'am," began the young officer, "I'm Officer Gonzales. Please tell us what happened as specifically as you can."

Emma sighed. "I was walking from the museum to my car. I'd parked it about four blocks away, and . . ."

"Why?" interrupted the officer.

"What?"

"Why did you park so far away?"

"It's cheaper." Emma looked at him, but he said nothing further, so she continued. "I was walking toward my car. I tripped over a crack in the sidewalk and dropped my things—my purse and umbrella. As I bent to get them, someone came up behind me, shoved me to the ground, and grabbed my purse." The two officers stared at her as if waiting for her to continue. "That's it."

Emma reached for the coffee in front of her, needing something to do with her hands, and sipped it quietly. She concentrated on the heat from the mug as it permeated her fingers.

"Did you get a look at the mugger?"

"Not really. I'm pretty sure it was a man; I think he was wearing a suit jacket. Dark—blue or black. Maybe gray. Medium height and weight. I couldn't tell any more than that."

"Young or old?" the older cop asked.

"Young? He ran quickly, easily. Moderately athletic, I think. I just don't know. I'm sorry."

"And you didn't see him, Detective?"

Ian shook his head. "I arrived too late."

The woman looked back at Emma. "Did the assailant say anything to you?"

Emma shook her head. "Nothing."

"Did he have a weapon of any kind?"

"No, he just shoved me out of the way, took the purse, and ran."

The older officer dropped her eyes in a quick assessment. "You look pretty scraped up. Are you sure that's all there was to it?"

Emma curled her fingers over her scraped hands. "Like I said, I fell. Before he shoved me."

"Convenient he was there, right at that moment," the other woman told her without hiding her skepticism.

"Coincidences happen," Ian inserted firmly.

"Of course, Detective." After a brief moment of eye contact, she turned her attention back to Emma. "Which direction did he go?"

"Toward Carry Street, but it was raining pretty heavily. I could only see him for a block or so."

"Is there anything distinctive about the purse or contents?"

"Not really. It was just a purse, dark blue suede with a silver buckle. It had my wallet—it's black, just a cheap one—with my credit card, driver's license, discount cards, maybe twenty in cash . . ." Emma thought for a moment. "My phone was in there, a red Android, a paperback, and my key ring—car key, house key, and a singing skull key chain."

Officer Gonzales, who had been taking diligent notes, paused at this. "A singing . . ."

"Skull. Key chain," Emma repeated. "It plays 'I Ain't Got Nobody,' and the eyes blink red."

Emma caught a small smile from Ian, but the older officer nodded, unfazed.

"Well, Ms. Reilly, we'll file a report, but—" The officer was interrupted by a mechanical voice from Gonzales's belt. She jerked her head in a clear order, and the man stepped away from them as he retrieved his radio. "But unfortunately, the odds of finding your purse are slim. My guess is someone just saw you trip and seized an opportunity. Cancel any credit cards that you had with you and contact your bank. Change your locks, just in case. You may want to consider a credit monitoring service, as well."

"That's it?" Emma asked.

The officer glanced at Ian, then back at her. "Do you need a lift home?"

Officer Gonzales returned in time to hear his partner's offer. "Actually, ah . . . we just got a report of a drug deal going down up the block."

"That preppy Ken Doll, again?"

"Ah, yeah." Officer Gonzales's forehead crinkled with a frown. "So . . ."

"Oh. No, it's fine. I'm fine. Thanks anyway. I can . . ." Emma's voice faded as she realized that without a phone, keys, or money, there wasn't anything she could do. She could borrow a phone and call . . . someone.

"I'll make sure that she gets home," Ian offered. The woman glanced at her, and Emma offered a fleeting smile.

"Okay, then. Detective. Miss." The two officers nodded and left the diner, a small bell chiming their departure.

Emma dropped her head back, exhausted both by the attack and the evening of social interaction. Ian cleared his throat awkwardly. "Shall I take you home, or—" Ian added quickly "—call you a cab?"

Emma kept her face turned away as she felt her cheeks heat. "There are people I could call," she said quietly.

"The man from the gala? I saw you with him . . . blond . . . tall . . ." Ian trailed off at her obvious bewilderment.

"You mean Rory? No, he's—" Emma stopped. Probably out with someone else, she thought. Rory didn't like to be alone. Her stomach clenched at the idea of interrupting him, the pitying look, the annoyance from whoever he was with . . . She shook her head. "No. Not Rory."

"Do you want a ride, then? I'm happy to."

"You don't need to . . ." Emma felt something swirl in her chest and looked down, suddenly very aware of how dirty she was. She felt a burst of embarrassment as she realized her backside must be covered in grass stains and mud.

"Then, can I—" Ian sounded uncertain. "Would you like some pie?"

Emma looked up, startled by the unexpected offer. "What?"

"No, of course not. You've just been assaulted. You're wet and probably cold and . . ."

"Kind of hungry, actually." Emma spoke without really meaning to. She started to retract her comment, then registered the flash of relief on Ian's face. "Pie would be nice."

He smiled. "Apple or lemon meringue?"

"Apple, with whipped cream."

When Ian arrived back at the table, each hand holding a plate of apple pie, Emma had her foot on the chair next to her, examining her torn stockings and bloodied knees.

"What's the damage?" he asked.

She quickly pushed her dress down over her leg, hiding the wounds from his assessing gaze, and turned back to the table. "It's not that bad."

He sat stiffly, and Emma stayed silent, not wanting to make the moment even more uncomfortable with a burst of unruly words.

"What was the paperback?" he asked finally. "The one in your purse."

Emma's smile was small but genuine as he offered safe ground. She wondered if he'd hit on the topic through insight or luck. "*Jane Eyre*. Brontë. Have you read it?"

He nodded, swallowing a bite of pie. "In college. I remember liking it."

"It's one of my favorites. The copy was one I got when I was about thirteen, the first book I really loved."

"Why do you love it?"

"The Gothic mansion, the mysterious madwoman, the brooding hero with a shadowy past who dresses up as a fortune teller and falls in love with the—" Emma paused, unsure how to explain what she felt seeing the bright, rejected figure of the plain governess get a happy ending. She shrugged. "I was thirteen. And I related to Jane a lot at that age."

Ian nodded in understanding. "I always had a book with me growing up. Usually Tarzan."

"Tarzan? I would have guessed Sherlock Holmes."

"Tarzan was my grandfather's favorite. He gave me the full series when I was a kid. Now, I'm more of a Philip Marlowe guy."

"Never met a simile he didn't like," Emma quipped, lifting her fork, and letting some of the tension leave her muscles, "and he never could resist a damsel in distress, especially if it was a bad idea."

"'She was worth a stare. She was trouble.'" Ian smugly took a bite of pie as Emma's eyes widened. "You're not the only one who can quote the classics."

"*The Big Sleep* is definitely a classic." Emma returned Ian's smile, and they finished their pie in comfortable silence as the noise of the diner hummed pleasantly around them.

Sliding her finger around the rim to catch the last bit of apple filling, Emma pushed away her plate. Ian rose and helped her out of the booth when her raw knees protested. He fished a few dollars from his wallet and placed them on the table beneath a water glass.

"Let me give you a ride home. I'm parked just up the street."

She considered for only a second. "Okay."

Emma waited at the door of the diner as Ian jogged to his car. She watched the headlights flash on, cautious affection growing as he signaled to pull away from the curb and again as he slid into an empty spot in front of the diner. She stepped into the rain without waiting for Ian, but he still made it to the passenger side door in time to gently help her into the car. The rain beat heavily as a squeaky windshield wiper hurried to sweep it away. Emma guided him through the darkened streets to her house, her voice hushed by the storm. Ian dedicated himself to steering through the downpour to her modest two-bedroom house, the blue-gray structure vanishing into the dark and rain. Emma paused with her hand on the door handle to peer at the familiar facade. She took a deep breath and tried to quiet the narration in her head that was steadily identifying all of the places someone could be hiding.

"Do you want me to check, see if everything is okay?"

"I'm sure it's fine." Her voice sounded doubtful even to her.

"I'm happy to check . . ." She watched a debate play across Ian's face as he studied hers before it settled into reassuring confidence. "I'm sure everything is okay. A mugger isn't likely to take a chance on B and E. He saw an opportunity and took it, that's all. Still, maybe change your locks," Ian said as she nodded. "I'll call tomorrow and ask if the officers have found anything."

"Thanks," Emma replied, opening the door. Ian turned back to the steering wheel. "Wait here. Just for a minute," she said on impulse.

She climbed out and ran across the short distance to her porch without bothering to open her umbrella. She found the spare key under a statue of a self-satisfied cat on the front porch. Opening the door and flicking on a light, Emma hurried to the kitchen, her spontaneous decision chasing any thoughts of the bogeyman from her mind. She yanked open the junk drawer, looking for a notepad. Seeing a stray business card, she grabbed that instead and scribbled her number on the back. She dashed back down the rain-darkened sidewalk, not bothering to close the front door—not letting herself pause and think—and pulled open the passenger door. She leaned in, her hand extended. Ian took the small card from her, glancing at the embossed name and contact information.

"I owe you for the pie." She was surprised by the flirtation in her voice and brightened her smile to match it. Then panicked. Without waiting for him to respond, Emma shut the door and ran back through the storm to the halo of light that beckoned from her front steps. She'd wished for a precipice; now, she hoped she was ready for the fall.

Chapter 7

"I knew something was wrong," Lily Ellis, Sarah's roommate, told Ian for the second time. "When I reported her missing last week, the cops told me I was overreacting."

He and Mike had identified the girl from the barn that morning: Sarah Weston, twenty-one, had been a junior at Carlisle College. Her parents lived in Milwaukee. Her father had been stoic when Mike had called them; her mother had keened.

She continued. "They said she was just a college student who took off for a few days, probably with a boy, and she'd come back on her own when the fun was over. But that wasn't like her. Maybe she'd stay out for a night or two, but not three days." Lily clenched a tissue in her hand, her reddened nose and puffy eyes a testament to her grief.

"When did you last see her?"

"Last Friday. I went to a movie with some friends. She wasn't here when I got back."

Ian noted everything the girl told them as Mike asked gentle questions. Mike had a way of putting people at ease, making him an asset in any interview. Ian struggled with this part of the job.

"So," Mike continued, "she'd never done anything like that before? Never disappeared or took off with someone?"

"No. Never. She was really thoughtful. She'd never want to worry her family or me. Oh, god." Lily put her fingers to her lips. "Do her parents know?"

"They've been notified."

Lily nodded, silent.

"Had she been in any trouble?" Mike prompted.

"She . . . she had a rough time last year. Sarah was this amazing athlete, softball, track, golf—anything she tried, she was just golden. She had a full athletic scholarship and everything. But last year, she tore something in her knee, and the doctors told her she couldn't play anymore. She was devastated. She got really depressed, and with the pain from her knee . . ." Lily stopped to swipe the tissue under her nose. "She was on a lot of painkillers. They just made everything worse."

There was a long pause. Ian and Mike watched quietly as a tear streaked down the young woman's cheek.

Lily took two deep breaths and brushed quickly at the tear. "But she had been doing really well lately. She'd gotten treatment, stopped using, and she was seeing a therapist regularly. She was doing really well."

"Okay," Mike said soothingly. "Can you think of anyone who might have wanted to harm her?"

"No. Sarah was so amazing, and she didn't hang out with anyone sketchy. She had a prescription, so back when she was dealing with all of that, it's not like she was out buying meth in a parking lot."

"Did she have a boyfriend or anyone she might have contacted? Anyone who might know where she was heading the night she disappeared?"

"There was a guy, someone she'd been seeing last spring, but I don't know who it was."

"She never mentioned a name?"

"No. She said she didn't want to jinx it. And then they broke up at the start of summer, and she didn't talk about him after that."

"Did she end it, or did he?"

"Her, I think. She wasn't that upset."

"Did you ever meet him? See him pick her up? See a picture?"

"No. Never. I think he was older, though."

"What makes you say that?" Ian asked, speaking for the first time since he had introduced himself.

"She'd talk about the nice places he took her: ballets, symphonies, museums, fancy restaurants. Guys our age are more beer than Beethoven, you know? She said he'd always order fancy wine at dinner and buy her gifts—jewelry, expensive lingerie." Lily gave a wan smile. "Not the kind of things that college boys can afford."

"Anything else you can tell us about him?" Mike asked.

Lily shook her head. "Like I said, Sarah didn't talk about him much. Maybe if I had asked . . ."

Ian cut off the thought. "Do you know if she kept the gifts he gave her?"

"Maybe? I don't think she'd have thrown them out."

"Is there anyone else who was important in Sarah's life?"

"No. After she stopped playing sports, she lost touch with most of her teammates. There were a few people she'd study with, but no one close. It was just me, really." Lily's face began to crumple again.

"Do you know if Sarah had on anything distinctive when she left? Jewelry, special clothing . . . ?" Mike asked his question carefully.

"Um, she sometimes wore earrings or a necklace. I don't think her clothes were anything special, jeans and a shirt. She did have her nails painted, though."

"Her fingernails?"

Lily shook her head. "Toenails. We did pedicures while we were watching a movie. She used lime-green polish. I told her it was so ugly, but she . . . That was the last night I saw her." The girl's voice caught on a rough laugh that melted into a soft sob.

"Thank you, Lily. You've been very helpful. Can you show us her room? Her parents gave us permission to look through her things, in case there's anything . . . anything that might help."

Lily stood, nodding, and led them to a small room just off the living area where they'd been talking. Sarah Weston's room was done in pastels, with a pale green bedspread and floral curtains. There was a beaten-up desk and a wooden chair in one corner, a single mattress on a metal frame, and a blue beanbag chair against the opposite wall. A bookcase stood next to the desk and was crammed with a collection of textbooks and well-loved novels, obviously worn from years of use. A giant bulletin board was centered above the desk and covered with the flotsam and jetsam of her life: ticket stubs, newspaper clippings, graded assignments, photos of Sarah smiling. A stuffed rabbit had fallen from the bed and lay in the middle of a polka-dot floor rug.

"If she kept any of his gifts, they'd be in her closet," Lily told them, not entering the room. Keeping her eyes averted, she pointed at the closet door, then turned and walked back to her own room.

"So," Mike said when the girl was out of earshot, "what do you think of our mystery man?"

Ian reached for a cardboard box tucked behind a stack of precisely folded sweaters. "Her toenails weren't painted."

"Nope. Think our guy removed it?"

"Maybe. He might have wanted to hide any identifying features. Or maybe it just didn't fit the scene he was creating."

"So, he's either very careful or has control issues." Mike nodded to the box Ian was opening. "Keep an eye out for her phone. We didn't find it at the scene."

"Yeah, I requested her phone records, but it sounds like they're going to make us get a warrant."

"Fucking sticklers," Mike muttered.

Ian lifted the lid, revealing a jumble of jewelry boxes, playbills, ticket stubs, and take-out menus. Beneath these lay a stuffed turtle, a sweatshirt with *Carlisle* emblazoned across it, a handful of wine corks, and a pair of red high-heeled shoes. Mike took out a jewelry box and opened it, revealing a silver charm bracelet. He ran his finger across the tiny heart, music note, and tennis shoe that were attached.

"My Sabina has one of these. Brian gets her a new charm every time she gets straight As on her report card," Mike said softly.

Ian watched his partner's face soften at the mention of his husband and daughter and looked away, reaching into the box to retrieve more of the jewelry. He found a gold heart-shaped pendant, a garnet tennis bracelet, and a ring made from twisted silver. "The roommate was right; these aren't the gifts of frat boys."

"He's either got rich parents . . ."

"Or he's old enough to have a well-paying job," Ian finished. "So, what, older boyfriend gets dumped by his teenaged girlfriend and takes revenge?"

"Lot of effort for revenge. Seems more likely a boyfriend would beat her and toss the body in a dumpster. You know, she's trash and all that? The setup in that barn—that was more like worship . . ."

"Or domination," Ian countered. "He could make her into whatever he wanted."

"Well, it makes more sense than a pissed-off drug dealer unless he's dealing until his art career takes off. But I'm still betting random crazy."

"It's never a random crazy," Ian protested. "There's always a motive."

"Son of Sam, Co-Ed Killer, Bundy, Night-Stalker . . ."

"They all had motives."

"Random, crazy motives."

"Alright, so it's an unknown boyfriend, an unknown dealer, or an unknown somebody else."

"Good day's work, then," Mike said, repacking the box. "Let's see if we can't narrow down that list from every-fucking-body in the county. I'll take the closet; you take the desk."

The two spent the next hour going through Sarah Weston's belongings, bagging and cataloging anything that might be useful. Periodically, they could hear Lily Ellis approach the door, hesitate, then move away again. When they finished, they stepped back into the living area carrying the cardboard box, a few journals and notebooks, a photo album, the girl's computer, a bottle of green nail polish, and an envelope containing the contents of Sarah's bulletin board. The room had looked oddly subdued without its cluttered presence.

Lily looked up as they entered. "Did you find anything?"

"Maybe," Mike responded. "We're going to take some of her notes and pictures to see if we can figure out who her boyfriend was."

Ian shifted the box in his arms so that he could pull a card from his jacket pocket. "If you think of anything . . ."

"I'll call right away."

"Good. Thank you, Lily. I know this isn't easy."

"I'll do anything I can." Lily reached out to take the card and surprised Ian by grabbing his hand.

She looked him directly in the eye for the first time since he and Mike had arrived. "Sarah was special. She was smart and strong and kind, and . . ." Lily's voice broke, but she didn't look away. "And loved. You need to find the guy who did this. You need to."

"We will do everything possible," Mike responded when Ian remained silent. "I promise."

Ian nodded without breaking eye contact with Lily. "Everything," he said softly.

Then, as if the need to say that had been all that was holding her together, she sank down into a worn futon. Her body folded into itself, and she began to weep softly. Ian and Mike closed the door gently as they exited, not wanting to intrude further on the grief that shrouded the small apartment, now all too quiet.

Chapter 8

Emma felt him watching her but didn't dare look in his direction. He'd approached during the middle of class and leaned against the door frame. He'd silently watched as she guided her students through the text, an almost imperceptible smile flickering across his face whenever she made a particularly enthusiastic comment. Almost imperceptible—but Emma caught each one. She faltered as the smile sparked again; then, taking a breath, she pulled her attention back toward her class with what seemed like physical effort. Ian remained motionless where he stood.

"Okay, so . . . Poe's narrators. We saw a great example of the unreliable narrator in *The Tell-Tale Heart*. Most of you suspicious souls decided that he was lying, but some of you made strong arguments that he was unreliable because of his disconnect from reality. Both are possible, and remember when we're talking about literature, you're just deciding if your understanding of the text is justifiable—"

Her eyes landed on Ian accidentally, and she forced herself to look away, flustered. "Or, uh, not justifiable." She took a breath. "Poe loved an unreliable narrator and is actually credited with developing a new type: The Watson."

"Like *Sherlock's* Watson?" Olivia asked. The brunette looked both eager and uncertain as she offered the guess.

"Exactly like. But Poe used this technique in the mysteries of C. Auguste Dupin more than forty years before Doyle. This narrator doesn't lie to the readers but always misses clues or focuses on the wrong things. He doesn't have the objectivity to solve the crime, so he misses the obvious."

Emma ran her eyes along the rows of students, checking their engagement. A handful were taking notes; one watched the baseball fields through a narrow window; a girl in the back stared at her lap, trying to text on her poorly hidden phone as her rainbow-colored hair framed her face like a curtain in an incense shop; another was just staring intently at Ian. Two freshmen in the middle row were focused on a tablet screen. As Emma watched, a girl to their right slid her chair closer to them. Emma frowned. She was one of her brightest and usually stayed engaged in class discussions.

Emma raised her voice slightly. "Ethan, Lacy, Hallie—thoughts?"

"What? Sorry." Hallie looked up, guilty.

"Whatever you're reading can wait until after class . . ."

"But, Professor Reilly," Ethan interrupted, eyes wide with excitement, "the body they found last Thursday—they're saying it was a student from Carlisle College."

"And she was murdered," Blake added softly.

Murmurs spread across the classroom. Emma glanced at Ian. He frowned and subtly shook his head.

"Alright, Ethan—Blake. I'm sure there's nothing to worry about. If there was a murder, the police will investigate. Try to stay focused—" Emma glanced at the clock "—for another five minutes. Are there any questions about unreliable narrators?" As she expected, no one raised a hand. "Good, then your homework should be easy. Submit your reflection on 'The Purloined Letter' by the end of the week."

Ian moved out of the doorway as the students gathered their books and bags. Emma sorted papers with unwarranted concentration.

"Interesting stuff," Ian said, pausing as the girl with the rainbow hair, still texting, walked by him. He closed the door after the last student and crossed toward Emma. He was holding a small paper sack down at his side.

"Uh, thanks. How did you find me here?"

His lips quirked. "I'm a detective."

Emma felt her chest tighten and immediately looked away. "Did you . . . want something? To talk? We can go to my office. Or get a coffee?"

"No, I have to get back to the precinct. This will only take a minute."

"Oh," Emma responded, swallowing her disappointment.

"Officer Gonzales found your purse in an alley a few blocks from the museum. No wallet, phone, or keys, unfortunately." He pulled her clutch, worse for wear, from the bag.

She sighed as she took it. "Yeah, I expected that. I've canceled the cards, and there wasn't much cash. And I bought a fancy new phone this morning." Emma didn't mention the locksmith was still on her to-do list. She didn't want to explain how anxious cold-calling strangers made her—she was trying to seem at least mostly normal. "All of my pictures and contacts were backed up. Everything else was replaceable."

"Except for your book." Ian held out the paper bag. "First loves can never be replaced."

Emma gave him a quizzical look. Ian shrugged, so she opened the paper sack, looking back with delight when she saw a well-worn paperback of *Jane Eyre*.

"Is it my copy or—?"

"It's yours. They found it with the purse. You said it was special, so I thought I'd bring it over."

"Thank you." Emma ran her fingers along the edges of the cover before looking back to him. "Why'd the officer call you?"

"Uh, I called him."

"No case too small?"

"I had a personal interest." Ian shrugged. "Officer Gonzales gets the credit, though. Sounds like he spent his night rummaging through trash cans."

"You could have just called to tell me." Emma fought a smile, catching her bottom lip in her teeth, and dropped her eyes to the book cover.

"You lost your phone."

"I have an office number; it's on my card."

"I was in the area."

Emma glanced up, her face suddenly stark. "So that girl really was a student here?"

"What?" Ian asked, startled by the shift in her tone. "No. I mean, I wasn't here for . . . I was just . . ."

"Right, I understand—just curious, though I imagine everyone will be."

"Of course. I just really can't discuss that right now. But I . . ." He pushed his fingers through his hair. "Look, I know last night wasn't great . . ."

"It wasn't *all* bad." Emma tried for flirtatious but wasn't sure she hit it.

"Really?" Ian sounded skeptical.

"I mean, getting mugged wasn't great, but there was also art—and pie."

"There was indeed pie." Ian definitely managed flirtatious. His smile was just a hint. "How would you feel about dinner?"

"Are you asking me on a date?" Emma needed to make sure, not trusting her read on the conversation.

"Yeah. I am. Tomorrow night, seven o'clock? We could grab dinner at Valentino's?"

She hesitated. Besides a few stale coffee dates, she hadn't been out with anyone since . . . Rory. Four years ago. She frowned, remembering his jabs about Emily Dickinson.

"Or someplace else if that doesn't sound good," Ian quickly amended, misinterpreting her silence. "Or I could cook if you don't like eating out."

Surprise distracted her. "You cook?"

"Does that shock you?"

"Is there any way to admit that it does without being insulting?"

"Not really. But let me prove you wrong."

Emma looked up, caught suddenly in Ian's gaze, and felt a buzz of anticipation. She smiled slightly.

"It's only dinner," Ian assured her. "But we can go someplace else . . ."

"No," Emma blurted. She pictured them at Valentino's, the sleek clothes and clinking silverware in low light . . . She felt a string of trepidation plucking in her chest.

"No, to dinner or . . . ?"

Emma took a deep breath. She held his eyes briefly, watching the confusion playing across his face. She needed to accept—or decline—or do something other than stare at him.

"Emma? If you don't want to, it's okay. You don't need to make up a reason. Just 'no' is good enough."

"I don't want to say no." She dropped her gaze, focusing on her fingers as she twined them in her sweater.

"Then . . ."

"I'm . . . not good at this." She risked a glance up.

Ian shook his head, not understanding.

"Dating. I'm not good at dating."

"Is anyone?"

Emma's laugh was a bit harsh. "Yes. Believe it or not, some people can accept a dinner invitation without making it *really* awkward."

Ian laughed softly. "Emma, I want to spend time with you. However you want to do that. If you want to do that."

She did. She really, really did. And she didn't want to take safe, careful steps. "Okay. Then, dinner. You cook."

"How's paella?"

"Good. Perfect."

"Perfect," Ian repeated, his gentle smile flashing into his eyes. "Can I pick you up?"

"Thanks, but I'd rather have my own car . . . in case I need a quick escape." Emma's joke was clumsy—and maybe too honest—but Ian smiled.

"Fair enough." Ian pulled a card from his pocket and plucked a pen from Emma's desk. "Here's my address," he said, scribbling. "Come over around seven."

"It's a date," Emma said, accepting the card.

"Yes," Ian responded, holding her gaze, not letting her look away. "It is."

Emma reread the address printed in Ian's neat handwriting. She looked up at the house again. Clearly marked by the same numbers was a quaint white and green cottage with a neat stone walkway and old-fashioned roses growing in great bunches by the front door. It was oddly charming and not at all what she'd imagined.

She'd thought she knew exactly what to expect as she'd tried on and rejected several outfits earlier that evening. She had settled on a sweet but casual lace top and jeans with ballet flats, adding funky jewelry to offset the Victorian image. She hadn't wanted to be pre-cast as the doe-eyed romantic who'd spent too much time reading Jane Austen. She'd planned her approach, her first words, how she'd respond to his greeting as she walked into a cool, austere, minimalistic bachelor pad. She had played it out in her head a dozen times and was prepared for all contingencies. Except this. She was not prepared for a man who grew roses.

Emma took a deep, centering breath and climbed out of the car, grabbing a bottle of red wine from the passenger seat as she did. She approached the door with steady steps and paused on the little wooden porch to smooth her blouse before knocking. Ian opened the door almost immediately. He wore suit pants and a crisp white button-down rolled up at the sleeves. As Emma stepped into the living room, she saw the matching jacket and tie slung over the back of an armchair. Ian's eyes ran over her in a quick appraisal, his mouth tightening slightly as he took in the scrapes on her palms. She tightened her fingers, obscuring the healing scrapes, and he glanced up again.

"How are you?" The question was more than just polite.

"Still a bit sore, but fine."

Ian took her jacket and purse, laying them neatly on an entryway table. Emma turned slowly, taking in the rest of the room. It was sparsely decorated but inviting, with richly colored furniture, rows of well-worn books covering the shelves, and a faded damask rug spread across the dark wood flooring. The leather couch that filled one wall looked well-worn; Emma imagined Ian stretched out with a book and a cup of tea. The room looked more like a BBC re-creation of a Dickensian den than the living room of a no-nonsense cop. Emma smiled, enjoying his defiance of the cliché. Ian lifted his eyebrows in a silent question. "I like it," Emma responded, "very much."

Emma watched Ian's stance soften and realized that he had been nervous. She held out the bottle still clutched in her hand. "I brought wine," she said unnecessarily. "I hope it goes with paella." The soft scent of cooking spices warmed the air.

"Actually," Ian said, taking the bottle, "I ended up working later than expected, so I'm making pasta primavera instead. I hope that's alright."

"Great." Her voice was pitched too high. "Perfect."

"I'll get you a glass." Ian returned to the kitchen and picked up an apron that had been cast across the countertop. "It will be just a few more minutes. Make yourself at home."

Ian returned to the stove, where something was bubbling, and Emma drifted to the bookcase. Ian had a broad collection, including history, classics, and art. Everything was neatly organized by genre, then author. Emma noted several titles focusing on the Pre-Raphaelite Brotherhood, a shelf devoted to classic mystery authors—including Raymond Chandler—and another filled with texts on criminology and forensics. Ian brought her a glass of wine as she browsed, told her to help herself, and returned to the kitchen. Emma could hear the sounds of plates and silverware being laid out.

Pulling a dog-eared copy of *The Big Sleep* from the shelf, Emma moved toward an overstuffed chair beneath a broad window. She reached to shift a stack of papers from the coffee table's surface so she could set her wineglass down but hesitated, curiosity overriding manners. They were photos of a painting, a close-up of flowers, purple, yellow, white, and green. Emma smiled at the array of flowers.

"You've been doing your homework," she called over to the kitchen, moving to the next image that showed a swirl of river around the roots of a tree.

"What?" Ian called back, sounding puzzled.

"Ophelia. The pictures you have of the Ophelia painting." Emma flipped to the next picture, a close-up shot of what looked like a rope dangling from a broad-leafed tree. Emma tried to identify the specific artist but couldn't remember seeing that in any of the canvases she had studied. Hoping for more clues, she slid the image to the back of the pile and turned to the next picture. For a timeless moment, Emma was captivated by the photo in her hand. Blank, hooded eyes looked up from the face of a young girl. Water droplets clung to the too-pale skin, damp hair spinning out around her. Emma reached her fingers up to brush her own cheek, suddenly overwhelmed by the memory of being wet and scared in the darkness outside the museum. The photos slid from her fingers and scattered across the floor.

"Shit," she hissed, snapping back to the moment. She'd carefully curated a polished, sophisticated version of herself for tonight, and she was messing up already. The clumsy ingenue was only appealing in fiction. Emma knelt hastily to collect the photos and put things back to rights.

This clearly wasn't some research project Ian was working on in his spare time. That was the girl—Emma turned the staring face toward the floor as she reached for the other images—the girl her students were discussing in class, the one who'd been murdered. But—Emma's brain insisted—she was also Ophelia. She felt a familiar jolt as her mind seized on the paradox. She began to mentally annotate the images. Why this character, this play? What did the pose signify? The stream? The tree? And why was Hamlet's doomed love missing her crown of flowers?

With a glance over her shoulder to where Ian was still working on their meal, Emma skimmed through the pile of photos quickly. She sorted the ones that actually showed—her brain skipped over what she knew she was looking at—Ophelia into a face-down pile next to her. She flipped through the others, convincing herself she could risk a few more moments and satisfy that itch in the back of her skull. Then, she could focus on Ian, on dinner, on being normal for just one evening.

She just needed to focus for a few moments—tree, stream, flowers, a rope where the coronet should be. And there was something . . . something else . . .

"With fantastic garlands," she murmured aloud.

"What are you doing?" Ian's voice was sharp behind her.

Emma jumped.

"Sorry, I—" She tried to wade back into reality, to find the emotional markers in his tone that would cue her reaction, but her mind had crept inside the text.

"The flowers," she rushed to explain, hoping insight would grant absolution, "the flowers in the picture, they're the ones described by Gertrude in *Hamlet* when she's telling the court of Ophelia's death. The crowflowers, the nettles, the daisies for innocence . . ." Emma glanced at Ian and her clear, bright knowledge scattered away. "The pictures of this . . . girl . . . the garlands of flowers . . ."

His face was dark with—surprise? Irritation? Emma thought she recognized fear sparking beneath the other emotions as he reached past her to collect the images. His movements were tightly controlled, but Emma could feel the strain as he brushed against her. She recoiled.

"I'm sorry. They were on the table, and I recognized . . ."

"It's work. You shouldn't be . . . I shouldn't have . . ." He shook his head, taking in a deep breath. "I'm sorry. I didn't mean for you to see any of this."

"It's fine," Emma said softly. "I mean, it's . . . upsetting." It was, Emma registered, or would be. But— "But, I'm fine. And Ian—the scene. It's Ophelia. I'm sure of it." She tried to level her tone, to not sound excited even as her mind danced with theories. "This is the girl that they found, isn't it? The one my students were talking about."

"I can't comment on that."

"You can't—" Ian's tone of icy professionalism scraped against her mind. It was the same tone used by every teacher who told her to calm down, every professor who told her to focus, every elbow-patched man who'd dismissed her ideas, dismissed her with a condescending "young lady" even after she'd shown her work, her evidence. She lifted her chin. "Ian, I know what I'm talking about. This is what I do."

"Homicide investigations are not what you do." He turned away.

"That's not what I meant. If you would just—"

"No," he cut her off. "I'm not letting you get involved."

"Letting me? You're not *letting* me? Fine." Emma heard her voice rise but didn't bother to modulate it. "Tell me what it means, then. Tell me what it says—"

"Emma, I can't talk about an active investigation. I shouldn't have left those pictures on the table—that was a mistake—but we can't discuss this." He strode into a small dining area, leaving Emma to follow behind. "Dinner's almost ready."

Emma shook her head, flustered by Ian's reaction. She knew she was right about this, that she could help if he would . . . "Listen. I can figure this out. I know it. I just need to spend a little more time with the images. The symbolism in Ophelia's death scene is—"

"Emma, please, let it go. Whatever you think you saw in those photos, you don't know anything. *We* don't know anything yet." He let out an exasperated huff. "This is a homicide investigation. You're talking about a homicide. Do you get that?"

"Technically, I'm talking about a photograph of a homicide. I'm not suggesting that I head out and go look for the killer."

Ian's head snapped back toward her, the irritation and—Emma was sure this time—fear claiming his expression once more.

"Stop. Just stop, Emma. Please. I'm not playing a game here. I see people—women just like you—brutally murdered every day. Beaten. Stabbed. Shot—" His breathing was rapid and unsteady as he broke off.

"I understand, and I'm not saying—"

"But you don't understand, that's my point. Maybe you know what death is like in novels, but this is real life. Real murders, real victims—real killers. And that means anyone who gets involved could be in danger." He was almost pleading with her now.

"I'm not some helpless maiden up in my ivory tower," Emma countered. "And I'm not foolish enough to get myself—"

"Emma, you're an English professor. I—do this . . ." Ian slammed the stack of photos onto the already set table ". . . every day. This is *my* job. Trying to find out what happened to this poor girl. Why someone took her. Drugged her. Strangled her—"

"And posed her like Ophelia," Emma shot back. Closing her

eyes for a moment, Emma tried to barricade her rising frustration behind a clear line of reason. "I don't need protection from the real world, Ian. And if this killer is really that dangerous, you should be doing everything you can to catch them, using every resource available. I—"

"Don't." Ian's jaw clenched. "I have been working my ass off for days, doing everything I can to figure out who did this. So has my partner and every other cop and scene-of-crime tech on this case. But *you* think *you* can find him? You're smart. Okay, I get it. But there's a difference between having a really clever take on some Shakespearean death scene and actual detective work."

Emma flinched away from his derision. "You're right. I'm not a detective. And maybe I don't understand your world. But you clearly don't understand mine either. Maybe my *really clever take* means that I can see things in those photos that you can't." She crossed to the door, snatching up her purse and jacket on the way. She paused, her hand on the doorknob, and looked back. "I may not have your years of investigative experience, *Detective*—" She filled the word with the same contempt she'd felt from him. "But I know my Shakespeare. And so does your killer."

Wrenching the door open, Emma stepped into the darkness, adrenaline from the confrontation quickening her steps and trembling her fingers as she dug for her keys. Ian was still standing, silhouetted in the open door, as she drove away.

Chapter 9

Ian dumped the pasta in the trash.

Scrubbing his hands over his face, he pulled out a bottle of whiskey and poured himself a glass. As the first drink hit, he grabbed bread and peanut butter as well. Alcohol on an empty stomach wasn't going to help anything.

He'd handled that about as badly as possible, he knew. It had been foolish to bring the photos home. It had been even more so to forget them on the coffee table. He'd gotten home from work, figured he could go over the file one more time—he hadn't been able to get Sarah Weston's face out of his head. And he'd spent too long fixated on the photos, looking for clues, looking for anything that would point him in the right direction.

Looking for exactly what Emma had seen.

He collected the prints and turned away from the carefully set table. Taking his sandwich and glass to the sofa, he grabbed his laptop and searched for image after image of Ophelia. He knew—trusted—that Emma was right, but he needed evidence to prove it to himself. It wasn't hard to find. The picture of

Sarah Weston's face poised to sink beneath the water was echoed in countless paintings of Hamlet's dead lover. The flowers, the stream, the frail, fragile face—they were all there. Centuries of men had tried to capture Ophelia with brushstrokes and pigments. This killer had done it with drugs, rope, and a corpse.

He reached for a close-up photo of Sarah's face, feeling again an uncomfortable sense of familiarity. He tried to convince himself that it didn't affect him. The similarities were superficial at best—blond hair, fair skin, similar build. If he went to campus tomorrow, he'd see a dozen copy/paste duplicates of her. A week ago, he might have seen Sarah Weston among them. Six months ago, he might have seen Zoey Turner.

Knowing he was just torturing himself—hell, wanting to after tonight—he searched for the news article he'd nearly memorized: *Carlisle Honor Student Killed in Drug Deal Gone Wrong*. The brief article laid out the on-record details. Zoey Turner had been killed by a drug dealer after she'd tried to buy some MDMA and a few ounces of cocaine, something her distraught family described as "uncharacteristic." What the article didn't say was that she'd been there as part of a sting set up by the CPD's narcotics unit. A detective named Bruce Devlin had caught her with a baggie of pills and threatened her with prison if she didn't agree to help them get her dealer. Ian had worked with Devlin in Narcotics before transferring to Homicide, and he was the kind of cop with a thick file the public was never told about. He'd half-assed the sting, didn't put enough men on Zoey, and lost track of her when their communication system failed.

They'd found her body three days later, shot with an unregistered gun.

The article also didn't mention that Ian had been the one who'd first brought Zoey in as a CI when she'd been little more than a kid. He'd gotten a few names from her in return for helping her into a counseling program in lieu of charges for possession. The program hadn't worked. She moved on to harder drugs, started selling—small-time shit—and then showed up at Ian's desk asking for help, offering to be his CI again if he'd get her out of this new mess. He'd sent her away.

So she turned to Devlin.

Ian told himself that what happened wasn't his fault, tried repeating the party line: He'd done what he could. He'd already given her one chance to get back on track; he didn't owe her a second one. She was in college—an adult. She'd agreed to the deal with Devlin. He'd been the one in charge of the sting. Some neo-Nazi selling meth to teenagers had been the one who actually pulled the trigger. Everyone said it wasn't his fault, but Ian couldn't shake the guilt.

And he couldn't bear the thought of another innocent person getting involved, getting in the way—getting killed.

Ian thought of Emma at the front of her classroom and tossed back the remaining whiskey. He pushed the photo of Sarah Weston away.

Sitting in the precinct the next morning, stale coffee souring on his tongue, Ian couldn't stop replaying the moments that had haunted his night—Zoey's face, destroyed by a bullet. Sarah's blank eyes staring at the painted tree. And Emma, in Ophelia's gown, being dragged beneath the water, the weight of her garlands pulling her down.

His subconscious wasn't being subtle.

He had a sickening feeling that his warnings weren't going to keep her away. Worst of all, he told himself, she was right. This killer had more in common with her world than he could imagine, which meant that Ian was competing on an unfamiliar field, playing by rules he didn't know.

Something had drawn the killer to the image of Ophelia, driving him to re-create that scene in the back of a decrepit barn. Was there a connection to the victim, something that had aligned her with Ophelia? Ian had found both art and literature classes on her Carlisle transcript. Had she done something or said something in one of those classes? Had the mysterious "older man" taken her to see *Hamlet* and tried to re-create the memory? Was she a random victim caught in someone else's darkness? The report a silent lab tech had slipped onto his desk revealed that the killer had torn Ophelia's death announcement from the blood-soaked play he'd left by her side, then pressed it into Sarah Weston's mouth. He'd forced those words, those images, into her still-cooling body, blocking her mouth after stopping her breath. He'd made her into an object, a decoration, posed and put on display, carrying the message of her own degradation.

He was scrolling through an image search of "Ophelia" when Mike dropped into the chair across from him. After a reluctant moment, he added "Pre-Raphaelite." The potential connection to the gala opening made Ian uneasy.

"We got our first batch of fan mail." Mike cut through his reverie. "Two crank confessions, a couple of zealots with God on their side, and a marriage proposal—for you. Apparently, she saw you on the news this morning and recognized you from a past life. Got some uniforms following up."

"No proposals for you?"

"Apparently, I'm a new soul. What are you up to?" Mike craned his neck to see Ian's screen. Ian turned it toward him.

"The lab report came in. The pages in the girl's mouth were from *Hamlet*, Act Four, which includes the death of a young woman. So, I thought that might have inspired the crime scene." Ian was reluctant to tell Mike that Emma had been the one to identify the connection. "Turns out the death of Ophelia is a popular topic for painters."

"Creepy," Mike offered.

"Yeah, well. There are commonalities with half a dozen famous pieces, but none of them are exact. He put his own spin on it."

"Would he need to have specialized knowledge about this stuff?"

"Not to know the story. Lots of people study *Hamlet* in college or even high school. As for the art—" Ian hesitated, once more reluctant. "There was a portrait of Ophelia at the museum gala."

"The one you went to?"

"It didn't look like our scene. That artist had painted her before she drowned, but there were other images referenced." He found the museum guide in the piles on his desk and tossed it to his partner.

Mike flicked through it and then turned it back toward Ian, his finger pressed on a painting by Millais. "This didn't strike you as interesting last Friday?" Mike's tone was flat, but Ian bristled.

"I didn't read the guide, okay? I just . . . looked at the paintings. Besides, the exhibit opened after the girl was murdered. The killer couldn't have seen it."

"Unless he's connected to the museum or the college. Where the girl went to school."

Ian was saved from responding by a wave from the desk sergeant. Mike rose and met him halfway across the room, bending his head in a brief conference before returning to Ian's side. "Any other insights that might have been helpful while I was working all weekend?" Mike asked.

Ian shook his head. If he had flipped through that booklet rather than flirting with Emma, they might have gotten this lead four days earlier. He'd literally been holding a clue in his hand and hadn't noticed. Mike was right. "It might not be related."

"Sure. Well, we've got a guest in room three. Come on." He tossed a folder to Ian and started off, leaving Ian to catch up as they walked.

The young man seated at the table was not afraid. His bottle-blond hair had been carefully styled into disarray, name-brand glasses framed his hazel eyes, and his ripped jeans doubtless bore a designer label. The smug surety of an expensive lawyer one call away relaxed his shoulders and raised his chin.

"So, Alex," Mike began, taking his seat in the interview room. Ian remained standing and leaned against the wall as he read through Alex Carmichael's file. "According to the folks down in Narcotics, you're the go-to guy if someone needs a little pick-me-up."

"What can I say? People love my effervescent personality." Alex grinned.

"And your illegal pills."

"No idea what you're talking about."

Ian knew that the kid would keep bantering until he got bored. Then he would shut up for good. Normally, Ian would tease this out, get as much information as he could. Try to ensnare him in his own arrogance. Instead, Ian found himself leaning forward with intentional menace. He lifted himself slightly, broadening his stance. "Look, kid," Ian snapped. Mike side-eyed his play. "We're not interested in whatever side business you've got going between trips to the mall. We just want to know what you did to the girl."

Ian slid a close-up shot of Sarah Weston's face, taken in the morgue the day before, across the table. Alex immediately recoiled.

"Shit, she's dead."

"Yes, she is. You know her?"

"I—I mean—I might have sold to her. Nothing like— Look, if she OD'd, that's on her."

Ian tensed. "What'd you sell her?"

Alex hesitated, visibly uneasy as his eyes strayed back to the photo. Corpses have a way of reframing a situation, Ian thought with grim satisfaction.

"Prescription shit, nothing hard," Alex conceded and leaned back, crossing his arms protectively against his chest.

"What kind of prescription shit?" Mike asked dryly.

"Oxy, mostly, though I got her some Adderall occasionally. But everyone does that stuff. Even some of your buddies in blue buy from me. Nothing I gave her could have killed her unless she just downed the fucking bottle."

"Your pills didn't kill her—but maybe you did?" Ian pressed, wanting to shock the smirk off the kid's face.

Alex whipped his head toward Mike, looking for an ally. "No fucking way."

"When did you see her last?" Mike asked, his tone even.

"Month or two. Not recently."

Mike tossed a glance at his partner. "Know anything about a party on a farm just south of town last weekend?"

"Naw, why would I?"

"We heard it's a popular spot."

Alex's confidence returned in a flash. "You guys don't know shit. Besides, I don't hang out with drunk townies. I'm Studio 54, not Levi's 501."

Mike snorted. "What do you know about Studio 54? You're, what, twelve?"

Alex's smirk fell away. "I'm old enough to know my rights. You can't hold me. I didn't have anything on me when you violated the Fourth Amendment and dragged me in here."

"Didn't you?" Ian asked.

Alarm flashed in his eyes.

Mike pushed Sarah's picture closer to Alex. "Someone killed this girl. We need to know who. Just think for a minute. See if anyone comes to mind."

Mike and Ian rose and left the boy staring at the table. Once the door was shut behind them, Mike raised an eyebrow at his partner. "Well, that was an interesting approach, Boy Scout. TMC play a James Cagney marathon last night?"

Ian shrugged. "I'm just sick of these smug assholes."

Mike gave Ian a doubtful look, then walked farther up the hall to a table decked out with chipped mugs and an ancient coffee machine. He poured a cup, sipped, and winced. "Well, this asshole was genuinely surprised by that picture. No disgust, no pride—just . . ."

"Horror. Yeah." Ian sighed. "But the toxicology report said that the victim had Percocet in her blood; oxycodone's the main ingredient."

"Which means Trainspotting in there could have done it. But the drugs could have been hers, too." Mike balanced his hip on the edge of the table. "Look, I know that you're not Devlin's biggest fan, but . . ."

Ian's jaw tightened as Mike unknowingly struck a freshly opened wound. "He should have lost his badge. IA didn't do anything with my report."

"They investigated," Mike responded on a sigh. They'd been over this before. "Sting went bad. It happens. Wasn't his fault."

Ian didn't respond.

"Wasn't yours either."

"This vic . . ." Ian changed tacks without acknowledging his partner's absolution. "She looks a lot like Zoey Turner."

Mike's eyebrows rose. "You think a drug-related shooting and this fucked-up art project . . . were done by the same guy?"

"We don't actually know what happened to Zoey," Ian protested without real reason.

"We know it wasn't this."

"Maybe she was a first attempt. Maybe Devlin . . ."

"Ian. You're about to say something real shortsighted."

"No. You're right." Ian shook his head. "You're right. Sorry."

"You never did take the lieutenant up on her offer to get someone in to talk to . . ." Mike's tone was casual.

"I'm fine. I just wasn't thinking." Ian avoided his partner's eyes.

"I'll check with Narcotics, then," Mike said without inflection. He cleared his throat. "I got a hold of the victim's therapist yesterday after you took off. Confirmed she was a patient but pled confidentiality."

"Did he tell you why Weston was being treated?" Ian gratefully accepted the change of topic.

"She—and no. But she did ask if it was a suicide. She was shocked as hell when I told her homicide. So we got a penny-ante dealer and a mysterious boyfriend."

"Looks like. Anything from the cell records?" Ian asked.

"No. There are a bunch of unidentified calls from the right time period, but they traced to a burner. Bought it with cash, likely tossed it when they broke up. Jewelry and tickets he bought for Sarah are a wash, too. All cash, no records. If there was surveillance footage, it's long gone."

"Sounds about right," Ian said dryly.

Mike walked down the hall and peered in the window at Alex. "Still squirming," Mike announced, returning to where Ian waited. "Did you hear anything back on the previous up north?"

"No ID. The detective wasn't in the office when I called, but he said he'd get back to me as soon as he could. It sounds like there's more than one case that's connected."

"So," Mike said, thinking through the implications, "if that is our guy, either he relocated here after those attacks or . . ."

"We found his practice ground up north."

"Makes sense. This is a big production for a beginner—anything sexual in those cases?"

"No rape kit reported, but the victims were all women."

"Maybe those women were practice or role-play. Then, once he's built his confidence, he heads home, meets a vulnerable girl, on meds, and he . . . decides to seize the opportunity." Mike punctuated the statement with a slight shrug.

"Wouldn't be the first time." Ian raised a hand at Mike's expression. "I'm not comparing him to Devlin. Just agreeing she might have been vulnerable. But if she took the meds voluntarily, it was someone she knew and trusted. You don't pop drugs in front of just anyone."

"Unless you're an addict," Mike countered.

"Still, it seems like an awfully lucky break to stumble upon the perfect girl." Ian rubbed the back of his neck. "Unless he was hunting on campus already. He sees her, follows her, waits until she's alone and vulnerable . . ."

"So, someone—we don't know who—killed a coed—we don't know why—and left her for us to find. Fuck, I feel like we're talking in circles." Mike jerked his head toward the door of the interrogation room. "Think it's worth holding him any longer?"

Ian moved to look through the window. Alex had turned the photos over on the table and stood in the far corner. "Probably not."

Mike nodded in agreement and pushed the door open. Alex whipped around to face them. "I want to talk to my lawyer," he bleated as soon as he saw the detective.

Mike opened the door wider and gestured through it. "Give him our regards."

Alex blinked, then scampered over, regaining his swagger as he crossed the threshold. "Waste of time," he muttered as he passed.

"Agreed," Mike said mildly.

Alex crossed the room at an unhurried pace, pausing to make eye contact with a young dark-haired officer that Ian vaguely recognized. Only the man's back was visible, but Ian could see surprise snap his spine as Alex jutted his chin up in greeting.

"Gotta admire his commitment to the bit," Mike said, following Ian's eyeline. "Say you sell to cops, act like you got a friend on the force . . ." He shook his head. "Well, what now?"

"We have the Ophelia connection," Ian replied.

"Whatever the hell that means."

"It means something—something important to whoever did this. He placed the girl in a trough with candles and flowers and a book page shoved in her mouth. He painted a goddamned mural. You don't do that unless you're trying to send a message." Ian felt unreasonably defensive of the theory, especially given it wasn't really his.

"Too bad we don't speak his language," Mike drawled.

Ian thought of Emma's face as she'd challenged him the night before. "Maybe we're not the ones he's speaking to."

Chapter 10

Emma arrived at work with her face pinched and bruised from lack of sleep. Fall was settling in, and the growing cold had emptied the expanse of lawn, leaving the brick facades and gray sidewalks starkly contrasted against the dying green. The clock tower at the center of the campus reverberated with its resonant call, and she quickened her pace. She hadn't done her usual course prep the night before. She knew the texts well but still wanted time to gather her thoughts and rebuild her armor before greeting her students.

She had never been shy in the classroom, but the bright, engaging figure she showed to her students was a persona she had crafted with years of practice. She donned it like a mask every morning, both disguise and protection. As she stepped into her office, hung her bag, and began her routine, she felt the mask slipping. She reached out to touch the desk, finding balance in the familiar eddies of wood. Today they were supposed to start Poe's poetry, usually a highlight for Emma. She had fallen in love with Gothic Romanticism before she ever knew the term, only knowing that the ruined castles, desperate romances, and tortured heroes could carry her away, that the rain-swept moors and darkened manor houses were someplace to safely wait in the shadows until she could find her way in the real world again. Today, though, the shadows offered little comfort.

She'd spent the night online researching death and decomposition, falling into murderous rabbit holes, clicking along dark pathways with morbid desperation, hoping that somehow more knowledge could make sense of the images that she'd seen. Emma's instinct was to focus on the puzzle—the threads had been weaving in her brain all night—but Ian's words had left her off-balance. She knew he was right. That girl had been murdered, and Emma didn't know that dark realm of the world. She had only met death in the curated spaces of funeral homes or fictionalized worlds. She didn't know how to process that kind of pain, of violence. She'd made herself remember the images—a too-still face, the eyes blank and cold. Water tracing along sickly grayed skin. Twisted flowers twined in blond strands. But instead of frightening her imagination into an obedient repulsion, Emma found her mind spinning with more questions.

Because she was pretty sure that she'd seen that face before.

Emma didn't think the girl had been in one of her classes, but she was fairly certain she was a student at Carlisle or had at least been on campus. She had racked her brain, trying to pinpoint the moment, the scene from which she recognized the girl—walking across the quad or sprawled across the green grass below her window? At an event, maybe, or passing through the labyrinthine hallways, books in arm? Whoever she had been, now she was just an impression, a shadow of memory that had slipped away. She'd become nothing more than an image to be studied, replaced by a photo on Ian's coffee table.

Her mind jerked away from the thought of Ian like a child touching a hot stove. The swift transition from hope to rejection had left her feeling vaguely nauseated. She'd wanted that—that rush of potential and promise—more than she wanted to admit. Not just romance; she had wanted to be at the start of something, to feel that hope and trepidation. But here, too, the past had been rewritten, a palimpsest of memory with Ian's angry dismissals effacing the gentle optimism that had come before.

She crossed campus to the main hall and climbed the stairs to the uppermost floor, cradling her books like a shield against her chest and stitching together her mask with each step. She opened the door to the classroom with a confident smile, the night's worries tucked neatly away. The students were mostly seated as she moved to the front of the classroom and greeted them. They all stared up with equal parts caffeine, hangover, and youthful confidence.

"Alright, everyone." Emma began to bring all attention forward. "'Annabel Lee': Like so many of Poe's works, it's focused on . . ." A beautiful dead girl, Emma thought. So many stories about beautiful dead girls. She cleared her throat. ". . . on a grieving lover. Initial thoughts?"

"It reminds me of *Romeo and Juliet*," a petite girl with a pixie cut said from the back row.

Emma smiled encouragingly. "Good, Madison. What makes you think of that play? Can you point to something specific in the text?"

"Well, it's a love story, and they both die."

"He doesn't die," Olivia reliably objected. "He just sleeps by her grave. That's not romantic; it's creepy."

"He says 'they love with a love that was more than love,'" Madison protested. "That's not creepy. It's beautiful."

"But it doesn't say she loved him back," Olivia said.

"She does love him, though," Madison insisted.

"Does it even matter?" Ethan asked. "The poem's about his love, his desire. Who cares what she feels?"

"Well, Poe certainly doesn't," Olivia agreed.

Emma interrupted the exchange before it could grow too heated. "How many of you read this as a romantic story?" About two-thirds of the class raised their hands. Madison looked smug.

"But there's nothing romantic about how he talks about her," Olivia objected. "He talks about her like a fairy tale. He never actually says anything about what she's like or who she is except that she loved him and she died. He talks about his love like it's all romantic, but it's not. It's all about him. She's just a body."

A dead girl strewn with flowers reached out to Emma through her student's words, flooding her mind with pieces of a pattern she couldn't quite see. Just a story—Emma tried to focus on what was being said, but she couldn't hold her thoughts still—the story of a dead girl's body.

"They're star-crossed!" Madison insisted.

"He's a stalker," Olivia retorted.

"Or an incel," Aiden added. Olivia shot him a conspiratorial smile and got a chin nod in return.

"No," Madison pressed. "They're like Romeo and Juliet."

"Romeo and Juliet killed themselves, Madison," Olivia countered. "Death's not romantic."

"Sure it is—" Ethan jumped fully into the fray. "If you're a necrophiliac."

That earned him a laugh.

Other students joined the debate, but Emma remained quiet. There was something she had missed—not just a body, not just . . .

"He *sleeps* by her *grave*."

"He loves her."

"He's unhinged."

The specter of the murdered girl rose again, clear and solid. Something she had seen . . .

"Just look at what the poem actually says . . ."

There.

"Okay," Emma said, her voice too sharp. Everyone stilled. She could feel a trickle of electricity beneath her skin and needed to catch it before it faded. "You've all raised some good points. In fact, I think that that is an excellent topic for your next writing exercise."

Emma glanced at the clock, which showed thirty minutes of class time remaining, and felt a rising desperation. "Actually, let's make this a research exercise." A soft groan rose from the class, and Emma felt a twinge of guilt. But the revelation was already wending through her brain; she couldn't fake her way through another half hour. "I know, I know. But I'm going to let you use class time to do it. Head over to the library. I want you to include—and cite—at least one source to support your ideas. Use the library databases, not Google. Off—go. I'll see you next class."

As soon as the last student had exited, Emma rushed to her office, stumbling at corners as she sped down the stairs. Annabel Lee's co-opted corpse had jarred something loose, leaving her humming. She had spent most of her life running through worlds of image and symbol; this was her domain. She felt oddly energized—knowing what to do, how to do it. There was a pattern here, in the text, and she could find it. She had to.

Maybe she couldn't reset things with Ian. She couldn't bring the murdered girl back to the bright future that she'd lost. But this, this she could do—research and semiotics, finding the meaning, the truth hidden in metaphoric and oblique creations. No matter what Ian said, she wouldn't stay locked away in ignorance—couldn't. Emma would always sacrifice paradise for knowledge, whatever the consequences.

She had a good memory for details and an adequate talent for drawing, so she grabbed sheets of paper from the printer and tried to re-create the pictures she had seen. First, she sketched a river with flowers on the bank, filling in details as she waited for something to strike her. She next moved to the tree hanging with garlands—she paused, closing her eyes as she tried to focus her memory. It wasn't a garland. It was a circle, a noose, a noose made of flowers where Ophelia's coronet of greens should have hung. She continued sketching, more slowly now as her mind worked: the churning water at the base of the tree, frothing around exposed roots; the thick trunk and sweeping branches, dipping to the surface of the water; the broad leaves—

Emma froze. There it was—that was what had been buzzing through her mind, trying to find the way out. She turned to her computer, quickly searched "willow tree." As images populated the screen, she stared at the familiar cascade of green tendrils, each delicate leaf a different shade ranging from emerald to silver as it was captured, shivering and weeping in the light. The broad leaves in her memory were grotesque and distorted by comparison. They were wrong. She brought up a bookmarked page—saved months before for an article she'd been writing about Shakespearian symbolism—and saw Ophelia's flowers: The small, yellow crowflowers, the stinging green nettles, the pale white daisies, and the long purples. She looked back to her sketch, then tried again to conjure the image in her mind. How had someone who had depicted the exact flowers named in the play, these tiny obscure little blossoms, gotten the wrong tree?

Emma sat back, her lip caught between her teeth as she continued to work through the problem. Either the painter had made a colossal mistake forgetting the iconic image of the weeping willow in Ophelia's death scene, or this new tree—whatever it was—meant something. She felt that same exhilaration that had sent her stumbling through the photos at Ian's house. But Emma didn't know enough about trees—let alone tree symbolism—to read the image, so she grabbed her sketches and went to find someone who spoke this language natively.

After jogging up two flights of stairs, Emma made herself pause before knocking beside the open door. She took a breath, set her body into practiced professionalism, and then stepped into the reception area of a gently worn office suite. Carolyn Matthews, Rory's administrative assistant, was talking patiently with an undergrad who seemed determined to see the dean. Carolyn was a dark-skinned, stylish woman in her late twenties who exuded calm and confidence. Despite her youth, she reminded Emma of a troll guarding a bridge, demanding that riddles be solved before admittance. Apparently, the hapless undergraduate at her desk had failed the test because she turned dejectedly away and slumped off down the hall. Emma hid a smile as the girl passed by and stepped up for her turn at the bridge. Carolyn had been hired to assist Rory's predecessor two years ago and had immediately welcomed Emma into her life with the easy confidence of a natural extrovert. They'd hung out socially a few times, always at Carolyn's invitation, but Emma always felt out of place among Carolyn's friends, like a character who'd slipped into the wrong story.

Emma thought back to the diner as she wondered who she should—could—have called for help and wished she'd tried a little harder to fit in.

"Dr. Reilly, how can I help you?" Carolyn smiled, dimpling at the formal greeting.

Emma returned the smile and gestured toward Rory's door, just past Carolyn. "Is he in? I have a research question." She could hear a muffled expletive from his office. Carolyn winced.

Rory had been an art professor—an extremely popular one—before being promoted rather against his will to his current position at the start of the term. He still taught a few seminars and advised graduate students, but mostly, his life now consisted of mediating academic squabbles and filling out paperwork. But beneath his well-tailored tweed, which Emma suspected he wore ironically, there was an artist and a scholar who could match Emma point for point whether they were debating the hermeneutics of Pre-Raphaelite art or allegory in *Dark Shadows*.

"Sorry, Emma, he's on a call right now." Carolyn's face radiated apologetic disappointment.

"Do you know when he'll—" Emma was cut short by a string of colorful profanity from behind Rory's door.

He pushed into the main office, still muttering, the door banging as he threw it open. His sandy hair looked like he'd been pulling at it. "That infant in IT insists that the email system is working and keeps repeating 'user error' like some damned mantra. Why we need to email people who work twelve feet down the hall is beyond me."

"Some of us are better in writing." Emma widened her eyes innocently.

Carolyn hid a smile. "Dr. Tamblyn, Dr. Reilly is here to see you."

"Did you hike up all those stairs to mock me?" His voice mellowed as he moved toward her.

"Of course not. I can mock you by email. Actually, I was hoping to borrow a book—"

"A book! See, Caro, there are still people in this technology-obsessed world who read actual, physical books."

"—on plant symbolism in art," Emma finished, unperturbed by the outburst.

"What era?"

"I'm . . . not sure. I came across this depiction of Ophelia's death scene, and a few details are puzzling me."

"Your brain stuck on an intellectual roundabout again?" Rory smiled lightly.

Emma shrugged, an acknowledgment of the accurate description. "Brain gremlins. It's just something I can't quite place, and it's bothering me." She handed a sketch to Rory.

"A sketch? Ever heard of a copy machine?"

"What happened to your rebellion against technology?"

"Anything invented before 1985 doesn't count as technology."

"Well, copying wasn't an option. It's . . ." Emma paused as she debated how much truth to tell him. "It's a mural, but not much is known about the artist."

Rory set the picture out on Carolyn's desk. Emma had sketched the mural in as much detail as she could remember, leaving a careful blank at its center. "What's here?"

"Some . . . abandoned household items," Emma said. "It was in an open space."

Rory nodded. "So, modern, then? Some Victorian influences, but definitely modern, maybe even postmodern. If I had to slap a label on this guy, I'd say 'contemporary, done in the style of the Pre-Raphaelite Brotherhood.' What is it about the plants that's bothering you?"

Emma smiled at his eager engagement with the puzzle. "He didn't use the tree cited in the text. I'm trying to decide if it's important or just sloppy."

Rory lifted the sketched tree to the light. "I'd have to see the original to give you anything specific, but I do have a very long and boring volume on arboreal symbolism that will at least put you to sleep tonight." He started to reach a hand toward her but pulled back. "Looks like you could use it."

"Brain wouldn't shut off last night," Emma said with a shrug.

"The curse of academia," Rory replied, "the surest cure for which is reading deadly dull texts about the meaning of trees. Hang here for a minute while I dig it out."

Rory disappeared into his office. Carolyn shook her head patiently at the heavy thump of books being tossed about and turned to her computer. As Emma dropped into one of the stiff chairs in the waiting area, a harried-looking boy in his early twenties rushed into the room. He was lanky and angular, a made-to-order Ichabod Crane with unkempt brown hair and the tell-tale backpack that marked him as a student. His clothes were clean but rumpled, and a forgotten price tag marked his shoes as both new and deeply discounted.

Carolyn looked up and frowned slightly in recognition. "Good afternoon, Malcolm."

"I need to see him."

"I'm sorry, Malcolm, but Dr. Tamblyn is meeting with Dr. Reilly, and then he has to attend the Instructional Leadership Council. You'll have to wait until your appointment tomorrow morning."

"I can't. You don't understand. It's about my thesis project."

"I do understand, Malcolm, but . . ." Carolyn trailed off as Rory stepped out of his office with a text in one hand.

"Malcolm. We don't have an appointment today." Rory's usually easy manner had faded.

"I know, but I need to talk to you about . . . about my project. My thesis." Malcolm dropped his eyes to his scuffed sneakers.

"Malcolm. We've discussed your barging in here before. We will talk tomorrow during your scheduled appointment."

"But I—" Malcolm caught something in Rory's expression, and disappointment slumped the boy's shoulders, giving him the distinct look of a puppy who'd just been smacked with a newspaper. "Fine. Whatever. It doesn't really matter anyway." Malcolm retreated with a final glance over his shoulder.

Rory and Carolyn exchanged a look.

"Problem child?" Emma asked after he was out of earshot, keeping her voice light.

Rory sighed and walked around Carolyn's desk toward Emma. "He's one of my grad students. A very bright young man, but . . ." Rory paused as if searching for an appropriate phrase. "He's not very self-sufficient. I get the impression that he's always had problems solved on his behalf. He was the star student as an undergrad, but now that he has to complete original projects independently, he's floundering."

"He took a few classes from me, I think." Emma vaguely remembered him as eager but unimpressive, the kind of student who always volunteered ideas confidently, whether or not they were on topic. She was surprised to see him so harried. "Grad school's a big adjustment." She remembered the years of trying to twist herself into acceptability.

"He doesn't have much of a support system, so he comes here. A lot." Rory sighed again, combing a hand through his messy curls.

"You're a good advisor."

"He's not much of a scholar—he lives solely online—but he's got incredible promise as an artist if he can just learn to work without the training wheels."

Carolyn cleared her throat politely behind him. "Dr. Tamblyn, the ILC meeting starts in ten minutes."

"Nymph, in thy orisons be all my appointments remembered."

Carolyn snorted. "In your calendar be all your appointments written down."

Rory grinned, Robin Goodfellow showing through once more, and handed Emma the book he had brought from the office. "I wish you joy of it. I'm off to annoy administrators." Rory turned with mock dignity and strode back into his office.

Emma shook her head. "Thanks," she called to his back.

"So, what's the new project?" Carolyn asked with open curiosity.

"Right now, it's just a picture that doesn't make sense," Emma replied, trying to keep her voice casual.

"But it might be something interesting later?"

"I doubt you'd—" Emma broke off suddenly, resisting the impulse to protect herself with distance. "Actually, is there any chance you're free for a drink later—or something?" Her voice lifted hopefully on the last word.

Carolyn's face brightened and then fell. "Crap. I have to take off straight after work, dinner with a new guy I met online. If I don't get murdered and chopped into tiny pieces, though, how about coffee tomorrow afternoon?"

"Perfect. That would be perfect." Emma's voice was breathy with relief. "You can tell me about your adventures in modern romance, and I'll talk about books by dead white guys."

"Dead white guys can be interesting, too," Carolyn offered.

"Sometimes. Yeah. Coffee's on me." Emma smiled at her small triumph as she stepped into the hallway. She was about halfway to the stairs when she heard her name. She stopped and turned back to see Malcolm jogging toward her. The dark-haired boy from her Gothic Literature course stood just behind him. She waved, and Ethan waved back. So did Malcolm. Too late to escape, then, Emma thought.

"Professor Reilly? I'm Malcolm Haynes. I took Brit Lit with you and World Literature. And I audited your class on novels last year . . ."

"Yes, of course, Malcolm. What can I do for you?" Emma smiled.

"Well, I wanted to take Postmodern Literature with you . . ."

"I don't teach that until spring."

"I know, so I had to take a film class with Professor Jacobs instead because I need some interdisciplinary courses for my thesis." He took a breath. "She's doing a guilt and innocence theme. All of the movies she picked are super depressing. And we just covered *Hamlet* . . ."

Emma tensed for a moment, hugging the book like a secret before reminding herself that nearly everyone on campus had been made to read Shakespeare at some point. She let out a breath. "How can I help?"

"Right, so Professor Jacobs said that the girl—Hamlet's girlfriend—is an example of true innocence. But when I pointed out that her rejecting Hamlet started everything, she shut me down. I mean, the girlfriend set it all in motion by listening to her dad. Plus, don't the gravediggers say that she committed suicide? Which is a mortal sin? I mean, I only watched the movie, but in the scene where she dies, there's literally a noose made of flowers in the tree branches when she dies. It's so obviously a metaphorical hangman's tree. But Professor Jacobs only pays attention to the language." Malcolm's tone was noticeably derisive. "She says she's a special kind of critic who doesn't have to look beyond what's on the page . . ."

"It's called New Criticism; it's a kind of formalist interpretation," Emma filled in automatically, but her brain tilted away from the conversation, tangled on something Malcolm had said.

"Right, that. But this is a *film* class!" Malcolm's voice filled with indignation. "Shouldn't you also consider the film? 'Cause the framing of . . ."

"Malcolm," Emma interrupted a little too loudly. "What did the scene look like when Ophelia dies? In the movie?"

"What? Oh. Ophelia's singing to herself, kind of gibberish, and she has a long rope of flowers. She tosses them over a branch, then falls beneath it. I don't know the play that well, but the filmic language is distinctly suggesting suicide. Don't you . . ."

"What does the tree look like?" The question was too abrupt, and Malcom stuttered into silence, his mouth still open.

Ignoring his reaction, Emma awkwardly opened the book Rory had given her. She flipped through the pages, looking for familiar trees. She spotted the image from Ian's photo almost immediately: a fig. She turned the book to Malcolm. "Like this?"

Malcolm looked confused. "No. It was, um, like a willow? You know—long drooping branches, kind of shiny leaves."

"But the flowers were a noose, not a crown?"

"Definitely a noose. That's why I think that—"

"You're sure?"

"Really sure." Malcom waited for a beat as Emma looked back to the book. "So, do you think I'm right? That she might not be 'a true innocent,' whatever that means." Malcolm sounded hopeful.

Emma glanced up, not really registering the boy any longer. "There's always room for interpretation. That's why the play's still worth discussing."

"So, I can tell Professor Jacobs that you said I was right?"

"Yeah, sure. Tell her I agree with you."

"Yes! I knew it. I knew you'd be on my side. Thank you, Professor." Malcolm jogged off confident in resting his justification on her shoulders.

Unable to wait, Emma sat down against the wall so that she could read more easily. A few drifting students glanced at her questioningly, but she ignored them. The tree Malcolm had described was definitely the expected willow, but the one she'd seen was decidedly not. And then there was the noose—

Working on a hunch, she turned to the page about fig trees, skimming over the historical meanings and allusions. The possibilities narrowed down like a game of Guess Who? but there were still too many unknowns. Setting the book on the floor, Emma dug her cell phone from her pocket. She impatiently punched in the numbers, and after four rings Ian's calm voice instructed her to leave a message.

"I know that you want me to stay away from you and your case, and you don't think I can help, and you think I couldn't possibly be good at this kind of thing because of how—because I'm just a literature professor. But you don't know everything about me, who I am, or what I can do, and—I—I'm close to figuring this out, Ian. And you need to hear it. You need to listen." She took a breath to stop the tumble of words. "Sorry. This is Emma. Please call me back." She hung up, sped to her office to grab her purse and her coat, and then ran out to the pale yellow sunshine outside, the wind biting as she stepped into the autumn air.

Chapter 11

"Detective Carter?" The desk sergeant approached Ian from across the precinct. "There's a woman here to see you, a Dr. Reilly. She says she has information about the Weston case."

Ian stood too quickly, sending his chair sliding backward. Mike quirked an eyebrow but said nothing.

"Take her to the conference room," Ian said, adding a belated "Thanks" as the officer walked away.

"Key witness to the case?" Mike asked casually.

"She might have information." Ian kept his tone neutral.

"Yeah, I just bet she does," Mike replied.

Ian ignored him and went to see Emma, uncertain whether he would be met with apologies or recriminations about the night before. He hesitated with his hand on the doorknob, feeling Mike's eyes on him, then walked briskly through, squaring his shoulders. She wouldn't come to the precinct to discuss their personal . . . issues. She'd said she had information—she was a potential informant, he told himself, just an informant. He'd listen to her. Stay professional. Then send her home.

Emma spun from where she had been pacing. "Did you get my message?" she asked, without preamble.

Ian took a step back, thrown. "What?"

Emma lifted her chin defiantly. "I know that you think I can't help, that I'm just some awkward book nerd with no real-life experience . . ."

The accusation struck him in the chest; professionalism lost to an irresistible impulse to reassure her. "Emma, that's not what I—"

"It doesn't matter. I'm not here for—" she vaguely waved her hand between them "—us. I'm here as a member of the public who has information about your case. So, will you hear me out? Or should I just call Crime Stoppers and hope someone there actually wants to find this killer?"

Emma's speech—she'd rehearsed it, he thought—left Ian feeling like a kid who had just stepped off a merry-go-round. He'd lost control of the conversation before he'd even had a chance to speak. Just an informant, he told himself. But he recognized his own lie.

"Why?" he finally asked. "You saw those pictures last night. You know what this—monster—can do, has done. Why would you want to get involved with—" *me*, he swallowed "—any of this? It's not fun, Emma. It's not like a mystery novel. It's dark, and nasty, and seeps under your skin in a way that makes you . . . shut down or go mad. Why would you choose to do that to yourself?"

"You did," Emma said softly.

"Emma . . ."

"It's already there, Ian." Emma took a deep breath, choosing her words with obvious effort. "My brain, it's—I'm not wired like other people. Sometimes, my brain . . . clings to things. Words, pictures, puzzles. That girl, she's in there. I couldn't let go of her if I tried. My brain is going to play with those images until I figure out what the picture is supposed to be. Whether I want it to or not. And honestly? I want it to. Because there's something there, something I *can* figure out. I know it."

Ian knew that she was expecting a reply, but he was distracted trying to read her—the tensed brow, the flickering hands, the tilt of her mouth, the lift of her chest as her breath hurried to catch her thoughts. He recognized her need to be heard and respected. But if something happened to her— Ian stopped the thought before it could run away from him. Zoey was just a kid he knew once upon a time, though her death still thrummed beneath his skin.

He reminded himself of his plan. Listen. Send her home. For her sake. "Okay. Ophelia's flowers." He gestured to a chair.

Emma let out a breath but didn't sit. "Okay, I was talking to a student . . ."

"About the case?" Ian interrupted.

"No, of course not," Emma objected. "We were discussing Shakespeare, that thing I teach, and he mentioned Ophelia's death—then I remembered something. In the photos, the flowers were hanging from the tree. But it isn't a coronet like in the play, like it should be—"

"The flowers are shaped like a noose, not a crown," Ian affirmed, wanting her to think less of her discovery.

But Emma just nodded tightly. "Yes. But here's the thing. One reading of the text—of the play—is that the queen's story about Ophelia's death being accidental was a lie. It's arguable that it was suicide. I think the . . . this person . . . is saying that Ophelia, and by extension his victim, is responsible for her own death."

Ian didn't know the textual nuances, but he understood violence. The idea of a killer placing the blame on his victim—the ultimate *she was asking for it*—made sense. He felt instinctively that Emma was on the right track. But he shook his head. "I'm sorry, I'm not with you."

Emma frowned, whether in response to his reaction or her own theories, Ian couldn't tell. "He's—I think he's trying to tell you that your, *our*, perception of the victim is wrong. That we should question the accepted narrative about her and her death.

But—" she lifted her hands, palms up, in supplication "—the text needs to be read holistically. Each piece—each word or symbol—connects to the work's larger themes. That means the noose—it's part of a larger message that he is communicating."

"Which is . . . ?" Ian asked, his voice noncommittal, not wanting to encourage her too much.

"I don't know." Emma's voice hummed with frustration. "That's why I'm here. I'm working from memory, and I just saw a small part—it's like reading a book with the pages ripped out."

Ian thought of the crime scene and wondered if Emma had seen that detail or if she was closer to understanding the killer than she knew. "Emma, I can't show you pictures of a crime victim."

"I've already seen them," she protested.

"You weren't supposed to. I shouldn't have left them out, and I'm not going to compound that mistake by showing them to you—again."

"Fine," she responded after a moment. "But just tell me this." Emma pulled a thick book from a satchel lying on the table and flipped it open to a marked page. "Is this the tree that he painted?"

Ian dropped his eyes and saw the unmistakable broad leaves and thick tree trunk that framed Sarah Weston's body.

"I'm good with details," Emma said, reading the question on his face as he glanced up from the page.

"Apparently."

"It's a fig tree," she told him, shifting the book toward him again. "Fig trees, fig leaves are often used to represent a loss of innocence or rejection of morality. Shakespeare frequently used symbolic elements, like plants, in his texts. Remember, at the museum, I told you—" Emma broke off, shaking her head. "Here, instead of a weeping willow symbolizing grief, whoever did this used a fig tree. It's a message."

Ian recognized that she was right, that she'd figured out what he never would have. She waited, watching him with the same wariness, he suspected, with which he'd been watching her.

"Ian?"

"Okay," he said, not hiding the doubt in his voice but hoping it would be misinterpreted. "Let's say you're right."

Emma finally settled into the proffered chair, allowing Ian to do the same. "So, the flowers in the photos were from Ophelia's death scene, right? Exactly those flowers. That means that whoever painted the mural knew the text. They got the details right."

He thought of the dozens of paintings he'd spent the morning poring over. "I'll trust you on that."

"The tree, then, should be a willow if the . . . artist . . . is following the text."

"'There is a willow grows aslant a brook.'" Those were the words on the page pulled from under the dead girl's tongue. At Emma's look of surprise, Ian reluctantly explained. "There was a note left . . . at the scene. It quoted that line."

Emma looked triumphant. "Then it's not a mistake; it can't be. And he left the note so you would know that."

Ian shook his head discouragingly. "How does that help us find him?"

"Think about it—Ophelia's death isn't really about Ophelia. It's about her lover, and her brother, and her father. She's a mirror reflecting everyone around her. But she also reflects Shakespeare's views of her, of women and how they exist in the world. And every artist who paints her reveals their own perceptions and biases—they show themselves in their art. Do you see?"

"So you think—" he made his voice skeptical "—solving this riddle might lead us to the killer?"

Ian saw something shift in her face, a decision being made. She was nervous, scared even—but she'd come anyway. She'd fought to keep emotions controlled—concealed—but in that moment, she let her longing, her regret, her determination play across her face. Emma offered that, he thought, to convince him.

"I know I'm not a detective—" She pressed her lips tightly together. "And maybe I'm not all that street-smart—"

The words trembled like an echo, and Ian wondered who she was hearing in her head.

"But this—" She met his eyes. "I'm good at this, Ian. I can help. I can help you find him."

Ian studied her face. He understood why she was here, recognized the flair of conviction and hope in Emma's face. And he deliberately crushed it. "Thank you for your thoughts, but we won't be needing any further assistance."

Indignation replaced hope in an instant. "You don't need any more *assistance*? I figured this out—I found the inconsistency in the painting—you had no idea. I don't need your protection, Ian. I need you to hear what I'm saying."

"Emma—"

She cut him off. "What if the killer is connected to the college? You must have considered that. Sarah was a student there. I recognized her."

"Wait. You know her. From where?" Ian leaned toward her.

Emma shifted back. "I don't— I'm not sure. I don't know her, really. But I know I've seen her."

"Or one of the hundreds of other young blonde women who go to Carlisle. That doesn't mean there's a connection with the school."

Emma's expression hardened. "But she *was* a student. The newspaper said so. And Carlisle sponsored the Pre-Raphaelite exhibition—the Ophelia painting was central to that. You can't have missed that connection after we—after seeing the exhibition."

Ian tried to hide his flinch—he had missed it. He'd been distracted. All the more reason to keep Emma away from him—from the case. He couldn't risk another mistake.

"I'm not asking to join you on a stakeout. I could just be a consultant—that's a thing, right? Don't you think having someone who knows academia involved in the investigation might be useful?" Emma's voice was almost a plea.

Ian looked into Emma's eyes and lied. "No. I don't think this is a lead we're going to be following. But thank you for sharing your ideas." He made his voice brusquely professional.

"Ian . . ."

"Thank you, Dr. Reilly." He stood to leave. "I appreciate what you want to do here. But you should stop thinking about this. Go back to work; we'll handle things from here."

"I can't," Emma bit out. "I can't just . . . that's not how I . . ." Emma flexed the fingers on her right hand in what seemed like a habitual gesture, something to soothe. "I know these texts, these symbols, this world. Let me help you."

"I don't need your help."

"Then let me help her."

"You can't help the dead, Emma. All you can do is try to stop more people from getting hurt. You need to let me—us—handle this." Ian turned away, not wanting to see her face. "I'll show you out."

"Don't bother. I can find the door on my own." Emma stood, shoving the book back into her messenger bag, and brushed past him.

"Just try to—let it go. Please," he said softly as she crossed the threshold. "Don't think about it anymore."

"Her. You mean don't think about her."

"Yes."

"She deserves to be thought about."

Emma walked quickly away. Ian let her go.

"Any luck?" he asked Mike, trying to sound casual as he returned to his desk.

"Nothing new." Mike didn't look up. "You?"

"Maybe," Ian admitted. As succinctly as he could, he explained who Emma was and how she had seen the pictures.

Mike put on an unconvincingly sympathetic face. "You

showed her crime scene photos on a first date? I'm guessing there's not going to be a second."

"I didn't show her . . ." Ian protested. "I just forgot to put the file away. And no. No second date."

"Not like you to be so careless with evidence." Mike's voice was mild.

"It was a mistake." Ian's voice was uneven, and he took a breath. "At any rate, Emma found the photos, and she spotted the Ophelia connection immediately."

"And now she thinks she's going to solve the case." Mike gave him a thoughtful look. "Is she smart or just nosey?"

"Smart," Ian replied reluctantly. "Really smart."

"Then maybe it's a happy accident. If you and she aren't going anywhere romantically . . ." Mike let the statement hang. Ian shifted uncomfortably but didn't respond. "Then, maybe she can be useful. Our guy clearly has a thing for art and literature, and as many books as you have on your shelves, that's not our area of expertise. It sounds like it's hers."

"She teaches classes on it."

"Then maybe we should hear what she has to say."

"We can't use an unvetted, unpaid consultant in a high-profile murder investigation. Once the defense discovered how she got involved, they'd rip her—and any evidence based on her testimony—apart. And it would undermine my credibility as a witness," Ian argued. "She stays out of it."

"Alright, Boy Scout." Mike turned back to his paperwork, then asked nonchalantly, "What's her theory, anyway?"

Ian sighed, leaning back in his chair. "She thinks the killer is using artistic symbolism to tell us about the victim—the weird flower noose and the tree apparently suggest sin or deception. Or culpability. The killer wants us to question the way the world sees the girl."

Mike made a contemplative noise. "Star athlete with a secret drug habit—it fits. Maybe he matched the victim to the story."

"Mike . . ."

"Okay, Romeo. But I don't have a better theory. Do you?"

"Maybe if we focused on the evidence and did our jobs, we would."

Ian shoved Sarah Weston's boyfriend box across his desk to Mike, then turned his attention to the collection from her bulletin board. He kept his head down as Mike watched him for a moment. Then his partner shrugged.

The pictures and mementos told the story of a bright, eager young girl just beginning to taste life, and Ian thought of Emma's parting words. This was not a girl who should be forgotten. As Ian read through newspaper clippings detailing sports triumphs and campus celebrations, a sudden thought struck him. He turned to his computer and pulled up the page for a small-time local newspaper. He scrolled through Monday's articles until he found the one that Emma's student had mentioned while he had been watching her class: *Body of Local College Student Found*. It wasn't a full article, just a quick mention in the local news section. Shit. He should have noticed this before.

"Mike," he called.

"Solve the case already, Sherlock?" Mike's voice was tinted with annoyance.

"Shut up and listen to this: 'Police responded to reports that the body of a young woman had been found in an abandoned barn just north of Route 22. The victim is reportedly a junior from Carlisle College who was reported missing several days ago . . .'" Ian looked over.

"So?"

"So—they say the victim is a Carlisle student, but this was published on Monday. Before we released any information."

Mike came over to Ian's desk, his face darkening as he read the computer screen. He scrolled down, clicking a link. "It's worse than that."

A newly updated article replaced the brief notice Ian had been reading, images of the mural and trough in which Sarah

Weston was found filling the screen. "Those aren't crime scene photos. No tape, no tags. Those were taken before we got there."

"How the hell did this rag get them?" Mike demanded.

"Let's find out."

The editor of the *Daily Independent*, Bradford Mackey, stood behind the expanse of a desk shoved into his too-small downtown office. Ian and Mike loomed over him, the afternoon sun casting them in shadow. Mackey stood as tall as his compact stature would allow, glaring defiantly at the detectives.

"We're well within our First Amendment rights to publish those pictures. You should see the ones we didn't print."

"We intend to," Ian replied dryly.

"Look," Mike said, leaning in close and pressing his palms against the desk, "a young woman was killed, and you're playing pen pal with her murderer."

"No, you look," Mackey snapped back. "This is a story, a big story, and we not only have a right but an obligation to report it. I don't know why the killer sent the photos to us, but he did. We only printed the ones that were relevant to the story. We withheld the more . . . graphic images out of deference to the sensitivities of our readers."

Mike snorted. "Out of deference to the sensitivities of your lawyers, more like."

"Detective Kellogg, we have not done anything unlawful. We held the full story until we could verify its veracity and fully intend to cooperate."

"Good. Start cooperating. I want to see the photos and anything that came with them, including the envelope."

Mackey reddened. "Unfortunately, the mailing envelope was disposed of. We've been unable to track it down."

Ian watched a muscle in his partner's cheek jump as he ground his teeth. Ian subtly moved between Mike and the smaller man.

"Then get us what you have and send anything else you find to the precinct," Ian ordered stiffly. Mackey pressed the intercom button on the phone on his desk and directed his assistant to bring the materials to him. A middle-aged woman in a neatly tailored skirt opened the door a few moments later, handing over an unmarked envelope. Ian pulled a latex glove out of his inner pocket jacket.

Mike sighed. "Don't bother. Everyone and his dog have probably handled these by now. Prints will be worthless."

Ian didn't respond as he used the folded glove to gingerly open the flap. He emptied the contents onto Mackey's desk. Three photos and a piece of white computer paper slid onto the wood surface. Ian eased the photos apart and stooped to examine them. The paper was glossy but cheap, the kind sold at office supply stores. He immediately recognized the top photo from this morning's edition. The paper had printed it in full at the top of the page and cropped the lower portion, just the trough, as an insert alongside the column. The other three had not been printed.

The first was a close-up of Sarah Weston's face, water pressing around her cheeks and hairline. The next showed her full body laid out in the metal trough as if the photographer had been perched above her. Ian thought of the ladder he had seen leaning in the barn. The final shot showed only her right hand. The photo was angled from below, giving the impression that she reached up toward the noose arching across the frame. Ian imagined the unknown photographer squatting down, trying to capture this shot. He would have needed to lean into the trough, across the body, his elbow probably submerged. Effort had been made with these images.

Ian turned his attention to the sheet of computer paper. It was almost empty, with only a single line of text at the top of the page and a small block of print at its center. The top read simply: *Her name was Sarah. She was a student at Carlisle.*

"That explains that," Mike muttered, reading over Ian's shoulder. Ian's attention, however, was fixed on the middle of the glaring, white sheet.

"'Wise men know well enough what monsters you make of them.'" Ian read the phrase aloud and looked over at his partner. Mike shook his head.

"It's from *Hamlet*," Mackey said uncertainly as he eyed the two detectives. "You know, Shakespeare. We looked it up."

"Thanks," Mike replied tersely.

Ian slid the paper back into the envelope, gathered the photos, and tucked them inside as well. "We'd like to speak to whoever received the envelope originally."

"That would be Charlotte, our intern." Mackey hit the intercom button. "Dora, please send Charlotte in."

The three men waited in tense silence until a light tap sounded on the door. A sturdy woman—older than Ian expected for an intern, maybe midtwenties—stepped in. She wore a dress and leggings in two different patterns of plaid that clashed with her Fanta-orange hair. She was holding mail in her left hand and shifted it behind her back as she stopped in front of them, giving her the look of a soldier waiting for orders. "You wanted to see me?"

"Yes. Charlotte, these are detectives. They'd like to talk with you." Mackey's tone was careful in a way that reeked of condescension. The woman's mouth tightened almost imperceptibly. She turned toward the two detectives and offered her hand first to Mike and then to Ian.

"Charlotte Mason. Charlie," she introduced herself. "I'm working as an intern here while pursuing a journalism degree from Carlisle College. They only let me sort the mail. I assume that you are here about the photos."

Ian introduced himself and his partner, then asked Charlotte about the envelope.

"It arrived Friday evening as part of the regular delivery. There were no special packages that day. I checked." Charlotte's tone was straightforward and precise. "I collected the mail as usual. There was no specific addressee, just the paper's name, so I opened it to see which office it should be sent to. The inner envelope, that one there—" Charlotte indicated the one Ian was holding "—was addressed to Mr. Mackey, as you can see. I delivered it first thing that morning. When we found out what was in it, I went back for the outer envelope, but it had been added to the recycling and taken out. I'm sorry about that."

"That's okay, Miss Mason," Mike said easily. "You couldn't have known."

"True," Charlotte agreed, "but I did save this one for you. It arrived last night." Charlotte held forth the envelope that she had been shielding behind her back. Ian noticed then that she was gripping it with a tissue between her fingers.

"I recognized the handwriting," Charlotte explained simply, "when I opened the outer envelope. The inner one was folded like that, but it wasn't sealed. I did my best not to touch anything with my bare hands, but you're welcome to take elimination prints if it's helpful."

"We may need to do that." Ian laid the first envelope down on Mackey's desk and, mirroring Charlotte's technique, used his glove to take her offering.

"Charlotte," Mackey exploded, drawing himself up to his full height, "why didn't you bring this to me at once?"

Charlotte turned a wide-eyed face full of innocence toward her employer. "I thought the police would want it. It's evidence in a murder case, after all." A kind of steel in her tone undercut her expression, and Ian doubted that she was nearly as guileless as she pretended.

"Thank you, Miss Mason, for all of your help," Ian said gravely.

Charlotte smiled at him, apparently catching the note of amusement in his voice. "Just doing my civic duty. But detective . . ."

Ian quirked an eyebrow at her.

"I'm covering this story for the college paper, and I could

use a statement from the police. I hope to get picked up by a national publication."

Mike turned a snort of laughter into an unconvincing cough as the mail girl outplayed her editor, but Ian just retrieved a business card from his pocket and handed it to her.

"I can't discuss an ongoing investigation, but I'm your exclusive when we solve it."

"Deal." Charlotte nodded curtly and, resisting a glance at her boss, left the room. Ian and Mike followed her out, the envelopes now enclosed in evidence bags.

"Gimme," Mike demanded as soon as he slid behind the wheel of their sedan. Ian obligingly handed over the envelope they had resisted opening in front of Mackey. Mike handed the emptied envelope to Ian, who did a cursory inspection: cheap grade office supply, postmarked downtown, block printing of the paper's address in black ink. Despite Charlotte's diligence, they were unlikely to get much from this. He turned his attention to his partner. Mike was using a pocketknife to open the enclosed envelope, which seemed identical to the first one Mackey had given them. He eased open the flap and peered inside.

"Looks like more photos. Let's head back and see what they tell us."

Chapter 12

"This is the tree!" Emma's teacup rattled as Rory thrust a newspaper in front of her. She was sitting in the nearly empty café that occupied the basement of the faculty building. Most of the other professors had left for the day, so she'd commandeered a large central table that sat in a patch of soft afternoon light. Rory dropped into the chair opposite her, ignoring the cup in front of the chair.

"Hello, Rory. Would you like to join me?" Emma said dryly as she dabbed a napkin at the splashes of coffee on the table.

"It is, isn't it? That's the 'mural' that you showed me."

There was a fever-bright intensity in his eyes. Emma took the paper, the previous day's edition of a lowbrow local daily mostly read for the pithy movie reviews and vaguely creepy pleas in the "Missed Connections" section. Emma felt uneasy as she unfolded the front page, letting her breath out in a rush as she saw only the painted wall instead of the face of the young woman, exposed and exploited.

"Well?" Rory prompted.

Emma ignored him, skimming the story that accompanied the photo. A college girl had been brutally murdered, the article reported, and left in a barn outside of town. The paper described the mural Emma had seen but added that the victim had been placed in a water trough, surrounded by melted candles, a book, and a glass jar filled with dark liquid, which the newspaper speculated was blood in the most gruesome terms. Emma flipped farther back in the paper to see a close-up of the trough, clearly enlarged so that the more ghoulish readers could catch the glimpses of leg and the golden hair protruding from the metal basin. The article concluded that police had no leads and gave no information about where they had gotten the photos. Given their discussion that morning, Emma doubted Ian had handed them over. She tried to relax the tension digging into her muscles and school her expression so Rory wouldn't see the fissures in her facade.

"Rory—" She broke off, unable to read Rory's face. Irritation or hurt or eagerness or—apology seemed the best route. "I'm sorry I didn't tell you more. I didn't want to get you involved or make any . . ."

Rory waved a hand. "Forget that. I don't care. This is what you were researching, isn't it?"

"Yes," Emma confirmed cautiously.

"Hi, Dr. Tamblyn. That's, uh, my seat."

Emma looked up to Carolyn, hovering behind her boss and holding a plate of mini scones.

For the first time, Rory seemed to notice the coffee cup at his elbow. "Caro, sorry."

He pulled a chair from the table behind him, setting it close to Emma's elbow. Shifting over, he gestured for Carolyn to be seated next to him. Instead, she shifted to Emma's other side, then delicately slid her coffee to her new position.

"Tell me what's going on, Em. Are you in trouble?" he asked.

"No, of course not."

"You're involved in a murder . . ."

"Excuse me?" Carolyn interjected.

Rory turned to her. "That tree Emma asked about? It was painted next to the murdered girl."

He passed Carolyn the paper. "Shit," she whispered, taking in the headline. She glanced up at her boss. "Sorry."

"No," he replied. "That response is appropriate." He looked back to Emma. "So then you're not involved with the murder?"

"Are you asking if I killed someone and then came to you for interpretive insights into my crime?"

Rory huffed lightly. "No—but then you must be consulting with the police. These pictures weren't published when you asked about that tree." Rory tapped the photo.

"You're working with the cops?" Carolyn's voice was a mix of impressed and concerned.

"Why did the police come to you?" Rory pressed.

"They didn't—exactly. I mean, I'm not . . ." Emma put up her hands, overwhelmed by the barrage. The questions stopped, and she closed her eyes for a brief moment. She chose her words carefully, feeling like she was walking through a dark room. "I'm not working with the police. I saw one of the pictures . . . unofficially. I have, in fact, been specifically told by the police not to get involved."

"Emma." Rory waited until she looked at him. "Tell me."

Emma's knee bounced gently as she considered her options. She gave up on composure, sagging a bit in her chair. "Okay, you remember that guy you saw talking to me at the gala?"

"Yeah."

"Turns out he's a homicide detective. I went to his place for dinner . . ."

"You went on a date with a cop?" Carolyn interrupted.

"I don't think that's the point of the story, Caro," Rory reprimanded.

"No, it's not," Emma said. "He brought a folder home from work; I accidentally saw a photo of the crime scene. I noticed the tree and . . ." Emma shrugged.

"Brain gremlins?" Rory echoed her phrase.

"Right. So I thought I could help, but when I tried to tell Ian—"

"That's the cop?" Carolyn asked.

"That's the . . . detective. He said the police didn't need help from amateurs. I got bopped by a metaphoric newspaper and sent on my way. So, that's that. Alright?" Emma couldn't keep the hurt from her voice.

"That is ridiculous." Rory's tone was indignant.

"I know. I should never have . . ."

"Of course you should have. Do you know how rare it is for police to actually solve a serial murder?"

"It's not serial if there's only one victim," Carolyn interjected. "Do you know something we don't?"

"Look at this—" Rory positioned the paper in front of her. "No one starts here. He's killed before, and he'll kill again—unless he's caught. And with a serial, the odds are only about 60 percent that they'll find him."

"Weird fact to know," Carolyn replied.

"NPR has a great true-crime series going." Rory turned back to Emma. "Some of these guys get cocky and slip up—Ted Bundy, BTK—but a lot of the times, it's citizen sleuths . . ." He caught Carolyn's expression. "A term I did not come up with—it's these amateurs who solve the crime. A blogger developed the profile for The Golden State Killer. A podcast fan identified the Bear Brook victims. A teacher and his wife cracked the first Zodiac cipher over eggs in their breakfast nook."

"Are you actually arguing that I should try to solve this crime?" Emma asked, incredulous. She'd expected Rory to board up the door Ian had locked, not to pry it back open.

"What's even the point?" Carolyn asked. "I mean, it was probably a boyfriend, right? Like thirty percent of murdered women were killed by a partner."

"Weird fact to know," Rory said dryly.

"Not if you're a woman." Carolyn raised an eyebrow but kept her expression mild.

Rory snorted softly and then turned to Emma. "I'm not saying you should solve it. I'm saying *we* should. And it's a fig tree, by the way."

"I figured that out. Thanks," Emma relented. "But the cops don't want our help."

Rory shrugged. "They will if we solve it. Did you tell them about the tree?"

"I tried and—quote: You're just a professor." Emma hated hearing Ian's rejection in her own voice.

"And Miss Marple was just a spinster."

"Also? A fictional character. Rory, a girl's been murdered," Carolyn protested.

"Sorry, sorry. I'll stop being flip." He gave Carolyn a boyish glance of apology that Emma recognized before turning away again. "I just . . . We could do something that matters, Em, genuinely matters. And not in a theoretical, five-people-will-read-this-article sort of way—we could do something important."

Despite her defiance, she hadn't forgotten Ian's warning. She thought—for the hundredth time—of his face when he'd first seen her with the photos. She'd focused before on his anger, his rejection; now she remembered his fear. "It's going to be a lot harder outside of St. Mary Mead."

"A puzzle too hard for you? Never."

"I don't mean the puzzle. I mean the reality of it. Someone really killed her, and this girl—"

"Deserves to have someone listen to her story, Emma." Rory studied her face for a moment. "Be honest. Is your detective going to do that? Can he even? You're made for this. Trained for it."

Emma heard an echo of her own protests in Rory's words, his confidence in her abilities a siren's song to her wounded ego. It was what she'd wanted from Ian.

"I understand it's not a game," Rory assured them even as his zeal grew. "I do. But it *is* a kind of text, one that we have the skills and knowledge to interpret. Em, he's sending a message with all of this." Rory tapped the page. "And it's in a language that we speak. The police don't. When you came to my office, you said you were researching a depiction of Ophelia's death scene. That's the connection you spotted, isn't it? Did your cop friend have any idea before you told him?"

"No," Emma acknowledged.

"You figured out that Ophelia reference—you—and I'm willing to bet they didn't even notice the discrepancy with the tree. They're already further along because of you."

"I understand nobody is asking me," Carolyn finally interjected. "But this is a bad idea."

"Noted." Rory didn't look at her. "Em? What do you say?"

"We tell the police everything that we find and let them do the actual legwork," Emma finally offered. She wasn't about to prove Ian right by getting killed by some madman. "We just focus on the text."

"Well, that's what we're best at." Rory grinned, pulling the paper closer and pointing to the tree. "Okay, then. So, instead of a symbol of grief, we have a symbol of condemnation. The fig tree suggests a lack of innocence or a fall from grace." He glanced up at Emma, and she nodded her consensus. "This is emphasized by the fact that it's painted on a closed door. She's been barred from heaven."

"And," Emma added, "a noose of flowers hung in the tree instead of Ophelia's coronet. You can't see it very well here."

"Good thing you have insider information," Rory teased, clearly enjoying the challenge.

"But he included the daisies . . ." Emma noted. "Why not trade those out for one of Ophelia's other flowers—her withered violets or columbines? Lost modesty or foolishness would both make more sense if he's trying to question her virtue."

A flicker of annoyance crossed Rory's face, but he pressed on. "You're right. It seems contradictory. Maybe they're there to represent an innocence that's been . . ." His eyes scanned the image, trying to translate it into expressible thoughts. "Overshadowed."

"Literally overshadowed," Emma agreed. "The fig dominates the scene; everything else is in its shadow. And the daisies are caught in its branches. It's a strong reading."

Rory's mouth quirked, his momentary frustration erased by her praise. "What's this at the base of the trough?"

"The article says that there were candles, a book, and an inkwell at the scene."

"Burned-out candles can symbolize a lack of piety, especially in Renaissance motifs," Rory told them. "And this—" he tapped on the overturned glass jar "—it's tipped over."

"Or he knocked it over accidentally," Carolyn noted dryly.

Rory gave her a reproachful look. "You don't do all of this—" he gestured at the picture "—and accidentally knock over a prop. And I thought you didn't want to play detective?"

"I said it's a bad idea. It is, and I'm not risking my skin. But I'm not going to let you drag Emma off a cliff either. Consider me your resident cynic." Carolyn met his eyes, chin lifted.

Rory nodded, accepting her terms. "Welcome to the team, then. You can narrate and chronicle."

"I'm no man's Watson," Carolyn retorted.

Rory smiled an acknowledgment that Carolyn reluctantly returned.

"Okay. The book could represent knowledge, honor . . . or faith . . . Is it damaged or torn?" Rory's eagerness grew as he spoke. "That could symbolize a rejection."

Carolyn sighed. "Is she rejecting or being rejected?"

Rory shook his head. "Both? She rejects . . . some virtue . . . and the artist rejects her?" He pointed to the center of the image. "What's there? A water trough? Bathtub?"

"That's where the body was found," Emma told them.

Rory glanced up. "Could be an allusion to Lizzie Siddal. A postmodern take on . . ."

"Wait, Lizzie who?" Carolyn asked.

"Elizabeth Siddal," said an accented voice from above them. Emma craned her neck to see Niall Chadha looking back, clearly pleased with himself. "She was sort of a Pre-Raphaelite supermodel. She was married to Dante Gabriel Rossetti and posed for most of the artists of the day. She was a painter in her own right, too, but she's mostly just remembered as their muse. Millais's famous *Ophelia* was modeled after her, and he had her pose in a bathtub to get a realistic depiction of how the water would soak her gown and hair. It's probably why her arms are at odd angles in the painting, posed up by her head. It was the only way she fit in the tub."

The psychology professor was the proverbial tall, dark, and handsome, with a clipped Oxbridge accent that added gravitas to his speech.

"Sorry, I was blatantly eavesdropping and couldn't resist a dramatic entrance." He glanced around the table. "You all look intent. Can I play, too?"

"Of course," Carolyn offered before catching the sharp looks of her companions. "Or . . . is this a 'members only' sort of team? He might be helpful. He knew the bathtub thing."

"So did I," Rory retorted.

"Yes, many people have access to the BBC," Niall responded smoothly, "but Oxford does teach a few useful courses."

Emma rolled her eyes. "Rory, as a psychologist Niall does have expertise that we don't."

Rory nodded grudgingly. "I suppose we could use a profiler on the team."

"A profiler? Are we playing Cluedo?" Niall grabbed a chair from the table next to them, spinning it around like a seventies sitcom teacher.

Carolyn slid the paper over to him. "A student was killed. Emma's gotten involved in the investigation, and Rory's decided he's Sherlock Holmes."

"The consulting detective, eh?" Niall said. "Then, I guess I'm playing Freud."

"Not a detective." Rory frowned.

"The Seven-Per-Cent Solution."

Rory raised his eyebrows. "Point to you. So—" He slid the paper to Niall. "Emma figured out something we think might be useful to the police. We've been discussing the symbolic implications of the crime scene to see if we can glean anything else."

Niall tapped the page, considering. "The working theory is that whoever did this knows the Siddal story and used the water trough as a reference to Millais? Not very Victorian of him."

"As I was saying before you jumped in, it might be a postmodern visual commentary," Rory countered. "The mix of periods and media would suggest that."

"So, either he's interested in reclaiming the narrative or challenging it. Postmodernism is an interesting era, psychosocially," Niall responded thoughtfully. "It's a direct challenge to the modernist forebearers who insisted on a reification of both art and artist. Perhaps by adopting the persona of a Pre-Raphaelite, who were themselves rebels against the status quo, he's signaling a rejection of social structures."

"Such as?" Carolyn prompted.

Niall shrugged. "The artistic community, public mores—it could be anything that he feels has an oppressive power over him. He destroys what society values—a beautiful young woman—and remakes it in his own vision, reclaiming and redefining what art is. Postmodernism is too often just associated with Warhol's soup cans and fairy-tale retellings—but it's really destructive, deep down. They're not just rejecting the work of those who came before; they're taking it, killing it, and using its corpse to build something new. Quite literally in this case. It's all very Oedipal when you think about it."

"So he's mimicking these artists to, what, claim their status? Their acclaim?" Emma theorized.

Niall nodded. "By seizing the narrative, the killer can usurp his idols. Look at the parallels: Millais hired Siddal to model as Ophelia, and in an ironic twist, the water he placed her in nearly took her life. The candles heating the tub went out during one of their sittings, and the water grew cold." Niall pointed to the burned-down candles at the base of the trough. "Millais didn't notice, and Siddal ended up developing pneumonia. She nearly became another tragic maiden. Maybe the trough is a commentary on how one story connects to the next, itself a very postmodern concept. Siddal becomes Ophelia; this girl becomes Siddal. It's a never-ending chain of violence."

"'The death of a beautiful woman is, unquestionably, the most poetical topic in the world,'" Emma murmured. "Poe," she added at Carolyn's look of repulsion.

"Bit of a creeper," Carolyn noted, "but this guy actually killed a woman, a real person."

"He probably doesn't see her that way." Niall's voice was almost apologetic. "If you are right about the symbolism here, he likely sees her as disposable. She isn't real to him, so the death isn't either."

Emma traced her finger along the picture of the trough, conjuring the memory of a water-bound face peering sightlessly from within its murky confines. "It was real for her."

Niall reached and touched her arm in a silent question. Emma gave him a small smile as reassurance.

"So . . . what now?" Carolyn asked. Three faces looked blankly back at her. "I mean, Emma already tried to go to the police, and they weren't interested. We need to give them more than a psychological interpretation of a bathtub."

"Em," Rory asked after a moment, "do you still have access to the photos?"

"No. That's why I showed you a drawing."

"We need to see more than just black-and-white reprints," Rory insisted unhelpfully.

Carolyn reached for the paper, flipping away from the front page to the very back, where a list of names was printed in the bottom corner. "Damn it." She sighed. "Look, I'm still very much on the side of 'this is a bad idea,' but . . . Charlie works at the paper. I can ask her if she knows anything."

"Who?" Rory asked after a beat.

"My roommate, Charlie. Short, red hair—you've met her. More than once. She used to work in student services." At Rory's apologetic shrug, Carolyn turned back to Emma. "She's doing an internship at *The Independent* as part of her degree requirements."

"It's worth a shot," Emma said. "If you don't mind asking."

"We could also visit the actual crime scene," Niall suggested. "Primary sources are always best."

"Do you know where it is?" Emma asked.

"Bad idea," Carolyn declared simultaneously. She looked at Emma. "I thought you were leaving the gumshoe stuff to the cops."

"It's not like the killer's still there," Rory countered. "And I'm sure we can find it. It's a large barn surrounded by yellow crime scene tape. If not, we're pretty sorry detectives."

"You're *not* detectives," Carolyn pointed out as Rory and Niall rose, their excitement clear.

Emma followed more slowly.

As they crossed the campus, Emma felt the same eager energy as the day before. The grassy quad seemed slightly shadowed as the autumn darkness continued to creep in. Rory and Niall brainstormed approaches for the investigation, with the occasional quip from Carolyn, but Emma fell behind the group, distracted by thoughts of Elizabeth Siddal. She knew the Millais's *Ophelia* well, had spent more than one summer afternoon in London engrossed by its terrible beauty, and could easily picture the auburn-haired girl in a silver-blue dress sinking into the water, her hands lifted as if in supplication. For the first time, though, she wondered if Ophelia had been cold as the creeping water dragged her down.

Chapter 13

Ian stilled as he leaned over the photos scattered across the table.

"Jesus," Mike breathed, "that's not our girl."

After a mostly silent drive to the precinct, the two detectives had commandeered a conference room and laid out the contents of the two manila envelopes across two mismatched tables. First, Ian had opened the one they had gone over in Mackey's office, three photos and the bright, white sheet of paper. Then, Mike had carefully emptied the second.

A spill of blond hair, the glint of water, the heavy, archaic gown—but this wasn't Sarah Weston.

Again, three photos were included. A close-up of the girl's face, pale and frozen in death, was at the top of the pile. Her head lay on a deep red pillow, her face turned slightly away from the camera and pressed into the soft surface. Honey-colored hair, darker than Sarah Weston's, lay in wild spirals around her face, clinging to her skin as if it were damp. Her eyes were almost shut, with just a slit of green showing between the fair lashes. The second shot showed her full body laid out on a wooden surface and draped elegantly in a crimson gown with the skirt bunched around her knees. Her legs twisted awkwardly; her feet were bare. Around her legs, light bounced back at the camera lens as though a flash had struck glass or metal. Other bits of debris that Ian couldn't identify lay around her prone body, and she appeared to be tangled in some sort of string. Golden strands wound around her torso, serpentlike, as if holding her in place.

"S n'M?" Mike asked, following his partner's train of thought.

"It doesn't look . . ." Ian hesitated over the word. "Forceful. More decorative."

"More crazy," Mike declared. "Shit. The mayor's going to have a fit when he finds out there's a second one. Probably blame us. Fucking election cycle."

Ian frowned but didn't disagree. He stared back at the picture. The girl was resting in a wooden container, her arms splayed outward over the edges so that her hands escaped the frame of the photo. Wordlessly, he moved on to the third image. As with Sarah Weston, the killer had included a close-up of the victim's hand. It dangled beyond the edge of the wooden enclosure over a shifting, reflective surface that Ian identified easily as moving water. Something had been tied to the palm with the same string that wound about the body. The wrist was raggedly slashed, a small amount of dried blood evident on the pale skin. The rest, presumably, having been washed away in the current of water.

"I'm guessing we have cause of death," Mike offered.

"Unless it was done postmortem."

"What's she in? A rowboat, maybe, or a canoe?"

Ian stepped back and focused on the lines of wood at the edge of the image. "Rowboat, I think."

"First a water trough, now a boat. Our guy got a water fetish?"

Ian didn't reply, reaching instead for the piece of paper. At the top of the page, he read: *Her name was Phillipa. She was a student at*

Carlisle. "We'll need to contact the college for admission records. There can't be too many Phillipas registered there."

Mike nodded in agreement, knowing there was more.

Ian's eyes dropped down to the page once more. He read aloud: "'I love not to be constrained to love, for love must arise of the heart and not by any constraint.'"

Mike shook his head. "Recognize it?"

"No."

"Know anyone who might?"

"I'll Google it."

Mike let it go. "I've been wondering why our guy would send the pictures to Mackey. I mean, *The Independent* has limited circulation, fairly low readership—*The Post* would have gotten a lot more attention. Or even send it to one of the Portland papers. He might have gone national."

"Maybe he has a connection to someone on the paper? Or he wanted someone specific to see it? We could check out their subscription list."

"Or he knew Mackey couldn't resist the temptation to publish them."

"Could be. We should check Mackey, see if there's anything there," Ian said, distracted. There was something in the photos that was needling him. He turned the photo of the victim's face to see it from a different angle.

"See something," Mike asked over his shoulder.

"I don't know," Ian replied as he adjusted the image again. "She's familiar somehow."

Mike walked over to the door of the small room and leaned out. "Miguel," Mike yelled to a nearby officer, "get someone in here who's good with computers."

Twenty minutes later, Mike and Ian were studying an enlarged image of the photo that a young computer tech had projected on the back wall. Ian gave terse directions as the tech adjusted the image so that the girl's upturned face was centered, life-size, on the screen.

"I know her," Ian muttered for the third time.

"She looks a lot like the first vic."

"It's more than that. I'm pretty sure I've seen her someplace."

"Maybe on campus?"

"Maybe," Ian responded, unconvinced.

He thought of Emma, considered Mike's suggestion to call her about the quote, and rejected it again. A happenstance meeting at an art exhibit, and now she . . .

Ian's head snapped up almost painfully as the image hit him: Emma's flushed cheeks and long blue gown—over her shoulder, a dark-haired man in his early twenties grabbing the arm of a girl, a pretty blonde girl. The pretty blonde girl whose face now filled the wall on the far side of the room.

Ian stared at the image, straining to remember every detail. The young man had been standing next to the pretty blonde, standing too close, and she looked uncomfortable. She looked almost frightened. That's what had attracted Ian's attention, her expression—not unlike the one Zoey wore when she'd asked him for help. The man had grabbed her arm as if to pull her away, and she had resisted. The blonde had jerked her arm from his grasp, thrown an insult at the young man, and turned back to her friends. The scene had lasted only a moment before the young man had disappeared into the crowd of museumgoers, but she had been upset by the encounter; he was sure of it. Ian didn't think he would recognize the man's face. But he remembered hers.

Ian opened the door to his darkening house. He stripped off his jacket and tie, tossing them carelessly onto the sofa as he passed. Toeing off his shoes, he padded sock-footed to the kitchen. He pulled a potpie out of the freezer, leaving it on the counter as he preheated the oven. Then he just leaned against the counter and waited, head down. He knew he should go pick up his clothes or turn on the TV or check his email—but he didn't. He just stood and waited, empty, for the soft beeping of the oven.

He was not usually one for introspection. He was good at dissecting other people's behavior, knowing what they would do or say when he pressed them or cajoled them in an interview room. He could trace their steps, find their mistakes, solve their riddles—but he never felt the impulse to tear his own actions down in the same way. He was, he thought now, excruciatingly normal. He'd grown up in a middle-class family in a suburban home, gotten his degree, and joined the force. He'd walked his beat, kept a cool head, and worked his way up to detective—white-collar, then Narcotics, then finally Homicide. He'd decided at thirteen that's what he wanted to do and then stopped asking questions. He had a goal, made a plan, and just—

Ian crossed the galley kitchen and got a beer from the fridge, draining half of it in one gulp. The foundation he'd built his life on had cracked when Zoey was killed. He'd felt the trestles shaking when he'd looked down at Sarah Weston's face, brushing the hair back from her brow. The frame had rattled when he'd met Emma, bolts loosening with each excited word and nervous smile. The boards had split as he watched her hope and hurt the night she'd come to his house. And he'd broken apart when he'd sent her away. Ian took another deep drink as he thought of her face, fierce and wounded and determined, as she had turned from him.

He'd been right. He'd run the conversation through his head again and again, and he knew he'd been right. His guilt over Zoey was mixing into this in ways he wasn't fully able to sort out, but he could admit to himself—at least here, in the silence of his empty kitchen—that the fear he felt for Emma was different, personal. Letting Emma help would endanger her physically and emotionally in ways she couldn't anticipate. There would be no excuses, no party line that he could comfort himself with. She didn't know what she was asking for, and he was right to tell her no. He drank again, finishing the bottle. He got out another. The problem, he realized, was that he hadn't wanted to. He knew that if he'd said yes, she would have thanked him, her face bright with excitement. She would have shared her knowledge, herself, with him—and god, he wanted that. But not at the risk of her safety.

The oven chirped its readiness, and Ian slid the frozen meal inside. He grabbed his beer and went to the living room, dropping down onto the sofa. He pushed his jacket aside and swung his feet up, letting his head fall against the armrest. He thought back to the night she'd come, playing through the evening with an alternate ending. He wondered if she'd have liked him, if they'd have kissed, if she'd have stayed. He considered calling her now, asking her for another shot now that he'd convinced her to leave the murder investigation alone. He wondered briefly, but not for the first time, about the blond man he'd seen with her at the gala. A fellow professor, he guessed. Handsome, undoubtedly smart, far more suitable for her than Ian was. But she hadn't wanted to call that guy when she'd needed someone; when she'd been scared and hurt, she hadn't turned to him. She'd turned to Ian, even if it was just because he was there. For a minute, he let himself enjoy the idea—the lie—that if he solved the case, if he just kept pressing forward the way he always had, then they could just erase what had happened and go back to those first moments, before he'd told her he was a cop, before the mugging, before the photos, before the fights—before.

He thought of the two dead girls with a roll of guilt. Their stories had ended quickly, brutally—and he wished they could be more than a footnote in his. But he knew this case would end. As would the next one and the next. They would become two of any number of dead girls—and boys, women, men. The only offering he could make to their memory was to close their case, solve their mystery, and let their deaths fade gently into time.

As the last of the light dissolved into shadow, Ian silently vowed he would do whatever it took.

Chapter 14

For all their bravado, Rory and Niall hesitated as they stood outside the abandoned barn where the girl's body had been found. Police tape still encircled the perimeter, though tattered ends at the door suggested they were not the first to come. A padlock secured the heavy doors.

"This is a terrible plan," Carolyn said as she got out of her car, blinking into the morning light. "For the record."

"Chicken." They all turned as a woman dressed in mismatched paisleys stepped out of the passenger door. She had a thick spread of freckles and hair a shade of orange that wasn't pretending to be natural.

"Charlie, you remember Emma from the BBQ last summer? And Rory. He won't remember you, don't take it personally. And this is Niall; I'm not sure that you've met. He works at the college, too."

"A professor?" Charlie asked, her attention centered firmly on Niall.

"Yes, psychology. You're a reporter?" He stepped forward to shake her hand.

"Technically, I'm an intern." She shrugged. "I work in the mail room."

They all paused for more small talk, but Charlie just started toward the barn door. "So," Rory asked, jogging to catch up. "You found this place through your contacts at the paper?"

"What? No. It's all over social media. People have been posting selfies here." She stopped in front of the padlock and gave it a hard tug.

"The best-laid plans," Niall muttered.

"You give up too easily," Charlie said, crossing to the right. "There's bound to be another way in."

"Entering is one thing," Niall called as she disappeared around the corner of the barn. "Breaking moves us into felony territory."

There was no response. The four academics looked uncertainly at each other, then Rory shrugged and followed her. Niall was close on his heels.

Carolyn sighed. "Come on, then."

She gestured to Emma, and they followed, rounding the corner to see the other three crouched down. Rory was tugging on a board loosely attached to the side of the barn.

"Rory, are you sure . . ." Emma called, jogging the remaining distance. But even as she spoke, the board gave way and dropped Rory back hard into the dirt.

"What's done . . ." Rory grinned, crawling forward through the newly formed hole.

"We'll put it back," Niall offered as Charlie slipped quickly after Rory. Niall followed, his lanky frame twisting to fit. As his feet disappeared, Carolyn came up behind Emma.

"Are you coming?" Emma asked.

"Who else is going to keep you geniuses from getting yourselves killed?"

"Okay, then, here we go." A jolt of anticipation buzzed across Emma's brain. She ducked down to the jagged hole, hoping Carolyn couldn't see the eagerness in her face.

Emma blinked in the dim light as she emerged on the other side. She heard the scrape of dirt and gravel behind her as Carolyn followed. The dusky room was filled with shadowy figures that resolved into disused farm equipment as her eyes adjusted. Rory and Niall stood a few feet in front of them, looking unsure. Charlie was inspecting the ground nearby, her phone out. Nothing looked particularly significant until a glint of yellow caught Emma's eye. Niall saw it, too.

"There," he said, his voice hushed. "In the back."

Emma nodded and moved toward the mural that had dominated her imagination since she first saw it in Ian's photos. The ground around her showed evidence of commotion at odds with the decrepit setting, and Emma imagined the police searching their way through the dust as Ian directed the investigation; he stayed a ghost at the edge of her vision as she walked across the hollow space. Here was the mural she had seen, the same yellow and purple flowers, the vines shaped into a noose, the fig tree where a willow should have stood. A painted stream frothed around its roots. The rest of the scene, still clear in Emma's mind, had been claimed by the police.

"Can you remember what it looked like before?" a voice asked Emma from just over her shoulder. She jumped, and Rory steadied her.

Charlie answered instead. "There was a metal trough just in front. I saw the originals that the paper printed."

"Where, specifically?" Niall prompted this time.

Using the noose as a marker, Charlie walked the basic perimeter of the missing object. "From here to here." She paced its boundaries, then dropped down to rest on her heels. "Down here were candles, blown out. And a book. There was a quote included with the photos. Might be from the book."

"Do you remember it?" Emma asked.

Charlie closed her eyes. "'Wise men know well enough what monsters you make of them.' It's Shakespeare."

"Hamlet says it to Ophelia," Emma stated quietly.

"What's the context?" Niall asked.

"Hamlet is treating Ophelia cruelly, either because he knows her father and the king are watching him, and it's part of his planned 'madness' or . . ." Emma walked toward the wall and touched the painted noose of flowers. "Or because her father has made her reject him. She'd just given back some letters and keepsakes that Hamlet had given her."

"The second interpretation sure fits," Carolyn said softly. "She rejects him; he tries to hurt her."

Rory's mouth was set in a grim line. "Maybe the killer saw this as a punishment for betrayal."

"Or something he perceived as a betrayal," Niall amended. "Just because he saw it that way doesn't mean we would. Killers often live by rules of their own making."

"How so?" Rory asked with just a hint of challenge.

Niall looked over to him. "He's a classic narcissist. Anything that threatens his sense of supremacy has to be denigrated or destroyed. Clearly, women threaten his sense of self. He's made this girl a part of his creation, turned her into something he could control." Niall's voice became more animated as he continued. "And consider the way that he killed. A careful killer would hide his victims, disguise his identity. He's clearly organized—tremendous planning and discipline went into this—and he put his victim on display. He wants to be seen, recognized."

"And just in case anyone missed it, he sent pictures to the paper," Charlie noted.

"He quite literally advertised his work," Emma agreed. "He's more interested in fame than safety."

"Or, more likely, he thinks he's too smart to get caught. You see it in a lot of narcissistic killers—they send messages, taunt the police—and it brings a lot of them down." Niall stepped back from the wall. "It's cruder than I thought it would be."

"What is?"

"The painting. It's not . . ." He searched for a word. "Good. Technique-wise, I mean, it's just not very good. The composition is off-balance, the symbolism is too on the nose, the work is sloppy."

"I imagine he was painting under a bit of duress," Charlie said dryly.

"But this is his masterpiece," Emma countered, following Niall's logic. She stepped back to where he stood to take in the full image.

"Right. He's put this out there as a statement to the world, literally killed to create it, invited everyone to see it . . ." Niall shook his head.

"Maybe he does this because he couldn't make it as a real artist," Emma suggested.

"That would make sense," Niall responded. "If he felt rejected by the art world, then this may be his way of proving his worth. He's more famous now than most of his contemporaries."

Emma asked. "Do you think he'll do it again?"

"I think he'll do it until he's stopped. I think he has to."

"But why this girl?" Rory asked.

"Sarah," Charlie interrupted. "Her name was Sarah. The killer included it with the pictures."

Rory abruptly walked forward until he stood immediately before the painted wall.

"Tell me what to look for," Carolyn demanded suddenly, turning from the painting. "If I were to see him, how would I know?"

Niall sighed. "You probably wouldn't. He's someone self-absorbed or at least disconnected. Probably ambitious but insecure, not where he wants to be in life. His relationships with women would be limited or at least short-lived. He handles criticism poorly, centers his own emotions . . ."

"But how can I tell?"

"I can't give you a magic answer, Carolyn." Niall moved over to Rory and dropped onto his heels, studying the wooden boards.

"Then what is the point of all of this?" Carolyn asked.

"The other option is doing nothing, waiting for another girl to die," Emma replied.

Charlie lowered her voice, angling toward Carolyn. "Look, I'm not supposed to say anything because the cops don't want it out yet, but there's already been another victim. Another girl, just like Sarah. Carolyn—" Charlie hesitated. "I plan to write about this. And I'm not going to lie and say there isn't some self-interest here; it could get me picked up by the AP. But this is what I do. It's how I can help. I'm with Emma here; we have to try."

"There's another girl?" Emma asked, her voice loud in the open space. Niall and Rory both snapped their heads her way. She flexed and released the fingers of her right hand, channeling a surge of shocked energy into the repetitive movement. She took a breath and consciously moderated her voice. "Do you know who she was?"

"Phillipa something," Charlie replied with a frown. "She was a student at Carlisle, too. I— Look, this isn't exactly aboveboard, but I took pictures of everything the killer sent. The envelope was open, and I found it first. I don't know what it all means—but you all might."

Carolyn caught Emma's eye. "You don't have to—"

Rory broke in with a protest as Emma moved to stand beneath the painted leaves. "Yes," she told them softly, "I do."

The campus had emptied, and dusk had set in when the three professors returned to the college. Charlie had added them all to a group chat, much to Rory's dismay, and secured promises from each to keep the others updated. Niall tested his new line of communication with a quote from Freud, to which Charlie had responded with a mocking meme and Rory with verbal annoyance. Niall laughed and headed to his own car with a wave while Rory trudged back to his office. Emma was left alone in the whispering night. Emma felt entranced by the mural in a way she couldn't explain to even them. Niall and Rory were excited by the challenge, by discovering an intellectual test to be passed. But they didn't understand the compulsion she felt when her brain latched on to a textual problem. She'd tried to explain it to Rory before, but he'd just assured her that all academics felt passionate about their work, a clear lack of understanding blurring his words at the edges. The images in the mural had woven themselves into her, adorned with words she had memorized before she understood what they meant. They'd made her part of the tapestry, part of the story. Now, in the darkness, she still felt its pull, like the phantom brush of cobwebs after walking through a dark hall.

Emma followed the vacant sidewalks across campus toward faculty parking, dipping in and out of pools of light as the streetlamps flickered on. She was far too aware of the sound of her own footsteps, the beat of her heart, the wind through the trees. She thought of Irving's *Sleepy Hollow* and tried to distract herself with the tale of the ghostly Hessian who stalked the night, head in hand. But the low tone of footsteps fragmented as another set—heavier and louder—echoed just behind hers on the brick pathway.

She'd reached the edge of the campus, with only a stretch of grass between her and the parking lot. The halo from the streetlamps failed to break the darkness. The reaching branches of two large oak trees that offered students a shady place on hot days now only deepened the blackness. Emma stepped onto the grass, straining to hear the footsteps. She paused, and there was silence. She turned back but could only discern shadowy shapes, nothing that was definitively a person.

She had nearly reached the parking lot when she heard the breathing. Short, hard breaths that were not hers and were not imagined. A twig snapped behind her. She took off, fumbling for her keys as she sprinted to her car. She had them out of the bag by the time she reached the door but dropped them as she tried to hit the unlock button. They skidded under the car, and Emma dropped to her knees, wincing as she hit the still-raw skin from her mugging. She reached beneath the car, stretching her fingers to feel for the metal of the keys. She leaned down so that her cheek touched the asphalt. Darkness. She heard footsteps, swift and hard, moving toward her.

"Hello?" a voice called out.

Emma pressed herself against the car door, trying to hide in the shadows.

"Emma?" The voice was softer now, and Emma recognized it just before Rory's face appeared over the hood of the car. "Are you okay? I was heading to my car—" Rory waved vaguely toward the far end of the parking lot "—and I saw you running."

Emma felt relief wash over her like a physical sensation. She bent over, put her head on her knees, and let out a hard sound that was equal parts laugh and sob. Rory crouched down beside her and placed a hesitant hand on her back. "Are you hurt?"

"I . . . No." Emma took a deep breath and looked up. "I convinced myself that I was being followed, and then I heard something. I ran and dropped my keys under the car, and . . ." Emma trailed off as relief turned into embarrassment. "It was foolish."

"It was probably just me," Rory said soothingly. He stood. "Here," he said, holding out a hand to her.

Emma took it, and he pulled her to her feet. They were standing inches apart, chest to chest, and Rory lifted his arms awkwardly. Emma wondered if he was planning to hug her, but he stepped back instead and pulled his phone from his pocket. Turning on the flashlight app, he crouched down again and slid the light beneath the car. He twisted and reached under, leaning so that his shoulder pressed against the car door. He then stood quickly, looking pleased with himself. He jingled the keys he had retrieved before handing them to Emma.

"Thanks." She threaded them through her fingers.

Rory shrugged. "Always happy to rescue a damsel in distress."

"I'm not a damsel."

"Right, of course." Rory looked around self-consciously, then stooped to grab something from the asphalt. He held his hand out. "Yours?"

Emma took the tattered paper without looking at it.

"Souvenir?" Rory pressed, seeming hesitant to leave.

Emma glanced down, recognizing the image from the museum gala. "No, I lost—" She thumbed through the pages, stopping at a dog-eared image of *The Lady of Shalott* and another of *Ophelia*. "I lost mine," Emma finished quietly.

"Well, I guess the universe thought you needed another one," Rory said with forced cheer. He rested his hip against the car. "Em, are you really okay? Do you need me to take you home?"

"Fine, I'm fine." She could feel embarrassment clawing in her chest at the thought of being chauffeured home like an errant child. She raised her hands emphatically. "I'm fine."

"Okay, then." Rory slowly stepped away, looking uncertain. She climbed into the car, trying twice before getting the key in the ignition. Her headlights caught Rory as she drove slowly out of the parking lot, and he held up a hand. Emma forced a smile onto her face.

She knew it was probably a coincidence that the program from the Pre-Raphaelite gala had been by her car. She knew that a lot of people from the college had attended. The fact that she had dog-eared her program, that it had been in her stolen purse, didn't mean anything. But she remembered the echo of footsteps across campus and couldn't quite convince herself that they had been harmless. She felt a sick heat creep across her skin, her mind chasing a line of logic that placed her directly in the killer's view. If that had been him, if he had been on campus, then he knew who she was. He knew where she worked, what car she drove. He knew how to find her.

She was nearly home before it occurred to her that hers had been the only car in the lot. Rory should have been walking in the opposite direction, toward the lot on the other side of O'Malley, instead of toward her. She said a little prayer of thanks that he had seen her in the darkness.

Ian was standing beside the door when Emma pulled up to her house. He was leaning back against the wall, his arms folded across his chest and one foot braced behind him like a cowboy at a saloon. His eyes were cast down, but he raised them as Emma slid out of her car and closed the door. Her knees had started to stiffen on the drive home, and she stood for a moment looking at him, unable to will her body forward. He pushed away from the wall and took a step toward her.

During the drive, Emma's fear and embarrassment had congealed into anger. She hated feeling out of control—hated that some craven man had made her jump at shadows. Made her run and cower. She'd felt so confident when she'd spotted the fig tree, so certain that she could—would—figure out how to stop these murders. But the killer was writing this play while she just stumbled through the scenes, waiting for the next stage direction. *Exit, pursued by—*

Instead of confronting the killer—not even the killer, she taunted herself, an imagined phantom—she'd panicked. Shut down. Emma sucked in a breath. Like Ian had warned she would.

She stared at him, standing there cool and professional and completely unmoved. Irrationally—she recognized—she hated him in that moment. Hated the idea that he'd been right about her. And unable to shake the thought that if he'd just listened, just believed her, she wouldn't have been alone in that parking lot. She wouldn't have felt like prey to some nameless watcher. The killer wouldn't still be out there. The girl in Charlie's photos would still be alive.

"Emma?"

She didn't look at him as she crossed to the door, a small tremor jingling her keys as she snapped open the lock. She flicked the light on, revealing a small entryway that led to an open-concept living room with a small dining area to one side and a galley kitchen tucked behind a dividing counter. She walked in, leaving the door open behind her, and dumped her bag and keys on the neat kitchen counter. The front door clicked closed, and she heard the sound of Ian following her. Opening a cupboard, she took down a wineglass etched with a turtle, a souvenir her sister had bought her on a Florida vacation. The glass was half full of merlot when Ian stepped into the soft light of the kitchen.

Emma took a sip. "Wine?" She gestured toward Ian with the bottle, but he shook his head.

"I don't like to drink when I'm on a case."

"Of course you don't." Emma took a longer drink, then tilted the glass to finish it. She poured another.

"Look, I just wanted to explain. I know I was a bit . . . brusque at the station, but you have to understand—"

"Seriously?" Emma snapped, knowing it was unfair. "You came over just to tell me again how right you are? I'm tired, and I'm angry, and I'm sore and . . ." She stopped as her voice began to shake.

Ian's posture stiffened. "You're right. This was a bad idea."

"I don't filter as well when I'm tired. Sorry," she bit out. "You'll need to come back tomorrow if you want polite, smiling Emma."

She carried her glass into a living room comfortably filled with overstuffed chairs and a sofa upholstered in soft green. Sinking into it, Emma pulled a rose-colored, chunky-knit blanket around her, wincing as she tucked her knees up. She closed her eyes, focusing on the textures against her skin.

Ian followed her. "Are you alright?"

"Sure." She took another drink.

"You're bleeding," Ian said without inflection.

She met his eyes for a long moment before responding. "I fell."

"Should I go?" Ian sat down in the chair opposite her when Emma shook her head and waited in silence as she collected her thoughts.

"I don't want to talk about . . . before."

"Then we won't. Can we . . ."

"I know another girl has been killed. Phillipa something."

Surprise, frustration, and that now familiar trace of fear sprinted across Ian's face. Emma noted them with detachment.

"How do you know that?"

"I thought you couldn't discuss the case with mere civilians."

"Emma . . ."

"I can't stop, you know." Emma took another swig of wine. "Thinking about it. Doesn't work like that. My mind . . . grabs things, keeps them. So, even if you don't want me to tell you about it, I can't just . . . stop."

"I'm sorry."

"About my brain?" She took another drink.

"That you saw those pictures. I shouldn't have brought them home in the first place."

"Why did you?"

Ian didn't answer, just looked down, his hands folded in his lap.

"Sorry, not my business."

"You have nothing to be sorry for." Ian rose as if to leave.

"There was another quote, wasn't there?"

"Should I ask how . . . ? Never mind." He stopped at Emma's dark look. "Yes, there was another quote."

"Shakespeare again?"

"No, uh, Mallory, if Google can be trusted."

"*Le Morte*?"

"You know the book?"

Emma tossed him a contemptuous glance, the wine besieging her already damaged boundaries. "I'm a fucking literature professor. Who was she posed as?"

Ian said nothing.

"Should I guess?" Emma closed her eyes, mentally cataloging the characters from Mallory's famous collection of Arthurian tales. Her brain stuttered to a stop, the image clear in her mind. "Of course."

"What?" Ian's voice was soft but clearly curious.

"Elaine of Astolat."

"I don't know . . ."

"Yeah—you do." Emma felt a deep ache as she thought back to the night they had met. She half sang, half recited, "'She knows not what the curse may be; Therefore, she weaveth steadily. Therefore, no other care hath she . . .'" Emma paused for a drink, then finished in a bitter tone: "'The Lady of Shalott.' She was there, at the gala, right next to Ophelia. He's taunting us, Ian. You . . . me, maybe . . . who knows. It's a different version of the story, but—there she was, in all her desperate glory." Emma drank again, her head starting to feel light. "He's telling you something. Was there a letter with the body?"

Ian looked startled. "I don't—"

"There's going to be a note tied to her hand, explaining her death." A message, she thought. Just like the last time. "I went to the crime scene today."

"You what?" Emma could see the surprise on Ian's face and knew he hadn't followed her train of thought.

"Crime. Scene." Emma's voice felt big in the small room. She tried to moderate it. "Sarah's. Saw the mural. The noose, the fig tree . . . He's trying to talk to you. It may not be in your language, but it's there."

"That was reckless, Emma. And illegal." Ian started toward her but stopped himself. He shoved his hands in his pockets.

"Well, at least I'm doing something to solve this damned thing." Emma waved her glass in a wide arc, sloshing the little wine left. "Rory thinks . . ."

"Rory?" Ian's nostrils flared on a sharp breath. "That guy from the gala? Why are you talking to him about the case?"

"Because *he* thinks I'm worth listening to." Emma knew she sounded petulant but couldn't help herself.

Ian sighed. "I didn't say you weren't worth listening to."

"It was strongly implied." Emma downed the rest of her wine and started toward the kitchen.

"Emma." Ian caught her by the elbow. She jerked away. He let her. "This guy doesn't have your best interests in mind if he's telling you to break into a crime scene. You should keep your distance—from him and the case."

"Keep my . . ." Emma smacked her glass down on the counter, then whirled so that she was inches from Ian's face. "He's a respected professor. He's the dean of my department. And who are you to tell me what I should and shouldn't do? We went on one date—not even. Half a date. You're not my boyfriend. You're not even my friend. You don't know me. You don't understand me. And you don't understand—" she waived a slightly unsteady hand across the room "—this. Ophelia. Elaine. The quotes, the paintings. Any of it. It's been almost a week, and as far as I can tell, the only lead you have—you got from me."

"I didn't mean—"

"Yes, you did. And I'm not finished." Emma spoke over his objection, not even trying to keep her voice even. "This isn't just some case. Not to me. And not to the killer. Whoever's doing this wants his work to be seen, to be appreciated. He wants to be treated as an artist—and you're underestimating him."

"Believe me, I . . ."

Emma covered her face with her hands, trying to block out the light and sound and vibrating anger that were unraveling the threads of control. After a few shaky breaths, she made herself look up. "You want me to just . . . ignore all of this and go back to my regular job, my regular life—to just pretend everything is normal. But nothing is normal. I'm not normal, Ian. I can't be." Emma closed her eyes.

"I'm just trying to keep you from . . ." Ian spread both hands in front of him as if he were presenting all of the dangers he was holding back.

"What? Getting hurt? Seeing too much? Going crazy?" Emma spat the words. "I'm not fragile. I'm smart and capable and . . . and . . . I solved the damn puzzle. *His* puzzle. Not you. I can't stop thinking, stop making those connections, just because you want me to. That's what I do; it's what I am, and I can't turn it off. Symbolism and suicide and beautiful dead girls—I see them cold and wet and scared and dying on a loop in my head. I've spent my life reading and learning and teaching exactly this. And you know what? I'm not going to quit, and I'm not going to break. Because if I see them, I can see him, and I, I . . . You wouldn't know half of what you do without me. Admit it." Her voice was shaking, her breathing fast and hard.

Ian was standing stiff and still. "I know. I know that."

Emma scanned his face but couldn't find his emotions this time. She nodded tightly. "Please, leave now. I'm tired. And I'm not drunk yet, but I plan to be." Emma looked past Ian toward the window where night had darkened.

"Right. You're right. This was a bad idea. I just wanted to . . ." Ian paused, seeming to search for words. "I'm sorry for everything, Emma. That's all I wanted to say."

Emma didn't watch as Ian left the room. When she heard the front door click shut, she rose stiffly and went back to the kitchen. She reached for the wine bottle again but hesitated, looking at the label. She ran her thumb over the illustration, a writer at his desk, quill pen in hand. She had bought the wine just because she liked the graphic, the image of the writer hard at work creating worlds for others to escape into. Now all she could see was Shakespeare, Tennyson, Poe, and all of the others decorating their pages with voiceless women who died for the sake of some hero's journey—their stories untold, a footnote in someone else's story. All these women meeting the same end over and over again, leaving behind someone to pine and mourn . . . but what good was that, really? What good did it do all those women to be loved but still lost?

Emma smashed the bottle against the edge of the sink, splintering the glass. The smooth, red liquid pooled thickly before swirling down the drain. She watched with an odd sense of disinterest as blood from a gash on her thumb—split open by the jagged glass—slid down her wrist to mingle with the remnants of the lovely merlot.

Chapter 15

Ian and Mike got the call at 5:49 the next morning. An early jogger had found a woman's body in a boat floating in a pond just past the boundaries of the Carlisle campus. The runner had been on his usual morning jog around the circumference of campus, but in deference to the hovering clouds, he decided to take the shorter loop through the forested lands surrounding the old millpond. The area was woven with dirt paths used mostly by college kids looking to get high and the occasional fitness enthusiast. Mike corralled the hyperventilating jogger and set to coaxing what information he could from him. The man told the detective that he had spotted the abandoned boat and decided to investigate. After that, very little coherence could be gleaned through the dry-heaving.

Ian left Mike and navigated his way to the stagnant water. The small pond was strewn with the first leaves of fall, their gold and rust shimmering on the surface as a light breeze crept across the water's surface. Ian shivered. As he carefully edged his way down the eroding slope, dirt scattering beneath his feet, he could see a small group of blue-jacketed scene-of-crime techs clustered around a wooden boat, its boards long since faded to gray. The boat had run aground in the muddied grass at the water's edge, and three candle stubs had been placed along the gunnel. The melted wax mimicked trickling water where it had cooled along the wooden surface. Nearby cattails reached toward the rise of bloodred fabric that Ian knew covered the second victim.

Phillipa Minor looked slighter in person than in the images Ian had so carefully studied, but the details were bitingly familiar. Her honey-colored hair was stiff now, lying like fissures across the deep crimson of the pillow beneath her head, and her face had a gray pallor that Ian had seen too many times. A slick sheen marking the initial stage of decomposition glossed her skin. This was no sleeping beauty. Her scarlet dress was thick with water that had gathered in muddy puddles at the bottom of the boat.

Ian crouched down, balancing his weight on his toes as he bent closer to the body. He could tell now that the shiny objects that had bounced light back at their unknown photographer were shards of mirror that were scattered around her, caught in the folds of her dress and sparkling on her skin like diamonds. Looped around her body were thick cords of golden thread, binding her arms to her sides and tangled through her fingers. They gave the appearance that she was fighting their grasp, resisting the darkness. Her slack face and awkwardly tilted head belied any fantasy of success. Ian searched her face for the girl he had seen at the museum gala, definite and assured, but the waxy skin offered only a poor counterfeit of the laughing dilettante with golden hair.

"'The curse is come upon me,'" a sharp voice said from behind him. Ian nearly landed in the pond as he swiveled, startled by the quote he had been trying to remember. Emma had said the same words the night they'd met. He rose and nodded at the newcomer, trying to mask his awkwardness with a nonchalant stance.

Dr. Ivy Wollard's lips tipped upward briefly before her customary mask of indifference settled back on. "Tennyson. You're not the only one who reads poetry, Detective."

"I think he may be using a different version of the story." Ian thought back to his conversation with Emma. "Did your guys take the note that was bound to her hand?"

"We didn't *take* it. We did, however, collect it as evidence." Ivy pulled out the clipboard that she'd tucked under her arm. "Looks to be a book page." She glanced up at him. "I'll get more specifics once we get it to the lab. One odd thing, though. It looks like it had been aged with tea or something similar, like kids do when they make treasure maps."

"Did you unroll it?"

Ivy waved at one of her blue-suited crew, and the young woman trotted obediently toward her. She took a plastic sleeve and handed it to Ian wordlessly.

"Mallory." Ian scanned the page of text, the words recognizable as English but distantly. Emma had known it would be here. She knew there'd be a message.

"What the hell is this, Ian?" Ivy said, fatigue weighing her voice.

He just shook his head. "Honest to god, I don't know. Can you tell me anything?"

Ivy shrugged. "Cause of death likely to be exsanguination from the slit wrists, but there's too little blood here for this to be the locale, even assuming the boat isn't watertight. I'll have to get her back to the lab to do a full postmortem and tox screen, but there are needle marks on her arms. She was likely drugged and held, just like the last one. Autolysis has started, but there is minimal bloat—she's been dead approximately seventy-two hours. Do you know when she was reported missing?"

"Last seen Friday, the seventeenth," Ian replied after checking his notes.

"The day after we found the Weston girl. Was he waiting for the first one to be found before he took another?"

Ian just shook his head.

Ivy said what he couldn't. "If he was, there will probably be another girl taken soon. We can't keep this from the media much longer." Ivy stood. "I'll get the labs started today and the autopsy scheduled ASAP. She's going to get top billing." She turned and started toward the cluster of cars parked at the start of the path, pausing at the top of the slope. "And Ian?" He looked up at her. "Whoever's doing this? He's meticulous, focused—zealous even. He's not going to stop unless we make him. Work fast."

Tired and on edge after hours at the crime scene, Ian and Mike trekked to campus and climbed the stairs to Dr. Rory Tamblyn's office. A call to the museum had earned them a quick redirect to the college for any questions about student workers like Phillipa Minor. Tamblyn—as Dean of Arts and Media—was their first stop. Ian didn't tell Mike that he already knew the man's name, had in fact spent a night Googling him after Emma had mentioned him. Tamblyn was well-respected, prolifically published, and had remarkably little social media presence—much to Ian's disappointment. He'd been trying to trace Tamblyn's relationship with Emma, but her timeline featured almost no pictures of herself, filled instead with group shots and landscapes, nothing overly personal. Tamblyn was featured in several.

He and Mike sat uncomfortably close to each other as they stared across Tamblyn's well-ordered desk. The neatness of his office surprised Ian, who had memories of strewn papers and scattered books from visits to his own college professors. Everything here was precisely arranged: alphabetized books, labeled drawers, a trim stack of papers in his inbox. A few sculptures and acrylic paintings added color to the space, though there was nothing that Ian would have considered worth displaying. He wondered if they were Tamblyn's work. The only personalized item that Ian noted was a picture of Tamblyn and Emma, apparently on a trip together somewhere. He forced his eyes away from it when Mike raised an eyebrow.

The man himself was smiling courteously at the two detectives, his hands steepled as if he were playacting an intellectual. Ian studied him, trying to stay neutral. He was objectively good-looking—Ian's eyes strayed back to the photo. Tamblyn noticed, glancing at it as well.

"Have you ever been to England, Detective?" Tamblyn asked politely, a slightly puzzled expression crossing his face. "That was taken in Canterbury last summer."

"No," Ian said stiffly. "I don't get much chance to travel."

"Ah." Tamblyn looked unsure but seemed to want some authority in the situation. "Well, traveling abroad is a great way to expand your perceptions. You should go sometime." He wasn't nervous, Ian thought, but wary.

"My husband and I took the kids to Disney World last year," Mike interjected. His voice sounded genuine, but Ian could see the touch of a smirk. "Went to their UK Pavilion. Great fish and chips." Tamblyn looked confused, and Mike added, "That's what we'd call french fries."

Tamblyn had the grace to look slightly chagrinned. "I imagine that was a lot of fun. I was lucky to have my trip sponsored by the college. Study abroad."

Mike's nod acknowledged Tamblyn's unspoken apology. "It was a lot of fun, actually. You have kids, professor?"

"No. Not yet, anyway."

"Married?"

"No—I thought you wanted to ask about the student who was murdered." There was no question in his voice, Ian noted, pulling out his pad and pen. He clearly didn't want to discuss his personal life. Ian didn't look at the photo this time, but Tamblyn did.

"We do." Ian straightened. "Sarah Weston."

"We're also interested in another girl in connection to the case, a Phillipa Minor," Mike added. "Do you recognize either name?"

"Sarah's been in all the papers, of course. Is the other girl a suspect?" Tamblyn asked, his brow furrowing. "Or . . . another victim?"

"A person of interest," Mike said noncommittally. "So, you don't know them?"

"I— If you're asking if they've ever been in my classes, honestly, I'd have to check enrollment records. Undergrad sections sometimes have a hundred students each. I rarely speak to students individually unless they either seek me out or have . . . difficulties of some sort."

"You wouldn't see their names on assignments or tests, maybe?" Ian pressed.

"Honestly, most professors don't interact with students that often until they're ready for more specialized classes. For the first couple of years . . ." Rory shrugged. "We lecture; they listen. We have teaching assistants to grade their tests or—more often nowadays—they just take them online, and a computer does it. I'm sorry. I can check the records if you like."

"Please."

Tamblyn turned toward the computer and then hesitated, lifting the phone instead. "Carolyn. Can you check student records for two students—Sarah Weston and . . ."

"Phillipa Minor," Mike supplied softly.

"Phillipa Minor. See if they were in any art courses? Thanks, Caro." Tamblyn hung up. "She'll have that in a moment."

"Appreciate it. We know that Minor attended that art gala you all hosted not too long ago." Mike's voice tended toward a drawl whenever he was interviewing people. "Tell me about that."

"It's a special exhibition hosted by the museum in coordination with the college. We hold one every year."

"Same theme?" Ian asked, already knowing the answer.

"No. It rotates. This year—the Pre-Raphaelites—was quite a coup, actually."

"Who picked the Pre-Raphaelites?" Ian kept his voice even, but Tamblyn still tilted his head in regard.

"The museum board, a group of about nine people."

"You one of them?" Mike asked that one, making Tamblyn shift his attention.

"Yes. I represent the college."

"You vote in favor?"

"Yes. As I said, it was quite a coup. Detective . . ."

A knock interrupted him. "Dr. Tamblyn?" A young woman in a neat skirt and bright pink blouse leaned in. "The class records?"

"Thanks, Caro." Tamblyn stood and crossed to take the proffered papers, leaving a broad berth between him and the detectives as he did. She nodded, watching the detectives—particularly him, Ian thought—with open interest.

Tamblyn glanced at the pages as he sat and then handed them to Mike, who passed them to Ian with equal swiftness. "The course listed there for Phillipa is a museum work-study. That's likely why she was at the gala. Students help with the organization and setup and then get a free pass to the opening."

"Was she an art student, then?"

"Not necessarily. We have students from museum management, business, art . . . Sometimes, they just sign up because they think it will be fun or need an elective. There's no selection process—they just enroll on their own."

"How about Sarah Weston? Looks like she took two art classes, one from you."

Tamblyn held out his hand, and the papers completed the circle. "ART 101. It's an intro class; half of the college takes it to fill their general education requirement." He studied the page for a moment. "An adjunct professor was originally supposed to teach that section, if I remember correctly. I filled in after he had to withdraw last minute. Fell off a roof. The other course she took is also a freshman-level course, practical rather than theory. She may have been interested, but these aren't the classes of an art major."

"And you don't remember her?"

"No, I'm sorry. While I help out with the gala, I don't run the museum course—that's Dr. Dalton—so I doubt I ever met Phillipa. As for Sarah—" He shook his head. "If we spoke, I don't remember it."

"Anyone you can think of who might have worked with both girls?"

"Not off the top of my head. The registrar's office could cross-check their schedules, I'm sure. Wish I could be of more help."

"You've been very helpful, thanks," Mike said.

"Can you tell us where you were on the 10th and the 17th?" Ian asked, trying to make the question seem standard. Mike shot him a look.

"Uh, the 17th was the gala. I know I was here on campus in the morning and at the museum all afternoon. And in the evening, of course. The 10th . . . here, I would guess. My assistant can pull up my schedule." Tamblyn's voice was curious but not concerned.

Ian held his gaze for a moment, searching for tells. "Thanks. We'll ask her."

They all stood, offered polite goodbyes, and Mike left his card. Then, the two detectives stepped into the outer office. The assistant—Carolyn—spun her chair quickly toward her desk, clearly having been eavesdropping as well as she could without actually pressing her ear to the adjoining door.

"Everything okay, Detectives?"

"We're just talking to anyone who might have relevant information for a case," Mike answered easily. "Miss . . ."

"Ms.," the woman responded, her smile widening slightly. "Ms. Carolyn Mathews."

"Ms. Matthews. May I?" Ian gestured toward a chair clearly intended for students and sat at her nod. "As you heard, we're trying to learn more about two students who took classes in this department. Do you recognize the names the dean gave you?"

The woman's face stilled for a moment before she replied. "I don't know either of them personally. Dr. Tamblyn has really only worked with graduate students since being appointed dean last year. I didn't work with him when he was a full-time professor."

"Do you know if they were involved in any department activities? Or took any of the same classes?"

She shook her head. "Sorry. The registrar's office can check their schedules." She echoed Tamblyn's suggestion, adding, "Ask about TAs, too. They often get recycled through the courses, especially the grad students. If they lived on campus, check with Campus Life. They'd know where they lived, if there were any issues reported. And I'm sure you've already spoken to Campus Security. And the Health Center, of course."

Ian suppressed a grin. "All good ideas, thanks."

"Is there anything else I can help with?"

"No," Mike said just as Ian said, "Yes."

"Yes," Ian reiterated. "Can you pull up Dr. Tamblyn's calendar for the 10th and 17th of this month?"

Carolyn looked intrigued and excited but, like Tamblyn, showed no apprehension. She typed quickly. "Of course. Do you want mine, too?"

"That would be helpful. Thanks." Ian ignored Mike's look as Carolyn crossed to an elderly printer.

"Here you go."

"Can I have a card in case I think of something else?" She turned distinctly toward Ian, and he gave her one. Then he and Mike stepped into the nearly empty hallway.

"What did you think?" Ian asked.

"She'd say yes."

"What?"

"Matthews, if you asked her out, she'd say yes. Just wait until after we've closed the case."

"What? No. I meant about Tamblyn."

"You're not his type."

"Mike . . ."

"Okay, you want me to tell you, no, he's probably not involved? Or do you want me to tell you, yes, he's probably banged your professor friend?"

"Fuck you." Ian set off down the hall.

Mike paused for a beat before following. "Easy, man."

"There's something off about him. I can feel it."

Mike stopped, grabbing Ian's arm. "Hey, I know I've been ribbing you about this, but seriously, Ian—I saw your reaction to that photo. So did Tamblyn. It's not like you to show your cards in front of a witness. And the way you lost your temper with the drug dealer . . ."

"That was a tactic."

"Was it? And the fact you refuse to even consider the professor's ideas even after she pointed out the connection to the gala—a connection you missed, by the way—which strategy were you going for there?" Mike shook his head. "We need your A-game on this one, Ian. And this ain't it. The lieutenant is getting restless, and there's going to be a feeding frenzy when the media finds out about the second vic. Do we need to hand this case over to another team? Be honest with me."

"No, of course not." Ian pulled his arm away. "I'm fine; I just . . . It's not about Emma. I've just got a feeling about Tamblyn."

"Okay. Okay. We'll check his alibi, but I gotta tell you I don't see it. What I see is a detective who's letting his emotions cloud his view of the case."

"Let's get back to work."

Ian didn't look at his partner until they'd crossed the rainy campus and climbed into their car. When he did, the worry still hadn't left Mike's eyes.

Chapter 16

"We're here on the campus of Carlisle College as this close-knit community reels at the report of a second student being brutally murdered . . ." A slender brunette in a bold red blazer swept an arm over the expanse of the campus behind her, her too-bright tone at odds with the horror she described. Her cameraman followed the gesture, panning over a crowd of faces registering shock, fear, and more than a touch of excitement. News trucks had filled the streets, reporters swarming around the promise of a story. Outrage and innuendo floated on the air.

Emma moved quickly to the door of her building as the camera shifted in her direction.

The halls were full of whispers as reports of the new murder were spread, dissected, and reconfigured into a Frankenstein's monster of fact and fear. The excitement of the first murder had gained an edge, and as word of another victim began to spread, the students now recognized a danger among them. They clustered in hallways and gathered at doors, talking in hushed tones about who knew who among the dead. Everyone kept their bags and jackets tucked tight against their bodies, safeguarding themselves from onlookers.

The names of both victims, Sarah Weston and Phillipa Minor, had been spread online despite the reticence of the police. Their photos appeared side by side in a slew of social media posts, the comments filled with questions and semi-sincere offerings of grief. The police had yet to confirm any connection between the two murders, but rumor and conjecture hadn't waited. Descriptions of the two were teased and examined as amateur analysts searched among the clues, hoping to find the killer's tell—or at least a talisman against danger. Emma watched her female students spin out the details of the deaths: redheads hopeful at the news that the two victims were blonde; business majors with dark, tight smiles confirming the dead girls had studied art; slender, pale girls whose eyes were ringed purple by the knowledge that both Sarah and Phillipa looked just like them.

Trying to beat back the memory of her own panicked dash across the quad with enforced normality, Emma had come to work at her usual time, parked in her usual space, and tried to work. Her mind kept wandering, though, retracing the patterns they'd found so far. Hours of restless half attention had produced almost nothing useful. She was trying to prepare her lecture on Poe's poem "Lenore"—Guy de Vere stands beside the casket of a beautiful woman, his lover, refusing to mourn her death as the townspeople accuse him of callousness. Niall would probably call it denial; Emma saw fear shrouded by those words. Uneasy, she stretched away from her desk, arching her back against her chair as she tried to gather her scattering concentration.

This was usually her favorite section of the class to teach. Emma had loved these stories since she was a teenager, hiding from a world that wasn't kind to difference. She'd dreamt of Manderley with Rebecca, fled the Castle Udolpho with Emily, heard Mr. Rochester's voice call out to Jane, and wandered the House of Usher with the ghostly Madeline. She'd always read these heroines as tragically romantic, but now . . . Emma scrubbed at her eyes. Now, they just seemed tragic—they were gaslit, threatened, abused. Even those who didn't actually end up with their abusers—happily ever after, Emma thought darkly—would live with that trauma forever. And those were the ones who survived. How could she go to class tomorrow and talk about Poe's use of sonorous language when that language was describing a woman who had died too young and remembered only for her lovers?

Her phone chimed with a text notification, breaking Emma's reverie. Charlie's message was brief: **Photos? The Bean Bag. 6.** Carolyn's response was a GIF of a woman looking supremely skeptical while Niall opted for Hercule Poirot eating pastry. Rory just texted **Fine** with a period to punctuate his annoyance. Emma hesitated. If she was going to back out of this, now was her chance.

EMMA: I'll be there.

They were doing this. She was doing this—Emma hit Send and waited for the familiar anxiety to claw at her rib cage. Instead, she felt a flutter of excitement as her brain began instinctively searching for the corner pieces of the puzzle. She pushed back from her desk, and pressed her palms into her eyes, thinking of Ian, not wanting to. She wished she could parse him like she did her books, to understand what lay between the lines. She replayed last night's conversation, looking for the patterns and linguistic tells that she was so good at finding in fiction. But her brain offered no insights, only more questions.

Why had he come to her? He'd apologized at the precinct already, though they hadn't left things on friendly terms. He hadn't known about their field trip until she told him, so he couldn't have been there to chastise her. Did he want the last word? The upper hand? Or—Emma closed her eyes in dismay—had he been doing exactly what she'd so ardently hoped for, asking for her insight? She'd been angry and accusatory, but he'd still told her what she needed to know to keep investigating: the new victim had been posed as a character from Thomas Mallory's *Le Morte d'Arthur*.

"Shit," she whispered aloud.

Unwilling to consider the ramifications of Ian's possible overture, Emma rolled her chair the short distance across her office to an overstuffed bookshelf. Scanning titles until she found *Le Morte d'Arthur*, she dug it out and slid back to her desk. She felt confident that her deduction last night was correct: the killer was referencing the story of Elaine of Astolat. She was the ultimate beautiful dead girl of the Pre-Raphaelites. Tennyson's heroine was poetically tragic, dying for a chance at life. Mallory's was, Emma remembered, not quite as passive. She scanned the pages until she found the story of Elaine and Lancelot, the most famous knight of the Round Table. The page was thick with notes from her class last fall, and she skimmed through as Lancelot readied to leave for his quest, and Elaine begged him to stay. First, Elaine entreated him to be her husband, then simply her lover. Lancelot refused both, promising the beautiful girl—a child really, Emma thought—that she would love another and insisting that he was not husband material. He even offered to give her a thousand pounds a year if she would leave him be. Emma wondered wryly what to make of this gesture. Was it a bribe? Hush money—there was an awful lot of discussion of Elaine being a "clean maiden"—or pity? Was it just the chivalric impulse to save the damsel however he could? Whatever Lancelot's motives, Elaine was having none of it.

Emma had always dismissed Elaine as immature and spoiled in her determination that she could not live without Lancelot, seeing the idea of dying for love as somewhat pathetic. But as she read through the text again, Emma found herself drawn to the figure.

"'Why should I leave such thoughts?'"—Emma read to herself—"'Am I not an earthly woman? All the while the breath is in my body I may complain me, for my belief is I do none offence though I love an earthly man?'" When told to forget about Lancelot and move on, Elaine didn't just refuse the demand. She refused the premise.

Emma's mind flickered with memories of teachers telling her to just stop getting distracted, her graduate advisor telling her to just be more organized, friends telling her to stop being so awkward. Of Ian ordering her to stop thinking about the murders. *Why should I leave such thoughts?*—Emma pushed the question away and kept reading.

When Elaine was nearly dead after ten days of refusing food and water, she called her brother and father and gave them very specific burial instructions. They were to dress her in beautiful clothes, lay her in a boat, and send her downriver to Camelot. They were also instructed to tie a letter to her hand that told her story. When her boat was spotted by Arthur and Guinevere, Lancelot was summoned, and the queen accused him of not showing the dead woman "gentleness." He protested his innocence, claiming he could not be forced to love someone, which Arthur agreed with. Even in death, poor Elaine couldn't win that battle. But she did get to tell her own story, *written word by word like she devised.*

Emma closed the book, thoughtful. It had always struck her as an odd story to include in the tales of the great knights. It could be read as a revenge fantasy; Lancelot could have been easily blamed for her ruin despite the insistence on her continued purity. Her letter made sure of that. But it was also a story about a woman who defied the expectations of her status and gender. Mallory's Elaine was not the desperate recluse of Tennyson and the Pre-Raphaelites. She propositioned Lancelot, refused to be mollified, and insisted on being heard no matter the cost to others. Tennyson's unnamed lady had died hoping to see the world, if only for a moment. This Elaine had died insisting that the world see her.

Emma glanced at the clock, swearing softly when she realized the afternoon had slipped away. It was almost six. She quickly cleared her desk, tucking *Le Morte d'Arthur* into her messenger bag, and swung open her office door. Emma shrieked. The young man crouched at her feet stumbled back as he rose, luckily bumping into the door opposite hers before he fell over. Malcolm, Rory's graduate student, stood wide-eyed and panting as they stared at each other. In one hand, he clutched a piece of paper crumpled in his quick retreat.

"I was just sticking a note under your door. I thought you'd gone home." Malcolm's words tumbled out over his harsh breathing as he tried to steady himself. He crushed the note in his fist. "Sorry."

"No, it's okay. I'm just a little jumpy today."

Malcolm nodded in understanding. "I knew them—Sarah and Phillipa. They were both nice."

It was a simple eulogy for two lost lives.

"I'm sorry. This must be hard." They stood silently for a moment before Emma prompted, "Malcolm? Did you want to talk about your project?"

His eyes jerked to hers. "No, no. I'm done for now. I may come back to my project later, but . . . I just . . . I can't . . . My work, I'm not sure it's good enough. I tried to talk to Rory—" he broke off, looking sheepish "—to Dr. Tamblyn about it, but he's too busy." Malcolm shifted uncomfortably. "And I decided to drop Professor Jacobs's class because it just wasn't— Anyway, I just came to leave you a note, to tell you that I like . . . appreciate . . . that you don't need to worry about me."

"I understand, Malcolm. No one's at their best right now. Let me know if you change your mind."

"Maybe . . ." Malcolm made a gesture partway between a nod and a shrug. "Never mind." He shoved the crumpled note that was still in his hand into a pocket of his navy blue backpack, turning away. He took a few steps down the hall, away from Emma, and then stopped.

"I hope they find him soon," he said, not looking back at her.

"Me, too." Emma didn't think that he'd heard her.

As Malcolm disappeared around the corner, Emma double-checked her bag for her new wallet, phone, and keys and then locked the office door. The digital clock in the hallway glared 5:52 in bright, red lines.

Emma arrived late and out of breath. The Bean Bag was populated with bored-looking twentysomethings in dark-rimmed glasses and ironic T-shirts. There was a bearded barista standing in front of an oversized chalkboard that listed half a dozen pun-filled specials, each in a different color. But the atmosphere was bright, the crowd wasn't overwhelming, and the scent of coffee permeated the air. The walls were covered with the works of local artists, presenting an unbroken vista of impressionistic nudes and watercolor fruit bowls. Bare Edison bulbs hung from the ceiling, lighting a room full of mismatched chairs, rough-hewn tables, and faded love seats. She saw a few familiar faces from her classes and settled her friendly but professional expression in place. But before any of them spotted her, Rory caught her eye from his place in line at the front counter, and he waved her toward the back where Charlie, Niall, and Carolyn had claimed a booth. Gratefully, she joined the others, who had already gotten their own drinks and pastries, and dropped into an empty seat. Niall and Carolyn sat together opposite her, and Charlie had set a chair at the head of the table. An envelope was situated squarely in front of her; one hand rested possessively on top of it. No one spoke.

Rory appeared at Emma's elbow and slid in beside her. "Your usual, I believe." He smiled as he sat down, placing a tall Americano in front of her, but the grin faded almost immediately.

"Thanks," Emma returned the smile weakly.

"Rory and I were interviewed by the police," Carolyn announced without preamble as soon as Rory was seated. "We met your detective."

"Ian?" Emma flexed her hand.

"In the flesh," Carolyn responded. "He was very professional."

"What's he like?" Niall asked when her expression made it clear she wanted someone to.

"Tall, blond, rather lithe. Amazing eyes."

Rory snorted. "He and his partner just asked a few questions. Both students had enrolled in art classes. They were looking for connections."

"They checked our alibis," Carolyn added.

"I'm sure they check everyone's alibis," Rory countered.

"But it means they think the killings *are* connected to the college. It might be someone we know." Carolyn looked at Rory, expecting another parry.

"It's possible." His voice was subdued.

They sipped their drinks awkwardly, no one sure how to respond. They'd all thought it, but hearing it aloud was different. Eventually, Charlie took charge of the moment, tapping the envelope. "So, none of these are too bad—nothing gory."

"Maybe we shouldn't . . ." Carolyn broke off as a barista approached their table. They all looked up. Charlie slid the envelope closer to her.

"Professor Reilly?"

Emma plastered an unconvincing smile on her face. "Olivia, hello. I didn't realize you worked here."

"Yeah, well." She ran her hands over the apron. "I've had to pick up some extra shifts lately. Which is why I wanted to ask . . ." The girl cut her eyes toward the others. "Um, I just wanted to ask about an extension on the essay. I know it's almost due, but what with my job and now with all the rumors going around and everything . . ." Olivia trailed off meaningfully.

Emma strained to keep her face pleasant and encouraging. "Just turn it in when you can. I'm not going to deduct any late points this time."

"Thank you. Thanks." Olivia looked visibly relieved. "I've never been late on an assignment before, but I . . . with everything. Hey, I get a discount here. If you want anything else . . ."

"It's fine, Olivia."

"Okay. The essay will be great. I promise." A twentysomething man with bottle-blond hair and hipster glasses snapped his fingers pointedly from across the room. Olivia sighed and walked over to him.

"She seems devastated," Rory said dryly.

"She's a good student. Nothing seems real when you're that age."

"Well, it feels very real at mine," Carolyn said pointedly.

"Right," Charlie said. She pulled out a pen and paper, a list of notes already covering two-thirds of the page. "Let's do this."

"Wait." Carolyn covered the page with her hand. "Are you sure you want to do this here?"

"Should we go to campus?"

"No," Rory said quickly. "Our offices are too small for five; if we sign out a conference room, we'd have to give a reason."

"Your house?" Niall asked.

"No. I don't want to invite bad energy there," Carolyn said firmly. Rory rolled his eyes. "Mock me all you want. No postmortems in my living room."

"Plus, we don't have pastries at home." Charlie shrugged.

"We can go . . ." Emma started, but Rory lifted Carolyn's hand off the paper.

"We're here. We have pastries. No one is looking; no one cares." Rory gestured at the other patrons, most of whom were staring at laptops or phones, many with earbuds in. "Lay it on us, Nancy Drew."

"Nancy Drew?" Charlie asked wryly.

"Would you prefer Harriet the Spy?"

Charlie considered him for a second. "No."

"Then?"

Charlie shrugged. "Okay, first victim: Sarah Weston. Student at Carlisle College, twenty-one. Popular, seemed to have a number of friends and relationships . . ."

"How do you know that?" Rory asked, his voice surprised and impressed.

"You've never heard of social media?" Charlie smirked.

"He really hasn't," Carolyn replied. "What else did you find?"

"She was a promising athlete until she was injured last year. Her online presence decreased dramatically last spring; could be the injury, could be something else. A few vague mentions of a new boyfriend but no pictures. She was posed as Ophelia, who is—" Charlie pointed at Emma.

Startled, she responded like the well-trained student that she still was at heart. "Female lead in *Hamlet*, daughter of Polonius, sister of Laertes. She's both a motivator for Hamlet's actions and his foil—his madness is feigned while hers is real. She rejects him at her father's behest. Hamlet turns her rejection back on her with mocking and accusations, basically calling her a slut. She dies, either by accident or suicide."

Charlie had been taking notes. "Painting suggests suicide, though. Art guy, go."

"I'm not your dancing monkey." Rory's voice was actively offended.

Emma sighed. "Rory . . ."

"Fine. Postmodern, multimedia, inspired by Millais."

"That's it?" Charlie prompted.

"We've covered this already."

"Okay, then. Niall?"

"Using the victim as a prop suggests a product killer—interested in the result rather than the process of killing. The ostentation of the display, the positioning of himself as parallel to a famous artist—it suggests someone with antisocial personality disorder, probably with narcissistic tendencies. Likely male, white, middle-aged or younger—probably has short-term if any relationships . . ."

"Why?" Charlie interrupted.

"He's hunting these women, taking them, posing them . . . that takes both time and freedom of movement. It's unlikely that he has a wife and kids at home. If he does, the relationship is likely abusive, at least emotionally, to create an environment where his movements wouldn't be questioned."

"Smart." Charlie glanced up at him.

"Thanks." Niall's tone was genuine but amused.

Charlie grinned at him, her shoulders relaxing a fraction. "Anything else before we look at the next girl?" She waited for a beat, then nodded. "Okay, then." She slid out a neat stack of photos. The first showed a woman's hand, the flesh too, too pale.

"What's she holding?" Niall asked.

"A letter." Emma felt a thrum of satisfaction. "She's Elaine of Astolat."

"Whoa," Charlie said, eyebrows raised.

Emma shook her head, feeling a blush warm her cheeks. "Ian came by. He let it slip." She pulled out her copy of Mallory, flipping to the story. "Elaine of Astolat, the Lady of Shalott, is a figure that appears in literature from the medieval era onward—" She took a breath, trying to sort the information pinging in her brain into careful piles of "relevant" and "irrelevant."

"She's another darling of the Pre-Raphaelites," Rory guided.

"Right, she was probably more popular in the Victorian era than when she originated. There are numerous versions of her story—Italian, French, and English—but I think that it's most likely that the . . . this version is drawing from Mallory—" Emma tapped her book.

"Okay, and what's her deal?" Charlie prompted again.

"She was a young woman who, in the Mallory, fell in love with the knight Lancelot. He refused her, rather politely to be honest, and she died of love. As she was dying, she gave specific instructions that she was to be placed in a boat with a letter tied to her hand explaining her story."

Charlie looked up sharply, then reached for the photos. She turned the first one over, revealing another that showed a woman in a red dress stretched out in a boat. "Looks like you're right."

Emma inhaled sharply. "The letter is definitely drawing on Mallory, but that's—"

"Waterhouse," Rory finished.

"I was going to say Tennyson, but yeah, Waterhouse makes sense."

"Explain for the nonexperts in the room." Charlie glanced around. "Okay, explain for me."

"John William Waterhouse was a British artist in the Pre-Raphaelite school. He, like most artists of the day, drew on Alfred, Lord Tennyson's version of the story," Rory told her.

"So, is the Tennyson/Waterhouse version different from the other one?"

"Well, Elaine is different," Emma answered. "The Tennyson version of the story sees the Lady of Shalott—she doesn't get a name—locked in a tower. She doesn't actually meet Lancelot, just sees him from a distance before dying. In the Mallory, she's much more active. She proposes to Lancelot, then asks him to be her lover. He goes missing at one point, and she rescues him. And after she tells him that she's going to die if he won't love her, she rejects his solutions, saying—" Emma broke off as she found the page "—'"Alas, then," said she, "I must die for your love."' And he can't save her. She defies the conventions of her gender and won't play by the rules of romance. And then when she dies, she gets the final word."

"But she still dies," Charlie pointed out. "Sounds like she broke the rules, and the universe punished her for it."

"If the killer is drawing on this version," Niall offered, "he might be telling us something about . . ."

"Phillipa," Charlie supplied.

"About Phillipa." Niall nodded his thanks. "If the message about Sarah Weston is that she was sinful, then maybe the message about Phillipa is that she was too unwomanly. She broke the rules of femininity in some way."

Charlie pointed to her dress. "Maybe she was too forward? Promiscuous? Red can symbolize lust and sin, right?" Rory made a soft sound, drawing her eyes. She frowned. "Don't look at me like I'm a talking dog. Every high school freshman reads *The Scarlet Letter*."

"It's possible . . ." Emma began.

"Or," Rory interrupted. "It could be another homage to Waterhouse. He painted three versions of this story. The most famous is the one with her sitting in the boat."

"Ah yes, the centerpiece of many a dorm room exhibition," Charlie tossed in, earning a smile from Niall.

Rory ignored her. "The other two show her in the tower. In one, she's wrapped up in golden thread, which I believe—" he traced a finger over the image "—is what you can see there. And in the other, she's wearing a scarlet dress. These two also feature the cracked mirror from the Tennyson poem." Rory pointed to the bouncing reflections in the bottom of the boat. "I'd be willing to bet that's what those are."

"So he combined at least two texts and three images. Why?" Emma asked.

"To take control of the narrative," Niall explained. "He's claiming all of the versions—"

"Postmodernism," Rory murmured.

"—but superseding them with his own rendering. He's taken the elements he wants from each and remade the story to suit his message, his world view."

"The assertive, punishable Elaine from Mallory is placed alongside the constraining domesticity of Tennyson." Emma caught Charlie's quirked brow. "The threads. She's supposed to sit quietly and weave, and when she looks up at Lancelot—in defiance of her designated role—she gets tangled in the threads. And cursed," Emma added after a beat.

"So, in both versions, she is punished for rejecting the status quo." Charlie made a note. "This guy is picking misogyny from column A and from column B, isn't he?"

"He did the same with Sarah Weston's scene," Emma noted.

Niall looked pensive as he stared at the image. "Em, you said before that Ophelia's sin was suicide."

"Right. The gravediggers say she killed herself. The noose in the painting suggests the same."

"What if it wasn't just that? In the nunnery speech, Hamlet accuses her of being . . ." Niall paused, searching for a word.

"Slutty and devious?" Charlie supplied.

"Yes, that. Could the text be read so that's literally true?"

Emma looked down, running the lines in her head. "I mean, scholars pretty uniformly read the scene as part of Hamlet's performance of an 'antic disposition' . . ."

"Scholars, sure. But how would a woman-hating murderer read it?" Charlie asked.

"In the worst way possible," Niall answered. "He'd assume the man was telling the truth and the woman was conniving and sinful."

"Then, yeah. If we take Hamlet's words at face value—again, a poorly supported reading—then you could argue Ophelia led Hamlet on, slept with him, dumped him, then publicly rejected him when he was no longer heir to the throne."

"So to this guy, both stories are about women who break the rules, hurt a man, and then die by a river," Charlie summed up. "And you all read this for fun?"

Emma frowned, knowing her defensiveness was unreasonable. "Again, he's not *right* about that interpretation. The texts are tragic but not . . . hateful." She folded her arms tight as if she could guard the stories within her chest.

"Sorry, right," Charlie said into the awkwardness. After a moment, she reached out to flip to the next picture. Phillipa's blank eyes looked back at them.

"God," Niall breathed, reaching out abruptly to turn to the next photo.

Emma looked down to the new photo that had been revealed.

"There were two notes," Charlie explained. "One said her name and the school. This is the other."

"'I love not to be constrained' . . ." Emma frowned. "No. That's not her letter, that's not . . ." She broke off and reached for the book, flipping the pages again. "In Mallory's story, she gets to narrate her story. She writes it down and even hires a boatman who doesn't talk so that he won't speak in her place. She tells her story, *word by word*—her words. But here . . . This is what Lancelot says to justify himself, how he explains why he's not to blame." Rage rose in her chest. "He took away her words." Emma tried to shut down the unruly emotion without success.

"Emma? You alright?" Niall's voice was distant despite his nearness.

"Yes, I— No." Emma pressed her fingers against her forehead and scrubbed gently up and down. "No. He's robbing them, the characters, the girls. Taking their agency, their words, their . . ." Emma didn't finish the thought, she couldn't. She looked up at Charlie, who nodded her head in understanding.

"If we're going to solve this, we need to be thinking critically not emotionally," Rory reproved. "This killer is . . . a spider in the center of his web, planning his next move. We can't afford to get distracted if we're going to catch him."

"He's not a mastermind," Charlie rebuffed him firmly. "They never are. You read him right, Emma. He's a sexist asshole who doesn't really understand what these stories are about. He can only see things one way; that makes him predictable. Like Niall said, he's a narcissist. That means he's not in control of this—it's a compulsion, and that's going to trip him up eventually. And while Rory sees a postmodern intellectual, I just see someone who's not creative enough to come up with his own shit. He's a shallow, self-involved wannabe. A copycat. And you know what we are?" She leaned close, her voice just for Emma. "We're the bitches who are going to stop him. Stay angry."

Emma met her eyes, accepting her challenge and offering a promise in return. Unable to fully marshal her thoughts, she quoted Arthur's lines from *Le Morte*. "'Tide me death, betide me life, now I see him yonder alone he shall never escape mine hands, for at a better avail shall I never have him.'"

Charlie gave her a tilted smile. "I like the energy. I have no idea what it means."

"It means that if we want to find this guy, we don't stop," Emma replied, claiming a king's words as her own. "Whatever it takes, we do what we have to."

Chapter 17

Mike was already on the phone when Ian arrived at work the next morning. Ian had spent the night researching the story Emma had mentioned, trying not to play their conversation on repeat in his head. Every time he saw her, he widened the gulf between them. And she was right—he couldn't protect her. Or, it seemed, anyone else. Phillipa Minor had been taken the day they'd found Sarah Weston. If the killer stuck to that pattern, another girl was already gone. And Ian had no idea who she was or where to find her. Their attempts to trace the costumes, art supplies, and narcotics used on the first two girls had dead-ended. The killer had hidden all of his movements online. Their forensic clues had dried up as well—and from the bits of conversation Ian had overheard, the college wasn't much help either.

"Yeah, thanks." Mike finished the call as Ian was booting up his computer. "I finally pried their file cabinets open. A few students shared classes with both girls, and there was one TA who was assigned to both the museum thing and the undergrad art courses that Weston was in. Name of Haynes."

"Anything to suggest he's our guy?"

"Nothing concrete. Creepy little bastard, though. Several complaints for following girls, waiting outside classes, that sort of thing. One record of an actual conduct hearing, a girl said he spiked her drink, but nothing came from it. No assault—the girl's friend hauled her home when she started slurring—no witnesses. The school seems disinclined to follow up."

"Well, it's suggestive."

"Might get us in to search his apartment." Mike sounded hopeful.

"Only if the judge is late for dinner reservations and doesn't bother to read the paperwork. It's a weak rationale for a warrant."

"So, it's just a coincidence that the same weirdo shows up in both girls' lives?"

"No more of a coincidence than their connection to the same art professor." Ian immediately regretted the rejoinder. He turned to his computer and began studiously searching for a file.

"Ian, man . . ."

"I'm just saying that the connection's too thin for a warrant. We need something firm."

"Right," Mike repeated noncommittally. "Well, Weston's memorial is tomorrow, and Ivy's coming in over the weekend for the other girl's autopsy."

"You want the memorial or the autopsy?"

"Heads or tails?" Mike was digging in his pocket when a young officer approached from behind Ian. He held out a sheet of paper. "Detectives? The desk said to keep an eye out for anything that might be connected to The Artist."

"The what?" Mike demanded.

The officer hesitated. "That's what the papers are calling him."

"Damn it. I hate it when they name them."

"What'd you find?" Ian asked.

"Missing person report. A Carlisle College student, right age, blond hair. Could be nothing . . ."

"Could be something. Good work."

Mike read the report aloud as the man left. "'Dana Ackerman, twenty-two. Blond hair, green eyes, 5'4"—last seen yesterday morning wearing a blue jacket, green top, and jeans. Jesus, another one."

"Right on schedule," Ian said bleakly.

"Don't jump to conclusions."

Before he could respond, Ian's desk phone rang. Mike gestured for him to answer, turning back to the report.

"Carter."

"Detective Carter? This is John Hastings, Northport PD, returning your call about an assault case."

"Right." Ian reached for a pen. "Thanks for getting back to me. We're dealing with a series of murders here . . ."

"The girls from Carlisle College?"

"Yeah."

Hastings was silent for a moment. "You think it's connected?"

"It's the theory we're working with."

"Damn it. I knew he'd escalate. We connected three attacks, all women in their midtwenties."

"Blondes?"

"The last two were. The first was dark-haired."

"Anything that you can tell me about the MO?"

"The first girl seemed random. She was walking home from work—she lived a few blocks off—and he rushed her from the bushes. Knocked her down, tried to grab her purse. A neighbor came out when she screamed, and the guy just ran. We probably would have dismissed it as a simple mugging if not for the others."

Ian pictured Emma, looking up from the grass in a long blue gown, and felt a sliver of unease settle in his chest. He cleared his throat. "How did you put them together?" Ian asked.

"The guy's shoes."

"His . . ."

"Shoes. Guy had these ludicrous shoes. They were camo high-tops. The victim said they looked like a kid playing soldier. Luckily, there was an overeager officer who decided to take prints. I probably wouldn't have," Hastings admitted. "They were sold all over the place, so didn't narrow the suspect list."

"But they matched the next girl?"

"Yep. This one he grabbed in a dark alley. He hit her in the face, hard enough that she lost consciousness for a minute, and pulled her into an old warehouse. Then . . . he just left her there. We found vomit nearby. Figure he planned to assault her but lost his nerve."

"DNA?"

"Nothing on the victim. Barf was too contaminated by the time we found it. Looked like a dog had been at it."

"Did she notice the shoes?" Ian asked, scribbling quick notes as he listened.

"No. Kept her eyes closed through most of it, just saw enough to tell us that he was wearing dark clothes and a mask."

"Like a balaclava?"

"No, plastic. Like something from the dollar store. But since we were looking, they took shoe prints and got a match. That's also the case where we got the latent."

"How?"

"The victim's Fitbit. He left a partial on the face when he grabbed her."

"Any other forensics?"

"A few fibers. The girl had dressed and showered before coming in, so there was no DNA. Similar story for the third victim. Attacked at night, knocked out, taken to a secluded location. He'd gotten more efficient by then, though. She was hit from behind and was out before she knew what happened. She woke up maybe ten minutes later. This time, he'd stripped her, took her clothes."

"Was she assaulted?"

"Did a rape kit, but no. We think he was trying to take any evidence with him."

"He knew he left a print?" Ian's voice sharpened.

"Yeah, but before you go down any conspiracy rabbit holes, he knew because an idiot local politician announced it. Guy's up for reelection, and he announced that we'd found a print on something belonging to the victim. Wanted to look good to the masses before everyone filled out their ballots."

"So, no conspiracy, but definitely a guy who's following the news reports and learning from his mistakes. That says he can control his behavior, at least enough to plan and clean up after."

"And getting more confident. If you're right about the connection to your case, he was practicing on these girls."

"How far apart were the attacks?"

"Two weeks. And all of them on the weekend."

"So he'd have time to drive down and back." Ian ran a hand across his eyes. "It fits, but . . ." Ian tried to match the image of someone who got so nervous he had to barf in an alley to one who could kill and carefully arrange the bodies of his victims. One seemed new, uncertain in his approach. The other was organized, calculated, and callous—and murderous.

"Any of the victims drug users?" Ian asked. If not, he might be able to cross Sarah's dealer off the list.

"No arrest records, but the second two victims were taken to pretty shady areas. Drugs wouldn't be hard to find around there."

Ian sighed. Not much help there either way. "Can you send me the case reports?"

"Consider it done."

"Thanks," Ian responded.

"Of course. I wish I could have . . ."

"Not how this works," Ian interrupted, his voice gentle as he told the other detective the words he wished he believed himself.

"Yeah. Hope your luck is better." Hastings disconnected with a soft click.

Mike had been patiently waiting throughout the phone call, and Ian turned to toss the notes he had taken to his partner. "Muggings, not full-on attacks. Prints match the one we found at the first scene, but . . ." Ian shook his head. "If it's our guy, he's a fast learner."

"It's a big jump from simple assault to—" Mike waved vaguely at their case files, then looked back to Ian's notes "—nighttime attacks, assaulted, stripped . . . Maybe he had the rest planned out and just needed to practice the actual attack. You consider that your professor might have been another practice go? She was mugged, right?"

"Her purse was taken after she tripped. Seemed opportunistic, not planned. Besides, at that point, he'd killed Sarah Weston and taken Phillipa Minor. He'd already moved onto the full-scale displays. Why would he regress back to simple purse snatching?"

"Maybe he'd planned more, and you interrupted him," Mike rebutted carefully.

"She doesn't fit the profile." Ian's tone was final. Neither of them pointed out that the first of the Northport victims didn't either.

"I checked up on Tamblyn's alibi for the days Weston and Minor were taken," Mike said a little awkwardly. "He's in the clear for both. Do you want me to check on these days, too?"

"Read them to me."

Mike obliged, digging out his initial notes and reciting a string of dates from early summer.

Ian flashed back to their interview in Tamblyn's office. Summer term, study abroad—England. "Son of a bitch."

Ian navigated to Carlisle's social media pages, then scrolled back through their timeline until he found the right dates. Tamblyn's face grinned back at him. Ian scrolled through photo after photo of students with Big Ben, red phone booths, and the blue lines of Tower Bridge. Tamblyn was in most of them. Emma was only in one, smiling contentedly, Tamblyn's arm over her shoulder. According to the cheery posts, she'd spent her time behind the camera.

"He's in the clear." Ian knew he should be glad to cross a suspect off the list, but his gut twisted in disappointment. And then shame. "He was in another country."

"You're sure?"

"Yeah. Emma's his alibi."

Chapter 18

Rory had left the café to run errands after the first round of coffees—Emma suspected it was actually a date—but she, Charlie, and Niall had kept at it, coffee becoming dinner, and dinner becoming drinks. They'd ended up back at Carolyn and Charlie's, the latter not even pausing the debate as she unlocked the door and led them in.

"Freud doesn't make sense," Charlie called over her shoulder as she made her way into the kitchen. Without asking, she pulled a selection of sparkling water and soda from the fridge.

"In general?" Niall asked sardonically, grabbing a water.

"Yes, actually," Charlie answered with a cheeky grin. "But I meant for the case. Your idea that it's all mommy issues . . ."

"Freudian psychology is more than mommy issues."

"There's also weird sex stuff," Carolyn offered, all innocence.

"Neither of which apply here. He's killing young women—"

"Of course they do." Niall cut Charlie off. "He's taking out his anger about his mother by killing surrogates . . ."

"Like his mother was blonde, so he's killing blonde women?

Didn't Bundy do that?" Emma asked, hopping onto one of the barstools that lined the kitchen counter.

"Exactly," Niall said just as Charlie objected.

"No. Bundy was supposed to have killed women who looked like his girlfriend. And that's been debunked."

"Why are we assuming that there's only one killer?" Carolyn asked. "Maybe it's a Bonnie and Clyde thing. Killers in love."

"Like the Ken and Barbie Killers."

Emma sighed. "Please don't tell me they made Serial Killer Barbie."

"No. It's what they call a couple from Canada who killed people and . . ." Charlie paused. "Other really gross stuff."

"Ed Kemper, Henry Lee Lucas, Ed Gein," Niall exclaimed a little too enthusiastically.

Charlie looked at him for a confused beat before a tiny, smug smile crept out. "Did you just Google serial killers with mommy issues?"

"I'm a psychologist. We study people with abnormal . . . psychology."

"So, that's a yes," Charlie said, mugging at Carolyn.

"It's still a good theory," Niall defended himself, a little sheepishly.

"So, it's a single killer, or a pair of killers, obsessed with a mother or a girlfriend. Or working with the mother or girlfriend . . ."

"Or—" Charlie interrupted Carolyn "—just a non-Freudian weirdo who likes creepy texts about dead girls. No offense." Charlie shrugged at Emma.

"I'm not the one who's read up on Serial Killer Barbie," Emma retorted. "But I can't deny he's obsessed with art and literature that objectify the deaths of beautiful women," she acknowledged. "The key has to be in the way the victims are presented—the references, the quotes . . ."

"That's your area, I'm afraid," Niall told her.

"Believe me, I know." Emma smiled. "Which is why I'm going to call it a night—go home and stare at some Shakespeare for a while."

"And maybe get some sleep?" Carolyn suggested gently.

"'To sleep—perchance to dream,'" Emma replied as she buttoned her coat in preparation for the autumn chill. "'Aye, there's the rub.'"

She'd woken a few short hours later to the dinging of her phone from where it lay on her black-and-floral nightstand. She rolled over, hiding beneath her pillow, as another ding followed. After three more, she felt for the phone and held it close to her face, her brain struggling to catch up with her eyes. Charlie had started the exchange without preamble, and Emma fuzzily wondered if she'd ever gone to bed.

CHARLIE: memorial service this morning . . . we going?

NIALL: I think we should

CAROLYN: Is it too ghoulish?

CHARLIE: killers sometimes watch the mourning to see the impact of their crimes

NIALL: This one will.

EMMA: We should go. Sarah deserves to be remembered.

She paused for a moment, her thumbs still on the screen of her phone. If he can see us, we can see him.

She tossed her phone on the bed and rose, pulling a prim black dress from the back of her closet.

After dressing quickly and forcing her face and hair into acceptable respectability, she made the short drive to campus where the service was being held. She slowly scanned the faces present as she stepped into the already packed auditorium. The set for an upcoming production of *Twelve Angry Men* had been quickly covered by black bunting and vases of lilies donated by a local florist. A large photo of a smiling Sarah stood at the front of the stage. There had been discussion of adding Phillipa to the program when her death had been announced—the college president didn't want to extend the observance, having already allowed students one day off for Sarah's service—but the board of trustees didn't want any accusations that they'd prioritized the status quo over the life of a student.

Emma hesitated, unsure of where she fit into the assembled audience. She spotted Rory seated a few rows back from the stage with his head bowed. Emma looked hopefully for Carolyn's friendly face but couldn't spot her in the crowd. Her gaze lit briefly on Ian, but she turned away when he made eye contact. Malcolm Haynes was hunched in a back pew near Professor Jacobs and a few other faculty members she knew by sight. Several of her students sat near the front—Hallie, Ethan . . . She searched her mind for more names but couldn't find them. Emma felt her chest tighten with distress. If Sarah had been in her class, would she be one of the forgotten?

The provost mounted the steps to the stage, and the assemblage fell silent. After a few awkward words of condolence, she signaled to a local Episcopal priest who had been approved by Sarah's family. The clergywoman was calm and rather generic as she conspicuously tried to avoid mentioning the brutal crime with euphemistic phrases. It did nothing to distract them all from the whispered word that hung in the air: *murder.* Emma slipped out quietly when Sarah's friends and classmates began speaking. It felt intrusive, voyeuristic even, to stand there and watch the spectacle of their grief. She wasn't going to learn anything from their pain. If the killer was there, he wasn't making himself known.

Emma thought for a moment that Ian's eyes turned toward her as she fled but dismissed the idea until she heard footsteps following her across the parking lot. She stopped, straightening her back deliberately before she turned to face him.

It wasn't Ian who stepped up to her.

Ethan's dark hair fell across his eyes, eyes that were red and filled with rage. "Why are you here?" His voice was thick with grief, his hand shaking as he gesticulated toward her. "You shouldn't be here."

Emma stepped back in confusion. "Ethan, I—"

"You think this is a game? Or one of your ridiculous books?"

Emma shook her head, trying to catch up to the moment. "No. Not at all. Ethan—"

"She's not some fucking character!" he shouted, stepping closer.

Emma raised her hands between them instinctively. "I don't understand. Who? Sarah—?"

"No! Phillipa. The girl they found by the pond? Her name was Phillipa. She's my—" His voice broke. "She was my girlfriend. She was funny and smart and . . . and you don't get to talk about her like that. She's not yours to talk about." Ethan ran a hand across his mouth. "I heard you. At the café? You and your friends talking about 'the dead girl in the boat.' She had a name. Phillipa. I loved her."

"I'm so, so sorry—"

"Don't. Don't you dare."

Another boy—the one that Emma had thought of as his shadow—grabbed him by the shoulders. "Come on, man. Let's go. Let's go home."

Ethan pulled away. "She's not some pointless metaphor. You teach all these stories about dying, getting us to pick them apart, treat them like puzzles, laugh at their silly romances and melodramatic deaths. But—she was . . . she was . . . I . . ." Ethan bent forward on a low moan.

Emma couldn't find any words to respond.

"Sorry, Professor," his shadow softly said. He wrapped an arm around his friend and led the sobbing boy away.

Emma walked, eyes downturned, across the parking lot and slid into the driver's seat of her car. She pushed the key into the ignition but left the key ring dangling, not knowing where to go. Instead she sat, watching as a thin film of rain coated her windshield, flagellating herself with Ethan's words. He was right. They were doing exactly what Ian and Carolyn had warned them against. Last night—she'd enjoyed herself. She'd told herself it was the company, the feeling of acceptance and comradery. But it was the challenge, the puzzle—the game.

She was still sitting there when the auditorium doors opened. A mass of people stepped out into the rain, bodies pressing into each other, huddling under umbrellas for cover. She saw Ian step out behind the rest, squared and rigid, the collar of his dark coat turned up against the damp.

When the parking lot had emptied, she pulled her car carefully into the street. Her brain felt flighty and uneven, and Emma talked herself through every signal and turn as she drove. She knew from experience that if she let her mind loose, she could drive by rote, following paths and haunts that she had traced for years without ever really seeing the road. When she reached her house, she released the wheel, her muscles stiff with concentration, and found her way inside. She made it to the living room and dropped to the floor in front of her bookshelves. She wanted to cry—for Sarah, Phillipa, herself—wanted the same painful, heaving sobs of grief and rage that Ethan had. But she couldn't find her way through the protective walls she'd spent so many years building. As a kid, she'd cried whenever she got angry, when she couldn't explain or wasn't heard, and it had marked her as weak to those who didn't understand. It had meant that she hadn't translated the world correctly, that she hadn't been able to adapt, to keep her mask in place—it signified failure. So now she sat, letting all the dark voices fill her head until she couldn't take any more. Then she crept to her bedroom, cocooned herself in a weighted blanket, and slept.

Emma woke hours later, her eyelashes matted and her head throbbing. She hadn't bothered to change out of her dress before dropping into bed. Her keys, purse, and coat were abandoned unceremoniously on the floor just inside the door. Her shoes were somewhere in the hallway. Rising into the late afternoon light, Emma peeled off the black dress and stockings and left them on the floor, wrapping herself in a robe before padding barefoot to the kitchen. Her stomach roiled at the thought of food, so she just set the kettle to boil and reached for tea. She picked up the phone she'd left on the counter—wincing to see it was almost five—and found that she had missed calls from both Carolyn and Niall. She'd turned the ringer off when she'd gotten home, needing the quiet. She stared at the screen for a moment, then cleared the accusing "missed call" notifications, left the phone on Silent, and crossed to the bathroom. She started the water running and liberally doused the tub with bath salts.

Feeling too restless to stand and wait for the tub to fill, she went to the bedroom and laid out an old sweatshirt from her alma mater and a pair of yoga pants before crossing to the entryway where she had dropped her things after the memorial. Picking up her keys, she set them in the bowl she'd placed beside the door after losing them once too often and then gathered her coat and purse. On the floor just inside the threshold, Emma noticed a plain manila envelope. Wadding her belongings under one arm, she stooped to retrieve it. It was sealed with tape, but there was no address or name on it. She hadn't noticed it when she came in. So she couldn't have dropped it when she brought in the mail yesterday, Emma thought as she turned back toward the kitchen. Especially, she realized with annoyance, because she hadn't remembered to bring in the mail.

Frustrated by this small failure on top of everything else, Emma set the envelope on the counter with more force than was needed. She put her coat away and hung her purse on a hook by the kitchen door. The kettle bubbled, low and soft, as steam rose from the spout. She selected a bag of chamomile tea and reached for an oversized mug; then she stood, her mind chasing lost details until the warm stillness was broken by a harsh sucking noise, the too-familiar sound of the overflow drain in her bathtub. She rushed to the bathroom, knocking the mug onto the floor as she went. Twisting the faucet off, Emma dipped her hand into the tub. Her skin chilled in the water, which had gone from hot to barely lukewarm as she had dithered.

"Damn it." Emma felt a scream build at the back of her throat at this final straw and dropped onto the floor of the bathroom, sucking in deep breaths as she tried to quiet the overwhelming forces within her. When the sensations subsided, she simply sat, unmoving, as water trickled behind her. She closed her eyes and focused on the rhythmic sound of the slowing drip. The kettle whistled from the kitchen in a sharp counterpoint. Emma stayed on the floor.

Eventually, she forced herself to her knees, pulled the plug on the tub of now cold water, and returned to the living room. She could either wait half an hour for the water to reheat or just give up and dress for bed. Even that small choice seemed overwhelming. She moved the kettle off the heat and flipped off the burner. Needing the chamomile to settle her nerves, she retrieved the mug and tea bag and slowly poured the boiling water. She lifted the mug and sipped lightly, her tongue scalded by the heat. She sipped again, wanting the pain.

Looking for a distraction, Emma grabbed the mystery envelope and a glossy magazine from the counter, rescued the remote control from the seat cushions, and dropped heavily onto the sofa. She set the magazine off to the side and flipped open the unsealed tab on the envelope, flexing the paper to widen the gap. Four glossy sheets of blank paper slid onto the coffee table in front of her. Across the back of the top one, a message was scrawled:

Emma—"I loathe that low vice—curiosity."

Emma's breath sped into short, sharp rasps. She stared at the bleak whiteness of the pages as she tried to convince herself that they were something she had ordered, had forgotten, that someone had mistakenly delivered them to her door, that they were anything but what she knew that they had to be. Hands shaking, she flipped them over, one by one, like a macabre matching game. She could take in only flashes, details: a pale hand, dark hair, a thick pool of crimson velvet. Her mind refused to grasp the full image of what was before her.

"No. No, no, no," she whispered lowly, a desperate chant to keep the darkness at bay.

Pushing back from the couch, she knocked her tea onto the floor as she stumbled backward. She scrambled for her phone, knocking her purse from the counter and dumping the contents onto the floor. Emma scrolled to Ian's number, hit Call, and held the phone to her ear, her eyes still on the coffee table. The tone sounded twice before abruptly going to voicemail. She heard Ian's calm, steady voice.

"Ian," she whispered after the tone, "Ian. Please, pick up. I . . . You need to come . . . He . . ." Terror rose, and she hung up as her brain began weaving a tapestry of worst-case scenarios. *He knows my name. He knows where I live.*

She gulped in three deep breaths. She needed to call someone else. She dug her nails into her palm, centering herself on the sting. She struggled to remember the name of Ian's partner or the precinct where he worked, finally dialed 411 and managed to ask for the police.

A chipper voice connected at last and asked where she would like to be directed.

"Ian Carter," Emma requested, her voice sounding thick in her own ears. "He's a detective."

"Which department?"

"Homicide." There was a silence at the other end of the line.

"Is this an emergency? Do you need immediate assistance?"

"Yes— No. Please, I just need to speak to him. Or his partner, I don't remember his name. It's about the murders, the Carlisle students."

"I'll try to connect you."

A few beats went by, and then tinny music began to play a discordant disco beat. The anonymous voice returned. "Detective Carter is out, but I'm going to connect you to his partner, Detective Michael Kellogg."

A few seconds later, a gruff voice spoke, "Kellogg."

"Detective Kellogg?" Emma was breathing heavily through her mouth, but she kept her tone even. "My name is Emma Reilly. I know—I talked with your partner, Detective Carter."

"The professor?"

Emma gave a harsh laugh. "Yes. Yes, that's me. I need . . ." She paused, unsure of what to say. "I need you or Ian to come to my house. I've received, that is, someone . . . someone left . . . pictures." With the last word, Emma's control broke, and she whispered into the phone. "He was here."

"Ms. Reilly? Pictures? Pictures of what?"

"He . . . he's killed another girl. He left an envelope with pictures . . ." Emma felt fear twisting in her chest. "Oh, god, what if he's still here?"

"Ms. Reilly, Emma, I'm on my way, but I need you to give me your address."

"Ian . . ."

"I'll call him. Can you give me your address?"

Emma managed to get the address out, her clipped words a counterpoint to the rapid staccato of her heart.

"Okay, hang on, Emma. I'll be there shortly, and we'll have an officer there even sooner. I'll stay on the line until the dispatched officer arrives. Make sure your door is locked, and try not to touch the pictures or the envelope anymore."

"Okay," she whispered, more to herself than him. "Okay, I can do that." Emma moved softly toward the lock, shifting the deadbolt into place.

"You should be able to hear the sirens any minute now."

Emma strained, picking up a faint sound in the distance. "I can hear them."

"Just hang on. Officer Davis should be there in a few minutes. I'm right behind him."

She stared at the door, clutching the phone until she heard the police car arrive and heavy feet come up the sidewalk. The door vibrated as someone pounded from the other side.

"This is Officer Davis. I'm going to hold my badge up to the window, and then I need you to open the door."

Emma glanced at the proffered badge, then fumbled with the locks, throwing the door open for a broad-faced officer in uniform.

"Dispatch said there was an intruder. Are you hurt, ma'am?"

"No. He . . . he just slid the envelope under my door."

The officer's brow crinkled. "Envelope?"

"Is that Davis?" Mike's voice from the forgotten phone surprised them both. "Let me talk to him."

Emma handed over the phone, retreating so the officer could step inside.

"Hello? Yes, sir." His eyes scanned the room, coming to rest on the photos. "Yes, sir, I see them. No, no one I could see."

As he continued the conversation with Kellogg, Emma moved to the far side of the room. She pressed her back against the wall and then slid down into a seated position, tucking her knees up under her chin. She was seated like that, staring up like a child, when a large man stepped into her view. She recognized him from her brief visit to the police station—he had been sitting across from Ian.

Mike Kellogg squatted down so that his eyes were level with hers. "Emma? It's Detective Kellogg. First, are you okay? You weren't hurt?"

"No. I didn't—I didn't see him. But he was here. At my house."

"Maybe him. Maybe he had someone else drop these off."

"But why?"

Mike looked at her thoughtfully before shaking his head. "We don't know yet, but we're going to take care of it."

He touched her shoulder briefly and then moved over to the table where Officer Davis stood. Emma dropped her head onto her knees and hid her face in the soft terry cloth of her robe.

Chapter 19

It was late afternoon by the time the crowd had fully dispersed from the memorial, students lingering for comfort or gossip, Ian couldn't tell. But if the killer had come dressed as a mourner, he'd played his role well. There were a few reporters and the expected cadre of curious gawpers, but most of the attendees seemed to be there to genuinely mourn. His eyes sifted through the crowd for Emma, but she wasn't there. He'd known she wouldn't be—he'd watched her leave earlier, her face still and set into a mask of soft sorrow. Ian wondered what she was doing, worried that he knew. He felt aimless and uncertain as he stood beneath the flickering autumn leaves outside of the auditorium. Mike was reviewing files back at the precinct, checking notes and alibis against the information that Hastings had sent about the previous attacks. But Ian couldn't face the growing desperation of that room. The lieutenant had assigned another team to support their investigation, and while Ian knew that it was because of public pressure and the media coverage, it still felt like a failure. The one thing he could do, he reminded himself, was the work.

He headed to the spot where Phillipa Minor's body had been displayed, just blocks from where Sarah Weston's mourners now gathered. Ian lost his balance and nearly slid into the water as he edged down the bank toward the pond. He grabbed a low branch just before his foot hit the stagnant water, jerking himself to a stop. His momentum worked against him, and he swung backward, landing on one knee in the mud. He snagged his palm on the rough bark of a tree as he pulled himself upright, cursing, and made his way to the spot where the boat had been moored.

Ian knew how unlikely it was that he would find a new clue and magically unravel everything. Still, he crouched in the mud, tracing likely paths to the site. He scanned the ground for any notable footprints, hoping for a clear connection to the cases in Northampton, but the damp soil had been smeared into abstract smudges. When he had exhausted every possibility, he returned to his car and drove to the barn where they had found Sarah Weston's body less than a week before. He parked well away and walked to the site, still cordoned off with yellow police tape in a fruitless effort to keep tourists of the macabre from snapping pictures of the mural that adorned the back wall. The tape would have no effect, which—as Ian found to his annoyance—was why a police-issue lock had been placed on the barn door. He cursed himself for not checking first. Mike was right. His head was not where it should be.

Ian shook the lock, but it held firm. Knowing the futility, he instead decided to survey the surrounding area. At the back of the left wall, he found a board that had been pried away and clumsily put back in place. He knew that it had not been there during his initial visit. He should call it in, make it an official report—but he thought of Emma, describing her visit to the crime scene. Instead, he stooped down to the small opening. If he found anything, he'd have to explain the breach of protocol, convince his lieutenant—and later a prosecutor and possibly jury—that he hadn't broken in to plant evidence. He knew it was a bad idea, that it potentially jeopardized their case. He couldn't bring himself to care. He wanted—needed—to do something, anything, to find this killer. He'd deal with the consequences later.

His phone rang. Ian jerked back into the afternoon light and reached into his pocket. The caller ID read **Emma**. He thought of her voice the last time they'd spoken, her drawn face at the funeral. She might be calling to apologize, to forgive him. Or to tell him again how this was his fault and she hated him for it, that she'd be better off with the art professor who took her to Europe and didn't involve her in grisly murders. Because he so badly wanted to hear her voice, even if she'd called to tell him to go to hell, he pressed End and cut the ringing off abruptly. He watched the message icon appear on the screen. Whatever she had wanted to tell him, he could listen to it tonight with a bottle of whiskey readily available.

He tucked the phone back in his pocket and shoved his way into the barn, pulling another board out by the nails in his haste. The wide space was dim and empty, and he flicked on his phone flashlight to scan the ground as he crossed toward the mural. The mud near Phillipa's resting site had obliterated any hope of footprints; here, the hard, dry ground had resisted their impact. Either the killer had learned from his previous attempts, or he was getting lucky. They could officially add the footprints and the partial fingerprints that they'd gotten from the trough to the list of leads that were going nowhere.

The mural seemed smaller now that police lights didn't surround it. With the trough and body gone, it was simply a painting of a tree with a quaint river swirling at its roots. The flowers, which had set so much in motion, seemed drab against the weathered boards. Only the painted noose gave any hint at what the image had meant. Ian had memorized this image after hours of staring at photographs. He knew the messages it contained—the closed door, the fig tree's fall from grace—but it didn't speak to him. This was a language not his own. His phone rang again, but he ignored it. He reached out and traced the flowers with his finger. They, too, spoke in another language.

A third call finally convinced him to step into a small pool of sunlight and look at the caller ID. The precinct number showed in his messages; Ian swore, knowing he was about to lie to a fellow officer about his whereabouts. He called his voicemail and heard the voice of Aaron Parker, one of the detectives who had been assigned to join Mike and him on the case.

"Hey, uh, Ian. It's Aaron. Mike just ran out of here, said to tell you to meet him at the professor's house. He tried calling. And texting. Something about getting pictures, and . . ."

Ian pressed End, cutting off Aaron's voice midsentence. Ignoring Mike's messages, he tapped on the missed call from Emma.

"Ian. Please, pick up. I . . . You need to come . . . He . . ." Her voice cut off abruptly. Ian felt a wash of adrenaline as he scrambled out of the barn and ran toward his car. He threw open the door and sank down into the driver's seat, slamming into gear and hitting the gas at the same time. He drove by rote to Emma's house, pushing his speed just to the edge of safety. Pulling onto her street, he registered Mike's unmarked car out front, along with a squad car. He killed his car's engine and pocketed the keys with thick fingers. He walked up to the front of the house with forced composure, trying to block out the dread that had been building since he'd heard Emma's call end in silence.

The door was pulled open by a uniformed officer whom he vaguely recognized. The officer apparently had a better memory; he stepped aside with a mumbled *sir* and pointed Ian to the right. He saw Mike kneeling near a cozy, green sofa, his back to the door. Two officers hovered nearby as a third took pictures of the coffee table. Ian processed everything quickly, his trained mind taking over as his sensibilities were overwhelmed. Then he saw Emma wrapped in a soft robe. Her eyes were wide and shining, fierce against her pale face, and somehow darker than he remembered.

Emma looked over and met Ian's gaze. He could see her throat working as she swallowed hard. Her lips parted. She said nothing. He took a hesitant step toward her as Mike turned to see what Emma was staring at. Ian stopped still.

"Carter. It's about damn time." Mike's expression was hard fury as he stepped away from Emma. He grabbed Ian's arm roughly and pulled him into the kitchen. "What the hell are you doing, disappearing like that then not answering my calls? There's a homicide investigation ongoing here, or didn't you notice."

"What happened?" Ian was relieved to hear his voice sound cold, impassive as he spoke.

"She found an envelope by the front door—more pictures from our friend. We've got a new victim."

Ian shot a glance at Emma. "Was Emma hurt?"

"Scared to hell, but no. The pictures were dropped through the mail slot, no sign of attempted entry or anything else."

"Which of the victims was in the photos?"

"A new one." Mike let that sink in for a moment before continuing. "I need to get on the scene-of-crime guys. We took her initial statement, but see if there's anything more you can find out. And Ian—A-game, remember. We've officially got a serial killer out there." Mike left him standing alone.

Ian walked stiffly over to Emma, acutely aware of the officers crowding the small room. He sat lightly on the couch, his eyes scanning her, trying to find some solid ground, to focus on professional concern. Ian knew he should speak, ask her what happened, if she was alright. But Emma turned to him, her eyes strange and dark, and spoke first. "You didn't answer your phone."

"No." Ian felt himself flushing as Emma watched his face. He met her eyes, and she nodded.

"Mike did," Emma said finally.

"I know. Emma, I'm sorry—"

"Don't." Her eyes shifted from Ian to the scene at the coffee table.

"Mike said that the person in the photo is . . . new. Another girl was reported missing today, Dana Ackerman. Do you—"

"No," Emma said firmly. Ian stiffened. "No. It's not her. It's . . . I know who it is." Emma's eyes dropped to her hands, where she twisted the cloth robe between her fingers, the movements repetitive and focused. "She's a student at the college." Emma took a deep breath before speaking again. "Olivia Ballard."

"You know her?"

"Yes. She's in my Gothic Literature class." Emma's voice was just audible. "Was."

"Mike!" Ian called to where his partner stood talking to Officer Davis. Mike glanced over with a questioning look, and Ian gestured him over, then looked back to Emma. "Did you tell Mike that you recognized her?"

Emma shook her head.

"You recognize her?" Mike asked, striding over.

Ian answered. "A student in one of Emma's classes. Olivia . . ."

"Ballard," Emma supplied.

"Damn it," Mike swore softly. "Goddammit."

Emma looked at Ian squarely. "She was so, so smart. Eager. Funny." Grief began to fill her chest, seeping up into her voice. "I just saw her . . ."

"When exactly?" Ian straightened.

"Uh, yesterday . . ."

"Okay," Mike prompted. "Where were you?"

"Downtown, at a little café. She works—worked there."

"What's the name?"

"Uh . . ." Emma raked her hands through her hair. "Oh, god, it has a ridiculous name. A bad pun. Bean something."

"The Bean Bag," Officer Davis offered softly, hovering a few feet away.

"Yes, the Bean Bag." Emma shot a grateful look his way. Ian shifted uncomfortably next to her.

"Did she say anything to you? Did anything seem wrong?"

"She was worried about an essay; she wanted an extension."

"Was anyone hanging around? Or bothering her in any way?"

"I'm not sure. I—I don't think—" Emma broke off, clenching and unclenching her hands as they lay on her lap. "I didn't see anyone or anything that felt unusual."

"Was there anyone there that you recognized? Someone else who might have seen her?" Mike pressed.

"I was there with friends. Carolyn Matthews . . ."

"We've spoken with her," Mike encouraged.

"Niall Chadha, he teaches at the college as well. Psychology." Emma paused, slanting her eyes toward Ian. "Rory Tamblyn. And Carolyn's roommate, Charlie."

"Okay, we'll check with them. Is there anything else you can tell us?"

Again, the pause. "No, nothing helpful."

"Even if you don't think it might be . . ."

Emma shook her head slightly. "Nothing."

"Emma . . . I'm . . ." Ian stopped, uncertain what he could offer.

"Emma," Mike said softly. "We'd like to park a patrol car outside your house, at least for now. If you need to go out, go to work . . ."

"No. I can move my classes online. Rory—Dean Tamblyn—won't mind . . . He'll understand."

"I can stay," Ian interrupted. "You shouldn't be alone."

"No," Emma said firmly.

Ian shook his head. "But . . ."

"The car is fine. But as soon as you're finished, I'd like everyone to leave." Her voice was soft but firm.

Mike glanced quickly at his partner. Clearing his throat, he took a step back. "Of course. We're just about done. I'll leave my home and cell numbers. You can call anytime, day or night."

"Thank you, Detective Kellogg."

"Mike."

"Mike." Emma managed a small smile with genuine warmth. "Are you done with me? I would like to get dressed." She tugged her robe more tightly around her. "I was going to take a bath . . ." She looked over at the table where the pictures had scattered.

"Just one more question, if you can manage," Mike pressed gently.

Emma nodded.

"There were two notes this time. The one addressed to you and a second in with the photos. Did you read them?"

Emma looked up sharply. "Only the one on the back of the photo. It's a quote about curiosity."

"Does the quote mean anything to you?"

"Other than the clear warning to stop prying because he knows who I am and where I live?" Emma let out a humorless laugh. "It's Byron, I think. I can't remember which poem; I don't know him that well. I'm sorry."

"That's okay. Did you see the other note? In with the photos?"

Emma flinched visibly. "No, I didn't look at them after . . . after I'd realized what they were."

"That's okay." Mike kept his voice even. "This one is another quote, I think. It might tell us why he took—Olivia. It might help us find out where she is."

Emma nodded for him to go on.

"Okay, it says: 'Strangle her in bed, even the bed she hath contaminated,'" Mike read. "More direct than the last ones—" That to Ian. To Emma, he said, "Does it mean anything to you?"

Emma closed her eyes. *"Othello."*

"What?"

"Shakespeare's *Othello*. Iago says it before . . ." Emma fell silent, her eyes dropping to where her hands twisted in her lap. "I *think* it's from *Othello*."

"Okay, *Othello*. We can look that up." Mike sighed and ran a hand across his eyes. "We'll need you to come to the station tomorrow to make a formal statement. We appreciate your help."

Emma rose without another word and left the room. Ian took a step to follow her, but Mike jerked him back. "Come on; I'll buy you a drink. We could both use it."

Ian knew he should accept but shook his head. "No. If she doesn't want me here, fine. I'll keep watch from the car."

"You—" Mike laid his hand against Ian's chest "—are about to cross a dangerous line, Carter. We've got three dead women now. He's escalating. Both of the other victims were held for six days, and if Emma's right, he killed this one less than twenty-four hours after he took her. Less time, less planning—he may have made a mistake this time; we can't afford to do the same."

"I get that. I do. I just . . . I just need to make sure Emma's safe. I can't—" Ian broke off, unable to articulate a feeling he couldn't fully identify.

"Christ." Mike ran a hand through his hair, a habit that already had it standing on end. "Look, Ian, I don't understand what's going on with you and this woman. But tonight, you need to let her be. She's not Zoey Turner. This is not your do-over."

"That's not what— She's—" Ian stopped. "This isn't about Zoey."

"No. And it's not about you. Or even her." He jerked his head toward Emma. "It's about the three girls he's killed. And whoever he goes after next if we don't stop him." Mike started toward the door, leaving Ian to trail behind him.

The partners didn't speak as they left the house and climbed into their cars. Mike immediately started his engine and pulled off into the waning afternoon light. Ian sat for a moment before turning the key and slowly easing the car away from the curb. He flipped a U-turn in the empty street and then parked again on the other side, where he could easily see both the front door and alley that ran along the far side of the house. He looked toward the window that he thought belonged to Emma's bedroom and saw a small movement at the curtains. He waited to see if her face would appear, but the curtains stilled.

"Son of a bitch," he breathed. He turned his collar up and let his head fall back against the headrest.

Chapter 20

Emma watched Ian park across the street but couldn't summon any anger. Somewhere in this mess, there was an echo of a bright night of flirtation, champagne, and apple pie. Ian was a part of that, she reminded herself. Perhaps for him, the brightness was still there. Emma had a sudden urge to run down to his car and ask to start again, to go back to that night with the pasta primavera she'd never eaten, to sip her wine, to flip through Raymond Chandler instead of crime scene photos, and to end the night with a kiss. Then, Olivia's cold, slack face seeped into her vision, and she imagined Ian kneeling over the murdered girl's body, searching the folds of rich green velvet with clinical ease as he sought to understand her death. Emma felt the hysteria she'd battled back for the past hour rising again, and she closed the curtain against the fading light, wanting the darkness. She lifted a pillow to her face and let herself scream, harsh and ragged, until she felt empty and spent. The clothes she'd set out earlier were still lying on her bed, and she forced herself to dress. Settling on the bed, Emma picked up a well-worn copy of *Persuasion*, hoping to lose herself in a happy ending. The shortening autumn days had brought its eager darkness, and she didn't want to be alone.

She gave up an hour later. Her mind wouldn't steady with thoughts of Olivia so near the surface. She couldn't focus on the familiar words, and the characters weren't enough to keep the world at bay this time. She set the book aside and reached for her phone, realizing it wasn't in its usual place on the nightstand. She searched the bedroom but couldn't find it in the pockets of her discarded clothes or robe. She crept down the hallway, flipping on the light as she stumbled across her forgotten heels. It wasn't in the kitchen or on the end tables near the couch. She looked quickly at the coffee table, the memory of the photos that had lain there shifting across her vision like an apparition. But the table was empty as she knew it had to be. Taking a steadying breath, Emma forced herself to rethink the night's events. She'd gotten the pictures, gone to the couch, then . . . she took another breath . . . then, to the kitchen to get her phone. She'd called Ian. Emma stopped that train of thought. She'd called Mike. The cop had arrived. She'd . . . Damn, she'd given him the phone. Emma hoped that the police hadn't taken it with them. No. He'd talked to Mike, and then . . .

Emma crossed the room to the oversized chair that sat near the window. Her phone was set neatly in the center of the cushion. She picked it up and saw more missed calls from Niall. She wondered without much curiosity if the police had already called him to confirm her story. Knowing she should call him back—and Carolyn, she dimly remembered—instead, after only a moment of hesitation, she found Rory's name.

He answered on the third ring, his voice thick and groggy. "Em? What time is it?"

"Rory . . ."

"Emma?" Fear traced through his voice now, chasing out sleep. "What is it? What's wrong?"

"There's been another murder. The killer . . . he was here, Rory. He was at my house."

There was a moment of stark silence, then Emma heard a rush of breath on the line. "What? How . . . ?"

"I don't know how. The police were here . . . Rory, it was a student of mine. He . . . he left me pictures of her."

"He . . . Pictures? What happened?"

"Someone—most likely the killer—came to my house after the memorial. He—he slipped an envelope under my door with photos . . . of another victim." More silence and then a strange, muffled sound from Rory's end of the line. "There was another note, too. Addressed to me."

"He came to your house," Rory repeated in a voice almost unrecognizable as his.

"It's worse. The girl in the photos, she was one of my students. What if he picked her because . . ." Emma stopped, closing her eyes against the thought. "We need to figure out who he is, Rory. I need to."

There was a long moment of silence before Rory responded. "I'm coming over. We'll go over everything again, everything we know."

Emma didn't hesitate. "Come."

They hung up, and Emma padded barefoot to the kitchen. She began to pull out cups and tea bags but hesitated when she realized her favorite mug was still on the carpet, now stained with chamomile tea. She hadn't bothered to pick it up after the police left. Emma decided to put on coffee instead. With the soothing sound of water running through the coffee machine filling the room, Emma walked over to collect the fallen cup. She scrubbed at the tea stain until it was just a damp spot on the carpet and then spent a few minutes straightening furniture and tidying up. Rory wouldn't care—or probably notice—but Emma felt the need to make her house look clean, neat, organized. Normal.

Lights flashed through the living room window as a car pulled up outside. She heard a car door slam, but rather than the expected knock on the door, she heard two more car doors close in rapid succession. Voices rose outside, and Emma dashed to the window. Rory and Ian stood facing one another, each stiff with aggression. A slightly dazed-looking uniformed officer stood off to the side.

"Damn."

Still barefoot, Emma ran out the door. "Wait, Ian. Stop it."

All three men turned to look at her, and Rory started in her direction. Ian put up a hand to stop him, and Rory brushed him off impatiently.

"Emma." Rory sounded relieved. "Are you alright?"

"Yes, sorry. I forgot they were out here. Officer," Emma called, gingerly working her way down the driveway. "I'm sorry, I should have warned you. This is Professor Tamblyn, a friend. I asked him to come over."

The officer started to speak, but Ian cut him off. "I gave orders that no one was to be allowed in."

"I'm not under house arrest, Detective."

She saw a flash of hurt rejection on his face, and then it was cold and composed again. "He shouldn't be here."

"Why exactly?" Emma challenged.

Ian didn't answer.

"Enough, Ian. Just . . . enough." Emma turned to the officer. "He's a friend," she repeated. "I asked him to keep me company. There's a lot on my mind, as you might imagine."

"Of course, ma'am," the officer replied, clearly wanting to go back to his car and away from whatever was happening. "Just let us know if you're planning to have anyone else come over."

"Sure. Sorry for the trouble." She reached out and took Rory by the arm, guiding him up to the door. "Come on. I've got coffee started."

She heard Ian's deliberate footsteps as he returned to his car. The engine turned over, and the car sped off. Emma didn't watch it go.

Once inside, Rory went to the window and looked out at the street. "What the hell was that?"

"Sorry. That wasn't about you."

"Was it about you?"

Emma didn't respond.

"Emma? Are you . . . and he . . . ?"

"No, I . . . no. It's not like that." He looked at her closely, and she turned away.

"Sorry. You don't owe me . . . I'm just not sure what's going on." Rory raked a hand through his sleep-mussed hair. "Emma—I don't know how to ask this, but the detective . . ."

"What about him?"

"Are you sure he's . . . safe . . . for you to be around?"

"Of course he is!"

"Sorry, sorry. He just, he seemed . . . upset out there. And when you sent him away . . ."

"No. Ian's just . . . Three girls have been killed now. And he's the one who's responsible for stopping it. That's a lot to deal with."

"Fine, but it's his job. He should be able to deal with it." Rory's voice was hard.

"Just let it go, Rory. Please." She stepped away from him.

"Okay. So, maybe Inspector Bucket's a decent guy, even a decent cop, under normal circumstances. But this—" Rory waived a hand broadly. "This isn't normal, Emma. I just want to make sure you can really rely on him."

"He's not going to hurt me, Rory."

"But can he help you?"

Emma dropped her eyes.

"Those pictures were a message. You see that, right?"

Emma laughed. "Yes, Rory, the message was literal—*stop fucking with this.*"

"Are you going to?" Rory demanded sharply.

"What if I'm next? Or what if . . ." Emma's voice dropped to a whisper as she voiced her worst fear aloud. "What if it was my fault?"

"No. Stop that right now. You are not to blame."

"Aren't I? How do I know that he didn't pick her because we . . . because *I* decided to play detective?"

"And if he did? That means you quit? Run away? Pack a bag and take off, hope the killer just gets bored? You do that, he gets exactly what he wants. Because you actually have a chance of figuring out what he's doing, *why* he's doing this."

"I figured out Ophelia, then Elaine—Olivia's still dead. The fact I've read fucking *Othello* isn't going to stop him. It's not going to stop another girl from dying."

"But what if it does?" Rory asked, saying aloud the question that kept creeping through Emma's head. "The quotes, the pictures, the symbolism—it's all a game to him. If we quit, he wins. If we solve the puzzle, we do."

"Three girls have already died. How is that winning?"

"Because he gets caught. Those girls get justice. No one else dies. That's winning. Or at least it's not losing anymore."

Emma closed her eyes, picturing Olivia during class—her face avid, explaining her latest insight or ruthlessly dismantling an interpretation she found lacking. Smart and fierce. And now . . . Emma felt something hidden—trapped—clawing its way out from inside.

She took a steadying breath. Ian and Ethan and the tiny voice inside her head that told her to fit in, blend in, not be too much, they had convinced her that she was wrong to play this game, his game. But it was her game, too, and she knew she could win.

"Where do we start?"

Rory reached out and gripped her shoulder. "With the story. Don't focus on the girls—just read the story as a text or narrative to be analyzed. Scene One: A girl is found dressed as Ophelia."

She shook her head in frustration. "We can't keep covering the same ground. The quote he left me tonight was Byron . . ."

"Emma." He squeezed, his digging fingers just short of painful. "What would you tell a student struggling with a difficult text? Give up? Move on to something new?"

"To read it again, critically. Annotate. Ask questions." Emma shook off Rory's hands. "Point taken. Although, I'd be less patronizing about it."

Rory's smile was soft, but she saw a hint of triumph in his eyes. "Occupational hazard. Scene One, then. Ophelia."

"She's Hamlet's girlfriend, he rejects her, she dies of grief . . ." Emma began.

"No. He chose Ophelia for a reason—what does it mean? What's the story *he's* telling, not the one we already know."

"Right, right. She's deceitful, unfaithful. She represents innocence lost, rejection," Emma corrected, reaching for the character, the perspective she needed. "She's Eve, Pandora, the embodiment of Original Sin. She betrayed a man and paid for it." Emma could feel the anger coil in her stomach, but she reached beyond it to find his truth. "He's saying this figure of innocence—the girl and the character—was actually a figure of iniquity. It's a punishment and a warning."

"Good." Rory's voice was soft, coaxing. "Scene Two: Another girl, blonde, pretty. Posed as . . ."

"Elaine of Astolat. She pursued Lancelot, tried to get him to betray his code, tempted him to sin, she died out of spite." She felt goose bumps rise across her skin as she let herself sink into this dark mindset. "By mixing Mallory's version with Tennyson's, he's simultaneously exposing her true nature and taming it. She's an offering to those who see the world the way he does . . . and a warning to those who don't."

"Keep going," Rory encouraged. "How does the third scene fit in?"

"The third . . . Olivia." The name was like a blow to Emma's sternum. She hesitated.

Rory's face hardened for just a moment. "No, not Olivia. Who is the next scene about?"

"I—I don't know. She doesn't fit." Emma took a step away from him. "Olivia's not his type; he killed her too quickly..."

"Who was she in the pictures?"

Emma felt her breath quicken. "I didn't look at them properly. I should have, but I—couldn't. I was upset."

"Anything you remember?" Rory pressed, ignoring the show of emotion.

Emma took a breath, trying to focus. "Her hair was down, loose. She was in a green dress—brocade or maybe velvet. Thick, textured. There wasn't enough to identify any references."

"What else did he give you? You mentioned *Othello*."

"Another quote... about Desdemona..."

"Who was Desdemona," Rory pressed, his voice low.

"She was an innocent victim," Emma stated firmly, knowing it wasn't what he wanted, but knowing it was right.

"Em..."

"No." Emma stepped back, crossing her arms over her stomach. "No," she repeated. "There isn't another way to read Desdemona; there just isn't. The story isn't even about her." She closed her eyes as something whispered at the back of her brain. "The quote was something Iago says to Othello. He's convinced that Othello has betrayed him and decides to destroy Othello's life. He persuades him to strangle Desdemona in their marriage bed."

"Because she cheated on Othello?" Rory prompted.

"But she didn't. It's not like the other two stories: There's no ambiguity—at all. Iago knows she's innocent because he's the one who framed her."

"Emma..."

"Just listen. The story isn't about Desdemona. She doesn't matter to Iago. He barely knows her, doesn't care about her at all. She was just a pawn. This story's not about Olivia. But maybe she's the message."

"Then we need to decipher it."

"What if . . ." Emma's pulse sped as she felt something snick closer to its place. "Rory, the first quote, Sarah's, was something Hamlet said. The second was spoken by Lancelot. The killer sees himself in those characters as a tragic hero. But this time, he's cast himself as Iago, the villain— Why?"

"It's his story, remember. Othello is a cuckold, a dupe. What if he sees Iago as the hero?"

"God. You're right." She felt vaguely nauseated. Iago was a fascinating character because he was unreliable, unrelenting, unremorseful—because he was unredeemed. That's why he was terrifying. "One of the reasons that Iago lists for destroying Othello is a rumor that he slept with Iago's wife. He's a man betrayed by a faithless lover—just like the others." Emma could see the disparate pieces begin to form an image. "Is that what this is? A mediocre man taking revenge on women he thinks have betrayed him? But why not pose Olivia as Iago's wife, then?"

Rory shook his head. "Like you said, the story's not about her this time. What else is different?"

"Me," Emma whispered, with certainty. "The killer could have sent his message to anyone, to the newspaper, the police . . . But he sent it to me." She crossed the room and dropped into the sofa.

Rory sat down next to her. "Maybe it's not you, specifically. Maybe it's what you know—or who. Your relationship with the detective? He could be trying to distract Carter by targeting you. Or it could be jealousy. Killers aren't the only ones with obsessive devotees."

"But we're not . . ." But Emma couldn't finish. She shut her eyes.

"Emma. I'm not going to pretend that I understand the situation here, but he seemed ready to take me out—just for coming up your walkway. That's not the behavior of someone simply doing their job."

"But why not just kill me, then? Why not make me Desdemona? If the killer is Iago, then Ian is Othello, and I'm . . . The story would make more sense that way."

"Then we've got the story wrong." Rory took a slow breath. "We need to look at all three scenes together . . . Okay, try this. The detective's the foil; the killer's the hero. But he's more than that, right? Because he's not just a character, he's the author."

"Fucking postmodernism," Emma muttered.

"Okay, yes, it fits my ongoing theory. But hear me out—these stories are all about transformation in one way or another. *Hamlet* is about a descent into madness and ruin. Lancelot goes from defender to betrayer. Iago turns Othello from hero to villain."

"So the killer is transforming himself into The Artist . . ."

"At the same time, he's transforming the girls into something, someone new. What if that's your role here, too?"

"Murder victim?"

"No. Metamorphosis."

"I don't— What does that even mean?"

"After this past week—" Rory hesitated "—you're not Emily Dickinson anymore, Em. You've challenged yourself, pushed yourself. And now he's pushing you. Maybe . . . maybe he's trying to transform you, to create you just in a different way."

"So I'm just a puppet? Great, thanks for that."

"I'm not saying that's what you are, Emma. I'm suggesting that's how he sees you."

Emma felt a wave of disgust. "Why me, though? Why not someone famous, someone influential? It doesn't make sense. If he wanted to . . . create . . . someone, why pick me? I'm just a literature professor."

"And Miss Marple was just a spinster." Rory's mouth tipped up, and Emma realized he was echoing their past conversation. "But do you remember what else she was called?"

Emma shook her head.

"'One of my names,' she said, 'is Nemesis.' Maybe he picked you because he knew that you weren't 'just' anything."

"Wrong story," she whispered, shivering.

"Is it? Shakespeare, Christie—most unnatural murders, bodies in the library—they're all detective stories, really. What if we're being too pedantic, too focused on the texts themselves. Maybe we need to approach this from a different direction."

"So . . . what? We've got one part medieval romance and one part Elizabethan tragedy, with a little bit of Victoriana and just a dash of golden age detective fiction—" Emma broke off with a shake of her head. "The paintings, the quotes, the clues . . . it can't be random, Rory. There has to be a connective thread, something that ties it all together."

"Look, it's almost 2:00 a.m.—" Rory scrubbed at his face. "You're exhausted. And I don't even know what I'm saying anymore. Maybe we should . . ."

"You're right. It's too late for this," Emma agreed, but the tangled skeins of his theory were weaving through her mind. The killer's story—when did it start? With the first murder? At the gala? Had he watched her fumbling through her first conversation with Ian and then decided—? But Sarah was already dead by then. Was she—Emma—a later revision, a foil added to keep the audience interested? Had he chosen her—

"Too late," Emma repeated, breaking off the spiraling thoughts before they could draw tighter around her. Emma stood and walked over to the counter where the untouched coffee had cooled to an unappealing lukewarm. She debated reheating it but instead dumped it down the drain. "If you're right, that means I know him, doesn't it?"

"Maybe. But it could be someone who's made up a relationship with you, someone delusional—a store clerk, the mailman, someone who passed you in the street . . ." Rory rose and went to her. "I'm so sorry. I hate that you have to go through this." He drew her gently to him.

For just a moment, Emma let herself burrow into him, tucking her face against his chest and looping her arms around his waist. She felt his chin drop onto the top of her head as they stood quietly.

After a moment, Rory pulled back. Emma didn't let go.

"Do you want me to leave?" he asked.

"No."

"Do you want me to sleep on the couch?"

Emma thought for a moment, relaxing into his warmth. "No."

"Do you want me to get naked? We never did get naked."

Emma laughed against his shirt. "No. I just want to hear you breathe. Can you just stay with me for a bit and . . . ?"

"Breathe? Yeah, I can do that." He kissed the top of her head. "Come on, then. Let's hit the sack."

They moved to the bedroom, still touching. Emma straightened the mussed covers and crawled in. Rory sat at the foot of the bed, pulling off his shoes and unhooking his wristwatch. He set the watch on the bedside table and slid, still dressed, into the bed next to Emma. He reached over and took her hand. Emma reached up with her other hand to flip off the light, then hesitated.

"Would you mind if I left the light on?"

"No, of course not."

Emma curled into his warmth, clinging to that moment of normality, and finally allowed the weight of the day to press her into a dreamless sleep.

Chapter 21

Ian waited as Dr. Ivy Wollard stepped out of autopsy suite two, pulling off a set of latex gloves as she walked. His eyes felt gritty, and his neck was stiff after half a night spent in the car and the other half spent driving in circles. He'd finally gone back to Emma's house around dawn. Tamblyn's car was still parked outside. Part of him believed that the other man genuinely was untrustworthy, but he couldn't tell any longer which part it was. He hadn't been a cop, ready to brawl in the street outside Emma's house. He didn't know who he'd been. He'd come to the office early and left as soon as Mike walked in, choosing the fluorescent lights of the morgue over discussing his behavior at Emma's the day before. If Mike hadn't heard about his near altercation with Tamblyn, he would shortly.

"Detective," Ivy greeted him brusquely. The body of Phillipa Minor, still on the stainless steel table, was barely visible through the closing door. Ian felt a thick press of failure, knowing that she wasn't the last who would lie there.

"Doctor."

"I don't think it'll be worth your trip. There's nothing earth-shattering. Cause of death was extensive blood loss from a laceration of both radial arteries. No signs of sexual assault, well hydrated, ate within a few hours of her death, a lack of defensive wounds and injection marks in the arm suggest sedation—we're still waiting on a tox panel. My people are working the trace evidence, but from what they've said so far, nothing there will lead you to this guy. It might help you build a circumstantial case, but . . ."

"But first, we have to find the guy."

"Sorry, Ian. The best I can do is to confirm a pattern. Good luck." The small woman strode past Ian, leaving him alone in the chilly hallway. With a sigh, he began the trek back to the precinct.

Mike was at his desk. Seated next to him in a chair scavenged from the conference room was Emma. Both of them looked up as Ian approached. Emma's face was passive.

"Morning," Ian said, nodding at her as he sat down at his desk. He felt a flush of embarrassment and busied himself straightening papers so that he didn't have to meet her eye.

"Good morning." Her voice was soft and uninflected.

"Professor Reilly was just giving her statement about yesterday's events."

"I'm afraid that I don't have much to add." Emma didn't look at him.

Mike ignored the awkwardness and continued his questioning. "Can you think of anything that sets this quote apart from the others? Or anything that connects them?"

"I think that Desdemona was painted by at least one of the Pre-Raphaelites, but . . ." Emma shook her head. Her eyes flashed to Ian and then back. He was surprised by the urge to reach out to her. He picked up a pen and pressed the cap against his palm just hard enough to be distracting.

"And the Byron?" Mike prompted.

"I just don't know. He's not connected that I know of, but—like I said, he's not an author I've read that well. I don't teach him. I think it was just saying . . . stay away."

"Okay," Mike said. "Okay, I'm going to get your statement typed up. Sit tight for a few minutes." He got up, took the notepad that he had been writing on, and crossed the room.

Emma nodded, biting down on her bottom lip. She twisted a piece of fabric from her top between her fingers. "Ian, about last night . . ."

Her voice faded, and Ian felt an unreasoning burst of hope.

Then she continued. "I just want to thank you for keeping an eye on me. That was . . . kind."

He studied Emma—her breathing was rapid, nervous. There was something he was supposed to say, supposed to do. "Of course," he said instead.

He could feel the rigidness in his muscles and thought what he must look like to her: arms crossed, lowered brows, shifting weight. He had interviewed enough suspects who looked just like this to know what it said—guilt. He tried to relax his body into a neutral position.

Emma smiled uncertainly. "And to apologize for . . . everything?" She shrugged. "I'm usually more . . . composed than I have been since . . . honestly, since you met me."

The lifted eyebrows, taut forehead, arms pulled inward protectively—distress, Ian read. She was uneasy, unsure of what to say. And she was here anyway, offering to turn the page on everything that had happened.

Before Ian could marshal a response, Mike dropped the typed statement in front of Emma, startling them both. Emma offered Ian a tight smile, then looked away.

"Alright, Professor, read this over. If there's anything off, let me know. If it's all good, just sign there at the bottom."

She took the pages and read through them slowly before reaching for an offered pen and signing her name at the bottom.

Emma let her breath out slowly. "Is there anything else that I can do to help?"

"No, that's all for now. Thank you." Mike rose and gestured to the door. "Let me walk you out."

Ian watched as the two moved through the busy room, Mike's head bowed down toward Emma's. He reached over and lifted the signed statement from Mike's desk. He read it quickly. She had been clear and concise, walking them through the minutes as she woke from a nap after the funeral, made tea, found the envelope at the door, went to the sofa, opened the envelope to find the pictures—upside down—and slowly looked through them.

I tried to call Detective Carter, but he did not pick up. I then tried to reach him through the main line at the police station but was told he was not available. I then asked for Detective Kellogg . . .

Her words sounded sure and calm, as if she had simply called for a hair appointment and found out that the stylist was booked.

Ian skimmed the rest of the statement, which included Officer Davis's arrival, followed by Mike and the other uniformed officers. As he was finishing, Mike returned and dropped into his chair, which groaned under his sudden weight.

"What do you think?" he asked Ian, nodding toward the statement.

"Clear, concise. Nothing we didn't know."

"She hasn't done enough to solve the case?"

The dig hit uncomfortably close, but Ian just shrugged. "Any other new information?"

"I got more on the Ackerman girl, the one who was just reported missing. She fits the type. Good student, well-liked, last seen heading into town on her bike." Mike scanned a printout from his desk.

"Who made the report?"

"Roommate couldn't reach her and called campus police. They called us."

"Parents?"

"Live in Pennsylvania. They haven't heard from her either, and the phone's going to voicemail."

"Battery could have died."

"Could have." The men sat in silence for a moment before Mike added, "Patrols are looking for her. Anything from the delightful Dr. Wollard?"

Ian quickly summed up Ivy's findings from the autopsy. "Which leaves us pretty much where we were." He sighed. "Let me see the photos of Olivia Ballard. I didn't have a chance to look at them properly yesterday."

Mike lifted several plastic evidence bags from a pile on his desk and handed them across to Ian. "They've been dusted, no prints."

Ian spread them out, side by side. These seemed less expert than the last two sets. Those had been thoughtfully framed and shot, more art prints than snapshots. The photographer had taken time. These, though, seemed almost haphazard, like someone had just stood in a convenient spot, pointed the camera, and snapped. The lighting was uneven, taken with a flash that hadn't been properly adjusted for the location. There were four images in total, all seemingly from the same angle. One showed Olivia Ballard's torso from elbow to ankle, the focus on the emerald-colored gown. Ian bent close, looking for any identifiable details. The fabric looked relatively inexpensive and was bordered with gold lace. Her ankles were bare and smudged with dirt. The next image was shot slightly farther down the body so that the feet were visible. One foot was covered by a plain black ballet flat, decidedly modern; the other foot was bare—streaked with grass stains and marked by bruises that had just been beginning to rise.

The next two showed the upper part of Olivia's body, a closer shot of her chest and one of her head. The image of her chest focused on the gown's bodice, which dipped low over her breasts and featured the same gold lace as the hem. Her chest was crisscrossed with pale pink scratches, and bruises circled her throat.

The final image showed the woman's face quite clearly. She lay on bare earth, her hair down around her shoulders and matted on one side. A dried leaf was caught in the brunette mass. Her face had the unnatural, unmistakable pallor of the dead, the skin glossed with a waxy sheen. The brown eyes were open.

Ian flipped the photo over, reading the words printed there. This was the one that held the message for Emma. He scrutinized the images, looking for any indication of where they might have been taken. But for all their artlessness, the photographer had been careful to reveal just the body and the bit of earth that it lay upon. Ian turned his attention to cause of death. There was distinct bruising, but not enough to indicate blunt force trauma. There was no blood, no obvious wounds, though, of course, if she had been dressed postmortem, they might be hidden. The marks on her neck were the only clue.

Ian moved through the photos once more before sitting back and looking at his partner. "This doesn't fit. She's dirty and bruised. She's been dressed in a costume, but she's not posed like the others. Those re-created specific elements of the stories. This looks like she was just dropped on the ground."

"We've been tracing her movements," Mike added, "and there are witnesses who saw her after her shift at the Bean Bag. She wasn't taken and held."

"So, does Olivia's death mean that Dana Ackerman's not connected? Or are we just waiting for another set of photos?" Ian rose to get a cup of stale coffee. "Same look, same age—missing four days now."

"Ballard breaks the pattern. She was taken and killed on the same day. The staging is half-hearted at best, nothing like the detailed scenes he's set up before. Maybe she wasn't part of the plan. He snagged her for some other reason; killed her quick. He could still be holding Ackerman."

"Is that why the photos were sent to Emma rather than the tabloid? Because she's not part of his official . . ." Ian paused but couldn't come up with a better word. "Oeuvre?"

"Maybe it was because the paper didn't publish the last batch. Or because they were hoping to avoid the cops. Or it's a warning, to you—her—who knows. How much do you know about the professor's personal history?"

"Not much. But . . . I think there's something between her and Tamblyn." Ian tried to sound indifferent. Mike picked up a pen and printed something across his notepad. He held it up for Ian to see: *ALIBI*.

Ian lifted his chin. "Not for Olivia Ballard."

"You can't fit him to the original murders, so now he's a copycat?" Mike's tone was not amused.

"Just trying to keep an open mind," Ian snapped.

"Well," Mike replied sarcastically, "let's just assume that's a ridiculous theory. Killers like this want to be involved, yeah? They get their jollies from the attention, so they like to keep tabs on the case. He sends pictures to the newspapers to make sure everyone knows what he's up to, and then he watches the cops to see how we're getting on. Probably enjoys being close. How many people knew about you and the professor?"

"There's nothing to know."

"Look, Carter, I don't give a crap about your love life, but maybe someone out there does. There's no way this killer hasn't been keeping up with the case; he's gotta be living for the attention. And he clearly wants to have a relationship with us, or he wouldn't be leaving us love notes at every crime scene. He's seen you in the news; he knows who you are. He might be messing with her to get to you."

Ian pursed his lips, checking his instinctive retort. "We met at an art exhibit the night that Sarah Weston's body was discovered. A lot of people could have seen us. We went to a diner after Emma was mugged—there were a few customers there, waitstaff. Two officers took her statement. I went to the college that Monday; her students saw me. Maybe a few other people. Then dinner at my house, then she came here—you saw her, the desk sergeant, most of the precinct probably. I stopped by her house to apologize that night—it was a short visit. That's it."

"Really? You've been acting out a country-western song over a girl you ate dinner with once?"

"She left before dinner."

"Jesus, Ian. That's pathetic."

"Thanks. I'm aware. Look, there's nothing there. Someone might have seen Emma and me talking, but I can't see anyone thinking that Emma would be a way to get to me."

"Unless they've seen you over the past week."

Ian ignored that. "A better possibility is that someone's realized that she's been investigating the crime. She told me she went to the first scene. She—" Ian sighed. "I think she and Tamblyn have been working together to solve the crimes."

"Oh, fuck me sideways."

"I'm not accusing them of anything," Ian protested. "I'm just saying that maybe they weren't all that discreet."

Mike considered this reluctantly. "She did say that Tamblyn was part of the group that saw Ballard at the café. We should ask if they were sharing murder theories."

"Could be Olivia overheard something, and she passed it along to the wrong person," Ian speculated.

"Damned amateurs. So, what did they uncover that's worth killing for?"

Ian shook his head, picking up the picture of Olivia's face and flipping it over. "'I loathe that low vice—curiosity.'" The quote didn't fit in the rest of the puzzle. "Maybe it's not what they know. Maybe it's something the killer is afraid Emma will figure out."

Chapter 22

Emma stepped into the sunlight outside the precinct and stood for a moment, unsure of where to go. Her classes were canceled, and her home no longer felt like hers. The stream of people on the way to jobs and errands ebbed and flowed around her as she hesitated. Finally, she pulled out her phone, thinking of calling Rory or Carolyn. The sudden vibration in her hand as a call came in startled her to the point that she dropped the phone, and it skittered across the cement. Emma grabbed for it, catching it as it dropped off the edge of the sidewalk.

"Damn, damn, damn." A passing woman gave Emma a sympathetic glance as she stood up and wiped the dirt off the phone screen. A cheerful *ding* announced that the call had gone to voicemail. Before Emma could listen, a text appeared on her screen. It was from Niall and simply said **Call me**.

Shit. She hadn't called him back. Checking the log, she saw half a dozen calls from him and several from Carolyn. Emma quickly hit the buttons to redial the missed call, and Niall picked up on the first ring.

"Emma? I've been trying to call you since yesterday. What's going on?"

"Sorry, with everything that happened, I just didn't . . . but I'm fine. Shaken but fine."

"Wait, what happened?"

"What? The photos. What did you . . . ?"

Niall cut her off. "Someone attacked Charlie. That's why I've been trying to reach you. And then Rory left a message with Carolyn this morning saying that something had happened to you, and we couldn't reach you, and I thought . . ."

"Is she alright?" Emma asked, talking over him. "What happened?"

"She was walking home from the paper, and someone mugged her. Knocked her over and took her purse."

"Is she hurt?"

"No," Niall said, the edge of panic leaving his voice. "A bit bruised, but not seriously hurt." He paused a moment. "What was Rory talking about?"

"Another girl was taken last night or maybe early yesterday."

"Jesus."

Emma could hear voices in the background. "Where are you?"

"I'm at Carolyn and Charlie's. Come over?"

"I'll be right there."

Emma hung up before Niall could respond. Dropping her phone in her bag, Emma rounded the corner and quickly got in her car. In minutes, she was knocking at her friend's door. Niall answered.

He gestured her in, and Emma saw Charlie stretched out on a couch in the small but cheerful living room, with Carolyn seated at her feet. The walls were papered in retro flowers, bright yellow and pink splashing around the room. The couch was a slightly lighter shade of rose, with half a dozen multicolored pillows vying for attention. The surface of every shelf and table was covered with knickknacks, books, and cut flowers. Emma could smell the gentle fragrance of vanilla bean tea candles scattered around the room. Every chair had its own blanket and throw pillow, none of which matched. It should have been overwhelming, but each piece worked in concert to create an atmosphere of cheer.

Emma crossed the room, noticing the fresh bruise rising on Charlie's cheek.

"Are you okay?" Emma asked, dropping her purse on a side table, careful not to unseat the glossy oversized books stacked there.

"Sore, but fine."

"Did you call the police?"

Charlie nodded. "I made a report, but the guy was wearing some sort of mask, like a kid's school project. Creepy as hell. I couldn't tell them much. He just ran up behind me, hit me across the face with something, and grabbed my bag. I kicked him in the knee—dropped him for a minute; he yelped like a dog. But then a neighbor came out, and he got up and ran." Charlie sighed. "My phone and wallet were in my jacket, luckily, so he just got some story notes and research. Hope he's really into local news." She shrugged.

Emma thought of the night of the gala, the cold ground, the scrape of skin against pavement . . .

"When?"

"After work, around six."

"Then . . ." Emma took a breath. "Did Niall tell you another girl was killed?"

Carolyn looked at him, shocked. Charlie looked accusatory.

"I thought you should tell them. I don't know the full story," Niall apologized.

"A girl—Olivia Ballard, a student of mine—was taken sometime yesterday morning or the night before. I went to Sarah's memorial, then came home and took a nap. When I woke around six, I found an envelope slipped under my door." Emma met Charlie's eyes.

"Three pictures, two notes?" Charlie asked.

"Yes. Just like the other two victims."

Emma told them the full story. "I didn't look very closely at the pictures, just enough to recognize her. But the notes were different. He didn't include her name, just two quotes. One from *Othello*—and one from Byron, I think. Something about loathing curiosity. That one was . . . threatening. And addressed to me. By name."

"Three girls in, what, just over a week?" Carolyn's voice held the disbelief that showed in all of their faces.

"Ten days since Sarah Weston was found," Charlie confirmed. "Officially a serial killer, then. Serials usually kill random people—they used to call them 'stranger killers' because of that—but this doesn't feel random."

"No," Emma said. "Sending the pictures to me couldn't have been random."

"So, he knows who you are and . . ."

"And where I live. Yeah," Emma finished Carolyn's thought quietly. There was a brief moment of pause as the thought settled around the room.

"'I loathe that low vice—curiosity,'" Niall murmured. *"Don Juan."*

"That's it," Emma encouraged. Charlie looked impressed.

"Oxford, remember. That incestuous cad is mandated curriculum. If I remember my A levels, that's in a bit where Don Juan is complaining about intelligent women marrying uneducated men."

"Yikes," Carolyn said. "That sounds less like *stay away from that corpse* and more like *stay away from that man*."

"Detective Ian, maybe?" Charlie suggested cautiously. "Is there anyone who'd want to warn you away from him?"

"No, I mean . . . Rory suggested a stalker, maybe a colleague or a student. But I . . ."

"There's definitely an element of dominance in these murders that would fit with a stalker," Niall broke in. "He sees a woman, wants her, gets rejected—at least in his own mind—and then abducts and kills . . ."

"Okay," Charlie cut him off. "Let's say that's the case. Emma, can you think of anyone who fits the profile? Knowledge of art and literature, connected to the college, has shown an interest in you or your life . . ."

"Malcolm," Carolyn said confidently.

"Rory's grad student?" Emma's surprise was clear. "He took a few classes from me, but we've barely spoken outside of class. Why would he care about my love life?"

"Hot for teacher?" Charlie suggested. "A little 'To Professor, with love'?"

"I heard him talk to Rory about you," Carolyn explained. "He was going on and on about how great you are. You make more of an impression than you realize."

"He wasn't particularly adept at literary analysis," Emma protested. "I'm not sure—"

"Does he really need to be good at analysis?" Charlie broke in. "He's basically just misinterpreted a bunch of literature and plagiarized some artwork."

"Or he could be smarter than he lets on," Carolyn added. "And we still haven't really considered the partner angle. Oh! What's that film class he's taking? I saw it when Rory approved his course schedule. Guilt in Media or something . . . Maybe he met a kindred killer there. A *Murder by Numbers* sort of thing."

Niall and Emma exchanged a glance; Niall shook his head.

"It's basically *Rope* with Sandra Bullock," Charlie supplied.

"Of course you nerds only watch Hitchcock," Carolyn scoffed. "But, really, he could have a partner. He knows the art; his other half understands the literature."

"Okay. But why would both of them have the same—weird—MO?" Charlie asked.

"*Folie à deux*," Niall offered. "A shared delusion."

"Thanks. But you don't get credit for the theory just because you speak French," Carolyn informed him dryly.

"Touché." Niall grinned at Carolyn's eye roll. "But a crush on Emma isn't much of a motive if there are two people involved. This still feels like a loner to me, someone metaphorically killing his father by remaking their work in his own image."

"Either way," Carolyn circled back, "it could be Malcolm. If ever there was a loner . . . and the way he begs for Rory's attention screams daddy issues."

Emma shook her head. "I don't know."

"What about the other quote?" Niall asked. "Maybe there's something there."

"Something Iago says to Othello. I think he posed Olivia as Desdemona. I didn't see much in the photos, but she was in a green-and-white dress, I think."

Niall straightened, then reached for his phone. He typed for a minute, then showed Emma a portrait of a young woman with dark hair, her chin resting on one hand. She wore a white silk gown with a green brocade overdress. "Something like this? He's cribbed from Lord Leighton this time."

"A levels again?" Charlie asked.

"Home field advantage. It's on display in London."

"That's her," Emma interrupted their banter softly. "Desdemona. But he . . . just copied it, I think. There was no setup that I could see, no scene. Just . . . Olivia . . . on the ground. In the dirt." Emma felt her throat tighten.

Carolyn glanced discretely at Emma and cleared her throat. "Maybe enough murder for one day."

Seeing the concern on her roommate's face, Charlie quickly got onside. "Right. Absolutely. Let's just order Thai and watch something pointless."

The four of them spent the rest of the afternoon pointedly ignoring the world beyond their walls, debating the merits of the British bakers as they watched the rise and fall of unfortunately named cakes. Despite the easy banter, though, Emma could tell the distraction had failed. Charlie's thumbs sped across her phone every few minutes, jotting down insights as they came to her. Niall tried to scroll unobtrusively, flashes of pale Pre-Raphaelite heroines betraying where his mind was really at. Carolyn kept displaying bright smiles, too tight around the edges, as she offered Emma food and drinks and blankets and anything else that might bring comfort. And Emma's own brain insisted on reciting Iago's soliloquies on repeat, adding a sinister undertone to the crowing of that week's best baker.

As dusk began painting the sky, Emma was sent off with a bag of leftovers and a mandate to keep the others updated, even if nothing happened. She promised that she would and assured them all that she would be fine under the protection of her designated patrol officer. She didn't mention that she planned to invite Rory over or that Ian would probably be lurking in the darkness under the guise of surveillance.

She texted Rory from the car, and when she got home, he was waiting with burgers from her favorite guilty pleasure place. He looked pointedly at her bag of Thai.

"Dinner?" he asked, gesturing.

"Leftovers. But a burger sounds great."

He shifted the burgers to one hand and reached for the Thai food as Emma unlocked the door. Rory followed her in, not commenting as she hesitated in the foyer. He moved around her, setting the food down in the kitchen, then moved swiftly through the house as Emma waited.

"All good," Rory said, holding out a hand.

Emma let out a breath she hadn't realized she'd been holding. "Silly of me."

"No," Rory said simply. Then, "Let's eat before it's cold."

They ate their food in the kitchen while talking about inconsequential things, then moved to the living room. Rory turned to one of Emma's many bookshelves and pulled out a book on the Tudors. "Quiet time?" he asked, holding it up. "I think I could use a night off from . . . everything."

"Perfect," Emma responded with a grateful look. Rory settled onto the couch while Emma took *Jane Eyre* from her purse and turned to her favorite scene, allowing herself to settle into the world. They had been reading in companionable silence for about an hour when Emma flipped a page and saw faint blue script stretching above the printed text. The writing wasn't hers.

"'From false to false, among false maids in love . . .'" She read aloud.

"Sorry." Rory glanced up from his book. "What?"

"Rory, have you read this?"

"*Jane Eyre*? I'm sure I did in some undergrad class or other. Why?"

"But have ever you borrowed my copy?"

"No. I've never really been into the Romantics. Too much tortured symbolism. Why?"

"Do you recognize this writing?" Emma passed him the book.

Rory looked at the page, his eye scanning the scribbled annotations. "It's yours, isn't it?"

"The one on the top . . . in blue."

"Maybe a student? You're one of the professors who make the rest of us look bad with open office hours."

"I keep this in my purse most of the time. Rory, what if it's . . . ?"

"Is it recent?"

"I don't know. I haven't read it in . . . months? Longer?"

"I'm sure it's nothing. Someone vandalized a book," he soothed. "Not every Shakespearean reference is about murder."

"You're right; I'm just . . . tired. Chasing phantoms." Emma rose and placed the book on one of the wide shelves already stuffed with books. "I think I'm done for the day."

"Shall I stay again?"

"No. No, I'm fine alone."

"I'll text you when I get home," Rory said, sounding subdued.

"Thanks, Rory," Emma said, finally meeting his eyes. "Genuinely. For everything. I'll send an SOS to the group-chat if anything happens, and I'll call you tomorrow."

"Try to get some sleep." Rory reached out and slid his hand along her arm. Leaning in, he brushed a kiss across her cheek. "I'll go full white knight if I don't hear from you, just remember."

Emma laughed dutifully, but stayed where she stood as he gathered his things and headed to the foyer. She heard the soft thud of the door closing, then quickly followed his steps, locking the deadbolt behind him.

Chapter 23

"Couple of kids just found a body in the woods. Matches our vic."

Ian looked up as Mike entered the conference room that Ian had commandeered to organize their investigation. "Was she posed?"

"God, you look like shit," Mike said.

Ian lifted a brow. "You want me to dress up to go see the corpse?"

"So, it's fun-time Ian today. Okay." Mike sighed. "Not posed, but it's a dark-haired woman who is, quote, 'dressed like some chick from the Renaissance faire,' unquote."

"Olivia Ballard."

"Likely. Come on."

Ian grabbed his jacket from where it had fallen on the floor and shrugged it on.

"Now you look like yesterday's shit."

"I crashed on the couch in the break room. Didn't have time to go home and change."

"Would it help if I tell you that you're being an idiot?"

"No." Ian pointed to the door. "Are we going?"

"Lead the way, Boy Scout."

Ian left the room, Mike trailing behind. The ride to the crime scene was silent except for Mike's off-key whistling. Ian caught his occasional glances in his periphery but stared resolutely ahead.

A small patch of forest about a hundred feet from the road had been cordoned off with yellow scene-of-crime tape. As they approached through the underbrush, Ian could see a bright patch of bold green cloth against the browning detritus of the forest floor. He felt an odd sense of vertigo as he ducked under the tape and approached the body, the face pressed into the dirt. The last time he'd seen this girl, she'd been arguing about literature in Emma's class.

He crouched down to look at Olivia Ballard's blank, dew-dampened face. Her dark hair was matted and tangled; her skin was smudged with mud. Debris clung to the cheap fabric of the gown, the emerald now clotted with earth.

Ivy Wollard stepped over to Ian and Mike. "This one's definitely not like the others."

"No fancy setup," Mike said, looking around the clearing. "More like a convenient body dump."

"It's more than that. Cause of death is blunt force trauma to the head. My team is searching for the weapon. Lividity suggests she was killed late Thursday to early Friday like you thought. The body was likely carried from the car, then dropped about five feet back, and dragged the rest of the way here." Ivy pointed to where a group of CSI techs had gathered.

"Suggests someone working alone," Ian offered.

"And someone in a hurry. Either we've got a copycat—" Mike glanced at Ian "—or, more likely, our guy's been seriously thrown off his game. The photos were noticeably different from the earlier crimes, too—basic framing, no angled shots, poor lighting. They could have been taken with a phone."

"A copycat's possible; this is definitely the kind of killer to have a fan club," Ian agreed.

"Thanks to Mackey's journalistic integrity, a lot of the details were published with the photos."

"But not my connection to Emma. That's one hell of a lucky guess if it's not our guy." Ian turned to Ivy. "What do you think?"

"Occam's razor."

"What?"

"Occam's razor: the simplest answer is most likely the correct one."

"So, you're guessing a single killer?" Mike asked.

"I'm not guessing. I'm evaluating the information with which I've been presented."

Ivy held out a plastic envelope with a piece of paper sealed inside. "There was a paper shoved in her mouth. That wasn't in the news."

Mike took it from her, quickly skimming it. "Looks like Othello is just about to kill his wife."

"Same MO," Ian pointed out unnecessarily.

"So. We're back to an unknown killer, targeting students at the college, either randomly or not. Good work, team." Mike turned back to the body with a sigh. "Costume looks like a cheap Halloween deal, dollar store variety. Not the same quality as the others."

"The shoe looks modern, likely just whatever she was wearing." Ian moved down toward her feet, scanning the ground around him. "Any sign of the other one?"

"Techs found it a few feet back. Probably came off while she was being dragged."

The two detectives stepped over to the secondary scene, where a black flat lay half embedded in the ground with a yellow evidence marker set next to it. "Sloppy, rushed," Ian noted.

"Whoever he is, something's spooked him," Mike said, looking toward the road.

"Good."

***

They drove back to the precinct on edge, their conversation terse. The desk sergeant informed them that Phillipa Minor's boyfriend, Ethan, was waiting in the interview room, and Mike swore. They'd both forgotten the appointment. He looked up as they entered, and Ian recognized him from the gala, the boy who had tucked Phillipa against his side as she had stared down her would-be assailant. All his bravado was now gone.

Mike led the young man through background questions. The two had been friends for most of their freshman year before Ethan had gotten the nerve to ask her out, just weeks earlier. He described a cheerful girl, always smart and a little mischievous, full of life and promise, a college sophomore excited by her studies and new love. Ethan gave them a list of Phillipa's friends and acquaintances, roommates, classmates, fellow pep squad members. Ian jotted down the names of two boys that Phillipa had dated previously; Ethan reported there was another, an older boy, who had been briefly on the scene at the end of the summer, but he had no details about him. Phillipa, he said, had been serious about none of them. She was too excited about the adventure of college to focus on a relationship. Ian painstakingly matched this list to a similar one he had made for Sarah Weston. Other than a vague reference to an "older boyfriend," there were no common links.

Mike stepped out of the room to get Ethan a soda, and Ian pulled out five pictures and placed them on the table in front of Ethan. The first two were of two officers, included as controls for the lineup. Then, he laid down one of Alex Carmichael, Sarah Weston's dealer. Next was Malcolm Haynes. Ian hesitated for a moment before laying down the last, Rory Tamblyn. He felt vague guilt over the subterfuge, but there was no way Mike would agree to this. Not only would including Tamblyn piss his partner off but showing Ethan the other suspects risked tainting any future lineups that might be held. Ian recognized his own desperation, but the knowledge that three victims had now been found and Dana Ackerman was still missing spurred him on.

Ethan pulled Alex's picture closer, then shook his head. "Sorry, I don't recognize him."

"Not a problem," Ian said. "How about the others?"

The young man considered them all in turn. He paused at Malcolm's photo long enough for hope to build and then shook his head. "He looks kinda familiar. I might have seen him around?"

"Any idea where?"

"School probably, but . . ." He shook his head again. "He's pretty normal looking. I don't know."

Ian repressed a disappointed sigh. "No problem, Ethan. How about the others?"

Ethan reached out again. "I recognize this one. He's a professor." Ethan tapped Rory's photo.

Ian swallowed, trying to suppress a burst of eagerness. "Did Phillipa know him?"

"Did he kill her?" The stoicism disappeared abruptly, and Ian could see the rage and grief simmering in Ethan's eyes as he looked up from the image.

"We . . . have no evidence of that. We're just looking for connections. Did Phillipa ever mention his name, Professor Tamblyn?"

Ethan shook his head once slowly, then again with more confidence. "No. Not to me."

"Okay. Do you know if Phillipa was friends with the other victim, Sarah Weston?"

"Sorry, I— If she knew her, she never said."

"How about Olivia Ballard? Or Dana Ackerman?"

"No. Are they . . . Have there been more murders?"

Ian hesitated just an instant. "We're just looking for possible connections. So Sarah never mentioned any of those names?"

"No. I mean, I don't think so?"

"And you don't know any of them?" Ian threw out the question without any particular purpose and was startled when Ethan visibly tensed in his chair.

"What are you saying?"

Ian raised a placating hand. "Nothing, like I said . . ."

"You're looking for connections, yeah. I heard. But I want to know why you think I'm that connection." Ethan's voice was shaking with emotion, but Ian couldn't tell if it was grief or anger. Both, he thought.

On impulse, Ian switched tracks. "You were at the art gala last week, weren't you?"

Ethan looked confused. "Yes. Why?"

"There was an incident there. Phillipa had some sort of altercation with a man . . ." Ian trailed off as Ethan leaned forward, his shoulders softening as some of his outrage seeped away. "Yeah, some loser was hitting on her. She said it wasn't a big deal. She laughed it off."

"Did you recognize the guy?"

Ethan's eyes dropped to the pictures, clearly picking up on an eagerness Ian was trying to keep from his voice. He scanned the photos, and Ian thought his eyes paused briefly on Malcolm's picture. But he shook his head, his expression returning to confusion, then frustration.

"I didn't pay much attention to him. He was just some guy. Brown hair, I think? I just thought he was some loser." Ethan looked up, his eyes damp.

Mike came in just as Ian swept the photos away. He handed over the soda with a quizzical look, taking in Ethan's distress. The young man set the drink, unopened, on the table.

"Is there anything else? I—I'd like to go now if I can." Ethan seemed deflated.

"Of course," Mike said. "We'll call if we have any other questions."

An older officer escorted him out, and Ian watched them cross the precinct in silence.

"So what now? We wait for the next body?" Mike asked, sinking into his desk chair and running a hand across his face.

"Unless he slips up," Ian agreed.

"He has." Both men turned to see Ivy Wollard walking up to them. "We found skin under the victim's fingernails. She fought back."

"Good for you, Olivia," Mike said softly.

"He took her in a hurry," Ivy continued. "There was no sedation. We can definitively tie whoever this is to at least this victim."

"I could kiss you," Mike offered.

"It would be the last thing you do."

"Tease."

Ian interrupted. "Any hits on the DNA, Ivy?"

"Still running it, but nothing so far."

"Keep us posted," Ian told her. "And Ivy . . ." Ian didn't finish, but he saw her tight nod. Time was running out.

Chapter 24

Having taken a long, circuitous route to the college, Emma arrived feeling foolish. No one had followed her. She pushed open her car door, a sharp wind shoving back against her as she stepped out. The morning was eerily quiet without the usual laughter and chatter of students. Reports of the murders had been picked up by the national news after videos of Sarah's memorial went viral, and college administrators had released a flurry of statements trying to balance calming assurances with legally sufficient cautions that would inoculate them against future culpability. Emma assumed they knew about Olivia by now as well.

With the flyers for the first memorial still fluttering on light posts and a second already scheduled, they'd abandoned any attempts at normalcy and given the professors the option of moving their classes online. Most had, and those who hadn't faced empty classrooms as students fed both each other's paranoia and determination to not waste their one life. An informal buddy system had been organized among the few stalwarts still on campus, and the sharp glint of keys pierced the fisted fingers of any girl who walked alone. Someone had chalked "Gather ye rosebuds" onto the sidewalk next to a makeshift memorial that had been set up at the center of the quad, and Emma felt a thrum of pain as she remembered Olivia's passionate discussion of the poem last term. She'd hated it, truly and deeply. The world was now a little less fierce with Olivia gone.

Emma had decided that she wasn't going to just sit and wait for something to happen, so she sought out the closed and careful realm of her office. She gathered the stack of reference texts that she had brought from home, tucked her purse awkwardly on top of the pile, and crossed quickly from the parking lot to the liberal arts building where she and Rory both had offices. The door was locked when she tugged on it. She leaned forward, bracing the books between her body and the glass of the door as she burrowed into her purse, digging one-handed. She felt the jagged edge of a key and pinched it between her fingers, dragging it upward. Emma grunted in frustration when she found herself holding her car and house keys; her work keys were tucked in her messenger bag at home.

"Dammit," she muttered. She pulled out her phone, debating whether she could call Carolyn or Rory to come to her rescue. She swirled her lock pattern across the screen, but before she could dial, a message popped up.

CHARLIE: I made a murder board.

A link brought up a full record of their theories, complete with pictures and connecting lines.

Niall responded with the expected red-string meme, while Carolyn added: Working from home . . . this is ALL she's been doing. Send help.

Emma smiled and began scrolling for an appropriate gif when a voice interrupted her reverie.

"Are you okay?"

Emma shrieked, spinning around toward the voice. Her phone, books, and purse spilled into a jumble on the pavement. Malcolm stood, his mouth slightly agape, hand raised in a defensive posture.

"Sorry! I didn't mean to scare you. Here, I'll help." He dropped to his knees and began to gather Emma's things, shoving them gracelessly into her purse by the handful.

"Not your fault. I seem to be doing this a lot lately." Emma looked at his shaggy head bent as he scrambled on the sidewalk and struggled to match the image with the previous night's suspicions. She dropped down beside him and began to gather the books into a pile. "What are you doing on campus today?"

He shrugged. "I don't like hanging out at my house, and it's nice here without all the people. Quiet. I'm glad to see you, though." Malcolm thrust her purse forward before she could respond and then held out his other hand. "Your keys."

"Thanks," Emma said, dropping them into the bag. She stood and started back to her car. Malcolm walked in step with her.

"Weren't you going in?"

"Wrong keys." Emma tugged her purse close. "I left the others at home."

"Oh, wait. I have one." Malcolm pulled a ragged navy backpack around to the front of his body and rummaged through. He pulled out a neon keychain. "Dr. Tamblyn gave me a copy so I could get in on weekends and grade exams for his class." He jogged back to the door, slid the key into the lock, twisted, and jerked the door open. He held it open for her expectantly. "It's okay. I'm allowed."

Emma tilted sideways so that there was space between them as she walked through the door. "Thanks." She paused before adding, "I'm glad you were here."

The boy looked pleased at the acknowledgment. "Do you need a hand?"

"No. It's okay."

"Are you sure? I don't mind."

"No, Malcolm." Emma heard the sharpness in her voice and offered a smile. "I appreciate the offer. But I'm fine."

Emma tugged the door closed between them as he shrugged, looking disappointed. She watched as he started down the sidewalk, then stooped to pick something up. Tucking it in his pocket, he continued around the corner and out of sight. Emma turned away from the hallway leading to her own door and trudged up to Rory's office, trying to shake off the uneasy feeling Malcolm left in his wake. She'd spent the morning organizing her house, feigning control by putting things where they belonged. Feeding her brain an organizational task sometimes distracted it enough that she could focus, and Rory's unreturned book was a nagging loose thread. She would leave the book by the door if it were locked.

To her surprise, not only was the door unlocked—it was standing open. Rory looked up as she knocked lightly on his door frame.

"Emma," he said, his face open with shock.

"Hey. What are you . . . ? Are you looking for something?" Emma tried to keep her face from betraying her concern but knew she'd failed as Rory's eyes dropped from hers. The customary neatness of his office had been replaced with chaos. Drawers hung open, papers were scattered and falling on the floor, and the computer screen showed a dozen open windows. Rory was seated at his desk, books strewn around him. He ran a hand through his hair, the usually artful strands already cast into disarray. Purple smudges shadowed his eyes, and taut lines cut along an unconvincing smile.

"Yeah, I was just . . ." He faltered. "Nothing. It's nothing, just a bad idea."

"Is everything okay?"

Rory hesitated, then seemed to decide on something. "Carolyn told me you were all at her house the other night discussing theories." His voice was slightly accusatory. "She insinuated you thought Malcolm might be . . . It's not him, Em. It can't be. He's a good kid, deep down. I know it. I was trying to find a record of an appointment or notes somewhere that could provide an alibi or prove . . ." He shook his head.

"I wanted to bring your book back," Emma evaded, feeling a sliver of guilt that Rory hadn't been at Carolyn's to offer an initial defense of Malcolm but knowing, too, that the conversation would not have gone well.

"It's not him, Emma."

She wavered for a moment. Rory seemed certain. She trusted his judgment, she did, and she didn't want to hurt him. But something had kindled at the back of her mind, and she couldn't resist touching the flame. If Carolyn was right—if there was a chance they could stop this before another girl died—the burns would be worth it. "Rory, did you know that he had keys to the building?"

"What? Maybe. A lot of the TAs do." His face tightened. "You don't agree with her, do you? He's just lonely, Em." He picked up a handful of papers from his desk and shoved them into one of the open drawers. "He told me how kind you were to him."

He watched her intently, clearly expecting a sharp retort. She picked up a photo from the nearest chair—a snapshot of the two of them on their study abroad in England—and placed it on the desk so she could sit. It was the only personal item in the professional space, and Emma felt a pang of sympathy. Maybe he could prove them wrong, prove Malcolm innocent. If not, Rory would need a friend, not an opponent.

"Have you found anything?" she asked, keeping her tone soft and noncommittal.

Rory let out a breath. "Not really. I dug out the newspaper article to check the dates, thinking that I could prove that Malcolm . . . and anyway, I started thinking about the photos again. Then I started thinking about this." Rory reached for a book. "Did you know that photography played a significant role in Victorian art? Some Pre-Raphaelites even used daguerreotypes to paint from. Look." He showed her a sepia-toned photo of a woman in a boat, a leafy tree centered behind her.

Emma felt a chill dash across her skin. "She's not . . . ?"

"Dead? No. It's a tableau. At the same time our friend Millais was painting, photographers like Cameron and Robinson—" he tapped the page "—they were re-creating the same stories using live models and photography."

"So . . ."

"So, maybe the killer isn't just imitating famous paintings like Charlie suggested." Rory was excited by the idea, leaning close to Emma as he explained. "The photos, Em. This must be why he's taking photos. It's someone who knows the period, the history. He's a scholar."

Emma lifted the open book to see the image better. "Does Malcolm have access to all of these?" She tried to keep the question casual.

"I already told you, Emma, it can't be him. Think about what I was saying the other night about you playing a role in his story. If he's a scholar, then it might be someone you know from a conference or grad school. Maybe someone who's read your work or saw you present or—"

"Or maybe it's someone who knows me from Carlisle. Carolyn thinks maybe he has a partner who's helping him, someone he met in a class—"

"What about your students, then?" Rory crossed his arms over his chest, his voice hard.

"What?" Emma flinched back, startled by the challenge.

Rory grabbed another newspaper from his desk, thrusting it toward her. "You recognize him?"

Emma took the paper. It was open to the obituaries, and Emma saw the smiling face that she now recognized as Phillipa Minor. She was wearing a Carlisle sweatshirt, clearly posing at some tailgating event. Beside her, smiling just as big, was Ethan. "He's in my Gothic Lit class," Emma told him. "But you can't be suggesting . . ."

"Why not? He's got a better motive than Malcolm does. Wasn't Carolyn's *first* theory the boyfriend?"

Emma remembered Ethan sobbing outside of Sarah's funeral. "No. There's no way. I saw him the other day; he was devastated."

"So is every grieving husband who pushes his wife down the stairs or drowns her in the bathtub and then sobs to the media about how he'll never forget her. He was manipulating you."

"You weren't there, Rory." Emma set the paper on the desk, turning the photo face down. "You don't know him."

"But I met him, remember? He practically challenged me to fight him behind the middle school. I'm guessing he's one of those students who like to be the center of attention, makes outlandish comments, pushes back on your ideas just to challenge your authority . . ."

"He's just—" Emma tried to defend Ethan, but Rory cut her off.

"A classic narcissist, isn't that what Niall said? He hits on the girls, dominates the other guys—"

Emma thought suddenly of Ethan's shadow, Blake, always a few steps behind. Something must have shown on her face because Rory reached out and grabbed her arm, triumph in his face.

"I'm right, aren't I?"

"He has this friend . . ." Emma shook her head.

"That kid who was hiding in the hallway? Let me guess, he's always in the background, worshipping, obeying. Hanging on Ethan's every word. It's classic narcissistic manipulation."

"That's not—" But it was, Emma recognized. Niall would have agreed with Rory's assessment of the two. Still, Emma couldn't reconcile that two boys who discussed stories in her little garret could be cold-blooded monsters. She pulled her arm away. "I can't believe Ethan could have murdered his own girlfriend."

"But Malcolm could kill some girl he met once?" He threw his hands up. "You don't understand. Malcolm, he's—he's not untalented, but he's playing with paint spatter and TV screens. This isn't his work—he's not at this level." Rory's voice was etched with emotion. "Leopold and Loeb are sitting in the back of your classroom, and you're pointing the finger at a kid who's just trying to figure himself out."

"He asked me about Ophelia right after Sarah Weston died. Malcolm did."

"A lot of people study *Hamlet*," Rory countered, circling around so that the desk was between them. He turned the paper over so that Ethan's face was staring up at them again. "Your students, for example."

"Yes, but . . ." Emma shook her head in frustration. She couldn't offer anything more than her feelings, her instincts, and she could see on Rory's face how unconvincing that was.

"You know you're not always great at reading people, Emma . . ." Rory looked away, quiet for a moment. "He's not a killer. He's just a weird kid who's not great with people."

Like you. Emma heard the unstated accusation.

"Okay. Point taken. It's just—I hate this. Not knowing. Suspecting everyone." Emma leaned back against the chair, her shoulders curling forward. "Maybe it's not him."

"It's not. But if even you can't understand . . ." He shut the book and began stacking papers. "This feels pointless. I think I'm going to head home."

"Sure." Emma tried to make her voice soothing, not quite understanding the emotional eddies that swirled around her. "Rory? Do you want to come over for dinner again? Talk some more?"

"Tomorrow, maybe."

"Yeah, of course. Right. Just . . . let me know."

Holding her purse tightly, Emma rose and walked quickly out the door, a hollowness growing in her stomach. She felt unbalanced. Rory was so certain about Malcolm, but she couldn't believe that Ethan was a killer. Maybe Rory was right. She wasn't great at reading people or understanding social rules. Maybe she'd missed something. Or misread it. She jogged down the stairs, catching herself as she stumbled on the last few steps. Images of awkward moments and missed cues pelted her brain. Rory was right. She didn't really know Ethan. Or Malcolm. How could she . . .

As she came down the hall toward the main entrance, she heard a familiar ringtone. She dug through her purse. No phone. "Shit."

Realizing she must have lost it when she dropped everything outside, she pushed open the glass door. The ringtone grew louder as Emma moved forward, and she stooped down, picking through the leaves and trash that had blown against the edge of the building. She spotted the phone and reached for it just as the ringing stopped.

Emma pushed her slipping purse strap back up her shoulder and tapped the screen to see the missed calls. There were three, all from Ian. He hadn't left a message, but as she looked, a text notification popped onto the screen.

IAN: You're not safe. Go home now.

Emma felt her skin prick. She glanced quickly around but could see nothing out of the ordinary. The growing shadows of the campus menaced as she hit Redial, waiting through the ringing for Ian's voice. There was a quick, sharp click, a moment of silence, and then the line went dead. She called again. This time, the line went dead almost immediately. Still standing in the protected alcove by the door, she tapped out a text message.

EMMA: What's wrong?

The response came quickly.

IAN: I'm waiting at your house. Come. Now. I'll explain.

Emma considered going back up to Rory and asking him to take her home, but she remembered the locked door, which had swung shut behind her while she had looked for her phone. She again cursed the forgotten keys. Taking a deep breath, she pulled her car keys out of her purse and clutched them tightly between her fingers. She ran more than walked to her car, unlocking the door while still feet away and locking it again the moment she slid behind the wheel. Her hands shook as she fumbled to start the car, the keys dropping to the floor. She forced herself to breathe slowly as she reached down to collect them. She was safe. The doors were locked. Ian was waiting for her at her house. She managed to start the car and slide the gearshift into Reverse. She slowly backed out of the parking spot and turned toward home, the sound of the turn signal filling the too-silent space.

Emma parked in front of her house, surprised to see the porch light on. She didn't remember turning it on as she left, though she was glad she had. Ian wasn't there. The contrasting light made the surrounding shadows even darker, and she couldn't make anything out.

Uncertain, she slowly climbed out of the car, pausing to scan the shadows once again. "Ian?" There was only silence. "Ian?"

Forcing herself away from the security of the car, she dashed up the sidewalk to the door. Her keys were ready, and she shoved the door open with enough force that it slammed into the wall behind it. Stepping across the threshold, she turned back to the empty porch to call one more time. "Ian? Are you there?" There was no response.

A creeping unease spread across her shoulders as she closed the door behind her, clicking the deadbolt into place. She crept out of the entry to the edge of the living room. The darkness of the night was growing, with just enough twilight spilling in the windows for her to see. She pulled out her phone, dropping her keys and purse on the floor as she dialed Ian's number. As soon as she heard the tinny ringing through her earpiece, a blaring noise sprang to life just behind her. Shrill and electronic, the sound of a phone playing Mozart's *Requiem* overwhelmed the small space of the entryway. The harsh noise cut off abruptly, and a strangled breathing took its place.

"Ian?" Emma whispered.

"No."

Emma lunged forward toward the light switch and caught her foot in the strap of her abandoned purse. She pitched forward and landed hard on her knees, her phone flying from her grasp. She felt fingers snake through her hair before her head was jerked painfully backward. Her hands groped in the darkness, searching for anything she could use as a weapon. Something came down hard on her fingers, and she cried out in pain.

"Don't." The voice was breathy but tinged with clear excitement. Emma felt a weight, then the bruising pain of a knee pressing into her spine. The hand yanked her hair, arching her back as her head was wrenched backward. Then, with driving speed, the pressure reversed. Emma's face slammed into the floor, a sharp pain lighting up her skull before the world sank into blackness.

Chapter 25

Ian jolted awake, struggling for breath as the smell of sweat and cologne burned his nostrils and from the thick fabric covering his mouth and nose.

"Hey, Boy Scout. Nap time's over." Mike's voice was muffled by the old sweatshirt that he had thrown in Ian's face.

Ian rolled over and dropped onto his hands and knees next to the beat-up leather couch that was shoved in the back corner of the break room.

Ian peeled the rank cloth away and threw it back at Mike. "I'm up. Jesus, Mike. That stench is not normal. You should get yourself checked."

"It's Benji's."

"Christ, I should have guessed. What time is it?" Ian ran a hand across his face.

"Nine fifteen."

"A.m.?"

"Yes. Man, when's the last time you went home?" Mike's brow creased with genuine worry.

"I have a change of clothes here. I can shower at the gym."

"Shit. Well, get yourself in shape. You have a visitor."

"Emma?"

Mike shook his head. "A patrol officer. Says he has info about the case, wants to talk to you specifically."

Ian stood slowly, his muscles stiff. He rubbed futilely at his clothes, trying to smooth the wrinkles, but gave up as Mike scoffed.

"I think we're past that trick," Mike said dryly.

"Whatever." Ian was too tired to really care. "Where is he?"

"Desk." Mike turned and walked away, leaving Ian to trail him like a recalcitrant child.

It took him a minute to place the man by his desk, but the name came to him eventually. "Officer . . . Gonzales."

"Yes, sir."

Ian waved vaguely at Mike. "My partner. Gonzales here took Emma's statement after she was mugged."

"That's ah . . . that's what I wanted to speak with you about." Gonzales ran a nervous hand through his dark hair. "There's something I think you should know—something I should have told you. That night, after I took Ms. Reilly's statement. We got a call about a drug deal in the neighborhood."

"I remember. Your partner called him—" Ian stopped short as the memory clicked into place. He glanced at Mike. "She called him a preppy Ken Doll."

"Shit," Mike replied. "This dealer's name Alex by any shot?"

"Yes, sir. Alex Carmichael." Gonzales shifted his weight. "I just found out that he's connected to the case, so I—"

"Good man," Mike said. "You were right to come tell us."

"That's not all I need to tell you." Gonzales shifted his attention to Ian. "The day after the mugging, I brought you Ms. Reilly's purse."

"Right," Ian encouraged.

"I told you I found it. I didn't. Alex did."

"You on a first-name basis with this guy?" Mike's tone held a clear warning.

"I know him from school," Gonzales told him apologetically. "I . . . My partner was dealing with the buyers, and when I was alone with Alex, he told me he had information about a crime. He'd tell me about a mugging he witnessed if I let him get away. So, I did. He told me where the purse was, gave me a description of the guy, and I . . . took the credit."

Ian leaned into Gonzales's face, and Mike put a warning hand on his shoulder. "You got a description of this guy?"

"Nothing helpful," Gonzales said, not stepping back. "Medium build, brown hair, Caucasian. It was dark. I didn't think Alex would ID him. And he'd make a lousy witness if he did."

"Jesus, Gonzales. Ms. Reilly's involved in a murder case. You know that, right? You realize this might be connected?" Mike demanded.

"I didn't know. I just found out. I'm sorry."

Ian dropped into his chair, frustration drawing his brow down. "So you were just doing a favor for an old friend?"

Gonzales hesitated. "No. Sir. I thought if I found the purse on my own, you might be impressed. I want to be a detective someday."

Ian just shook his head.

"Go tell your sergeant, Gonzales," Mike instructed him. "We're going to have to report this. It'll be better coming from you."

The young officer nodded and left in silence.

"At least he had the balls to own up. Better than most." Mike sat across from Ian.

"Hell of an endorsement for the CPD." Ian let his head drop back against his chair. "So you think the dealer was involved?"

"If it was just Weston, maybe. He doesn't make sense for the other victims." Mike shook his head, studying an array of notes on his desk. He tapped one with his finger. "Speaking of, you heard from your girl this morning?"

"She's not my—" Ian straightened. "Why?"

"I've been trying to set up another interview to confirm some details about those photos. But she hasn't gotten back to me. You know if she was planning to go anywhere?"

"No. And she wouldn't just leave." Pushing away from his desk, Ian jerked open the top drawer and dug for his keys.

"Alright, cowboy. Settle down. She probably just turned her phone off. A patrol car has been driving by the house every couple of hours; I'll get them to check on her."

"Like hell." Ian stood and headed toward the door, not waiting for an answer.

"Okay, okay. Let me get my jacket." Mike jogged to catch up, shoving his arms through the jacket sleeves as he went. Ian slammed into the parking garage and climbed into an unmarked car, barely giving Mike enough time to close the door before taking off. They hit every stoplight for the first half mile, and Ian flipped on his turret light, zipping around the line of cars in front of them. Mike remained silent.

"What?" Ian asked testily.

"Nothing."

"It's my fault, you know, that she's involved in this. Whether the bastard's using her to get to me or not, she wouldn't be anywhere near this if not for me. She's a fucking English teacher. She shouldn't be . . ." Ian trailed off. "It's on me. If something's happened, it's on me."

Mike didn't respond.

Ian glanced at his partner, then back at the road. "Thanks."

"For?"

"Not patronizing me."

"Sure."

Ian pulled up to Emma's house with jarring speed, threw the car into Park, and covered the ground up to the door with long strides. Mike was a few feet behind when Ian reached into his holster and drew his service weapon. Mike immediately did the same. Ian turned to him and called out in a low voice, "Door's ajar."

Mike nodded and followed Ian, gun ready, as he slowly pushed the door open with his foot and stepped into Emma's house. He kept his weapon up as the two men moved methodically through the small space, checking for signs of an intruder. Ian checked the coat closet before moving into the living room while Mike proceeded to the kitchen.

"Clear," he called.

"Clear," Mike responded.

Mike gestured Ian toward the bedroom while he entered the bath. Ian stepped carefully over the threshold, gun raised, sweeping a glance over the space. There was no sign of Emma or anyone else. Mike stepped up behind him.

"Bath's clear."

Ian nodded once, then turned toward the closet. With Mike taking a position to cover him, Ian reached out one hand and pulled open the closet door. He pushed against the line of clothes, checking to see that no one was hiding in the darkness. Ian turned to Mike, shaking his head. "Nothing."

Mike gestured to the bed, then changed his stance as Ian knelt and pulled up the dust ruffle. "All clear."

Ian stood. "She's not here."

"What are the odds that she left and just forgot to shut the door?"

Ian returned to the entry. Emma's purse was on the floor, tipped over at the edge of the living room. A jumble of loose coins, bits of paper, and cosmetics was strewn across the floor. "Not good."

"Keys are on the counter," Mike called from the kitchen.

"Wallet and purse are over here. There's a set of keys here, too. Looks like she dropped them." Ian tipped up the purse and quickly sorted through the remaining contents. "Any sign of her phone?"

"Not in here," Mike called back.

Ian stood, pulled his phone out, and called Emma. The chirping sound of a cartoon theme song played in response. Tucking his phone in his pocket without hanging up, Ian followed the sound into the living room. Shoved against the edge of a bookshelf, Ian saw Emma's flashing, singing phone. He lifted it by the edges. "Damn."

"Either she dropped it, or someone was smart enough to leave it here." Mike came over to Ian. "We need to get everything photographed and dusted, just in case. I'll put a call into CSI."

Ian nodded, crossing into the kitchen as Mike made the call. Carefully opening drawers, he found a plastic sandwich baggy and dropped the phone inside. As he zipped it closed, he pressed on the screen and was surprised to see the home screen light up.

Mike stepped up behind him. "Who doesn't lock their phone?"

Ian shook his head. "Not Emma. She's too protective of her privacy. But if she had it in her hand, and it was still unlocked when this guy picked it up . . ." Ian tapped into the settings. "He's disabled the security so that he'd have full access."

"So, what, he grabbed it from her, played with it for a while, and then threw it on the floor?"

Ian shook his head. He opened the recent calls and scrolled through.

He saw several with the precinct's number from that morning. Mike calling to set up another interview. Below that, he saw his name repeated three times from the night before. He tapped again to look at outgoing calls. Again, his name was listed. He pulled out his cell phone to confirm what he already knew: he hadn't missed any calls from her. Finally, he opened the screen to her text messages. The last exchange that it showed was between Emma and him.

IAN: You're not safe. Go home now

EMMA: What's wrong?

IAN: I'm waiting at your house. Come. Now. I'll explain.

Ian stared at his name, small and clear on the phone screen. She'd come home thinking that he'd be here. He felt a twisting pain in the center of his body.

"When did you send this?"

"I didn't. Check the time stamp. I was with you at the precinct."

Mike took the phone from him and tapped on the screen. "It's not your number. Someone else's number's been saved under your name." Mike looked at Ian as he put the pieces together. "He didn't change the security settings after he attacked Emma. He'd already done that. He'd already been in her phone."

"Then pretended to be me, lured her here, and took her." Ian's voice was clear and steady.

Mike shifted his weight as he watched his partner. "Scene-of-crime is on the way. I'll get an APB out."

"Her car's out front," Ian offered. "He must have had his own vehicle."

"We'll canvas the neighbors, see if anyone noticed anything." Mike hesitated. "Ian . . ."

"Don't." Ian took the phone from his partner and brought the text exchange onto the screen again. Mike moved back into the living room without another word.

Ian took a deep breath and began to check the house more methodically. Nothing in the kitchen seemed to be disturbed. There was a single glass, washed and turned over to dry on a dishcloth next to the sink. A box of crackers was out on the counter. Ian opened the dishwasher, careful not to disturb any prints, and peered in. Half of the space was unfilled, clearly waiting to be washed. Either Emma had found a reason to wash this one glass all by itself, or someone else had. Was he here, having a snack, when Emma had rushed home? He spotted a scrap of white, half-hidden beneath the oven, and leaned down. He picked up an order ticket from a local burger place, read the name scrawled across the top, and tucked it in his pocket. Ian moved quickly back to the front door. There was no sign of damage to the lock or the door frame. He looked again at the spilled purse. The contents spread away from the door toward the living room. The phone had been found in that direction, too; maybe it had slid from her purse or been dropped as she came in. Ian stepped from the door to where the purse lay, shortening his stride to approximate Emma's. The purse suggested that she had been coming into the house. Three or four steps in, she had stopped. Ian stood in that position, then twisted to look behind him. The coat closet would have offered a perfect position to hide before coming up behind her.

He'd been here waiting. Emma had obviously had her keys with her; they'd dropped near her purse. "Mike," Ian called out. "You said you found a set of keys?"

"On the kitchen counter."

Mike trailed Ian as he returned to the kitchen. On the counter sprawled a handful of keys connected by a key chain with a tiny skull attached. Ian reached out and touched a small black button just above the plastic head. Tiny red LED lights flashed from the eyes, and it began to croon.

"I ain't got no body . . ."

"That's creepy," Mike said. "Think they belong to our guy?"

"No," Ian replied with surety. His mind filled with rain and apple pie, with Emma bruised and dripping as she gave a statement to a young cop in a dingy café. "They were Emma's. They were stolen the night of the gala. The night that she met me."

Ian watched the scene-of-crime techs methodically search Emma's house as Mike arranged for patrol officers to question the neighbors, his hand tight around the receipt. He watched, almost passively, as Emma's phone was collected, trace was run, and the inevitable report came that the number belonged to a burner phone that had since been disconnected. He barely spoke as they drove back to the precinct and updated the detectives from Missing Persons. He was silent as he printed off a copy of a picture of Emma from her online faculty profile and taped it to the murder board alongside Sarah Weston, Phillipa Minor, Dana Ackerman, and Olivia Ballard. He said nothing when, at the day's end, they all dealt with the realization that they had very little to go on, no ransom demand, and Emma was very probably going to be transferred from Missing Persons to Homicide in a matter of days. Then, with equal calm, he logged into the DMV database, looked up Rory Tamblyn's address, drove to his house, and kicked in the door.

Rory stood in a designer kitchen wearing boxer shorts and a tight blue T-shirt. The smell of onions permeated the air, and a pan hissed and sizzled on the stovetop. The tasteful open-concept design provided Ian a clear sight line from the front door. As he crossed the living room, quickly closing the space between them, Rory scrambled back from the counter where he was preparing dinner. He reached for the knife on a nearby cutting board and raised it in his right hand, his left going up in a vague position of defense.

"Put down the knife, Tamblyn."

"Like hell. What are you doing in my house?"

Instead of responding, Ian lifted the cutting board, scattering a pile of neatly chopped vegetables, and used a two-handed grip to smash it into Rory's arm. He cried out and twisted away from the blow. Ian grabbed Rory and easily forced the knife from his hand, dragging the arm back with bruising force. He pushed Rory from the kitchen into the more open space of the attached dining room. As Rory stumbled, Ian grabbed the fabric of his T-shirt, spun him around, and pressed him against the wall with one forearm against his throat.

"Where is she?"

"What the fuck?"

Ian jerked him forward and back, slamming his head against the wall. "Where's Emma?"

"Emma? I have no idea. What the hell are you talking about?"

Ian slammed him again. "I know that you're behind this, you prick. I found the receipt you dropped. Now tell me where you've taken her before I reach down your throat and pull your balls out through your esophagus."

Rory brought his knee up, managed to strike Ian in the thigh, and created enough space between them to get a hand up and push against the bottom of Ian's chin. The detective stumbled back, and Rory escaped his grasp. He dashed into the living room, and Ian followed, catching him from behind and knocking him to the floor. Rory gasped for breath as Ian drove a fist first into Rory's ribs, then—as he rolled him over—into his jaw. Ian straddled Rory's legs, then dug his fingers into his shirt front.

"Tell me where she is."

"I don't fucking know what you're talking about!"

Ian heard Mike enter the house, his voice vaguely registering as Ian punched Rory again, splitting his lip. He wondered distantly if something had tipped his partner off or if Mike had just followed him on a hunch. Mike was an intuition guy. But he still had to clear the living room before he would reach them. Ian wasn't done.

Rory spat blood into the detective's face and pushed him away. He made a lunging motion toward the counter, and Ian raised his arm again. Before he could drive his fist down, Mike caught him from behind, and he jerked him back. Ian lost his balance and stumbled, slipping on the tile floor and tumbling back against the wall. Mike stood over him, chest heaving from exertion.

"Jesus Christ, Carter, what in god's name do you think you're doing?"

"He knows where she is, Mike. He killed Olivia Ballard, then took Emma. I know it. Just give me . . ."

"Fucking nothing. That's what I'll give you. Do you have any idea how much damage you've done here?"

Rory had scrambled to his feet and now stood with his hands pressed to his bloody mouth. "I have no idea what he's ranting about. He broke in and attacked me."

"You asshole," Ian reared up and made a move toward Rory, but Mike wrestled him back and shoved him through the door.

"Out, Ian." Mike turned toward Rory. "On behalf of the department, I apologize. If you'd like to make a complaint, I'll take you down to the station." He turned back toward Ian. "Out," he ground out. "Now."

Ian staggered out the door, bending at the waist as he struggled for air. The skin across his knuckles had split, and a flash of pain lit up his hand as he flattened his fingers against his thighs, trying to keep himself upright. Acid burned the back of his throat as nausea swept through him. He gagged.

He could hear Mike's and Rory's voices as a distant hum behind him. Lights began to flick on across the pleasant suburban neighborhood as concerned citizens stepped onto their dusky porches. His head jerked up as he realized what they were seeing: a bloodied vandal who'd broken into a house just like theirs, a corrupt cop brutalizing an upstanding college professor. Mike was right; he'd done irreparable damage to their case. Ian swallowed hard, forcing down the bile, and made himself stand and walk to his car. He saw a middle-aged man across the street stiffen, then pull the woman next to him closer in a protective gesture.

Ian got in his car and drove, with no particular destination, until his breathing slowed, and the adrenaline faded to a brief tremor in his hands. He pulled the car to the side of the road, set the hazard lights, and let his head drop back against the seat. He had, more than likely, just ended his career. He had gotten nothing from Tamblyn, and he had screwed up any case that might be made in the future. And Emma was still gone.

He didn't know how long he sat there in the growing cold, but when the phone rang, his hands had stiffened into fists. The number showed the precinct. He ignored it. It rang again. Then, the phone beeped to indicate a text message.

MIKE: Call me. Now.

Ian debated ignoring that, too, as he indulged in a brief fantasy of going home and drinking until he blacked out. But that wouldn't help. He called Mike.

He said nothing when Mike answered on the first ring. "What the hell was that?"

"He knows something." Ian breathed deeply, trying to keep his tone even. He needed Mike on his side.

"He has an alibi for last night. He was with some coed. We called, and she backed him up."

"She's lying," Ian said too sharply. He tried again. "Romantic partners are terrible alibis."

"It was a one-night stand; not until death do we part." Mike's tone was grim. "Why would she lie for a guy she barely knew?"

"I don't know. But I found a receipt at Emma's. Tamblyn's name is on it. He was there, Mike. At her house." Ian thumped his hand against the window, forgetting his damaged fingers, then pulled the phone away from his face as he hissed in pain. He didn't need to remind Mike what he'd done.

"There a date?" Mike asked after a pause.

Ian froze. He hadn't checked. He'd seen the paper, seen the name, and—he pulled the paper out of his pocket, scanning it quickly. "Fuck." He'd gotten it wrong.

"Jesus, Ian. They're friends. You know he's been to her place before. You never thought maybe he dropped it some other time?"

Ian didn't say anything. He couldn't say anything.

"And now we can't even ask him." Mike's voice rose with every word. "No way IA lets us near him, not to mention his lawyers. Because you fucking punched a suspect in the face."

"I know." Ian felt the cold, bone-deep and numbing.

"He's alleging police brutality, and given the state of his face, he's got a pretty damn good case. They're shoving his blood-soaked T-shirt into an evidence bag as we speak."

"He'll win his case," Ian said simply.

"This could be your career, Ian," Mike said on a sigh, the anger draining from his voice.

Ian ran that thought across his mind, deliberately and brutally spinning out what it would mean. Best case he'd lose his job, his pension, his reputation. Worst case he'd go to prison, probably landing in solitary. Cops don't do well in gen pop. "It doesn't matter," he said finally.

Mike's voice was steeped in exhaustion. "Go home. Sleep, drink, whatever. Get your head in the game."

Ian hung up the phone without arguing. He knew his partner was right. Unwilling to seek out the warmth and comfort of his home while Emma was somewhere scared and alone, he drove to a nearby park, pulled an emergency blanket out of his trunk, and curled his long frame into the back seat of the car. He lay in the creeping autumn cold, fighting sleep until his body couldn't hold out any longer. He dreamt of darkness.

Chapter 26

Ian entered the doors of the police station just after 4:00 a.m., the collar of his coat turned up, and his head down. He didn't want to catch anyone's attention. The night duty officer gave him a nod as he went by.

"Early start, Detective."

"Got a thought that won't let me sleep," Ian said, not pausing.

He avoided the elevator, instead jogging up the back stairs to the precinct office. The room was dark except for a lone desk lamp someone had forgotten. Ian didn't turn on the lights.

He'd woken that morning with stiff limbs, gritty eyes, and a phone bursting with missed calls. There were three from Mike, one from the union lawyer advising him to call before speaking to anyone, and two from his commanding officer. Lieutenant Fletcher was brief and profane as she informed Ian that he was restricted to desk duty with a likely suspension to follow. Internal Affairs would be contacting him tomorrow—Ian mentally corrected that to today—to set up an interview.

All of which made his current presence in the darkened office somewhat questionable. The lieutenant usually showed up around six to work through her regular pile of paperwork before the morning briefing. That was a meeting Ian planned to miss. Moving quickly, he crossed to the conference room that they had been using for the murder investigation. The door was locked, and Ian dug out his keys, wincing as their jangling seemed to fill the empty space. He glanced over his shoulder before entering the small room. Pulling out his phone, Ian snapped pictures of the murder board and each individual item. He then moved methodically through the files, photographing notes, lab reports, and witness statements. He briefly paused when he reached the copy of Emma's statement after the photos were left at her door, then forced himself to keep going. He could dwell on recriminations later.

Once he had documented everything there, he stepped out of the room, locked the door, and moved through the darkness to his desk. He opened the top drawer and grabbed three legal pads containing his personal notes. He circled to Mike's desk and tugged on the drawer where he knew his partner kept his own notepads. It didn't open. The lock would be easy to jimmy, but Ian was walking a fine line as it was. He debated logging onto his computer and emailing files to his personal account but hesitated—he hoped he could stay under the radar for a while, but if they were going to build an IA case against him for assaulting Rory Tamblyn—and he had no doubt that they would—then there was a good chance they'd go over his email to look for anything incriminating. He'd have to rely on hard copies and his memory.

Tucking the legal pads under his jacket, he stepped out into the hallway and quickly descended to the lobby. He paused briefly in the main floor stairwell as he heard the familiar voice of a fellow detective pass by the door. A new officer sat at the main desk, and Ian glanced at his watch. It was ten after five. Photographing everything had taken longer than he had expected. He gave the officer a tight nod, resisting the impulse to pick up his pace as he approached the door. The cold air was a shock as he stepped outside. Keeping his head down, he turned up the street and walked with forced casualness two blocks north to where he had left his car. He drove home, careful of every stop sign and turn signal.

Once there, Ian cleared a wall in his home office, moving the furniture haphazardly and stripping the surface of art and mementos. Then he downloaded the images from his phone to his laptop, printing copies of each piece of evidence and organizing them back into the careful piles and folders he had assembled at the station. He found a pack of thumbtacks and re-created the murder board on the now empty wall. Soon pictures and notes filled the space as Ian used a felt tip pen to scribble on the pale cream surface. He annotated each photo with dates and details. First, the victims: Sarah, Phillipa, Olivia. And then the missing: Dana, Emma. He wrote a question mark under the photo of Dana. They'd heard nothing more from Missing Persons or her family so far.

Next, he labeled the potential suspects. He started with all of the girls' past and present boyfriends and the classmates that they'd interviewed, sorting out those who had alibis or were only connected to one of the victims. Phillipa's boyfriend, Ethan, stayed in the pile along with a question mark to stand in for the "older boyfriend" that had been mentioned for both girls. He hesitated over a picture of Gonzales's drug dealer friend but kept him in play as well. They hadn't found a connection to Phillipa, but he knew Sarah and had been in the area during Emma's mugging. Next, Ian picked up a picture of Malcolm Haynes, the kid Mike had called a "creepy little bastard." He was connected to the first two victims, but rather tangentially—he'd been their TA—and being creepy wasn't exactly damning evidence. Ian pinned Malcolm off to one side. He hung Rory Tamblyn front and center. Tamblyn had an alibi for both Sarah Weston and Phillipa Minor's abductions and, according to Mike, for Emma's. But not Olivia. And maybe Emma's abduction was something different.

Ian's phone buzzed against the desk. He picked it up, and the screen showed his lieutenant's extension at the precinct. Resisting the impulse to swipe to ignore, he answered briskly.

"Yes."

"Damn it, Carter."

"Look, Lieutenant—"

"Save it, Detective. Internal Affairs is officially investigating your tantrum yesterday," Lieutenant Fletcher told him. "You're on paid suspension as of this morning. Call your department rep. Don't speak to IA without someone there. And Ian . . ."

"What?"

"Stay the hell away from this mess. I know you have a personal relationship with the victim here, but that's all the more reason you can't touch this case. Mike's on it, and Jason and Aaron will pick up the slack."

Ian said nothing.

"You hear me, Carter?"

"I hear you."

"Good. Come to the precinct, sign the paperwork, and turn in your badge and gun. If you're bored, you can get a jump on your anger management classes. I have no doubt that there will be some in your future."

"Yes, ma'am." Ian hung up before Lieutenant Fletcher could comment on his sarcasm.

He turned back to the wall displaying the evidence connected to the serial killer. Somewhere on that wall was the detail that would make all of the pieces fall into place. He reviewed each picture and every note. Emma didn't fit the pattern. She was the wrong age, had the wrong appearance. Her abduction didn't match the style of the others. Even Olivia Ballard had just vanished. There was little physical evidence; there were no witnesses. They didn't even know from where they had been taken.

But Emma had obviously been taken from her home. Her abductor had left her purse spilled across the floor. He hadn't picked up either set of keys. He wasn't pretending she'd just left town. He hadn't even bothered to close the door.

The keys, though, and the text messages showed premeditation, so it wasn't just a spur-of-the-moment action. Had it been planned as far back as the gala? Ian reached for stacks of papers on his desk and quickly rifled through them. He cursed himself. He hadn't copied the incident report from that night. They hadn't considered it part of the case. It was an error, he knew, that had come from Ian seeing Emma not as a witness or even a victim but as . . . Ian struggled to complete the thought and pushed it firmly away. He didn't have time to sort out his feelings for her. She was missing; he had to do his job. Ian closed his eyes, steepling his fingers against his brow, and tried to focus on the details of that night of the mugging. Emma had told the officer that she'd caught her shoe and tripped. Then, after she was already down, someone had shoved her and taken her purse. It had seemed like a crime of convenience. He had missed the significance.

The kidnapper could have gotten her address from her license, but Ian's number wasn't in the phone he'd stolen, so whoever had taken her needed access to Emma's new one. Ian grabbed his phone and scrolled through the call history. His actual number had been there the night she'd gotten the photos of Olivia. She hadn't called him, nor he her, the following day. That meant that her abductor had gotten Emma's phone, switched the number, and put it back sometime between Friday and Monday. Ian paused to add that note to Emma's wall.

Tamblyn certainly had opportunity. He'd come to Emma's house after the photos were left and had presumably spent the night with her. Ian rolled his shoulders uncomfortably. Emma had come to the station the next day to give her statement, likely bringing her phone with her. Ian didn't know where she'd gone after she left the police station or the next day—she hadn't wanted to talk to him by that point. He needed her phone records; he just hoped he hadn't burned all of his bridges. He dialed the familiar number quickly.

"Hey, Mike."

His partner didn't bother with a greeting. "Have you been officially suspended, or are you just hiding?"

"Personal day. It seemed like a good idea."

"No shit."

"Mike, I need you to check something for me."

"No."

"Mike . . ."

"You can't work this case anymore, and you know it."

"Fine. Then just check for yourself. Emma called me the night of Olivia's abduction when the photos were left for her."

"Right," Mike said cautiously.

"Three days later, someone had changed my number in her phone. Whoever took her must have had access to her phone after she left me that message."

"The guy had her keys. He could have broken in at any point."

"But she probably wouldn't leave her phone at home, so he would have had to come in contact with her at some point. I need you to find out where she went during that window. Did she make or place any calls? Get any texts?" There was silence on the other end. "Mike? Have you checked her call record?"

"Of course I have. I'm not the fuckup here."

Ian let the insult pass. He deserved it. "And?"

Ian heard a shuffling of papers. "Incoming call from a Niall Chadha—would have been right after she came to the station. Then a text from Chadha, then an outgoing call to the same. A text to Tamblyn that night, another the next morning. Nothing the next day, other than the three texts from not-you."

"Have you contacted Chadha to see why he called and texted?"

"We left a message."

"That all?"

"He probably heard about the Ballard girl."

"She texted Tamblyn, too. You talk to him?" Ian's voice was flat.

"Yeah, right."

"Mike, you can't just not investigate him . . ."

"He's not home."

"Think he did a runner?"

"Or he checked into a hotel after some Neanderthal busted his door in."

"Look, Mike, feel free to kick my ass whenever you like. I've got it coming. But first, track down Tamblyn."

"Even if I do, he's not likely to cooperate. The last cop who interviewed him punched him in the face. Leave it, Ian. This isn't your case anymore." Mike hung up, leaving Ian listening to silence.

"Fuck." His assault on Tamblyn had cut off their best lead.

Carolyn Matthews recoiled when she opened the door to Ian's knock. He stepped back and ran his fingers through his hair, suddenly very aware of his many recent sleepless nights.

"Uh, Ms. Matthews," he said haltingly. "I don't know if you remember me . . ."

"You're the detective investigating the murders," she responded carefully.

Before Ian could reply, a tall, stylish man appeared in the doorway behind Carolyn. "Here to interrogate us, Detective? I'm happy to offer my insight."

"And you are?"

"Niall Chadha."

"Right, Emma's friend. Have you seen her recently?"

The man's smirk dropped immediately. "Not since Saturday. Is something wrong?"

"Tamblyn didn't say anything to you?" Ian responded indirectly. "Either of you?"

"No. He told me to work remotely until things . . . get back to normal," Carolyn responded. "What's happened?"

"We're not certain. I was . . . following up on the case, and . . ." Ian trailed off again. He was struggling to guide the conversation like he wanted. "There was an altercation."

"What did you do? Punch him?" A voice asked from behind him. Standing on the walkway was a small woman with unforgettably colored hair.

"Charlie," Carolyn warned.

"We've met," Ian said, trying to place her in a new context. "You're the intern . . . ?"

"Charlie Mason, *Daily Independent*." Charlie gestured him out of the way and stepped inside. "Hey, I get it. Rory's got Backpfeifengesicht." At his blank look, she explained, "His face is very punchable."

"Can we get back to Emma?" Carolyn demanded. "What's going on?"

"None of you have seen her, then?" Ian evaded.

"Not since Saturday." Niall glanced at the others as they each shook their head, the implications of that gap creeping into each of their faces. He cleared his throat roughly. "Something's happened to her, hasn't it?" Niall finally said.

"She didn't respond to the text I sent Monday. I just thought that maybe she didn't want to . . ." Charlie canted her eyes toward Ian. "That she needed some space after what happened to Olivia."

"Something happened to her," Carolyn said flatly.

"We don't know anything yet . . ."

"Based on the fact that you're here asking vague questions and giving vaguer answers, we can assume that something's wrong. And if there is, if something's happened to Emma, we need to know—we can help." Charlie strode into an adjoining room, taking for granted that they'd follow. When Ian entered, she'd already set her laptop on the coffee table and was busily opening files. "So, who are your suspects?"

"I can't . . ." Ian began out of habit, then stopped. He was out of ideas, out of leads. Emma had trusted these people enough to share what she knew, trusted them to understand the crime scenes the same way she did. She'd been right about every riddle that the killer had left so far—maybe she'd left a clue of her own. He looked at each of their faces in turn: expectant, fearful, determined. If she had, this is where he'd find it. "Fuck it. What's your number?" Charlie recited it, and Ian texted her the picture he'd taken of the original murder board. Charlie glanced at her phone with clear surprise, tapped the screen, then turned back to the computer. In a few keystrokes, the image was on her monitor.

"So, if I'm honest, we don't have a lot," Ian began. "The first victim had been involved in drugs—that's the dealer—" He pointed to Alex Carmichael's photo. "But he's not connected to any of the others. We found a few people who knew both girls—" He pointed to the boyfriends. "But nothing panned out."

"Rory's on there?" Charlie said, her voice a question.

"He was connected to both girls tangentially, but he has an alibi."

Carolyn sat down next to Charlie and leaned close to the screen. "I fucking knew it." She turned the screen so that Niall could see as she pointed. He shook his head. "Right, you don't know him." She turned it to Ian. "Malcolm. Rory's TA. I told you he was creeping on Emma."

Ian sat on Charlie's other side. "Haynes? He's been on our list, but we couldn't find a motive."

"He knew the first two girls through Rory, and he audited some of Emma's classes. He talked about how much he liked her. Often," Carolyn said.

"It's still not much of a motive," Niall countered gently.

"You're the one who said this was about control, rewriting his own narrative, right?" Carolyn retorted.

Ian glanced up at the other man appraisingly. "You have a theory?"

Charlie snorted. "Everyone has a theory." She clicked across her screen, pulling up a document. "And you're not the only one with a murder board."

Ian studied the screen. The document was divided into three sections, each headed with the name of a victim. The first displayed an image of Millais's *Ophelia*, along with the quote that had been sent with the paper with the black-and-white images from the front page of *The Independent*. Below, Ian read an impressive profile of the killer, notes on the painting, and analysis—clearly Emma's, he thought—of the story. The second column was similar to the first but included three paintings and all of the pictures of Phillipa Minor that had been sent to the paper. He raised an eyebrow at Charlie, but she just shrugged. The final column had the two quotes sent to Emma, a painting of a woman in green, and two stanzas of a poem.

"You've been busy."

"You want to hear what we think or . . . ?" Charlie was definitely in charge of the conversation.

"Go."

"Okay, Niall's a psychologist. According to him, the killer is likely a narcissist, has a poor track record with women, and is using the killings to take control of his own narrative—basically, his life isn't what he wants, and he's using the fantasy of the stories to make himself less of a loser." She looked up at Niall. "Right?"

"Essentially. He feels out of control in real life, so he uses his art—the murders—to display dominance over people he thinks have slighted him—or his art. He makes them into what he wants them to be."

"Does that fit Haynes?" Ian asked the other man.

"I've not met him, but from what Carolyn says—possibly. He's socially awkward, particularly with women. He's been floundering in his own artistic endeavors, and he has little social power. He's the proverbial mediocre white man who feels like he is owed a piece of supremacy, but instead—he's failing. Do you know if he has a history of violence, Detective?"

"No police record, but more than one student—all female—have filed complaints about stalking."

"That could be an initial step toward something like this. Many mass or serial killings begin with gender-based violence because these men feel they're owed women's bodies."

"He fits the narrative profile, too." Charlie enlarged the second column. "We think the first murder scene was inspired by Ophelia—Emma told you about that?"

Ian nodded.

"The second one is drawing from multiple places: a poem, a medieval story, and three paintings. Rory says it's postmodern. Seems like cribbing to me. Either way, it means that whoever did this knows art. But—" Charlie scrolled down "—Emma said that he's misinterpreting the texts. He's applying his own very misogynistic lens to the stories. So he's probably someone who knows the texts but not how to analyze them. Someone smart enough to dig his way through Shakespeare but not someone who's really studied him. Malcolm's a graduate student, so he's got the brains—"

"Rory's always complaining how he won't do the reading, though. Says he just looks things up online but never actually bothers to research his ideas," Carolyn interjected.

Ian nodded. "What about the third column?"

"These are the photos that were sent to Emma." Charlie scrolled. "So we don't have copies. You probably do, though." Charlie clicked back to Ian's murder board, zooming in with satisfaction.

"Niall, you were right. It's a match to the painting you suggested." Charlie clicked back to her file.

"Desdemona," Niall confirmed.

"This one breaks the pattern of the other two." Charlie continued her summary. "Emma and Rory came up with a theory that the killer was sending a message not about Olivia but with her. A message for Emma. Rory's theory was more postmodern bullshit, but basically, he thought that the killer was letting Emma know she was part of his story. That she had a role to play."

"If Haynes was fixated on her," Niall offered, "then it would make sense for him to want to draw her into his new narrative. He may have seen the murder of her student as a gift of sorts, an offering."

"He's getting closer to her with each one," Ian speculated. "The first girl is a student at the college, someone Emma might have seen but didn't really know. The second attended the gala the night that Emma was mugged—"

"That was connected?" Niall's head snapped toward him in surprise.

"It looks that way."

"Malcolm was there that night, too," Carolyn said. "I know he was the TA for that class."

"And the third girl was Emma's student."

"And now he has Emma," Carolyn finished for him.

"We don't know that for sure," Ian tried. Carolyn just shook her head, the full implication hitting her all at once. The energy that Charlie had brought suddenly dissipated, and they sat for a moment in silence. She shut her laptop, and Niall reached a hand down to Carolyn.

Ian stood. "Whatever it takes, I'm going to find her. I promise."

"Promises are dangerous things, Detective," Niall said quietly. Ian simply nodded, knowing just how true that was.

Chapter 27

Emma woke with the thick grit of mud in her mouth, a cloying taste that didn't mask the tang of blood. She was lying on her stomach, her cheek pressed against bare earth, and her hands were bound tightly at her back. Her shoulders ached from the pressure. The air around her was heavy with the scent of dirt and decay. A weak stream of gray light seeped in behind her, only enough to reveal the rough edges of her surroundings. A long stretch of packed earth lay directly in front of her, ending in the rise of a wall. She couldn't make out the details, but with a sick sense of certainty, she knew that it, too, was dirt. She was underground. She pulled a deep breath in through her nose, held it, and released it again, trying to stay calm, to figure out—something. There had to be something. But all she could see was dirt. The dense earth muffled the sound of her uneven breaths and blocked any outside noise from reaching her. Which, Emma realized with a sickening feeling, probably meant that no one outside could hear her.

Her head throbbed from a star of pain at the center of her forehead as she gingerly shifted to look to the other side. Her hair, loose and long, tangled around her face. Instinctively, she tried to raise her hand to brush it aside, and the bindings on her wrists pulled tight. She pulled again, this time with intent, and the ties cut against her skin. Her feet, too, were bound; she flexed her toes, and a bright sting of pain scattered up her limbs as blood circulated through the numbed flesh. She gave a quick cry, and the throb of pain in her head spiked, bringing with it a wave of nausea. She could feel bile building in the back of her throat and made herself focus again on breathing.

When the throbbing receded to a bearable level, she forced herself to focus on each site of discomfort along her body, shifting and flexing muscles from her toes upward. The hum of pain in her feet had subsided as blood flow continued, but her shoes and socks had been removed, and she felt the sting of scrapes along the side of one foot and a narrower press of pain in the sole of the other. Her legs felt relatively sound, except for her knees, which she must have bruised when she had fallen. The memory of that moment—the voice behind her, the hand in her hair—rushed at her, and nausea returned, triggering a surge of adrenaline that left her shaking.

Instinct overriding reason, she abandoned her careful assessment and instead rocked her body sharply, using the momentum to roll herself over on her back. Fabric tangled around her as she moved. Her hands were crushed at the small of her back, and she lay panting. Using one elbow as leverage, she pushed herself into a seated position. She could still see little of the room around her, but the new position allowed her to look down at her body. Not only had her shoes been taken while she'd been unconscious, but so had her clothes. She was now dressed in a heavy brocade gown, the rich plum fabric like spilled wine flowing around her legs. Small touches of silver glinted in the wan light. Goose bumps crawled along her skin as she realized that whoever had taken her had stripped her and then slid this fabric along her skin, pulling it tight against her body. And that those same hands had likely dressed the other girls, arranging their limbs and hair like pretty dolls. She wished she'd dared to ask Ian if it had been done before or after they'd been killed.

The thought of Ian gave her a brief flash of hope as she remembered his promise to meet her at the house—before the heavy realization set in that it had been her captor, not Ian, who had lured her home. So no one was looking for her; no one even knew that she was gone.

Brutally shutting down her self-pity, she began shifting herself by digging her bound feet into the dirt floor. Inch by inch, she pushed until she could see the source of the light: a large door made from wooden slats leaned at an angle across a broad opening in the dirt wall about a foot up from the floor. A thick, rough-cut beam protruded above it, supporting a heavy, rock-marked swell of dirt that led up the ceiling. Emma recognized the entrance of an old-fashioned root cellar. The aged wood of the door had bent and warped, leaving gaps between the boards. The light was weak but clear, and Emma realized for the first time that it must be morning. She wondered if only a single night had passed. Or more.

Digging her heels into the hard turf, she tried to drag herself forward toward the door. She felt a slick warmth coat her right heel as she struck it against a sharp stone. She dug her feet in again, slowly struggling forward until the sweat rising on her forehead mingled with blood and dirt smeared along her face. She scrubbed her cheek against her shoulder in a vain attempt to clear her vision as it dripped into her eyes. She blinked rapidly, and tears rose against the invading filth. Then, as she braced herself to move another painful inch, Emma heard a dull scraping sound. Surrounded by thick earth, the sound would have to be close by to reach her. Too close. The noise rang in her ears and raised the hair on her arms. Holding her breath, she shifted as close to the door as she could, straining to hear. A hollow, hesitant sound reached her, growing closer: footsteps, shuffling and awkward.

Emma tried to push back from the door but, in her haste, tipped sideways. She rolled gracelessly into the shadow, pressing her face back to the dirt. With her face toward to door but shielded by her tumbled hair, she tried to appear as still and small as she could. The door rattled and creaked, swinging open with a heavy thud. The full force of the morning light broke into the cellar, and Emma shut her eyes involuntarily. Afraid to open them again and alert the intruder to the fact that she was conscious, Emma strained her ears. The footsteps that had paused as the door opened resumed with the same awkward gait, but now Emma could hear another sound as he moved into the enclosed space, a steady rustle like something being pulled across the ground. No, Emma realized, like something being dragged. There was a heavy thud a few feet away from her; this was followed almost immediately by a second, softer thud. Thick, labored breathing was interrupted periodically by small, rough grunts. An uneven beat thumped out against the floor, and Emma felt something warm brush her side. She flinched, every muscle tightening in revulsion. She heard another grunt, and the warm object pressed solidly against her. Something dropped, soft and slightly damp, against her cheek. Emma held her breath.

The heavy breather walked toward the door, his footsteps now lighter and even. She heard a brief crunch, then the distinct sound of the solid door dropping closed. There was a thick bang against its wood surface, and Emma knew that she was locked in. Slowly, she opened her eyes to see what was pressing against the cool skin of her cheek. She shifted slightly, and the object dropped away, landing just in front of her. A cry caught in her throat as she recognized it for what it was: a human hand.

Emma rolled farther into the darkness, then stilled, listening for the sound of breathing.

"Please, please, please," she whispered to the darkness.

A soft moan responded.

"Are you awake?" she asked softly. "Are you okay?"

"Who . . . ?" The voice was groggy and rough.

"Shhh. He might come back. Are you hurt?"

"No, I . . . Who are you?"

"My name is Emma."

"Emma?" The figure made a sudden move. "Ah, god." There was a groan, then stillness.

Emma's breath sped up, bile rising at the back of her throat as recognition hit her. Her lungs burned, and she had to try twice before she could speak. "Rory?"

"Emma . . . This wasn't . . . You aren't . . ." His voice was flecked with pain and anger.

"Do you know who it is?" Emma asked after a moment.

"No. I was at home, having a scotch. Then everything started . . . swimming. I blacked out." Rory groaned softly. "I think I was drugged, but I don't know how he could have . . ."

"He was waiting for me in my house," Emma said. "He didn't even . . . He just grabbed me. I don't know how he got in."

Rory was silent except for the sound of quick, shallow breaths.

"Rory?" His breathing seemed deeper; Emma wondered if he'd lost consciousness again. She wriggled closer. Bracing herself against his shoulder, she tipped her body over him so her fingers could reach his throat, breathing a sigh of relief as she found a fluttery pulse.

She shifted again to face him, and in the dim light she could see his face was heavily bruised, his lip split. His eyes were closed, and his muscles slack. She felt the familiar creep of panic and tried to bind it back in place with the threads of a plan. She scanned her surroundings again, forcing meaning onto objects obscured by shadows—dirt walls too thick to dig through, a lock she couldn't pick, a door she couldn't break . . . and beyond that, an enemy she didn't know.

"Rory?" she tried again, the panic winning, clawing against her voice, making it small. "Please. I don't think I can do this alone." He didn't respond.

Emma rolled so that her back was to Rory's motionless form and curled her knees up toward her stomach, hiding as well as she could while still keeping her eyes trained on the door. All she could do was wait. When Rory woke up, they would make a plan. They would find a way out. They would fight back.

If he woke up.

Chapter 28

Ian tried not to react to the stares when he stopped at the precinct to surrender his badge and gun. He avoided eye contact with his fellow detectives as he crossed the room, ignoring the remarks—not all of which were whispered. He knocked on the lieutenant's door and didn't wait for an answer before entering.

"Carter. I assume you understand why you've been suspended." Lieutenant Fletcher was seated at her desk and didn't bother looking up.

"Yes."

"You want me to walk you through the process, the investigation, appeals, and all that?"

"No need." Ian kept his expression passive.

The lieutenant's face hardened as she finally met his eyes. "Where are you from, Detective?"

"I'm sorry?"

"Where'd you grow up? What'd your parents do?"

"I grew up in a suburb of Milwaukee. My dad worked in an office. My mom was a bank manager." Ian gave a soft head shake, confused. "I don't see what my background has to do with anything."

"You really don't, do you?" Lieutenant Fletcher gave a soft, mirthless laugh. "No. Guys like you never do. Badge and gun on the desk. Sign this to say you've been notified that you have a right to a union rep and lawyer if you need one." She spun a paper around so that it faced him. "Initial the top, date the bottom."

Ian stood, drawing his weapon from his side holster and placing it, with his badge, on top of the signed document.

"Well, Carter, you're now officially on suspension, which means that as long as that's the case, you are not allowed to represent yourself as an officer of the law or perform any actions in that capacity. Do you understand? As of right now, you are not a cop."

"Yeah, I got it."

"Then I sure as hell expect you to act like it." Fletcher rose for the first time, her smaller stature doing nothing to undermine her authority. She wrapped her fingers on the edge of her desk, giving Ian the impression that she was trying to restrain herself. "I find out you're still investigating this case, I'll toss you out on your ass myself."

"Noted." Ian crossed his arms, staring just above her head.

"Jesus, Ian," Lieutenant Fletcher pushed back from the desk and turned away from him. She settled her hands on the small of her back, waiting a beat before turning to face him again. "Do you even understand how bad this is?"

"Yeah, Lieutenant. I do." Ian kept carefully still, a study in contrast to the lieutenant's frustrated gestures.

"Then get the hell out of my office." She waved a hand at him. "Your rep will be in contact. So, doubtless, will IA." Fletcher dropped back into her chair.

Ian nodded. He turned, pausing by the door. "For what it's worth, Lieutenant, I am sorry that this will blow back on you."

"Unfortunately, Carter, that's not worth a lot. Just don't make it worse. Go home, drink yourself into a stupor, and leave this alone."

"That's the plan."

Ian crossed the room, formulating an explanation to Mike as he walked, but his partner had left his desk, likely, Ian admitted to himself, to avoid a conversation. He pulled at the drawer of his desk and was surprised to find it locked. With an embarrassed glance over his shoulder, he shifted to Mike's desk and grabbed a pen. At the very least, he owed Mike a note of apology. Mike's legal pad was covered in writing, three words prominently printed at the center: *Medium—brown—Caucasian*. Gonzales's description of the mugger.

"Shit," Ian said aloud. He pulled out his phone and scrolled through the photos he'd taken of the murder board, heedless of the attention he was drawing. The man who told their witness about the party at the barn . . . *Medium build, brown hair, Caucasian*. The man who harassed Phillipa at the gala . . . *Medium build, brown hair, Caucasian*.

Ian strode from the room, flipping through images as he walked. As soon as he was out of the building, he dialed the number on his screen.

"This Alex?" Ian demanded without preamble.

"Who this?" came a voice filled with affected laziness.

"Detective Carter."

"Then I think this is a call for my lawyer."

"Just—" Ian moved farther down the block, farther away from the precinct "—listen. Your friend Gonzales told us that he let you off a drug charge because you witnessed a mugging."

"So? No evidence."

"I'm not interested in your petty dealing. I need you to ID the mugger."

"Not sure I can."

"Try."

"What's in it for me?"

Ian swore under his breath and ran his free hand through his hair. "If you can ID this guy for me, I'll make you a confidential informant."

"So what, I get to be your puppet?" Alex scoffed.

"It's a get-out-of-jail-free card, you asshole. You get busted? If you're a registered CI—I make it go away." Ian made the offer he hadn't been willing to give Zoey.

"Okay," Alex said after a beat. "What do you want me to do?"

Ian exhaled and closed his eyes for just a moment. "I'm texting you three pictures. Tell me if one of them is the guy you saw."

Ian selected pictures of Ethan, Malcolm, and Rory and sent them to Alex, pacing during the minutes it took him to speak again.

"The one in the blue shirt," Alex said finally.

Ian ended the call abruptly. "You son of a bitch," he told the picture on his screen.

Ian double-checked the house numbers. The address he had pulled from the copied files had led him to a squalid little duplex with chipped paint and a smear of dirt and gravel where the lawn should be. He climbed from the car and straightened the neatly pressed jacket that he had thrown on. Since he'd lost his badge—and with it, the authority of the police department—Ian needed to rely on assumption and intimidation to get what he needed. He walked up the cracked sidewalk and knocked loudly on the door. There was no response. Ian knocked again.

"Malcolm Haynes," he called through the door. "This is Detective Ian Carter. Open the door." Ian turned his knock into a firm bang. "Haynes."

When there was still no answer, Ian moved quietly around to the side of the house. A small window, smeared with grime, was set several feet back from the front stoop. Ian peered through cautiously. The window opened into a mirthless kitchen. The drab walls held no decoration, packaged food boxes filled the counters, and dirty dishes sat abandoned in the sink. There was a small table with a single chair in the far corner. Ian couldn't make out any sign of movement, so he retreated back along the wall to another dingy window.

Ian could see a single bed with a coarse blue quilt thrown haphazardly on top and a single yellowing pillow scrunched at the headboard. A scratched wooden dresser, pushed against the far wall, was the only other furniture. The walls themselves were covered almost completely with cheap art reproductions. Ian recognized a Van Gogh, the *Mona Lisa*, and something he thought was by Jackson Pollock. Others were more obscure: a Madonna with child, a ship battering against a stormy shore, a black-eyed woman in a street scene. All of the posters had been taped or tacked to the wall, frayed edges curling with age. Ian could see the outline of a single frame hanging just above the bed.

The door to the bedroom was ajar, and Ian could see another closed door across a small hallway. He stepped around to the back of the house into an alley filled with garbage cans and loose debris. There were no windows, so Ian moved gingerly through the mess to the other side. The sole window revealed a tiny bathroom with a sink, toilet, shower, and just enough space to turn around. A single toothbrush was perched on the sink's rim, and a single towel hung from a crooked metal bar screwed to the wall just above the toilet. None of the rooms showed any sign of Haynes or anyone else. The house was marked by neglect that went beyond the typical college crash pad.

Ian returned to the front of the house and quickly scanned the living room. No one was there either. He jogged back to the door and—looking quickly around to see if there were any spying neighbors—jammed his shoulder against it. The cheap lock gave immediately. Ian waited a beat, but if anyone had seen him, they didn't care enough to interfere. He stepped into a living room that looked much the same as the rest of the house. A shabby love seat was tucked against the back wall with a pressboard coffee table set a few feet away. The once beige carpet was gray with ground-in dirt. The wall opposite the kitchen was covered by a rough bookshelf made from concrete blocks and mismatched boards that looked to have been salvaged from an alley or a dump site. The boards warped and sagged beneath the weight of dozens of books crammed helter-skelter onto their surfaces. Ian crossed the room to look more closely. The books seemed to be in no particular order. Art tomes were mixed in with paperback fiction. Textbooks lay on top of well-read copies of *National Geographic*. Every inch of space was filled.

Ian quickly surveyed the rest of the room and then moved into the kitchen. A few minutes of searching revealed nothing of interest. The cupboards were largely bare, with a few cups, plates, and pots that Ian guessed had come from the local thrift shop. He moved to the back half of the house, first going through the minute bathroom. Other than cheap toilet paper, off-brand soap, and some over-the-counter medication, the bathroom cabinets were empty. Crossing the narrow hall, Ian entered the final room of the house: Malcolm's bedroom.

Ian quickly took in the rumpled bed, beaten dresser, and mishmash of art posters that he had seen from the window. He flipped a light on, startled for a moment as the framed painting over the bed came into view. A woman stood at the center of the image, wind whipping her auburn air so that it clung to skin paled by moonlight. Grass and trees were gray with the settling darkness, and the sky was a deep, bleak charcoal beyond the withered circle of a waning moon. It was a stunning image painted in the school of the Pre-Raphaelites, but that wasn't what made Ian's breath catch. The face of the woman, though turned slightly away from the painter's vantage point, was very clearly Emma's. Her feet were bare beneath a blue gown, and there was a tension in her body that suggested surprise or fear. It was as if she'd been caught a moment before fleeing, Daphne about to beg salvation from a pursuing Apollo. Ian felt his skin prick uncomfortably at the mix of fascination and repulsion that it aroused in him. The painting could have been beautiful, but something in the hard lines and bleak colors made it seem predatory.

Ian moved closer. He could see the slightly raised lines where the brush had slid along the canvas. This was not a print, and it was doubtful that Malcolm could afford a quality original. Ian wondered if Malcolm had painted it himself. He leaned in, looking for a signature. There was a small, illegible swish that might have been lettering, but Ian couldn't read it. This close to the canvas, Ian could read the details of Emma's face. Her eyes were angled backward to look over her shoulder, and her lip was caught between her teeth in a gesture Ian recognized. One hand was raised to her breast, fingers clenched. A painful heat settled into Ian's chest. He'd been wrong about Tamblyn.

No longer bothering to be careful, Ian crossed to the dresser and dumped the contents of the top drawer onto the floor. Using the toe of his boot, he sifted through the mess: underwear, socks, and worn T-shirts. Nothing that would help him. The second drawer joined the first, adding pants, shorts, and flannel pajama bottoms to the pile. The bottom drawer offered nothing more than a few worn sweatshirts. Ian banged on the drawer bottoms, then swiftly ran his hands along the inside of the empty dresser. He turned to the bed, frantically stripping the stained sheets and tossing them to the floor. He felt along the surface of the mattress and then muscled it over to check the bottom. He flipped the box-spring, tearing the flimsy fabric to check inside the frame. Nothing.

Frustration mounting, Ian began pulling posters from the wall. Carolyn had been right: Malcolm was the key to finding

Emma. Malcolm, who had been at the gala. Malcolm, who was known for stalking women. Malcolm, who could easily have been lurking around campus, waiting and watching. Ian turned to the painting with a sudden flash of surety and yanked it from the wall. He flipped it over and tore open the brown paper that lay neatly against the back of the frame. Inside, there was a manila envelope thick with papers. Ian shook the contents onto the top of the dresser. Glossy pictures, book pages, handwritten notes, and pencil sketches spread over the cheap veneer. Ian immediately recognized the images of Sarah Weston and Phillipa Minor. There were photos that matched those sent to the newspaper, along with sketches that seemed to be preliminary designs for the scenes. Some had notations—suggestions for revisions and additions—written in the margins. The book pages were torn from Act Two of *Hamlet*. Ian didn't doubt that they would match the book that had been left at the first crime scene. He rapidly sorted the contents into piles, grouping those that seemed to be connected to Weston and those that matched with Minor. He was left with a handful of sketches and notes that depicted another scene, but it wasn't the final moments of Olivia Ballard.

He laid the pieces out side by side. These sketches seemed less sure than the others, less confident. The first drawing showed a dilapidated structure in a broad clearing. It looked to Ian like an old homestead. Off to one side, a neat grouping of leafy trees backed up to a pine forest. The next depicted a closer view of the small grove, revealing it as an orchard. This drawing had less detail than the first. It looked like a sketch rather than a completed piece. In the center, Ian could make out two figures, a woman who seemed to be sitting or kneeling in long grass—or possibly flowers—and a man who was stretched out before her, lying on his back as he looked up into her face. Ian moved to the third and final picture. This was a close-up of a woman's face, unmistakably Emma. But unlike the painted scene that had hidden these pages, here Emma looked powerful rather than frightened. The face was at once impish, regal, and somehow otherworldly. The artist had captured a mischievous glint in her expression that showed her both playful and seductive. Ian flashed suddenly to the night at the gala. He had seen this same expression on Emma's face as she glanced up at him as they talked. Here, though, the small smile was for the man who lay in the deep grass beneath her.

The final page in the group was not a full sketch but rather a series of lines and brief notes. It took Ian a minute to recognize it as a map. Two serpentine lines represented a river, while two straight lines ran alongside, showing the rough boundaries of a road. Two more lines crossed those, with an arrow that Ian assumed showed a turn. Notes across the top of the page read *90, L MM26. R Robin Hill. L Sharp.* Beneath the sketch, someone had written a single word: *Barrows.* Ian picked up the first image again and felt a sharp hit of recognition. He knew where this had been drawn. And at least in the world of the sketch, that meant that he knew where Emma was.

Gathering the four images, he tucked them back into the envelope. He left the other images and pages on the dresser. Walking quickly to the front door, he let himself out and pulled the door closed behind him. When he reached his car, he climbed in, pulled out his phone, and dialed Mike.

"Ian, how—"

"Later. Right now, you need to get a warrant to search Malcolm Haynes's house. You'll find everything you need to tie him to the murders."

"What? How the hell do you know that?"

"Gut feeling." Ian tossed the envelope onto the passenger's seat and started the car.

"Ian, if you've done anything—"

"Mike, you can lecture me, or you can call a judge, get a warrant, and do your damned job. He's your guy. I'm sure of it."

There was a pause before Mike spoke. "Ian, you're on suspension. You can't be anywhere near—"

"I promise, Mike, when you show up, I won't be anywhere near the house. Just tell the DA you got an anonymous tip." Ian hung up, jammed the car into gear, and headed toward the interstate.

Chapter 29

Emma had lost track of time. Rory had woken briefly but had been largely incoherent. He kept repeating that Emma was not supposed to be here, mumbling about the other girls. She had soothed him as best she could, but she didn't think he'd heard her. After Rory had lost consciousness again, she'd given over to the panic and pain and screamed until her chest ached with the effort of each drawn breath. No one had come.

When her breathing steadied, and slow tremors began to rattle down her body, she stayed there, still and silent, her cheek pressed against the hard soil. The small beams of light that worked their way through the door shifted, marking time, and the ground beneath her cheek grew cooler. At last, her aching muscles demanded that she move, and she rocked herself back into a seated position. Her whole body had become a constant throb of pain.

She had never been athletic or particularly popular—her companions growing up had largely been fictional—but she'd always been the smart one. She was the one who had the answers, the one who could solve the problem. She had to solve the problem. Closing her eyes against the hopeless situation—the locked door, the tight bindings, Rory injured and powerless beside her—she searched her mind for the answer she needed, for some missed thread that would lead her from this dark labyrinth. But she had nothing. She let her head drop forward as she ran through every scenario, again and again. And again.

Emma didn't realize that she'd dozed off until the rattle and scrape of the door jolted her awake. She rolled as carefully as she could into a position where she could peer over Rory's prone body. Boots appeared in the dusty light, and the door swung up and back, creaking on its hinges. A man dropped a foot down from the edge of the opening to the floor of the cellar, his knees bending slightly as he landed. He was slim and, judging by the easy movements, fairly young. Emma could see a swath of dark hair and pale skin, but his face was turned away as he stepped from light to darkness. He moved first to the far corner where Emma had lain this morning before pulling herself to the door. She could see him tense, then jerk around as he realized she wasn't there. He moved farther into the shadows along the wall, tracing its length, looking for her, before spinning abruptly and almost running over to where he'd left Rory, just visible in the rectangle of light released into the small space. Emma shrank down, sliding back from Rory's side as the man approached. He moved with a slight hunch as he ducked his head to avoid the low earthen ceiling. Because of this posture, Emma could see him before he saw her, but she destroyed any advantage she may have had when she let out a muffled cry of recognition.

Malcolm was smudged with dirt and sweat as he breathed heavily three feet above her. Emma instinctively ducked her head away from an expected blow. Instead, she heard a scuff of feet and a high-pitched yelp. She twisted around to see that Malcolm had fallen back, his face pale and slack.

"No," he cried with plaintive anger. His eyes were wide and moist. "You're not supposed to be awake."

"Malcolm, I . . ."

"Shut up!"

He made a sudden move toward her, stumbling over Rory's body. He landed hard at her side, and Emma kicked out. Crying in surprise or pain, Malcolm rose to his knees and struck at her wildly. His hand connected with her temple, and she fell back, unable to catch herself before hitting the ground. She rolled onto her stomach, trying to crawl away, but Malcolm grabbed a fistful of her dress and yanked her toward him. He twined one hand in her hair and wrapped the other around her shoulders, drawing her tight against his body. Emma could smell the tang of sweat and stale body spray.

"Stop it! Stop." Malcolm's breath was hot and moist against her cheek as he spoke. He shook her.

"Malcolm, I'll stop, I promise. I—" Emma was silenced as Malcolm's hand slid from her hair to her mouth.

"I'm sorry. I'm sorry, Professor." He dropped into a squat with one foot on either side of her hips. "But I'm going to fix it. Fix everything. I promise."

"Malcolm, you don't need to do . . . anything . . . Just let us go. Please."

"I can't. I can't do that. This wasn't how it was supposed to—" His face was inches from hers, but he was speaking to somewhere just over her shoulder. "I found this place. I found that dress. This is going to be even better." His eyes dropped to hers. "Do you remember The Fairy Queen from that poem? The one we read in class."

"La Belle Dame Sans Merci."

"Right," he agreed, his voice unnervingly normal. "The Fairy Queen enthralls a knight and tries to lead him to his death."

Emma's heart sped with the small thrill of hope. There was no damsel there, no victim other than . . . "But the knight doesn't die, remember, Malcolm? He survives. So does the queen." Emma tried to hold still beneath him, to keep her expression soft and encouraging.

Malcolm smiled. "That's why it's perfect. You can't just— You can't keep telling the same story." He lifted his palms in emphasis, fingers spread and shaking slightly. "It needs a new perspective, a new— I tried to—" He pressed his fingers to his lips as if trapping his tumbling words. After a silent moment, he tried again. "It's always been the girl, right? Always. Over and over, every story, every painting. But now, this time—I reverse the narrative. *He* becomes the art; he's the story. When they find him, find the photos, but you're gone . . . He'll be left to tell the story, again and again, people doubting, suspecting—he'll be mad Ophelia, abandoned Elaine—he'll live their story. You see? The perfect postmodern reinterpretation of the narrative." Malcolm snuck a finger between his lips, biting the nail.

"And where do I go, Malcolm?" Emma's eyes swept the dim space. Would he just leave her here to die? Board up the door and walk away?

"That doesn't matter. You're not the story, not in this version." Malcolm's voice was frustrated. "You get it, don't you? What I'm doing—saying? I don't—I don't want to hurt you. I like you—a lot. You've always been kind to me. But the *art* . . ." Malcolm banged one hand on the dirt floor. "The art is what's important. Everyone will see the art, *my* art. They'll see me."

"I see you, Malcolm. I understand—not fitting in, wanting to be accepted. I do. I see you. So does Rory. You don't have to—"

"No. You don't see. But you will."

Chapter 30

Ian's car bumped along the dirt road following directions that Malcolm had coded onto the sketch—*90, L MM26. R Robin Hill. L Sharp.* A left turn at mile marker 26 on I-90, then a right brought him to Robin Hill Campground, a place he had grudgingly gone to on several holiday cookouts with Mike's family. Scanning the left side of the road for anything that might indicate "sharp," he drove a slow two miles before turning around and retracing his path. Dusk was beginning to fall, and Ian flicked on his headlights, chasing the shadows out of his way. After half a mile, his lights hit a brown metal sign half hidden in the bush. He parked in the shallow pull-off and shoved the car door open with enough force that it ricocheted back at him. He caught it with a booted foot and climbed out of the car, leaving the engine running. He jogged across the road and pushed the leaves aside to reveal a historical marker that detailed the story of the Sharp family homestead.

Ian sprinted back to the car and jerked the keys out of the ignition. He dug a small Maglite out of the glove compartment, and—cursing himself for not bringing a better weapon—shoved a small knife into his back pocket. He locked the door and crossed back to the sign; he could just make out a faint trail through the brush. He clicked on the flashlight and aimed the beam low across the path, gently pushing at branches and foliage as he moved. About a hundred yards in, he reached the side of a hill and looked down to a view he recognized. Painted gold in the dusky light lay the remnants of a farmhouse and barn—and a grove of what Ian now realized were apple trees just behind them.

The same grove, he knew, that Malcolm had sketched with Emma at its center.

Flicking off the flashlight, Ian loped softly down the hill toward the structures. The house was dilapidated and gray, with gaps of light showing through cracked and missing boards. The squat two-story building would have projected an image of wholesome familiarity in its prime but now lay as a haunted reminder of things lost. A large tree, leaves slipping free from the branches, hovered over it like a specter, blocking the front door from Ian's view. The barn, waiting just to the east, was eerily similar to the one where they'd found Sarah Weston's body. Bracing himself, Ian lowered into a half crouch and crossed the unprotected space to reach the weather-beaten structure.

He cautiously approached the backside of the old barn and stole around to the side. Pausing at the corner, he leaned around to surveil the area. He had a better view of the house from here and could see the porch, stark and pale in the fading light. The door stood open. He held his breath, straining for any sign of movement. A light wind fluttered across the valley, stirring grass and leaves with a gentle hush. The whole homestead seemed lifeless. Ian slid around the corner, keeping his back firmly to the wall, and crept along the far side of the barn, pausing again as he heard a vague sound across the clearing. The orchard's trees had dwindled to dark lines against the sky, lifeless fingers reaching for salvation. Nothing moved. Chalking the sound up to an animal skulking in the twilight, he moved to the faded door and pulled gently on the splintered wood. The door swung outward with a groan, and Ian paused again, listening for any indication that someone inside the dilapidated structure had heard him. He counted off a careful ten seconds of stillness, his heartbeat outpacing the numbers, before stepping into the darkness of the barn.

The thick scents of mold and mud saturated the air. Ian risked turning on the flashlight, but kept the beam low, as he scanned the large space, his light catching on rotting hay bales and rusted farm tools. The barn was empty, a large expanse of shadows that deepened where the floorboards had cracked and fallen away. He moved slowly through, checking for hidden spaces or concealed hides, until he was sure that there was no place Emma could have been locked away. He snuck back into the dusky air.

Outside, he stopped again to survey the open spaces before walking quickly toward the farmhouse, knees bent to stay low. The light had faded enough that the flashlight was no longer optional, and the beam swung across the tall grass, bouncing as it hit the dead trees in the distance. He cleared the area surrounding the house, pausing only to inspect an old VW Bug that was parked next to the side farthest from the barn. There was a brown jacket in the front passenger's seat and fast-food wrappers scattered over the floor. Much of the yellow paint had rusted off, the door was locked, and the license plate was obscured with mud. Ian debated trying to clear it to read the numbers but didn't want to waste time. He'd return if—when—he'd located Emma. He shifted his attention to the partially collapsed porch at the front of the house.

Ian walked up the front steps, testing his weight on each board before moving forward. The porch was cracked and broken, and Ian had to skate along the edges to reach the door that hung crookedly on its hinges. The threshold had caved in, leaving a jagged hole. He traced his steps back to a shattered window and crept over the sill, stumbling as a piece of the frame splintered in his hand.

He scanned the space, the shaft of light revealing fallen boards and heavy cobwebs. Recessed into the back wall was an alcove, the remains of a bookshelf or pantry in better days. Ian inched forward, keeping to the sturdier boards near the wall. Keeping his Maglite trained on the spot so he wouldn't lose it in the darkness, he slid his feet along the unseen floor, feeling for obstacles. The sound of his breathing filled the space, muffled by layers of dirt as it echoed back to him. His foot struck something heavy, and he lowered the light. In the stark illumination, he could see a makeshift bed of straw and coarse blankets; a winter coat was rolled up at one end like a pillow. Someone had been squatting here for several days. A dark blue backpack lay on the ground, and the remnants of several take-out meals filled the corner. Ian made a cursory search of the meager belongings. The backpack was stuffed with clothes—Ian shook them out, surprised to see they were all women's things. Then he recognized a blouse from Phillipa Minor's BOLO description. The girls had probably been held here. And Haynes had kept their clothing as trophies. In the front pocket of the pack, Ian found some crumpled dollar bills and Malcolm Haynes's school ID. Leaving the grimy pile behind, Ian continued around the edge of the room until he reached the alcove. It was empty.

The dusty floor had been visibly disturbed, but there was nothing that resembled the mass that Ian had spotted from across the room. Ian searched the floor, but no footprints were heading either out into the room or along the wall. He turned and scanned the space from this new vantage point, tracking his own footprints from the window, past the blankets, to where he now stood. There were no other signs of inhabitation, but a small metal latch at the back of the alcove flashed his light back at him. A door hinged on one end. He flicked the latch open, and—stepping back so that he would be partially covered should someone be waiting on the other side—he pushed hard. The wall swung out into the darkening night air. Whatever steps had once led to this entrance had disappeared, and Ian was faced with a two-foot drop onto the dirt. He slowly leaned out, hunting the shadows for any sign of Malcolm. The creaking groan of tree branches shifting in the wind seemed thunderous as Ian strained to find the danger that he knew waited for him. Crouching low, he hopped to the ground so that both feet struck simultaneously, keeping him balanced and ready to react. After a moment of stillness, he stepped away from the house toward the apple grove. A growing sense of dread rose in him like bile as he moved toward the shifting silhouettes of the trees.

Malcolm's drawings had shown Emma there, life made into art.

A hollow crack beneath his foot brought him to an abrupt stop. He had been moving down a gently sloped hill, and his flashlight revealed that the ground sheared off, dropping at a steep angle. He knelt to inspect the object he'd stepped on, his light exposing the lines and whorls of an old wooden beam. He shifted his weight and half jumped, half slid down the entrance to an old cellar. Recognizing its potential as a hiding place, he checked the area thoroughly before turning his attention to the door. It was roughly slatted and no longer airtight, with cracks showing inky darkness between the boards. A large tree branch had been slung across as a makeshift lock, preventing the door from being opened. Ian's heart sped up. The branch would be no deterrent for someone outside; it was designed to keep something, or someone, in. Ian leaned close and pressed his cheek to the boards. He could hear a soft sound on the other side.

"Emma?" he dared.

Silence stretched for long moments before he heard a voice, almost a sob, respond. "I'm here."

Forgetting caution, Ian muscled the tree branch from the door and wrenched it open. He moved the light haphazardly around the small space, searching until it landed on Emma's pale dirt-streaked face. She closed her eyes and dropped her forehead to the dirt ground. His stomach clenched as the light caught on the folds of rich fabric, the horror of Malcolm's artistic vision come to life.

Ian dropped into the dark space and immediately stumbled. He moved the light away from Emma, startled to find himself next to another prone figure. The face was turned away, and Ian reached to shift the body. A faint wave of shock registered as he recognized the slack features of Rory Tamblyn. "Shit," he muttered. Not only had he been chasing the wrong lead, but his prime suspect had been abducted without him even realizing it.

"Is he alive?" Emma's soft voice penetrated the darkness.

Forcing himself to move beyond self-recriminations, Ian moved his fingers to the side of Tamblyn's throat. A thready pulse beat beneath the sweat-slicked skin.

"Yes," he responded. Ian turned and crept toward Emma, keeping his light trained on her body but carefully away from her eyes. "Are you hurt?"

"Bruised, sore, not hurt."

"Can you move?"

"I'm tied. Ankles and hands." Emma spoke in short bursts as if the effort of sentences was beyond her.

The words sent a flair of anxiety through Ian, mixing with anger. Ian exhaled raggedly as he tried to maintain his facade of calm control.

"Hurry. He's still out there." Emma's voice was tangled in emotions that Ian couldn't stop to smooth and unwind.

He gently pressed Emma's shoulder down so that her stomach was to the floor. Holding the light in his teeth, Ian pulled the pocketknife out and slid the blade open. He ran it with quick, efficient motions against the ropes that bound Emma's hands, then moved to her feet.

"What about Rory?"

Ian nodded and—a little less gently—repeated the process to free Tamblyn. "We need to get you out first, then I'll come back for him. Do you think you can walk?"

"If I can't, I'll crawl," Emma replied, moving stiffly to her knees.

Ian reached a hand to her shoulder as she came to the entrance, stopping her from raising her head above the threshold. He couldn't see her expression in the darkness, but she froze at his touch and let him move in front of her. Ian slowly crawled through the door, staying as low as possible, did a rapid search of the surrounding area with his light, then reached down to Emma. She moved slowly as she rose and faltered as she tried to stand. But her grip on his hand was strong. Ian pressed his hand to her cheek for a brief moment and felt her lean into his palm. Then, sliding an arm along her back in equal parts protection and support, he turned her back toward the farmhouse. A gut feeling told him that Malcolm was in the apple grove, preparing.

Ian wanted to take Emma to his car, drive off, and let someone else be Tamblyn's white knight. As he reached the farmhouse, though, Emma pulled away.

"Rory," she said simply.

"Once you're clear," he responded. "Just up here." He found a deep shadow away from Malcolm's entry point to the house and car, in case Malcolm made a run for it. Ian's only weapon was the small pocketknife; he dug it out of his back pocket and pressed it into Emma's palm.

He sensed more than saw her tight nod. "I'll need the light. I'm sorry."

"The moon is more light than I've seen for a while," Emma replied.

Ian pushed down a surge of anger. "Don't move unless you have to. It's easier to hide than run. But if I don't come back, if something happens . . . my car's up through the trees, there." He pointed in the direction that he had come down the trail. "Run. Find my car, and call for help. Understand?" He dug for his keys and phone, handing them to her.

Emma nodded and pressed herself against the wall of the dilapidated house as Ian turned and moved as swiftly as he dared back to the still-open cellar. He dropped inside and crawled to Tamblyn's side. He felt for a pulse again and heard a soft groan in response. Ian shifted him roughly onto his side, stuck the flashlight in his own back pocket, then scooped him over his shoulder into a fireman's carry. Moving awkwardly in the small space, he inched toward the door. The other man's shallow breathing raked against his ear, and there was a stickiness on Rory's skin that Ian thought was likely blood. He stood slowly once he reached the entrance to the cellar and heaved Rory's weight to the ground at the front of the door. He pulled his flashlight out and swung it back toward where he knew Emma waited in the shadows.

Her scream reached him just moments before something hard and heavy struck the side of his face, shattering his vision and sending him down into the darkness.

Chapter 31

Emma curled her fingers into a tight fist around the knife that Ian had left her as she watched him move farther away. His flashlight skittered across the stiff grass, a pale imitation of the half-moon that had risen above the shaggy ghosts of the apple trees. Its weak light did little to dispel the blackness. Ian vanished into the shadows of the cellar. She pressed herself back against the coarse wood boards of the farmhouse as she fumbled with Ian's phone, trying to get a signal, all the while waiting for Ian to reappear. Finally, from the ghostly silhouette of the orchard, the shape of a man emerged, moving slowly. He stooped slightly forward as he walked, his back and neck rounding.

"Malcolm." Emma mouthed the name without a sound.

Her captor walked from the trees, maybe a hundred yards from Ian and Rory. Emma didn't dare call out. Moving as gingerly as she could, she began to steal back down the hill. Her bare feet were silent on the grass, but the heavy gown wrapped her legs as she moved and pulled her down as if she were treading through muddy water. Her breath was ragged with fear and effort. About halfway down the hill, she stopped, sinking into the shadows. She watched as Ian's form rose slowly from the cellar. His body jerked and heaved, and Emma realized he was struggling against the weight he was carrying. He leaned forward and slid Rory to the ground, his body rolling softly as it landed. Light rocked around him as he moved, the beam of his flashlight shining up his back and leaving his legs in darkness. Pulling himself out of the cellar, Ian reached for the light and drew it around toward where Emma stood. It caught the reflection of pale flesh as Ian swung around. Malcolm was no more than a foot away, and Emma caught the glint of metal as the light glanced over him.

Abandoning any attempt at secrecy, Emma stood to her full height and screamed, "Behind you!"

She took off at a full run. She reached the top of the cellar and looked over. The slanting door was flung open, and Ian's fallen flashlight showed his sprawled form on the earthen floor. Malcolm stood panting at the threshold, looking down into the cellar with a handgun hanging limply in his fingers. Without thinking, Emma hurdled herself the short distance toward him. She hit him without grace or precision, but Malcolm was caught off guard by the unexpected attack. They hit the ground heavily, rolling down a gentle slope away from the cellar door and tangling them both in the thick fabric of her gown. Emma scrambled on top of him. The small knife was still clutched in her hand, and she slashed the blade against his face. Malcolm struggled beneath her, and Emma lost her grip on the pocketknife. She scratched through the darkness, hoping to find his face, his eyes, anything that would give her the advantage. Her nails scraped a bloody path down his neck before he managed to shove her aside.

Emma's arms ached, and her head spun as she forced herself to her knees. She could hear Malcolm's harsh breath behind her as she frantically traced her fingers through the grass, hoping divine intervention would place the knife within her reach. Instead, her fingers wrapped around a branch as thick as her arm. She swung in a wild circle as his footsteps came up behind her, the branch slamming against Malcolm's shins with reverberating force. His knees buckled, and he dropped to her level. Meeting his eyes, Emma swung again. The branch collided with his temple with a moist crack, and Malcolm's eyes widened in shock before rolling backward. He rocked, then collapsed into the dust, stunned.

Emma shoved him onto his stomach. She ripped a slivered ribbon from her sleeve, roughly jerked Malcolm's arms behind him, and wrapped the ribbon around his wrists as tightly as she could, knotting the ends. Leaving Malcolm lying in the dirt, she scrambled back to the open cellar. She lowered herself into it, careful to avoid Ian, and reached for the flashlight that he had dropped as he fell. Emma ran her hands along his face to his neck, found a strong pulse, and ran them back to his cheeks. She moved her fingers along his face, searching for injuries, then spread them along his scalp. She felt warm, thick blood at the back of his head and moved the light around to assess his wound. Ian groaned as her fingers probed his wound, and Emma pulled back.

"Ian? Ian, can you hear me?"

Ian groaned again and shifted his weight away from the ground. Moving slowly and, Emma noticed, careful not to shift his head, Ian rose to his hands and knees. He paused there, breathing heavily before slowly rocking back on his heels.

"Where's . . . ?"

"Malcolm? Outside. I hit him with a tree branch."

Ian jerked his head to meet her eyes, then hissed with pain. He closed his eyes and took several deep breaths.

"Do you need to throw up?" Emma asked awkwardly.

In the small stream of light, Emma could see Ian's mouth quirk. "No."

"You probably have a concussion."

"Yes."

"I'm sorry," Emma said softly.

"Why? I might be a little foggy, but I'm pretty sure you saved my life."

"For before. For everything."

Ian didn't respond immediately. "We need to get help."

Emma rose to her feet and hauled herself up from the cellar. Ian followed unsteadily, ignoring the hand Emma offered to help. Once outside, Emma moved to stand over Malcolm. He lay still in the position that she had bound him. Using one bare foot, Emma pushed at his shoulder. He didn't respond. She turned back to see Ian reaching down to Rory.

Ian pressed his fingers to the other man's neck. "Still alive."

"Can you carry him?"

Ian hesitated a moment. "No." He gingerly tested the edges of the bruise that was blooming on his forehead. "I didn't see him coming."

"I know. You were looking for me."

Ian glanced up but didn't respond.

He rolled Rory over. "Hand me the light," Ian directed. Ian ran the light over Rory's face, and Emma sucked in a tight breath as the smeared blood showed against his too-pale skin.

"Can you make it up the hill, or should I try to find your car on my own?" Emma asked, keeping her voice neutral.

Ian responded quickly. "You're not going on your own."

Taking a deep breath, he bent slowly to check Malcolm's pulse and breathing. He tugged on Emma's knots and made a small, satisfied noise. "Those are . . . tight."

"I know."

Ian met Emma's eyes, then nodded, rising. "He's secure for now. Let's go." Ian took Emma's hand in his, and together with the weakening beam of the Maglite guiding their way, they trod up the hill. They passed the too-silent farmhouse and slid into the blackness of the forest on the far side of the clearing. The trail was barely visible with the moonlight unable to breach the canopy of foliage above them, and the trek back to the car was torturously slow. When they reached the far end, and Ian's car came into view, Emma let out a half-sobbing breath. Ian reached out in a seemingly impulsive gesture and pulled her to his chest. Emma wrapped her arms around him and dug her fingers into the soft material of his shirt. Ian's arms pulled her in tighter, and they stood silently.

They were interrupted by the *whup-whup* of a siren, a sound so out of place in the nightmare of Emma's last days that it took her a minute to recognize it. Headlights bore down on them, and Ian tugged Emma over to the side of his car. A park ranger in a telltale khaki Jeep pulled up beside them. He parked and climbed out of the vehicle. Ian shifted so that he stood between Emma and the young man.

"Evenin' folks. Don't know if you know this, but this is a restricted area. I saw your car earlier, thought maybe . . ." The ranger broke off as he flicked a flashlight their way and took in Emma's dress and Ian's bloodied face.

"Jesus fuck," the man blurted. "What the hell is going on?"

Ian moved his hands so that they were plainly visible. "My name is Ian Carter, and I'm a detective with the CPD. This woman was kidnapped; two injured men are down by the old farmstead." Ian pointed toward the trail they had just come up. "Do you have a radio with you?"

"Yes. I . . ."

"Good. I need you to radio for help. We need the police and an ambulance." Ian's voice was calm and steady. "Can you do that?"

The man didn't respond but moved back to the Jeep and reached inside the open window for a radio handset. "Hey, it's Jerry. We've got a situation out here. We're going to need the local PD and a medical response team." He paused as someone responded on the other end. "Yeah, I'm not sure—"

He was interrupted by the ricocheting sound of a gunshot.

The ranger instinctively ducked down beside his Jeep, and Ian moved to cover Emma with his body, pressing her against the door of his car. All three waited, frozen, as the sound echoed into stillness.

"Rory," Emma breathed.

"Get us some backup—" Ian barked at the still-paralyzed park ranger "—now." He ran toward the sound.

Emma dashed after him, and Ian whirled on her. "Stay here."

"Like hell."

"You can't run in that thing." Ian gestured to the brocade dress.

"Then you'll beat me there. But I'm still coming."

Ian's jaw tightened. "Stay behind me. Keep low."

Emma nodded, and the two moved back into the woods. They tripped and slid along the path, the sound of the ranger's radio pleas fading as the forest swallowed them. When they broke through to the other side, Ian picked up his pace to a steady jog, his gaze swinging from side to side as he scanned the open space with his flashlight. Emma heaved her skirts up and struggled behind him, her already torn feet rubbing raw with each step. As they reached the bottom of the hill where the root cellar lay, Ian slowed and pulled Emma in behind him. They moved in tandem—slow, cautious inches toward the door.

Ian's light searched the ground below them, landing first on Malcolm. He was face down in the dirt just as Emma had left him, but he had moved about five feet to the left, and his now unbound hands were flung out above his head. A dark, wet stain was spreading across his left shoulder. A foot away, his bloodied head buried against his knees, sat Rory. A gun lay at his feet.

Chapter 32

The darkness in the valley lifted as Ian watched the invasion of police and emergency personnel, bringing with them a storm of light—the beams of flashlights, headlights, and portable spotlights forced the shadows into submission. By the time he and Emma had managed to walk a shocked and injured Tamblyn up to the waiting cars, the panicked ranger had managed to rouse a battalion of officials in various shades of uniform. Paramedics arrived shortly after, assessing and treating each of them. Tamblyn's head wound had been marked as the most serious, and he was trundled into an ambulance minutes before Mike and members of the CPD arrived on the scene.

Ian could tell his partner—possibly former partner by now, he realized—was less than happy about the situation. Mike started toward where Ian leaned against the side of his car, a cold pack provided by one of the paramedics pressed to his head. A second ambulance rumbled up the dirt road, and Ian watched as Emma was transferred from where she had been sitting in the ranger's passenger seat to the back of the ambulance. An efficient paramedic whom Ian judged to be in her midforties hopped out and began a quick assessment of Emma's condition. Ian could see her mouth move as she responded to questions. She shook her head, held out an arm for a blood pressure cuff, then pointed down. The paramedic moved the heavy skirts up Emma's legs and reached for a medical kit. For the first time, Ian realized that Emma's feet were bare. Even from a distance, he could see the stain of blood on her soles. Her face registered pain for just a second as the medic cleaned and bandaged the wounds, then Emma pulled her expression into stillness as the treatment continued.

Ian heard Mike's footsteps as he approached from behind, but he didn't turn. The paramedic had wrapped Emma's feet, then progressed to other cuts and lacerations up her legs and arms. Emma turned her head, and Ian saw a wide scrape across her cheek where the skin had begun to darken to a bruise.

"So, you want a statement here, or do you want to wait till we're back at the station?" Ian met his partner's gaze without expression.

"What the hell were you thinking?"

"That a killer was holding her captive, and she didn't have time to wait for paperwork."

Mike grunted. "Deranged kidnapper, likely a serial killer, and you thought it would be fun to go off without backup? Or a weapon?"

"I'm on suspension. I couldn't call for backup."

"Bullshit. I would have come."

Ian nodded his acknowledgment of this.

"So, you wanted to play cowboy? Rescue the damsel from the railroad tracks? What then? She falls for you, and you ride off into the sunset. It was a jackass move, Carter."

"Yes." Ian paused, staring down at his hands, memorizing the tracks of dirt that ran across them. "She was barefoot."

"What?" Mike asked, startled by the non sequitur.

"Emma," Ian said quietly. "She was barefoot the whole time."

Ian could feel Mike staring at him and finally looked back up, bracing himself for his partner's fury. Instead, he read deep concern etched into the familiar face. "We'll need a formal statement later, but right now, you need to get to the hospital and have that head checked."

"I'm fine."

"You go to the hospital, or I arrest you for obstruction. Your call."

Ian nodded as he shifted his weight away from the car and moved slowly toward the ambulance.

The paramedic glanced at him. "Decided to get that checked?"

"It was decided for me."

"Good. Climb in."

Ian boosted himself awkwardly into the ambulance and took a small seat against the wall. Emma was lying back on the gurney that filled most of the space with her eyes closed. He turned to the paramedic as she pulled the doors shut. "Is she okay?"

"She's fine," Emma replied. "She's been kidnapped, beaten up, her feet hurt. And she's tired."

"Nothing life-threatening," the paramedic confirmed. "But since she has some gaps in her memory, we need to do a full physical workup." Ian knew they would also be collecting evidence, checking her body and blood for any sign of the man who had abducted her. He reached over and gingerly took her hand. Emma curled her fingers lightly over his. They sat in silence as the ambulance rolled into the coming dawn.

"What's the damage, Frankenstein?" Mike asked, pulling aside the privacy curtain to where Ian was still perched on an exam table. Ian turned to show off the shaved patch and line of stitches on the back of his head. Emma had been admitted for observation. Ian had watched her, too-still on the gurney, as she had been taken away.

"She's still being checked out," Mike said, following his train of thought.

"Can you tell me anything?"

Mike shrugged. "Nothing you don't know. Minor injuries from the initial assault and the constraints. She's got a gap in her memory, so . . . they're doing a rape kit. In case."

"Yeah."

"She's a fighter." Mike shifted his weight from foot to foot. "Tamblyn's been checked out and tucked in. Sounds like he doesn't remember much either."

"Convenient."

"Do not start that again." Mike dropped his voice to just above a whisper and stepped closer to Ian. "Tamblyn's agreed to drop the assault charges against you because you saved his life, but don't push your luck."

Ian pictured Tamblyn in the darkened cellar, skin slick with sweat. "You're right." Ian took a deep breath. "Did he give you anything more about the shooting?"

"Said that he woke, dizzy and disoriented, and started to make his way up the hill. He heard a noise from behind him. Haynes comes at him with a gun. They fight. The gun goes off."

"So, now what?"

"Now," Mike responded grimly, "I do my job. You rest that hard head."

Ian checked his watch. It was almost noon. "Not allowed to sleep."

"You got someone who can keep an eye on you? You want to go to the house? Brian will be there. Kids should be up soon."

"No, thanks. I'm going to grab something to eat here in the cafeteria. I'll be fine."

"She's on the third floor," Mike said, turning to leave.

Ian said nothing but headed toward the elevator.

He spotted the straight form of a uniformed officer as soon as he entered the hallway. He slowed his pace, once again feeling his limitations without his badge. Before Ian could speak, however, the officer addressed him.

"The nurse just left, Detective Carter," Officer Gonzales said. "Do you want to go in?"

Ian's mouth tightened into a line. "Hell of a coincidence, you being assigned here."

"I volunteered. Making amends." Gonzales's face said clearly that he wasn't doing this for praise.

At Ian's nod, the young officer knocked twice, then opened the door. Emma was dressed in a pale blue hospital gown, her hair damp and her face clean. She sat up as Ian entered.

Ian hesitated at the doorway, feeling like a teenager waiting for punishment. "How are you?"

She shifted in the bed, straightening her posture and tucking the gown tighter around her. "Better. You've got blood on your shirt."

Ian glanced down at his filthy clothes, surprised. "I haven't had a chance to change."

Emma shook her head, and Ian knew he'd gotten the answer wrong. But he didn't know what the right one was.

"Do you need a statement?" she asked blankly.

Ian studied her; the bruises and lines of exhaustion looked even worse in the fluorescent light. He remembered that she'd told him once that she didn't hide things as well when she was tired. He had a sudden, guilty urge to use that to his advantage.

Instead, he made his tone deliberately gentle. "I have a few questions if you're up to it. But mostly, I wanted to see if you're okay."

"The answer to your question is no," Emma said, meeting his eyes with sudden intensity.

"What question?"

"If he sexually assaulted me— No, as far as they can tell, he didn't. I can't remember."

"I'm sure he didn't. It's not part of his MO," Ian told her, trying to sound reassuring.

"That's what Mike said." She looked down at her hands. "I thought it was you, waiting for me. When he took me."

"I know," Ian replied softly. He moved over to a chair near the bed and sat down. "We saw the texts. I didn't send them."

"I figured that out," Emma said bitterly. She pressed her hand to her eyes. "I'm sorry. I'm tired."

"Do you want me to stay? Sit with you awhile?" Ian held his breath, his hands gripping the chair arms in preparation for flight.

Emma shook her head, lying down in the bed and turning her back to him.

"Okay." Ian rose stiffly and crossed the room, pausing with his hand on the doorknob. "Emma? I'm sorry."

"I know." Her voice was muffled against her pillow. "Me, too."

His arrival at the precinct the next morning was greeted by applause, although Ian recognized some of it as sarcastic. He may have caught a serial killer, but he made an absolute mess doing it.

"Hey, handsome," Mike said as he approached his desk.

Ian grimaced. He knew from the bathroom mirror that his eyes were circled and bloodshot, and much of his face was shaded blue with bruising.

"Have you seen this morning's paper? Our friend Mackey is going to make you a star." Mike tossed a copy of the *Daily Independent* onto Ian's desk. "And the intern, Charlotte, has left you three messages already— She wants to make sure that she gets her exclusive."

Ian lifted the paper as he sat. The headline read in bold letters: *Courageous Cop Catches Killer.* "God, that's awful," Ian muttered.

"The picture or the prose?"

"The prose. What's the picture?" Ian unfolded the paper so that the bottom half was visible. There, he saw a large picture of himself outside of the hospital, exiting the ambulance next to Emma's stretcher, her hand in his. He was muddied, bloodied, with an intense expression. "Shit. How'd they get it?"

"Must have heard the report on the scanner when Dispatch said which hospital you were headed to. They probably just waited till you showed."

"Could be worse," Ian suggested.

"Read the article."

Ian moved his eyes back above the fold and quickly scanned the accompanying story. Unsurprisingly, it was filled with purple prose and stretched truths. Malcolm was a mustache-twirling villain, Emma a helpless damsel—"She'll hate that," he muttered as he read—and Ian himself had been turned into a vigilante rebelling against the red tape and bureaucracy of the CPD. "Shit," Ian repeated.

"Fletcher wants to see you," Mike offered casually.

"I bet she does." Ian tossed the paper in the trash can beside the desk.

Mike reached into his top drawer, pulled out a second copy of the paper, and tossed it to Ian. "Don't worry about it. I got plenty."

"Bastard."

Mike laughed loudly enough for the other detectives in the room to look his way, some in curiosity, most in annoyance.

At that moment, Lieutenant Fletcher spotted Ian through her glass window. She ducked her head out the door. "Carter. Now."

Ian rose. "Time to meet my maker."

"Good luck, cowboy."

Ian crossed the room to his boss's office, entered, and shut the door behind him. "Yes, Lieutenant?" He stayed near the threshold.

"You are one lucky son of a bitch." Fletcher's face was thunderous as she watched him from behind her desk.

"What?" Ian took a step forward, startled by the words rather than the expression, before forcing himself into stillness again.

"You broke every rule in the goddamn book, assaulted a witness, broke into a suspect's house, and who knows what else." Fletcher reached into her desk, pulled out Ian's gun and badge, and slid them across the polished wood surface. "But I guess shit don't stick to you."

Ian stayed by the door. "I don't understand."

Fletcher laughed humorlessly. "Well, you stopped the serial killer, saved the girl, and the press painted you as John-fucking-Wayne. The commissioner decided that their story plays better than 'fuckup gets lucky.' So, I've been told to shine you up and get you back on the job. Tamblyn's dropped the charges, so IA's going to let things go. You're back on duty, but you'll be riding a desk until you get a clear psych eval. Now take your shit and get out of my sight." She stood and collected his gear. Circling the desk, she strode toward him and slammed the items against his chest.

Ian clutched at them before they could fall. "Yes, ma'am. Thank you."

"Don't thank me." She turned her back on him. "I wanted to boot your ass."

"I understand."

"Somehow I doubt that, Carter." The lieutenant dropped heavily into her chair.

Ian shut the door awkwardly as he left, his gun and badge cradled in his arms. As he crossed the room, eyes swiveled to avoid his. The lieutenant's office was not soundproof.

"So," Mike said as he sat down. "Still standing."

"Barely." Ian put his badge and gun on his desk and dropped into his chair in unconscious mimicry of his boss. "Seems I'm John-fucking-Wayne."

"What does that mean?"

Ian picked up the newspaper. "Commissioner decided vigilante hero might not be the worst look."

"So, you get to be a poster boy." Mike's voice was laced with the same disdain as Lieutenant Fletcher's.

"Seems like it." Ian scrubbed at his face, noticing his stubble for the first time. "Shit."

"Well, better a dancing monkey than a *former* detective."

Ian nodded, but he wasn't sure. The idea that he would be finishing the paperwork and just moving on to another case seemed impossible to him. "Did you find anything new while I was—"

"Going rogue?" Mike interrupted. "We located Dana Ackerman. She went out partying with some people she 'kinda knew' and decided she'd take an extra-long weekend. No phone chargers at the soirée, apparently. She's embarrassed and seems a little pissed at the kickup but not hurt. There's no suggestion that she was being held."

"So, we have the three college students, Emma . . ."

"And at least one of the girls up north that Hastings identified, likely all three," Mike added.

"You figure out motive?"

"Jealous? Spurned? Nuts? Weird little nobody gets rejected by the pretty blonde girls and takes it badly. It seems to be a trend these days. It works, Ian."

"Seems to. He just . . . I wouldn't have said that he had it in him. He was a messed-up kid, but . . . ?" Ian shrugged. "I missed it."

"He had at least one more on the agenda," Mike told him, ignoring the mea culpa.

"What do you mean?"

Mike pulled a folder out of his drawer. "The original's being analyzed, but they sent up scans. It's a journal that details each of the scenes." Mike spread a series of drawings out on the desk. Ian leaned over to look more closely. The first two showed a detailed colored image of the earliest crime scenes: Ophelia and Elaine of Astolat. They were more stylized than the sketches that Ian had found, with specific details of each scene and calligraphic lines of the quotes that had been placed with the bodies. Both of the women were clear and recognizable. The next page showed a woman who must have been Olivia Ballard, though her features were blank. This sketch seemed much more haphazard than the other two. Mike set a fourth page down. It showed another faceless woman. She wore a long medieval gown of soft blue, and her hair was pulled back from where her face should have been. A light veil was draped over her hair, making her look like a bride. At the bottom of the page, in looping calligraphy, someone had written three poetic lines in faint blue ink:

". . . as false as air, as water, wind, or sandy earth,
As fox to lamb, as wolf to heifer's calf,
Pard to the hind, or stepdame to her son."

"None of them match Emma's getup," Mike pointed out. "You recognize that last bit?"

Ian shook his head. "Find anything else?"

"There are two weird things, but don't read too much into them. There was a car at the homestead registered to Tamblyn, not Haynes."

"Tamblyn drives a VW?"

"No. A Beemer. It was parked in the bushes not far from where the cavalry found you. The VW near the barn was reported stolen a few months back. We're checking for prints or signs that the girls—or Dr. Reilly—were transported in it."

"If he drove Tamblyn's car out to the barn, then how did Haynes . . ." Ian just shook his head. He could have walked into town, hitched—hell—booked a rideshare. "Never mind. What's the second thing?"

"The DNA under Olivia Ballard's fingernails wasn't a match. Unknown subject." Mike shrugged. "Could be a screwup. We're having it retested."

"Good," Ian said vaguely. "Smart."

He reached again for the image of the woman in blue.

Chapter 33

Emma looked around her house and felt fear and rage crawl through her body, leaving a sense of nausea in its wake. Her hands were coated in the same fine powder that covered every surface in the kitchen and living room, a memento of the crime scene techs' search for fingerprints. The signs of invasion were subtle, like the traces of dust: pictures askew and items slightly out of alignment, footprints scuffing the floor, a glass on the counter that she had not placed there. Feeling a tremor sneak along her skin, she resolutely bent down to scoop up abandoned items from her purse that lay strewn across the floor. The purse itself was gone, collected for evidence, as was her phone. Charlie had gotten her a new phone, downloaded extra security apps, and refused to leave until Emma had added a more secure passcode.

Just as she set the gathered items on an end table, she heard a knock at the door. She knew it was locked and bolted, but Emma still felt a moment of panic at the noise. It was her space, her house, and she didn't want anyone in it right now. The knock sounded again, along with a muffled call. With a deep breath, she crossed to the door and moved close to its newly polished surface.

"Who is it?" For a mad moment, she thought of the opening line of *Hamlet*—"Who goes there?"—and wondered what ghost was waiting for her on the other side.

"It's Ian."

Emma snicked the lock open and slowly drew back the door. She studied Ian's face in the stark light and struggled to translate what she saw. He was visibly exhausted and injured, but there was more there, a sort of damage that ran deeper than his bruises. Emma recognized his pain in her own. Detective or not, he had been threatened, assaulted, and nearly killed. He'd crawled through the darkness and felt the warmth of his own blood. She stepped aside.

"Can I get you something? Tea? Coffee?"

"No, thank you." Ian took a small step forward, then paused uncertainly.

"Sorry, come in." She waved vaguely toward the living room and then turned to lead the way. She sat down on the far edge of the sofa and curled her legs beneath her.

"Did you have more questions?" she asked after he had settled himself in one of her oversized chairs. He looked stiff and uncomfortable against the soft fabric. She studied his face. "Or do you want to tell me what else you found?"

Ian looked startled before offering the ghost of a smile. "You would've made a good detective. We found a sketchbook with a new scene. It doesn't match any of the victims . . . or you. This woman is in a blue dress."

"Can I see her?"

Ian hesitated, then pulled out his phone. He flipped through several screens before turning the screen toward her. There was a picture of a colored drawing of a woman in blue, draped in sheer fabric.

"Faithless Cressida . . . It's Shakespeare again. Or it could be Chaucer, I guess. Or Joseph of Exeter."

"What makes you say that?"

"I've been to the Tate Britain, for starters." Emma rose and pulled a well-annotated text from her shelf. She flipped through until she found what she was looking for, then handed the book to Ian. "Malcolm plagiarized all of his poses. Ophelia from Millais, Elaine from Waterhouse—he probably thought he was clever drawing from all three versions—" Emma tapped the glossy image Ian was studying. "And now, from Opie. The dress color is different, but—there she is."

"You know the painting that well?"

"I love the Tate. I've spent hours in front of these paintings. It's like he curated it specifically for me." Emma dropped into the sofa. "Poor Cressida." She handed back his phone.

"Why was Shakespeare your first guess?"

"It's the cruelest version. In the story—all versions—Troilus falls in love with Cressida, but after they have a secret assignation, her father goes over to the enemy and takes Cressida with him. She promises to return to Troilus but doesn't; she betrays him and takes another man as her lover. Chaucer's Cressida is frightened and doing her best. Her love is genuine. His portrayal of her is sympathetic. Shakespeare's is . . . not. Critics have written entire papers asking why he's so bitter and hateful in his portrayal of her. She's a 'wanton,' in his words. I figured that the killer . . . Malcolm . . . was most likely to pick the notoriously misogynistic version." She shrugged. "Was there a quote?"

Ian took out his phone again, scrolled, and showed her the screen.

". . . as false as air, as water, wind, or sandy earth,
As fox to lamb, as wolf to heifer's calf,
Pard to the hind, or stepdame to her son,"

"It's part of a longer speech. Basically, the two lovers are pledging themselves to each other, and Cressida is promising to . . ." Emma inhaled sharply. She rose quickly and found her copy of Shakespeare, flipping to the scene. "Read that." She pointed to the beginning of Cressida's speech. Then returned to the bookshelf as Ian found the passage.

"Ah . . . 'If I be false or swerve a hair from truth, when time is old and hath forgot itself . . .'"

"Skip down a few lines: 'From false . . .'" Emma scanned the book spines, only half paying attention to what he was saying.

Ian read dutifully. "'From false to false, among false maids in love . . .'"

"Here!" she interrupted. She found her copy of *Jane Eyre* tucked randomly on a shelf after the night spent reading with Rory. She flipped through the pages as Ian watched, visibly confused. She showed him the page with the cramped blue script. "Same phrase."

"Okay?"

"I didn't write that. And I couldn't figure out who did. But that book was in my purse when I was mugged. He had it; he wrote that."

Ian studied the page. "When did you find this?"

"A few days ago. I thought it was odd, but—" Emma shook her head. "Why did he abandon his original idea? He'd clearly planned it out. He wrote this the night of the gala. He knew then what he wanted to do with me."

Ian shook his head. "It seems like the first two murders were carefully planned, every detail, but the third . . ."

"Olivia," Emma said.

"Olivia's attack and your kidnapping appear spontaneous. Like he told you. He had a plan but screwed it up. Maybe you spooked him by investigating, so he felt like he had to scare you, stop you. So he improvised."

"So I became the beautiful woman without mercy . . . a threat rather than a betrayer? I suppose it fits. *La Belle* isn't at the

Tate, though. I wonder how he picked her." Emma lifted the phone again and scrolled to the drawing that Malcolm had left behind. "His Cressida looks like me. It's not just the dress. She has my hair, my posture. He was talented." Emma touched the screen, flicking the picture away. "Was I the start of it all?"

Ian reached a hand toward her as she sank back onto the sofa. He stopped just short of her arm, curling his fingers back against his palm. "Sarah Weston was taken before the gala. Haynes probably chose her and Phillipa Minor long before that night. You just became . . ."

"Part of the collection." Emma wrapped her arms over her chest. "Was the purple dress you found me in meant for someone else?"

"It's possible."

"Then you saved two of us."

Ian looked surprised, then uncomfortable.

"Thank you, Ian." Emma's voice was soft but unwavering.

"You should never have been involved in the first place."

"Malcolm got me involved. He chose me, mugged me, left that message in my book. And then . . . then I *wanted* to be involved, wanted to help." Emma looked up, finding his gaze. "You didn't do anything."

"Sure," Ian said softly enough that Emma didn't think it was for her.

Emma studied his face for a moment. "Do you ever read mysteries? Anything like that?"

"Sometimes," Ian answered slowly. "I like noir."

"Chandler. Of course. How do you—" Emma broke off, uncertain of what she needed to ask. "How do you keep it all separate? The books and—"

"Real life?" Ian finished for her.

She nodded.

"It's never been hard, honestly. They're just stories."

"Are they?" Emma asked. "I can't—" She took a breath. "I wanted to read myself to sleep last night, but I realized that all of my favorites—they're all about death, people hurting each other. I don't know how to read them anymore. And I don't know what to do without them. I don't know where to go to escape—" Chaotic emotions threatened to overwhelm her and she broke off abruptly.

"Hopefully you can find new stories, new places to escape," he offered.

"Maybe." She smiled slightly, unconvincingly, as the last few days rolled over her again. She had unseen wounds on her now, bruises and cuts to her carefully curated sense of self. He didn't understand—how could he? She could think of only one person who might.

Rory answered the door at the third knock. He was bruised and moving stiffly as he stepped aside to let her in. "You look much better than I do," he said lightly.

"The magic of makeup. A perk of womanhood, I suppose." Emma flexed her hand, and Rory's eyes dropped to it.

"Can I get you something? A drink or . . . ?"

"No, I just . . . I just wanted to see you. To talk."

"Come to my library. The books might be comforting."

"They used to be." Emma followed Rory through a darkly decorated, starkly masculine main room and into a cozy room filled with high-backed leather armchairs. The walls were lined with floor-to-ceiling shelves, each one neatly filled with books but otherwise bare of decorative items. There was a faux fireplace against one wall and a large mahogany desk under the window. Papers were scattered across its dark surface, vying for space with stacks of books and journals.

"You've been working," Emma said, looking at the clutter.

"I needed a distraction."

"I get that. I've been wandering from room to room like Miss Havisham."

"Do you want a drink?" Rory reached for a bottle of scotch.

Emma shook her head. "I'm surprised you still have a taste for it."

"Why?"

Emma glanced over, surprised. "After you were drugged. You said you thought Malcolm put something in your scotch."

"Right, yes. Well, I'm not going to let that little bastard ruin one of my great pleasures in life." He saluted her with his glass.

"Ian came to see me this morning."

"Business or pleasure?"

"They found another drawing, another plan in Malcolm's things. There was supposed to be another girl. Cressida."

"One of Shakespeare's least popular. Malcolm was better read than I gave him credit for," Rory said before taking another sip of scotch.

Emma could feel Rory's eyes following her as she moved around the room, touching the books softly, testing her reaction to them. Emma had been to this room many times. She and Rory had planned and plotted and researched for hours here as they'd prepared for their study-abroad course. She moved to another shelf with uniformly framed pictures, seeking one she knew she'd find—the two of them outside of Agatha Christie's house, Greenway. She lifted the photo, scanning their happy faces. They hadn't waited for the tour, she remembered, just posed by the folly. Rory had insisted. It had become an ongoing joke that they visited all of the literary gift shops in England but none of the museums. Emma liked the kitschy souvenirs but never had the patience to read all the placards on the actual displays. Except . . .

Emma put the photo down, the trail of memories ending somewhere she no longer felt safe. She tried to distract herself by scanning the other photos, all familiar. "Wasn't there another one? Of all of us, at that faculty party?"

"What? Oh, I took it to the office." Rory tipped his head questioningly. "Why?"

"Nothing, no reason. I just noticed." Emma turned away, her terrier brain trying to find the missing picture in her memory of

Rory's office. She shook her head and moved to the desk, where he leaned casually. A series of sketches covered the wooden surface. "Are these new?" The images were drawn in clear, dark lines, stylized women in contorted poses. Their bodies were constructed of sharp angles; their faces were blank. One showed a young woman wrapped in diaphanous material, her body showing through the Greek draping.

Rory touched one gently. "I've been . . . processing everything. Drawing helps."

Emma looked up, noticing new lines where his mouth drew tight at the edges. "Are you okay?"

He shook his head. "I truly thought it was beyond him."

"I didn't really believe it either, but . . ." Something flickered in Emma's brain. "He told me that he'd never read *Hamlet*, just seen the movie. I'm surprised he knew Troilus and Cressida. And Mallory, for that matter."

"He kidnapped and assaulted both of us, Emma. It hardly seems a stretch to imagine that he would lie to you."

"No, I suppose not." Another flicker, this time closer. Brighter. "You knew it, though."

"What?"

"When I said it was Cressida. You knew it was Shakespeare's version that he'd drawn."

Rory raised an eyebrow. "You told me it was."

"No. I didn't." Emma inhaled as a monstrous theory sparked into life. "And when I read you that quotation written in my copy of *Jane Eyre*, you recognized it."

"I don't remember that." Emma heard Rory's breathing speed up.

"Do you remember going to the Tate with me? You teased me because I skipped the author museums but spent hours staring at the art." Emma lifted the image of the Greacen girl. "This is the Opie painting, isn't it? Of Cressida?"

"It's just some girl." Something dark burned across Rory's face, but he snuffed it out.

Emma held his eyes for a brief moment, then smiled tightly. "Of course. Sorry. I can't stop trying to find connections, even when there aren't any. Maybe I'm not ready for company after all." She dropped her hand to her side and stepped away from the desk.

"Emma?" Rory moved between her and the door. "My sketch."

"Sorry." She held it out, trying to display indifference.

He didn't take it.

"Was it really the quote that did it?" Rory asked after a moment of scrutiny. His voice was light, almost uninterested. "I didn't have him take your bag to get the book, but then . . . I couldn't resist a little clue. Childish, I suppose."

Emma followed his glance to the shelf of photos. "It's not at the office, is it?"

"No." Rory's smile was almost sad.

Emma felt another puzzle piece click into place—Rory, Carolyn, and Emma at a faculty party along with a young blonde girl that Rory had brought with him. He'd introduced her as a student worker. She'd seemed smitten. Sarah. They'd asked a cater waiter to take their picture; he'd used Emma's phone.

She began to laugh, harsh and not entirely controlled. "Really? All of that for the fucking photo? It wasn't even on my phone anymore, Rory. It backs up to the Cloud."

Emma watched confusion shadow his face.

"Luddite," she spat, darting toward the door with the sketch clutched in her hand.

Rory's fist snaked into her hair. She gasped and pulled away instinctively, and he tightened his grip and pulled her firmly against his chest.

"Where are you going? This is your triumphant moment. You've solved the case, Miss Marple." Emma could hear a smile in his voice. "Don't you want the grand confession?"

"Bastard."

Emma jerked in his grasp, but he wrapped one arm around her waist, pulling her tighter to him. He moved his hand from her hair to her throat.

"Don't you want to hear about the first time I killed a girl? How good it felt?" His voice was playful, puckish, familiar. "Or how I trained Malcolm? The first time he went out alone, he nearly got caught. Vomited all over his ridiculous sneakers. It's a funny story, really." He brushed a strand of hair back from her eyes. "No? I'm surprised. With your penchant for Gothic fiction, I would have thought you'd enjoy the cliché."

"Let go of me, you sick fuck." Emma struggled as he increased pressure on her throat; her breathing shallowed beneath his hand.

"I'm disappointed, Emma." His voice mocked her. "Blaming mental illness. I'm not sick; I'm a fucking artist. I took these worthless things, and I made them extraordinary. Killing is a rush—don't get me wrong—but it's base, facile. But this—they were the muse, the brush, the canvas for my masterpieces."

"They were innocent girls . . ." Emma whispered. She'd wrapped her hands around his, digging her nails in. She'd leave evidence, if nothing else.

Rory's voice was jagged. "Hardly. They were empty forms, pretty dolls with nothing to offer beyond a hard fuck. I bought them expensive gifts, took them to the theater, the museum. They were too simple to appreciate any of what I offered."

Rory abruptly spun Emma around and shoved her against the bookshelf, his hands gripping her shoulders. Emma gasped at the sudden return of air to her lungs.

"My art gave the world more than their lives ever did," he whispered damply against her cheek.

Rory pressed closer against her, forcing her body into stillness as his heat encompassed her. Threads of fear tightened in her chest. She closed her eyes, trying to hide her panic and quell the bile rising in her throat. Crawling her fingers along the shelf,

Emma dug at the spine of a book with just her nails, desperate for anything that could be transformed into a weapon. At the first tug, Rory snapped his hand to her wrist, forcing her arm up and bending it until she cried out.

"What's the plan, Emma? Are you hoping your knight in shining armor's going to come for you?" He smiled, a parody of the Rory she knew. "Or are we doing a feminist retelling where the damsel fights back? Do you want to fight me, Emma?" With his free hand, he pulled a heavy bookend from the shelf and held it aloft. "Or should we just make this quick?" He made a sharp downward gesture.

Emma tensed for the blow.

Rory laughed, making the gesture again and waiting for her flinch. Then, tossing the bookend carelessly to the floor, he wrenched her away from the shelf and released her with a shove. "Do you really think that I'm going to do something as witless as beat you to death? In my own study?"

She stumbled only a few steps before losing her balance. She hit the edge of the desk with bruising force and fell to the ground, landing on her knees. Crawling, she tried to seek refuge behind the mahogany structure but was stopped by the pressure of a boot that sent her sprawling toward the center of the room.

"Where's the fun in that?"

Emma turned to look up at him, searching for a hint of the compassion he had shown her so often. "Why me?" The question felt pathetic, but Emma couldn't let herself die without finishing the puzzle.

Rory looked genuinely confused. "Don't you understand? How alike we are? I see how you wear your mask, play your role. I do the same thing every day, feigning normality when we are anything but."

"I'm not like you. You're a monster."

"But you are—that's how I always know when you're playacting, pretending to be like the other girls. You can hide your real self from everyone else, but not from me—never from me. This was supposed to be a game for you. For us. I would show you the photos in the paper, cajole you into 'solving' the mystery with me, my partner in crime." Rory knelt beside her, a parody of a man proposing to his lover, and wrapped his hand around the back of her head. He lifted her face close up to his, and Emma could feel his sweat against her skin. "Instead, I saw you in your blue gown at the gala, staring up at that detective like a Victorian coquette—my beautiful Cressida."

Emma felt nausea rising as understanding hit. That was how he saw her now. Faithless, traitorous. His.

"So clever, so false—" He forced his mouth to hers, biting her lip when she tried to escape. Emma could feel warm blood on her skin as he drew away.

"So, I changed the game." Rory's voice was without malice. He kept Emma tight against him, stroking one hand lightly along her back. "When you asked me to stay that night, I lay next to you, listening to you breathe, knowing how easy, how satisfying it would be to stop that breath and watch you grow cold."

She felt her fear seep away, replaced with unadulterated rage. She thought of her family, her students, everyone whose lives would crack or break if he killed her. Carolyn, Niall, Charlie—Emma inhaled sharply. Charlie had been right.

"You're nothing more than a shallow, self-involved wannabe," she spat at him. "A pathetic excuse of a man. A derivative artist. A low-level administrator who will die having accomplished nothing. People will forget you the day after you're gone."

Rory shoved her away, and Emma felt a moment of triumph as she hit the floor with a crack. His petty, narcissistic soul had felt the blow.

He pinned her to the floor with his hands around her throat

as he tried to stop her words. "Nothing? I've accomplished nothing? I'm *The Artist*. No one will forget what I've done."

"What Malcolm did," Emma taunted, her voice tight. She balled her fists against his chest and shoved. His hands loosened just for a moment, just for a breath.

"It was *me*. I killed those girls. I made them art."

"Don't you read the papers? Malcolm is the killer, *The Artist*." She read the fury in his face and pushed harder. "He planned my kidnapping without you, didn't he? Your little puppet cut his strings. Then he caught you, too, and tossed you in a dirty hole. Was it really drugs in the scotch? Or did he just outsmart you?"

"He'd be nothing without me. It was all my plan, my vision. *La Belle Dame* doesn't even—"

Emma cut off his rant. "You're just another victim, trussed and tied and left impotent in the dark."

"I'm the one who killed him."

Emma's eyes watered as he squeezed harder. "You'll be nothing but a footnote," she gasped.

Rory abruptly pushed away from her, moving to his desk. He began to sort through the scattered papers, seemingly unconcerned that his latest victim was still alive. "No. He's nothing."

Heaving air into her lungs, Emma slowly leveraged herself up to a seated position. She was mere feet from the office door, but she knew she'd never make it out of the house. Rory was bigger, faster, and stronger. She quickly scanned her surroundings, looking for anything she could use to defend herself, and spotted the discarded bookend beside his leather-bound tomes. Using her heels, she pushed back slowly, careful not to draw his attention.

Rory turned, his face filled with satisfaction. "You've forgotten one thing. I still have you. If they find you, as Cressida, they'll know that Malcolm isn't The Artist. They'll know the real genius is still out there." He crossed slowly to Emma, dropping beside her again, pressing her down.

"Shakespeare and Chaucer leave out the best part of Cressida's story, you know. In the original, Cressida tries to hide from the world after her betrayal. Just like you, my little recluse. But God blinds her and disfigures her for what she's done." He traced a finger down her cheek.

"Rory . . ."

"It's harder than you'd think to strangle someone, but that feeling when the pulse stops beneath your fingers . . ." His voice was light as he placed one hand on Emma's clavicle, holding her still. He feathered the fingers of his other hand across her throat, hesitating at the pulse point. Emma's breath sped, but she remained still. Rory leaned down and kissed her again, licking at the blood he'd left there before. Emma forced herself not to pull away. He wanted her fear. As his lips moved against her, she stretched one hand toward the bookshelves and nearly cried out as her fingers brushed against a smooth, cold surface. The bookend was just out of reach. Rory sat up, giving her the inch of space she needed, and she pushed against him with as much force as she could muster. Without waiting to see his reaction, she twisted her torso around and flung herself forward. He wrenched her onto her back again and slammed his body down onto hers. But he was seconds too late. Emma hefted the bookend up and struck him on the back of the head as hard as she could.

Rory cried out and rolled away as Emma scrambled toward the doorway. The bookend had done little more than stun him, though, and he grabbed at her, catching her shirt. The fabric tore away, and the force sent her sprawling. She crashed toward the other side of the room, slamming into something sharp and hard. Disoriented, she pushed to her knees. She'd landed near the fireplace, with Rory standing between her and the door. There was no escape. Instinctively pressing herself to the wall, she watched him cross toward her. A soft clanging filled her ears. The world became still and silent for just a moment as she looked back at the fireplace tools in their neat brass holder: the tiny shovel, bristle brush, and jagged-tipped poker. Her fingers were pale against the iron as she lifted the poker, turned toward Rory, and swung her arm up as he reached toward her.

Chapter 34

The frost-bright air bit at Ian's lungs as he flung open the door of Mike's car and began jogging down the row of stately Victorians, the street lined with autumn trees and speckled with early Halloween decorations. The lights of a waiting ambulance were a glaring intrusion. Ian picked up speed; behind him, he heard Mike's footsteps match his own. They both recognized the house.

Two paramedics were laboriously working a gurney down the front steps, their breath puffing out in white clouds. A patrol car was parked on the lawn a few feet away with one door flung open.

"What happened?" Ian asked with poorly disguised panic in his voice.

"Male with a severe stab wound to the neck," a young patrol officer responded. "Alive, for the moment." She pointed toward the paramedics.

Male. Ian took a deep breath, fighting to slow his heart rate. "ID?"

The woman checked her notes. "Dr. Rory Tamblyn."

"Shit," Mike said, jogging up beside him. "What happened?"

"Tamblyn attacked someone, possible DV. Looks like self-defense."

"Who is the woman?" Ian asked, knowing the answer.

"Emma Reilly. Isn't that . . ." Ian watched the shoe drop. "She's the one who survived. And you . . . ?"

Ian cut her off. "Is she alright? Where is she?"

The officer straightened, her voice professional. "Minor bruises and abrasions, but she refused to go to the hospital. I put her in the patrol car to keep her out of view." She gestured to the people who had already begun to gather in the street. "She asked for you."

"Go," Mike said as Ian turned quickly. "I'll fill you in later."

Ian didn't care. He could now see Emma in the front seat of the patrol car with her feet out the door and a silver medic blanket around her shoulders. He could see blood staining her top and dappling her skin. She looked up as he approached.

"Are you hurt?" he asked without preamble.

Emma shook her head. "You were right."

"What do you mean?" Ian asked, kneeling down to her eyeline. He wanted to touch her but didn't.

"You told me not to trust him."

"Emma . . ."

"He did it all. He told me. Malcolm took the girls. But it was Rory, he killed them, he . . . They were just things to him, objects for his 'art' . . ." Emma laughed, a hard, broken sound. "I couldn't see it. That night, after he left me the photos of Olivia—I think he enjoyed hearing me describe it, discussing theories while he . . ." Here, at last, Emma's voice faltered. "He tried to kill me."

"You couldn't have known."

"You knew. You told me not to trust him, you saw through his story, you . . ." Emma's voice was rising.

"I didn't *know* anything. I didn't trust him; I didn't like him, but . . . God, Emma. I would never have let you near him if I'd known what he really was." Ian rocked back on his heels, looking away. "I don't know how to trust myself anymore. From the moment that I . . ." His voice trembled. "I didn't like him, but it . . . it wasn't rational. It was you. I let my feelings get in the way, and you were almost killed because I couldn't . . ." Ian broke off as Mike approached.

"Dr. Reilly," Mike said as Ian stood and stepped back.

"Detective Kelly." She offered him a small smile.

"How you doing?"

"I'm alive. Rory . . . Is—is—he—?"

"He's on his way to the hospital. But it doesn't look good."

Emma nodded but didn't speak. Ian's jaw clenched.

Ian felt Mike watching but didn't look up, keeping his eyes on Emma's face. Mike waited a moment and then turned with murmured well wishes. Grief washed over Emma's face as she nodded an acknowledgment.

"Emma, I know I fucked this up." Ian's words stumbled out. "All of it. From the jump. And I'm sorry, so sorry. For shutting you out, ordering you around, ignoring you . . ."

Ian hesitated, waiting for a response, but Emma remained silent.

Police lights whipped around them; in the house over his shoulder, Emma had lived a nightmare. The moment was all wrong, he knew. But the coiling emotion in his chest wouldn't stay still. He reached out and gently took Emma's hand, letting out a slow breath when she curled her fingers into his.

"The night we met, at the gala, you told me that the Lady of Shalott risked the curse, risked everything because she thought it would be worth it—that looking up and seeing the world would be worth it."

He paused, and Emma held his eyes. Her voice was low and even. "She died, Ian."

"But she lived first." Ian traced his thumb across hers. Dried blood speckled her fingers. "I can't promise a happy ending. I can't promise it will be worth everything that's happened, but I want to take the risk."

Emma looked down the street, away from the growing crowd of onlookers. "Maybe you're braver than me."

"No." Ian's voice was soft, but his grip tightened.

"Detective!"

Ian turned at the panicked call and saw Tamblyn's assistant and the intern—Carolyn and Charlie, his brain belatedly supplied. They were standing behind a police barricade, Carolyn waving desperately. Charlie had her phone out, and Ian suspected she was taking photos.

"Can I . . . Can they come through?" Emma's voice was small.

Ian hesitated only a moment. "Of course."

He stood, moving quickly to the crowd. "What are you doing here?" he asked, more abruptly than he intended. "I mean, how . . ."

"Police scanner." Charlie shrugged. "Carolyn recognized the address."

"Is Rory . . . ?" Carolyn's voice trailed off, her eyes on the ambulance.

Ian hesitated. He didn't want to discuss anything within earshot of the spectators. "Emma's over here. Come on."

He nodded at a patrol officer as he waved the two women through. Charlie looked around, piecing things together.

Carolyn looked dumbfounded. "Is she hurt? What happened to Rory?"

Ian drew them aside and lowered his voice. "Emma was attacked. She's fine, shaken up but . . ."

"It was him, wasn't it?" Charlie asked.

Ian glanced at her sharply but nodded. "Emma figured it out, and he attacked her. But she fought back."

Carolyn's face flashed with horror, then hardened. "Good. Is he dead?"

"No. Not yet, at least."

Ian led them to the car where Emma was waiting. Her face crumpled as Carolyn pulled her into a hug.

"We do what we have to," Charlie said, crouching beside her. "Remember? You warned him. And that's what you did. That's all you did."

"You're going to come stay with us tonight." Carolyn took Emma's hand and squeezed it. "We'll get takeout and watch movies and . . . Oh, god. Someone should tell Niall."

"Go," Charlie said, standing. "I'll stay with her while you call him."

Charlie moved next to Emma, but her eyes dashed across the scene, pausing at the window where the scene-of-crime techs had begun their work.

"Still looking for your exclusive?" Ian snapped.

Emma looked surprised by his tone, but Charlie just shook her head. "No. I'm not going to tell his story."

"Why not?"

Charlie met Ian's eyes directly. "Because he'd want me to."

"Then tell mine," Emma said.

"What?" Ian asked.

"You're sure?" Charlie dropped down to Emma's eyeline.

"Everyone else—they're going to write about him and Malcolm and all of the violence. I want you to write about me. And Sarah and Phillipa and Olivia. Tell that story."

"Word by word. I promise." Charlie looked away for a moment and cleared her throat.

"Do you need to go in?" Emma asked Ian. Her voice was tired but tinted with something Ian wanted to be hope.

He scrubbed a hand over his face. "I can wait until Carolyn gets back, but then . . ." He trailed off, not wanting to finish the sentence, to say that he was going to leave her.

Emma shook her head. "Go. Do your job."

He watched her for a moment longer, then turned to cross

the expanse of green lawn. Officers had set up barriers at its edges as people began to gather, camera phones held aloft.

"She alright?" Mike asked as Ian mounted the steps.

"She will be," Ian said. "Let's go."

Mike studied him for a moment, then nodded.

If not for the presence of police, the rooms would have felt rich and welcoming. Mike led the way to the office, where a busy swarm of officers and techs monitored, measured, and recorded the scene of the assault.

Ian looked down at a viscous stain soaking the ornate rug.

"She hit him with a poker. It was still in the assailant's throat." A nearby officer followed his gaze. "Not much blood spray. Smart not to take it out."

Mike had taken a slow tour of the room, scrutinizing the elements of the scene before coming to a stop beside the blood. "When you get all of this processed," he said to one of the investigators, "be sure to run his blood against the skin under Olivia Ballard's fingernails. We'll want to verify."

"Already called Ivy," a tall, white-suited woman said. "We've got a sample from this guy on file."

"From the medics?"

"No, assault case. I recognized his name from—" She shrugged uncomfortably, looking toward Ian. "Guess this means you're in the clear, though."

"Son of a bitch," Mike said, turning to Ian, "that son of a bitch. He gave us the evidence we needed himself, that damned bloody shirt."

"He thought he was smarter than everyone," Ian replied numbly, moving around Tamblyn's desk.

"He was. We've had all we needed to solve this thing, and we didn't see it."

"Emma did."

Ian turned away to look through the broad window. Emma stood, her arms tight around her middle, looking small as she stared toward the house. He wondered what she was hoping to see.

As dusk settled on the neat suburban neighborhood, Ian watched Mike and the others reflected in the glass, the image of them going about their tasks—marking, measuring, considering the evidence that had spread itself across the narrow confines of the study—superimposed on the outside world. The work he had dedicated himself to for so many years went on, blurred in the glass, seeming unreal and unimportant as Emma walked away.

Chapter 35

Emma was surrounded by books.

Carolyn and Charlie had taken her to their house, run her a bath, wrapped her in a fuzzy bathrobe and a fuzzier blanket, and settled her on the sofa. Tea and toast had appeared shortly after, and when that went untouched, it had been supplemented with bags of neon candy and sleeves of cookies.

Then Niall arrived, calm and reassuring on the surface with a buzz of anxiety underneath that he thought he'd hidden, Emma knew. His voice was pitched to a soothing tone that Emma had never heard before—one he used with patients, she guessed. He'd brought her books.

"I just got new ones," he said as he set down several plastic bags emblazoned with the logo of Emma's favorite indie shop. "I didn't want to accidentally pick up one that . . ."

"That Rory had added a special note to?" Emma picked up the cold tea and set it down again. She hated him for many reasons, but the fact he'd chosen *Jane Eyre*—that he'd corrupted that precious memory from her childhood—felt unbearably cruel.

He presented his collection, dozens of books that included everything from a biography of Elizabeth I to *The Baby-Sitters Club*. Emma picked up an illustrated edition of *Little Women*, tracing her figures across the idyllic image on the cover. "I sense a theme."

"Badass women," Niall acknowledged sheepishly. "I thought . . ." He shrugged.

"Thank you." Emma's voice was soft but clear. He touched her shoulder lightly, then moved away, claiming a chair across the room.

Charlie had settled on the floor, thumbing through *The Adventures of Pippi Longstocking*. "What's our game plan, then?" she asked, her voice neutral. "Ignore or debrief."

Emma looked down at the book, open now to an image of Jo and Laurie. She felt threads of tension binding her friends as they watched her. "Ignore. For tonight. Tomorrow, I'll—tell you about it," she added with a glance at Niall. "But tonight . . ."

"Tonight we eat and read and watch bad TV until it rots our brain and pretend we're kids again," Charlie announced, opening a bag of gummy worms.

"I'm in," he replied. "I never got the American high school experience."

"Gloriously bad YA novels, bags of junk food, nutrition-free takeout . . ." Charlie ticked off the items on her fingers. "This is pretty much it."

The trill of Emma's phone disrupted the banter. Emma checked the screen. "Ian," she said.

"You don't have to," Niall offered.

"I can talk to him," Carolyn said, "Or just let it go to voicemail."

"No." Emma unwound herself from the blanket as it rang again. "I'm okay."

She stepped onto the back deck and pressed the green button with a deep breath.

"Ian," she said without preamble.

"Emma." His voice was surprised. "I didn't think you'd pick up. I just . . . I . . ." He stumbled into silence.

Emma waited.

"I shouldn't have done this. I'm sorry. Again."

"It's okay. Again."

"I should just—"

"Ian," Emma interrupted. "Do you remember that little diner after the gala? You quoted *The Big Sleep*."

"It was the bit when Marlow realizes the girl he just met is trouble."

"And he can't resist trying to save her. That night, you . . ." Emma took a breath. "Did you . . . ? Were you . . . ?"

"Emma," Ian cut her off. "I didn't ask you out because I wanted to playact some noir fantasy if that's what you're asking. You're not a damsel. I asked you out because you're funny and interesting, and I wanted to see you again."

Emma was silent for a moment, needing to ask him the question that wouldn't let her go—not wanting to in case the answer was yes.

"Ian—when Rory was . . . He said that he and I, that we're the same. That we both hide who we are. And I don't know—maybe he's right. Maybe I . . ."

"No." Ian's voice was sharp and hard. "Men like that, they know how to read people. They know how to weaponize every insecurity you have. He lied to you every minute of every day. He's gone—don't let him decide who you are."

"Gone? Is he . . . ?"

Ian's voice was muffled as he swore. "Shit . . ."

"It's okay. I'm okay." She felt oddly numb as she mentally prodded the knowledge that she'd killed a man. Rory. "I survived."

"You fought like hell," Ian corrected her.

"I survived," Emma repeated, trying to use the words to shock the numbness back to life. "Now what?"

Ian hesitated. "I don't know. But I'd like to be there . . . if I can."

Emma shook her head, knowing he couldn't see it. "Ian, I don't know— After everything . . ." Emma closed her eyes as, for the first time since all of this began, she felt tears slip down her cheeks. She let them fall.

"Emma?" Ian's voice was hesitant. "Should I . . . would . . . tomorrow . . . ?"

His words failed to find their order, but Emma barely processed them. Her mind snaked off treacherously. "'Tomorrow and tomorrow and tomorrow . . .'" She heard her voice whisper as if from a distance.

". . . is another day. A new day. A mystery. We begin again," Ian pattered off quickly, a note of concern humming beneath the light words.

"What?" Surprise spun her thoughts away from their bleak path.

"You're quoting Shakespeare, right?" he replied. "Which means wherever that thought is going, it's probably about death or suicide or something nihilistic. So, I'm giving you and your uncanny brain some alternatives. *Tomorrow*—is only a day away. It clears away the cobwebs and the . . . something."

". . . and the sorrow," Emma finished quizzically.

"Right." Ian's voice was soft, serious. "It's not all darkness, Emma, even if it feels like it right now. Sure, there's Poe and Chandler and all the rest who want to burrow into the worst of humanity, but there's also—"

"*Annie*?" Emma felt a hesitant warmth unfurl just behind her rib cage. "You know Daddy Warbucks was a war profiteer."

Ian let out an incredulous huff of laughter. "Okay, but also—a kid sings to a dog. Both can exist in the same story."

Emma breathed deeply, chilly air filling the hollows of her chest. She wasn't ready for wit or hope or . . . whatever Ian was offering. But underneath the grief and fear and terror that still twined around her, there was something—gentle, bright. A vivid splash of color beneath the gray.

"Ian?" she said finally. "Not tomorrow. But—soon. Maybe. Once I put some pieces back together. I can't promise . . . anything. But . . ."

Ian's reply was immediate. "I can wait. Until you're ready, I can wait. Just . . . don't disappear."

"I won't." Emma hung up, wrapping herself in that promise. A chilling wind rippled her hair and fluttered the leaves that dappled the yard, a reminder of the winter darkness still to come. But in that moment, she let herself believe in the hope of returning light.

Acknowledgments

A special thanks to my parents for letting me brainstorm murders at the dinner table, to my grandmother, Patricia, for the eagle-eyed editing, and to my sister, Landy, for reading on despite the scary bits (with the doors locked, of course).

To Tegan and Isaac, just for being you.

To Monica for the texts, the cheers, the suggestions, and the insider knowledge of small-town journalism.

To Susannah from Mystery Loves Georgia, Kelly from SinC, and Abby for the helpful feedback in the early days when this book was merely a hope.

And, of course, to my editor, Meredith Clark, and her team at MIRA, and to my agent, Felice Lavern, at ArtHouse Literary Agency—thank you for your faith, support, and honesty every step of the way.

Without each of you, this book wouldn't be what it is. Neither would I.